Ma

The mage tournament

Book two

Chris Michael Wilson

Chapter 1

"Our first objectives?" Hadrik asks. "Did I hear him right?"

"That's right, you heard me!" Golmyck, the gnome king says, as if he were responding to Hadrik's question. "I am now going to announce the objectives of the tournament's first round, so you'd better pay attention, because I'm not planning to repeat myself. Are you ready?"

Golmyck makes a short pause before he continues.

"Very well, then!" he says. "Your first objectives are as follows. You will need to each find a glowing pinecone and bring it to the city of Galamir. Glowing pinecones grow only on the continent of Varathia, so most of you may not know much about them, but they basically look just like regular pinecones, except they start glowing brightly when you take them in your hand. There is no time limit for completing these objectives, but the earlier you bring the pinecones to their destination, the quicker you can begin your next objectives, which will give you a head start, compared to the latecomers. Lastly, I would like to mention that in this round you will be allowed to form teams with other participants. A team can have as many members as you want, and if you all confirm that you are part of the same team when you reach Galamir, you will pass the first round together, as long as you have at least one pinecone with you. That would be all for now. Good luck!"

"What?!" Hadrik shouts. "He can't be serious! How can they even call this a mage tournament with objectives like that? What's next? Are they going to tell us to go pick some flowers?"

"Hadrik…" Daren says, with a very dark look on his face. "I honestly could not give less of a damn about the tournament's objectives right now."

"Oh, I almost forgot something very important!" Golmyck says. "Daren, the healer in armor, and all the members of his group are to present themselves at the gates of the royal castle of Thilias in exactly five hours. This includes the dwarf, the artificial mage, and the lessathi. Failure to do so will result in their disqualification from the tournament. The little girl that travels with them may also join them if she wishes, but she is not required to. Thank you all for listening! Have a nice day!"

The gnome then presses a button and the transmission gets interrupted, while the holographic screens in the air start to disappear slowly, one by one.

"Wait, how did he know that Barry was a lessathi?" Hadrik says. "Didn't Barry himself only find out about this recently?"

"The fact that the king of Thilias knew both about Barry's and Kate's true identities strongly suggests that he's been keeping an eye on us for a while," Illuna says. "He must have spies that inform him of everything that goes on in his kingdom. I wouldn't be too surprised if he knew about my existence as well."

"Ah, crap," Hadrik says. "If that's the case, then maybe he also knows about me being a giant. Maybe they're calling me to the castle to kick me out of the tournament."

"They're summoning us because of what happened with the noble yesterday," Daren says. "They even have bounties on our heads. We shouldn't be too surprised that they'd want to interrogate us. Come on, let's head towards Rose's house. Going to the hospital now is out of the question without Rose to guide us, and it would be prudent to get our backpacks before we head towards the castle."

Daren pauses.

"One of us will also have to deliver the news of Rose's death to her siblings when we get there," he says.

I remain silent for a while after hearing Daren's question, and so does everybody else. Kate and Flower are both looking towards the ground, as Hadrik is scratching the back of his head uncomfortably.

"I'll do it," I say, eventually. "I'll try to break it to them as gently as possible."

Daren gives me a long look for a few seconds. He doesn't appear to be very comfortable leaving this matter in my hands, but he doesn't seem to want to be the one to deal with it either, and neither does anyone else, by the looks of it.

"Alright," Daren says, finally. "Barry will be the one to give the news to the kids. Any objections?"

Everybody else stays silent, as Kate and Flower are still looking towards the ground.

"It's settled, then," Daren says. "Let's get going. We'll take the same route that we took when we came here, to avoid getting lost. Follow me."

"Can I have Arraka back, please?" Flower asks Hadrik, as we start heading towards the mansion.

"Actually, I think I'd rather hold on to her a little longer, if you don't mind!" Hadrik says.

"Well, okay…" Flower says. "But make sure you keep an eye on her."

"Don't worry," Hadrik says, as he starts to spin the amulet again. "I'll be sure to give her all the attention she needs!"

We all follow Daren and go back the way we came, as we slowly begin to leave the slums behind us, and to enter the richer district that Rose's house is situated in.

Nobody said a single word while we walked down the alleys, not even Hadrik. Kate in particular seemed to be the most affected by what had happened, and the expression on her face was very painful to watch. Amidst the silence, an enraged Arraka would occasionally start showering us with a variety of insults and threats, as Hadrik ignored her and kept spinning her amulet despite her never-ending complaints.

"Will you shut her up?" Daren says, after a while. "I've already had enough of Arraka to last me for a week. I don't need to hear her constant yammering the entire trip."

"Oh, right, sorry…" Hadrik says, as he closes the amulet and then continues to spin it by the chain.

Arraka's shouting is still audible, but it's more of a mild annoyance now that the noise has become muffled.

"I think my wrist is starting to go numb from all the spinning," Hadrik says, a few minutes later. "Barry, what do you say? Do you wanna give this a try? I assure you it's a very rewarding experience!"

"I think I'll pass, thanks," I say.

"Suit yourself," Hadrik says. "But seriously, you don't know what you're missing!"

"I've been thinking," Kate says, all of a sudden. "Could Rose perhaps not be completely dead? Could she still be somewhere in there, inside her body?"

"Kate…" Daren starts to say, but Kate continues to speak, this time raising her voice a little.

"Maybe there's still some way to bring her back!" she says, looking at each of us in turn, seeking our approval. "Maybe if we defeat that follower of Ulruk who stole her body, we can bring her back to normal. We can't know until we try!"

"Kate, please…" Daren says, as he stops and looks Kate straight in the eye. "Don't make me say this again. Rose is gone. You can't bring back the dead, no matter how hard you try."

"But how can you know for sure that she's dead?" Kate says, with desperation visible in her eyes. "You heard what she said before she left. You all heard her! She told us to take care of her siblings. Why would she say something like that if a part of Rose wasn't still in there, somewhere?"

"Revenants are born with the memories of their hosts," Illuna says. "Because of this, it is common for them to be confused at first, and to have a bit of an identity crisis, as they struggle to differentiate between their own thoughts, and the ones that they inherited from their hosts."

"Then maybe we can still—" Kate starts to say, but Illuna cuts her off.

"Even if they may sometimes choose to uphold some of their old host's values and principles," Illuna says, "the revenants are still completely different entities than their bodies' previous owners. A revenant cannot be born if their host is still alive. The very fact that this revenant came to be is proof that Rose was already dead when the servant of Ulruk took hold of her body."

"But…" Kate tries to argue again, this time with a lot more hesitation in her voice. "But… maybe if we…"

She stops when she realizes that she no longer has any valid arguments to bring to the table. Instead of continuing her train of thought, her gaze turns towards the ground again, and she doesn't say another word.

"I'm sorry," Daren says, as he turns back and he starts to walk towards Rose's house again.

We all follow him one by one, with Kate being the last to move from her spot. The rest of our journey towards the mansion was spent in complete silence. When we got closer to the mansion, Rose's siblings noticed us from afar and came running to greet us.

"Where's Rose?" Suzie says, after looking around for

a few seconds. "Did she stay behind at the hospital?"

Everybody looks towards me, as I step forward and clear my throat nervously.

"What's wrong?" Suzie asks, starting to get concerned. "Did something happen to Rose?"

"Yes," I say. "We were attacked on our way to the hospital. We thought that Rose would be safe, but she..."

I pause, not knowing how exactly I should deliver the news to her without causing her a shock.

"Oh gods," Suzie says. "Is she..."

She stops for a second before she continues.

"Is she dead?" she asks.

Her direct question takes me by surprise. Before I get the chance to answer, Daren steps in front of me and he kneels in front of Suzie, with his head bowed down.

"I'm sorry," he says. "It was my fault. I promised I'd protect her and I—"

"Oh, it's okay," Suzie says, forcing herself to smile. "Rose told us long ago that we should always be prepared for this to happen. She taught us how to cook our own food, and how to clean the house, and everything else we needed to know, in case she never came back from one of her journeys."

While Suzie talks, her brother is trying hard to hold back his tears.

"We promised her that no matter what happened, we wouldn't cry," Suzie says. "We promised her that we'd stay strong and that..."

She stops talking for a second to rub her eyes with her sleeve.

"And that we would always remember her with a smile," Suzie says, with a much shakier voice than before. "And that we would keep living our lives and be happy, and... and..."

The girl can't contain her tears anymore and she

suddenly breaks down crying. Her brother, who was also at his limit, starts to cry as well, in a much louder voice.

"Hey, now," we hear a man's voice coming from behind us. "What kind of monsters would make such a beautiful girl cry like this?"

As we turn around, we see that the man who spoke is almost as tall as Daren, with a well-toned muscular build, wearing a shirt that is half-unbuttoned, with long black hair that reaches his shoulders, and a bristly moustache covering his whole upper lip. On his left hip, he is wearing a golden scabbard that appears to be holding a rather expensive sword, at least judging by the multitude of gems decorating its hilt. The man stops in front of Suzie, and he wipes her tears gently with his right hand.

"Did these mean people upset you, my dear Suzie?" the man asks her.

"Uncle Enrique," Suzie says, barely able to control her voice. "It's Rose. She…"

The girl struggles to get the words out of her mouth, as she is drowning in tears.

"She's dead, uncle," she says. "Rose is dead."

She then hugs her uncle as hard as she can, while she is still trying hard to contain her sobs.

"Rose is… dead?" Enrique says, with a mixture of both pain and shock in his voice.

His look then gradually darkens, as he looks towards us.

"Are they the ones responsible for this?" Enrique asks, as he starts to slowly pull his sword out of its scabbard.

"*No*!" Suzie shouts. "It wasn't them! They tried to protect her! They're her *friends*!"

"I am the one who let Rose die," Daren says, as he steps towards Enrique and bows his head before him. "I promised I would keep her safe, but I've failed her. I cannot even begin to express my apologies…"

After seeing the pained expression on Daren's face, Enrique slowly calms down, walks over to him, and then places a hand on his shoulder.

"There's no need to apologize, my friend," Enrique says. "It is I who should apologize, for jumping to conclusions earlier. It's clear that you've suffered a great deal from this as well."

Enrique then walks past Daren, and he takes a good look at each of us in turn.

"Cheer up, my friends!" he says. "Why all the long faces? Rose would not have wanted to see you like this. She would have wanted you to smile. We should not be mourning Rose's loss. We should be celebrating your safe return. And as Rose's friends, you are all my friends as well!"

He turns towards Suzie.

"Suzie!" he says. "Bring me the finest bottle of wine from the cellar. The one that we were saving for a special occasion. You know which one I'm talking about, yes?"

"Yes, uncle," Suzie says, as she wipes her tears with her sleeve again, and she stops crying all of a sudden. "I'll bring it right away!"

"Now, then, friends of Rose," Enrique says, as Suzie goes rushing towards the house, "Before we toast, I would like to hear your names. It would be unfitting to not know the names of the people I intend to share a drink with!"

"Is this really the time and place to have a drink?" I say, after we all just look at him, dumbfounded, for a couple of seconds.

"What are you talking about?" Enrique says. "It is always a good time and place to have a drink! Drinking brings people closer together. Just ask your dwarf friend. Dwarves are renowned for their excessive drinking habits, and yet they are one of the most united people in the world."

"Aye," Hadrik says. "Although there is a common theory that the only reason why dwarves don't carry grudges is because they're always too drunk to remember what they did on the previous day. My name is Hadrik, by the way. Pleased to make your acquaintance!"

Hadrik then shakes Enrique's hand and he introduces the rest of us in turn.

"This here's Barry," Hadrik says. "This is Daren. Over there we have Kate, and the little girl's name is Flower. Oh, and we also have two banshees. The one inside the girl's body is named Illuna, and the one in the amulet I'm holding is named Arraka."

There is a barely audible mumbling sound coming from the closed amulet, as Hadrik stops talking, but nobody pays it any mind.

"Two banshees?" Enrique asks, a bit shocked. "And Rose was friends with both of them?"

"Well, not both of them," Hadrik says. "The one in the amulet is more our prisoner than our ally, really, but Illuna and Rose were definitely very good friends."

"Well, in that case she will always be welcome here, banshee or no," Enrique says. "Ah, here comes our wine!"

Suzie is now hurrying towards us with a bottle of wine in her hands, while behind her, we can see Ella, who seems to have fully recovered after last night, and who is carrying a plate that has several wine glasses on top of it. When the two of them arrive, they place both the plate and the bottle on a picnic table next to us, and then Suzie starts to open the bottle.

"By the gods," Enrique says when he sees Ella. "My eyes have been truly blessed to bear witness to such beauty!"

He then bows gallantly and kisses her hand.

"If my heart didn't already belong to Rose for all eternity, I would have likely fallen for you in an instant!" Enrique says.

Ella is looking a bit confused after hearing Enrique's words, but instead of answering him, she decides to bow elegantly, and to introduce herself.

"My name is Ella," the girl says. "I've heard from Suzie what happened to miss Rose. I am sorry for your loss."

For a moment, there was a glimmer of sadness in Enrique's eyes, as he heard Ella's words, but he quickly forced back a cheerful smile on his face, before he spoke again.

"There is no reason for you to apologize, my dear!" Enrique says. "You had nothing to do with this."

"I assume you are the new master of this house," Ella says. "I believe I owe you an explanation for my being here. You see, Rose has only just hired me yesterday to work as…"

Ella pauses for a few seconds before she continues, as she slowly lowers her head.

"As a slave," she says. "I am well trained in house cleaning and cooking, and I also know how to read and write. If you will have me, I promise that I will serve you as faithfully as I've served her."

"I'm going to stop you right there, Ella," Enrique says, as he gently lifts the girl's chin with his hand, so she can look directly in his eyes. "You should not be telling such lies. The Rose I knew would never have hired a slave to work for her. No matter what your past may have been, once you became a part of this family, you did so as a free woman, and not as a slave. As long as you work in this house, you are prohibited to call yourself a slave any longer. Are we clear?"

"Yes, sir," Ella says, smiling faintly, as tears start to

form in her eyes.

"Very well, then!" Enrique says.

He then turns to us.

"Well?" he asks. "What are you all waiting for? This wine isn't going to drink itself!"

"Uncle," Suzie's brother, Kevin, says, as he pulls on Enrique's sleeve, while he's still sniffing, with tears in his eyes. "Uncle, what are we going to do? How are we going to live without Rose? We've tried hard to learn how to live by ourselves. We've handled ourselves for weeks while Rose was on her journeys. We learned how to buy food, and how to cook, and how to use the fireplace, but we can't… we can't—"

"Do not worry, my young little friend," Enrique says, as he pats Kevin on his head. "You will not have to live by yourselves, because starting tomorrow, I will move back in with you!"

"You… you will?" Kevin asks.

"Of course I will!" Enrique says. "Would I lie to you? Once I bring back all of my belongings, I will be living here again, and it will be just like the good old times!"

Upon hearing Enrique's words, Suzie, who was busy filling the glasses with wine, comes running to her uncle and gives him a big hug again.

"Thank you, uncle!" she says. "Thank you so much! I didn't think you'd ever come back!"

"I'm sorry to interrupt," Kate says. "But from what Rose told us, I understood that the reason you two got divorced was that you wanted to spend time with other women. Shouldn't you be discussing this with your current wife before making such promises?"

"Lover," Enrique says.

"I beg your pardon?" Kate says.

"Lover, not wife," Enrique says. "Rose has been and will always remain my only wife."

"Right," Kate says. "Your lover. What do you think her reaction will be to all of this? Can you be so sure that she will agree to move into this house with you, just to take care of your ex-wife's siblings?"

"Oh, she will be furious!" Enrique says. "She cannot stand children!"

"Then how could you make such a promise in her name, without consulting her first?" Kate asks.

"Oh, I never made the promise in her name," Enrique says. "In fact, I intend to break up with her as soon as I get back home!"

"You're going to break up with your lover… just to move in with Rose's siblings?" Kate asks, somewhat shocked.

"Of course!" Enrique says. "Why are you so surprised? She will be missed, but in the end, she's just another woman who only loves me for my money and my good looks! I should have little trouble replacing her. There are plenty of other fish in the sea!"

He laughs.

"Now, then, grab your drinks, everyone," Enrique says. "Today, we toast for Rose: the most beautiful and kind-hearted woman I've ever known, and the love of my life. May she always be remembered, and may she continue to live in our hearts, from now and forever more!"

After hearing Enrique's speech, we all decided to take our wine glasses, and to join in on the toast.

The next half of an hour was spent talking about Rose. We told Enrique of the adventures we've had with her for the past week, and he told us of their years together at the mansion. It was clear that none of us were in the mood for drinking, or telling stories, but it didn't matter.

Enrique was right. Rose would not have wanted us to spend our lives in regret. And we couldn't afford to avoid talking about her from now on just because it hurt to remember her. Rose did not deserve this.

While we talked, it was becoming more and more obvious that despite his cheerful act, Enrique was likely the one who was suffering the most from Rose's loss. However, whenever he talked about Rose, his smile would become genuine, and even Kate had managed to smile once or twice during our long conversation.

When time began to run out, we told Enrique that we needed to be heading towards the castle, and we each went to get our backpacks before starting on our new journey. As we were about to set out, Enrique took us aside for a moment to have a word with us, away from the kids.

"There is something that I did not dare to ask in front of the children," Enrique says. "I saw that you did not bring Rose's body with you when you returned to the mansion, so I assumed the worst, but I need to know. How did Rose die?"

We all exchange a few uneasy looks, before we finally decide to answer his question.

"This is going to be a bit hard to believe," I say.

"Oh, believe me, I am not a stranger to the world of magic," Enrique says. "I am prepared for anything."

"Well," I say, "what happened was that after Rose was killed, her body was… taken, by an entity that is called a revenant."

"When you say her body was taken…" Enrique starts to say, but Daren answers his question before he finishes it.

"He means that an evil spirit took hold of her body, after she died," Daren says.

"And I suppose that there is no way to bring Rose back, even if you kill this evil spirit?" Enrique asks.

"No, there isn't," Daren says. "I'm sorry."

"I understand," Enrique says.

He pauses.

"If the children ever ask me what happened to Rose, I will tell them that her body was incinerated," Enrique says. "I would rather have them believe this than give them nightmares."

"Then we'll make sure to tell them the same story, if they ever ask us," Daren says.

"Thank you," Enrique says.

He then turns to face all of us.

"My friends, I am sorry that we did not have the chance to meet under better circumstances," he says. "Just know this: whether you decide to remain in the city or to leave before dusk, you will always be welcome here, whenever you decide to come back. May the gods be with you!"

"May they watch over us all," Daren says. "Goodbye, Enrique, and good luck!"

Once we all say our goodbyes to Enrique and to Rose's siblings, we go on our way, taking the shortest route we know to the castle. According to Enrique, as long as we keep walking in the same general direction, we should be coming across a lot of signposts showing us the right way to our destination, so we shouldn't be too worried about getting lost.

"Do you think they'll be alright?" Kate asks me. "Rose's siblings, I mean. I'm not sure how much I can trust that man to care for them from now on…"

"Well, Rose definitely trusted him enough to leave him in charge of checking up on her siblings while she was gone," I say. "And his concern for the children looked genuine to me. Plus, the kids seemed to love him. I don't think we have anything to worry about!"

"I guess you might be right," Kate says. "He did seem serious when he said he'd break up with his lover to move in with them. Maybe I was just worrying over nothing."

“Look, there’s another one of those signposts,” Hadrik says. “We’re still on the right track!”

It takes us a little less than two hours to reach the castle of Thilias from Rose’s mansion. When we reach the front gates, Daren signals the guards to let us through, and once they confirm our identities, they open the doors. We then all step inside, slowly, as the gates slam shut behind us.

There’s something odd about this castle. I noticed it even before we went in. From the outside, the castle’s windows looked as if they were supposed to have precious gems encrusted on their frames, but the gems were all missing. It also seemed as if several decorations had been ripped off from the towers’ outer walls.

Now that we’re inside, I see that the castle’s interior looks even worse. The hallways are completely empty. There are no paintings on the walls, no carpets on the ground and no vases on the tables. The place looks more like a dungeon than a castle. There aren’t even any guards patrolling the hallways. I’m almost starting to wonder if we didn’t somehow end up in the wrong place.

“This feels like the ogre fort, all over again,” Hadrik says, as he opens Arraka’s amulet. “Hey, you! Arraka! Are you sensing any guards hiding invisibly around here? Answer me!”

Arraka makes no sound, acting as if she weren’t hearing a word of what Hadrik is saying.

“Giving me the silent treatment, eh?” Hadrik says, with a grin.

Suddenly, Kate freezes the whole area around us, making it look as if we were inside some frozen palace from a fairy tale.

“The area is clear,” Kate says. “There’s no one surrounding us.”

“Great,” Daren says. “Now unfreeze the damn hallway before anyone sees—”

Before Daren gets to finish his sentence, a door in front of us opens slightly, and a man that appears to be some kind of a servant from the castle, sticks his head out of it.

"The king will—" the man starts to say, but he suddenly stops talking, due to the shock of seeing the whole hallway completely frozen.

After a few seconds, the man starts talking again, choosing to act as if nothing had happened.

"The king will be notified of your arrival, shortly," the servant says. "Please wait in this hallway until it is time for your scheduled appointment."

He then closes the door without saying another word.

"Well, you heard the man!" Flower says. "We still have plenty of time left until the meeting. Let's go exploring!"

"What are you talking about?" Daren says. "He told us to wait here. And Kate still needs to unfreeze the hallway, before anyone else sees this!"

"I can't unfreeze it," Kate says. "It will melt on its own in a few hours."

"We don't have a few hours!" Daren says. "If the king sees this, he'll have our *heads*!"

"Relax!" Hadrik says. "What's the worst that could happen?"

"Good gods, man!" Daren says, exasperated. "Isn't there anything that ever sets you off?"

All of a sudden, the whole area around us gets covered in flames, and all of the ice quickly melts into water, which then almost immediately evaporates into thin air. The flames then disappear as quickly as they appeared, leaving the hallway in the same state it was when we first came in.

"There," Flower says. "I took care of it. Now, does anyone want to go exploring?"

"Sure, I'll go," I say.

"Perfect!" Flower says. "Follow me!"

"Oh, come on!" Daren says. "What are we supposed to tell that servant guy if he comes back and asks for you?"

"Tell him we'll be right back," I say. "And then give me a call through the transceiver."

Daren shakes his head in disapproval, but he doesn't say anything else. I go catch up to Flower, who seems to have stopped in front of a wall, not far from our original position. After looking at the wall from different angles, the girl starts to knock on the bricks, one by one, as if she were looking for something.

"Is there anything special about this wall?" I ask her.

"Shush, I'm trying to listen!" Flower says, as she continues to knock on the bricks.

After a few more seconds, the girl finally seems to have found what she was looking for, and she starts to pull one of the bricks out of the wall with both her hands. As she puts the brick down, I see that inside the hole left in the wall, there is a small wooden lever.

"Wow, you sure know your stuff, huh?" I tell Flower.

"Of course!" Flower says. "Petal and I have been through dozens of ruins with hidden passages before! It's sort of our hobby!"

"Less of a hobby, and more of a tendency to get into mortal peril on a weekly basis," Illuna says, as the girl's eyes turn bright blue again.

"I got it!" Flower says, as she pulls the wooden lever.

As soon as she releases the lever, the bricks surrounding it start to get pushed inside the wall, making way for us to pass to the other side. We both go beyond the wall, and enter a small dark room that has a stone pedestal in the middle of it. Upon closer examination, it seems that there is some writing on the top of the pedestal, but it is too dark to make out what it says.

Flower makes a small orb of fire, which she sends

floating above the pedestal, so I can read the writing on it. Now that I get a clear look at it, it appears that the text is written in the Common language.

"What does it say?" Flower asks.

"It says: 'Place your palm on this pedestal, if you like discovering secrets.' "

"Oh, I love discovering secrets!" Flower says, and she quickly places her palm on top of the stone pedestal.

Suddenly, a hole appears at the base of the pedestal, and two small objects get thrown out of it. As I reach to get them, the hole closes itself back up again. Getting a closer look at the two items, I see that one of them is a piece of a puzzle, while the other one is a small parchment. I hold the parchment in my hand, so that both Flower and I can see what's written on it.

As I read the text on the parchment, I notice that it's written in the Common language as well, and that it says: "Find all of the pieces of the puzzle, and I will share with you my greatest secret. I've left one of these in each of the buildings I've designed."

The parchment is then signed as simply: "This building's architect."

It would appear that this castle's architect is also the one who designed the ruins from the forest. I now have two of these puzzle pieces in my possession. I wonder how many of them are left.

"Hey, this sounds like fun!" Flower says. "I want one too!"

She puts her palm on the pedestal again, but this time, nothing happens.

"It doesn't let me get another one!" Flower says. "Barry, you try it!"

"Hey, Barry, can you hear me?" I hear Daren's voice, coming from the transceiver.

"Yeah, I hear you," I say, as I grab the transceiver in my right hand.

Flower frowns at me, for ignoring her, and she takes my left hand herself, placing it on the pedestal. Just like before, the base of the pedestal opens up and throws out another puzzle piece and parchment. Flower takes both items and puts them in her pocket.

"The castle servant came back," Daren says. "He said the king will see us now. Hurry up and get back here, will you?"

"Yeah, we're on our way," I say.

After we make our way out of the dark room behind the wall, Flower pulls on the lever again, and the bricks go back into their original position. She then grabs the brick off the ground, and carefully places it back into the wall.

"We wouldn't want anyone else to discover the secret before us, would we, Barry?" Flower says, with a smile.

"I suppose not," I say, as we start to head back to where everyone else was waiting for us.

"Well?" Daren says when we reach them. "Did you find what you were looking for?"

"Yep!" Flower says, with a cheerful smile.

"Spectacular," Daren says. "Now, let's get moving."

We open the doors that the castle servant used earlier, and we enter a long, empty hallway that seems to lead directly to the throne room. Before opening the last set of doors, Daren looks at each of us in turn, to confirm that we are ready, and then we all step inside the throne room, one by one.

The throne room looks just as empty as every other part of the castle, except there is a long, narrow, red carpet leading to the throne on the opposite side of the chamber, where the king is currently sitting. Standing beside him we can see the servant from before, and on the other side, an old man that I do not recognize, but who appears to be rather important, at least judging by his expensive clothing. The gnome is now dressed in a more kingly manner than when he made his last appearance, having a golden crown on his head and a red mantle on his shoulders. When we arrive in front of him, he greets us courteously.

"Welcome, friends!" Golmyck says. "Please, make yourselves at home! I'm sorry for the lack of chairs, but I've been told repeatedly that it would not be fitting for ordinary people to be seated in the presence of a king."

"Skip the formalities, king of Thilias," the important-looking man says. "This isn't the time and place to observe proper etiquette."

"Now, now, ambassador," Golmyck says. "Proper etiquette is always important, lest we descend into barbarism."

"You speak to me of barbarism, when the people standing before us are proven murderers?" the ambassador says. "I did not come here to hear your lectures. I came here in the name of the king of Ollendor, in order to make sure that the murderers of his majesty's brother are rightfully punished!"

"Murderers they may be," Golmyck says, "but they are also our esteemed guests, and I would like to at least hear their reasons, before deciding their punishment."

He then turns to us.

"What say you, brave warriors?" the gnome says. "What was your reason for killing the earl of Ollendor?"

"We killed him because he placed absolutely no value on human life," I say.

"Ah," Golmyck says. "I assume that you are talking about the slave girl he was with at the time. Tell me, young lessathi, are you aware of the laws in our city regarding slavery?"

"Your majesty," Daren interrupts us, as he places himself in front of me, and he bows before the king. "Please, allow me to explain what happened!"

"Psst!" I hear Arraka's voice coming from the

amulet, as soon as Daren begins to speak. "Hey, you there! Weakling! Stat wielder guy. Half-lessathi. Come here!"

"Half… lessathi?" I ask her, as I get closer to Hadrik and the amulet.

"Never mind that!" Arraka says, in a low voice. "We've got trouble. Eiden just teleported in the middle of the hallway, and he's hiding with that invisibility spell of his."

"Eiden?" I ask her. "Why would he choose to come now, of all times?"

"I don't know and I don't care," Arraka says. "I promised that I'd let you know when Eiden was near, and I've kept my word. Now will you tell this buffoon holding my amulet to stop spinning me with every opportunity he gets?!"

"Uh, right…" I say. "I'll see what I can do about it."

While I was talking with Arraka, it seems that the discussion between the king and the ambassador had gotten a bit more heated.

"You would defend this filth?!" the ambassador shouts loudly at the gnome king.

"I'm not defending anyone," Golmyck answers him, calmly. "I'm simply saying that before condemning them, they need to be offered a fair trial."

"These scum do not deserve a trial!" the ambassador shouts. "They deserve to be executed on the spot! Do you want war, king of Thilias? Need I remind you that I represent the king of Ollendor himself? I will not stand here to witness this mockery of a trial when we already have all the information we need to pass their sentence this very instant! You will have them killed right here and now, or there will be war! Do you hear me, Golmyck? *War*!"

"I'm afraid that I can't let you execute these people, ambassador," we hear Eiden's voice coming from behind us.

As we all turn around, Eiden starts to walk slowly towards the ambassador, and he stops right in front of him. The ambassador is now sweating all over, and it looks like he's barely able to maintain his composure.

"What's the matter, ambassador?" Eiden asks, with a smirk. "Aren't you going to bow before your Creator?"

The whole room falls completely silent, as the ambassador tries hard to force a humble expression on his face, while he bows slowly before Eiden.

"As always, I am but your humble servant," the ambassador says, sounding as if he were experiencing great pain with every word he spoke. "It is an honor to have you in these halls, oh great Creator."

"What?!" Flower and Daren both shout at the same time.

"Wait a minute," Hadrik says. "Creator, as in, the founder of Varathia's civilization? Is that the Creator we're talking about, here?"

"I'm surprised that you didn't know this by now," Eiden says, with a puzzled expression on his face. "Didn't Arraka tell you? She was there when it all began, after all."

There are a few moments of silence, during which we all turn our gaze towards Arraka's amulet.

"What, didn't I mention it?" Arraka says. "I guess it must have slipped my mind. Aha- Ahahahahaha!"

"So, you are the Creator that I've been hearing so much about," Golmyck says, while stroking his chin.

"I am indeed!" Eiden says. "And I must say that I am a big fan of your work. I heard that the first thing you did when you moved into the royal castle was to strip it of anything of value, sell everything, and then give the money to the poor. The nobility in all of Varathia had been in an uproar for months after the event. It was a most entertaining spectacle to see!"

"I was always of the opinion that the royal castle belongs not to the royal family, but to the people," Golmyck says. "I only did what anyone else would have done in my place, if they had been chosen by the people to represent their interests."

"I think you might be holding too high of an opinion of the people under your rule, king of Thilias," Eiden says, with a polite smile.

"Creator," the ambassador says, as he finally musters up the courage to speak again. "I know that your word is law throughout the whole continent of Varathia, but I must insist—"

"The continent of Varathia..." Eiden interrupts him. "You people always called it that, didn't you? But the size of Varathia is nowhere near the size of any other continent in the world. If anything, it's more of an island, really. In fact, if I recall correctly, that is how I named this place after the still winter. The island of Varathia. The island of freedom. Why did people start calling this a continent, I wonder? Was it because you felt left out, when you discovered that there was a world outside of Varathia? Was it perhaps to satisfy your own egos, fooling yourselves into believing that you could compare with the civilizations from the other continents?"

"Creator, please," the ambassador says. "I don't know what your affiliation is with these mages, but they have done us a great harm. A life has been lost that can never be replaced. It would be most tragic if the victim's killers were to be simply set free."

"Oh?" Eiden says, with an evil smile. "And what if I told you that I was in fact the one who gave them the ability to hurt the people of Varathia?"

The ambassador is now sweating even harder than before, and he seems to be too afraid to give Eiden an answer. Seeing the expression on his face, Eiden starts to laugh.

"Do not worry, ambassador," he says. "I never suggested that they should be set free. However, I believe we can all agree that an execution would be a dull way for such powerful mages to meet their demise."

"What do you… have in mind, then?" the ambassador asks.

"The arenas, of course!" Eiden says. "Have them thrown in the arena, and if they somehow manage to survive until the end, then it will mean that the gods have seen fit to acquit them of their crimes. The rules of the arenas state that you may not use magic during fights, so they won't get any unfair advantage over any of the other gladiators. There are even magic detectors placed all around the fighting area, to make sure that there's no cheating."

"Yes, but," the ambassador says, "if they somehow manage to survive, the king of Ollendor will—"

"Are you trying to say that the fabled arenas of Varathia, the pride of your 'continent', are not enough to stop a mere handful of mages that can't even cast any spells?" Eiden says, with a wicked smile.

"No…" the ambassador says. "No, of course not…"

The ambassador stops for a few seconds, to clear his thoughts.

"Very well, then," he says, finally. "The criminals will face their sentence in the arena. But I will oversee the proceedings personally. I want to make sure that nothing goes wrong."

"Of course, ambassador," Golmyck says. "The arenas are yours, for the duration of these events."

The ambassador pauses again.

"Three days," he says. "In three days, I will arrange the greatest arena event in the whole history of Varathia. Until then, the criminals are to be locked in the cells beneath the arena of Thilias, along with the other gladiators."

"It is settled, then!" Eiden says. "I look forward to seeing what you will have in store for us, ambassador. I will be seeing you again on the day of the main event. Do not disappoint me."

With these last words, Eiden teleports out of the room, without a trace, as he always does.

"You criminals are coming with me," the ambassador says. "I don't want you roaming the streets and putting any more innocent lives in danger."

"Actually, ambassador," Golmyck says, "I would like to have a word with them in private first, if you don't mind. I'll be sure to have one of my servants escort them to their cells shortly afterwards."

"Hmph," the ambassador says. "Do what you will. I'm not planning to waste any more time here. I've got business to attend to. Just make sure that they're all in their cells by midnight."

The ambassador then walks away from us and out of the room, slamming the door shut behind him on his way out.

"Alright, then," Golmyck says, as he gets up from his throne. "Follow me. I'd rather not have our discussion in this dull place. I am now going to lead you to my real castle, where we can talk to our heart's content, until it is time to lead you to the arena."

"What makes you think that we'll simply agree to be led to the arena?" I say.

"Well, you are free to resist arrest, of course," Golmyck says. "But that would also result in your immediate disqualification from the tournament. Is this what you want?"

I open my mouth to say something, but I can't think of any clever retort to give him. Instead, I choose to remain silent.

"Of course it isn't," Golmyck says, answering his

own question. “I do not know what any of your reasons or motivations for coming here might have been, but I would imagine that if they were strong enough to make you want to risk your lives in a tournament like this, then you would definitely not let such a minor obstacle stand in your way. If it helps, then you can consider this arena as an extra qualification round, of sorts. To get you warmed up for the main event. Now, where was that hidden lever, again?… Ah, yes, here it is!”

The gnome reaches behind the throne with his right hand, and he pulls on a lever. This causes one of the stone blocks forming the floor in front of us to move aside by itself, revealing a hidden staircase that leads to the lower levels of the castle.

“Barry, I leave the throne room in your care until I return,” Golmyck says.

“What?…” I say.

“Yes, your highness,” the king’s servant says, almost at the same time as me.

“Oh, my apologies,” Golmyck says, after he realizes the confusion he’s created. “I was talking to my servant. He is also named Barry.”

He then turns to face all of us.

“Alright, this way, if you please!” Golmyck says, as he starts to go down the stairs.

The rest of us exchange a few looks, and then we follow the gnome, until we reach an underground room filled with machine parts and prototypes, as well as various tools that seem to have been thrown around randomly after their use. In the middle of the room, there is a workbench on top of which we can see a large device that looks like a bigger version of Daren’s transmitters, with a green light at the bottom.

When we entered the room, Golmyck was in the process of taking off his mantle and crown, and putting on the oil stained lab coat that we saw him wear earlier, when he appeared on the hologram. Now that I look around more closely, I realize that this is in fact the exact room that he was transmitting from, and that the device on the workbench is likely the one that he'd finished fixing, right before the transmission.

"Welcome to my castle inside my castle," Golmyck says. "I found this secret room shortly after moving in here, and I quickly decided to take advantage of the large unused space in order to set up my new workshop. I haven't really been tinkering with devices as often as I would have liked since I became king, but I find that this place always relaxes me after a heated discussion such as the one that I had with the ambassador earlier."

"You said that you had something you wanted to discuss with us in private?" Daren says.

"Yes, I did," Golmyck says. "Let's start with your giant friend over there, who is currently shapeshifting into a dwarf."

"Damn it!" Hadrik says. "I should have known that it was all too good to be true. Is this the part where you kick me out of the tournament?"

"Of course not!" Golmyck says. "The rules of the tournament never explicitly stated that giants were not allowed in the tournament. We only avoided inviting giants to this contest because of the overwhelming advantage you would get from both your size and your strength. However, given that you have willingly shrunk yourself to the size of a dwarf, we have decided to make an exception in your case. You will be permitted to participate in this tournament, as long as you do not shapeshift yourself into anything bigger than what would normally be possible for a dwarf. And also, since you seem to be so fond of your dwarf form, this is how you will present yourself to all other participants from now on. I don't want any of the other mages finding out that you are in fact a giant. Are we clear?"

"As clear as can be!" Hadrik says, grinning happily.

"Well, in that case, you are free to go!" Golmyck says. "I no longer have any business to discuss with you."

"You mean I'm free to go to the arena, or…"

"No, I mean that you are free to carry on with the first round of the tournament," Golmyck says. "Unlike your friends, you were not present at the scene of the crime, so there is no reason for us to incarcerate you. There is no need for you to go into the arena."

"The hell there isn't!" Hadrik shouts. "Do you think I came all the way here to go looking for pinecones? I came here to fight, damn it! I swear, if you don't let me fight in this arena, I'm going to start thrashing the whole neighborhood until your guards throw me in there themselves!"

"Well, if you insist, then I can write a letter of admission for you, which you can give to the guards at the arena's entrance," Golmyck says. "They'll be sure to let you in once they see the royal seal."

"Perfect!" Hadrik says. "Much obliged!"

"Should I also be writing a letter for the girl and the banshee over there?" Golmyck says, as he looks towards Flower.

"Uh, well—" Flower starts to say, but Illuna interrupts her.

"No, we're fine," she says, as the girl's eyes turn blue. "We'll watch the show from the spectator seats."

"Very well," Golmyck says. "Then I'll be sure to provide you with a ticket."

"I see you've done your homework," Hadrik says. "I didn't think you'd also know about Illuna."

"My spies have been instructed to be extra vigilant when it comes to mages from other continents," Golmyck says. "They've been keeping a close eye on you ever since you entered the city."

"Does this mean that they were also watching us when we attacked the noble?" Daren says.

"Yes…" Golmyck says. "This is the second reason why I wanted to speak to you in private. First of all, I would like to offer you an apology. I imagine that the scene you witnessed that day must have been quite shocking for outsiders like yourselves."

"You don't sound like you approve of what was happening with the slave girl," Kate says.

"I do not," Golmyck says. "I personally find that the way our society treats slaves is sickening, and that we are all responsible in a way for allowing this system to continue. I, myself, am not much better than my predecessors, because I've barely done anything conclusive to address the problem since I moved into this castle."

"But why?" Daren asks. "Why haven't you done anything? You are the king. You could do so much to help these people…"

"Look up there," Golmyck says, as he points towards a metal device hanging from the ceiling.

"What about it?" Daren asks, after he gives the device a cursory glance.

"What you see over there is an invention of my own making, with the sole purpose of blocking communication towards the outside," Golmyck says. "I installed it here shortly after my arrival to the castle."

"You're saying that someone could be trying to listen to our conversation?" I say.

"Oh, they are most certainly trying!" Golmyck says. "You might not have noticed, but the room above us is littered with dozens of hidden devices, made for spying on conversations. Make no mistake, I am not the only person with an information network in this city. And the control I have over my kingdom is in fact a lot more limited than you might think."

"And who are these people that are keeping tabs on you, exactly?" Hadrik asks. "The other kings?"

"Yes, in a way," Golmyck says. "The ones in charge of keeping an eye on me are a group of lessathi who are allies with the other kings, but who work independently. They control a vast underground network of spies and assassins who rival my own, and their purpose is to make sure that I don't take too many initiatives that might 'endanger' the future of Varathia. If I try to take a decision as bold as freeing all of the slaves in my city, I may well get assassinated even before I manage to sign the decree."

"So, you're just going to stand here and do nothing, then?" Daren asks.

"Not at all," Golmyck says. "In fact, I have been working for years to improve our relations with the animal kingdom for this exact purpose. Their territories have been getting smaller and smaller due to the increasing number of monster attacks in recent years, so their negotiators have become a little less rigid lately. I promised to provide them shelter within our walls, on the condition that they help us clear the lessathi threat from our city. I will have a meeting in this very room with one of the representatives of the animal kingdom in a few days, where we will discuss this exact topic. If everything goes well, it is very likely that we will be reaching an agreement in the next few months."

"So, what you're trying to say here is that you've got everything under control, and that we should no longer interfere?" Hadrik asks.

"Yes, exactly," Golmyck says. "I wanted to make sure that you were aware of the whole situation, in case you'd be tempted to do something rash again."

"A few months is too long," I say. "Maybe we can take care of your lessathi problem, instead."

"Oh?" Golmyck says, while stroking his chin. "And

do you speak for your entire team, when you are making this proposal, young lessathi? Or do you only speak for yourself?"

The gnome's words took me off guard. While we've already been travelling together for a week, I'm not sure if everyone would agree to join me on this potentially suicidal mission.

As I stand there, and try to think of an answer to give the gnome, Daren takes my side, and he puts his hand on my shoulder.

"He speaks for me as well," Daren tells Golmyck.

"And for me," Hadrik says, as he steps forward. "After hearing what happened to the slave girl, yesterday, I would be more than happy to teach these bastards a lesson, if they are the ones responsible for what's going on in this city."

"Interesting," Golmyck says, and then he turns towards Kate. "What about you, artificial mage? Are you volunteering for this mission as well?"

"These lessathi you spoke of…" Kate says. "Do you know if they are working with other artificial mages? Is there a woman called Diane, who controls electricity, helping them?"

"As far as I know, the lessathi from my city are not using any mages as bodyguards," Golmyck says. "My spies would have certainly found out by now, if there were any other artificial mages in Thilias."

"I see…" Kate says, and she pauses for a few seconds. "Even if Diane is not in this city, there is still a chance that the lessathi might know something about her current whereabouts. If you're all planning to storm their headquarters anyway, then I'm coming as well."

"Well, if everyone else is going, then I guess we're going too, right Petal?" Flower says, enthusiastically.

The girl's eyes turn blue again, as Illuna takes a deep sigh, but she doesn't say anything.

"I'll have to admit that I wasn't expecting you all to offer your help so wholeheartedly," Golmyck says.

He takes a few moments to clear his thoughts before he continues.

"Very well, then," Golmyck says. "I will think about what you've said. We will continue this discussion further, once you return from the arena. After you manage to earn your freedom, you will need to stop by my castle again, in order to receive some documents which will prove that you've served your sentence for your crimes. While these documents will most likely not be needed in Thilias, they should help you deal with guards that might try to have you arrested in other cities, for the murder of the earl of Ollendor. Now, unless you have anything else to discuss with me, I will start writing on that letter of admission for the dwarf, and then you can be on your way."

Once he's done talking, Golmyck writes a few words on a piece of paper, stamps his seal on the letter, and then gives it to Hadrik, so he can show it to the guards at the arena. Just as we turn to leave, the gnome suddenly remembers that he forgot to tell us something.

"Oh, and one last thing," Golmyck says. "I believe this should go without saying, but I will mention it, nonetheless. You should never talk about anything we've discussed in this room as long as you are inside the city. Not even amongst yourselves. You never know when someone might be listening. I called you into this secure room to chat privately because I felt I could trust you with this information. I hope that you will not betray my trust."

"Of course not…" Daren says. "We will take care."

"Very well, then," Golmyck says. "In that case, I wish you luck in the arena, and may the gods be with you!"

"May they watch over us all," Daren says.

After we finish our discussion with Golmyck, we say our goodbyes to the gnome, and we leave him to work on his devices, while we start to climb up the narrow stairs, one by one. When we reach the throne room, we see that the king's servant was already waiting for us, at the top of the stairs.

"This way, if you please," the servant says, as he starts walking towards the exit. "Make sure that you follow me closely, so you won't get lost."

"Don't worry, Barry, we're right behind you!" Hadrik says, and then he grins at me widely. "Isn't that right, Barry?"

"Oh, shut up," I tell him, as we all start to follow the servant out of the room, and towards our new prison.

Chapter 2

"Listen, Arraka," Daren says, as we walk towards the arena. "Are you absolutely sure that the Eiden you've fought during the still winter is the same person as the one we're dealing with now? I mean, it's been six hundred years, right? No one would blame you if you were to make a confusion after all this time!"

"Damn it, this is the third time you've asked me this exact same question," Arraka says. "Yes, it's the same Eiden from six hundred years ago. Get it through your thick skull, already!"

"Daren, why are you finding this so hard to believe?" Kate says. "We already knew that he was six hundred years old and that he was an old acquaintance of Arraka and the golden fox. Given his power, it wasn't that big of a stretch to assume that he was the one who defeated Arraka all that time ago."

"It's not the fact that he could beat Arraka that I find hard to believe," Daren says. "It's the fact that he is known as the founder of this continent's civilization, when all we've seen him do so far is wreak havoc, for the sole purpose of his amusement!"

"People change over time," Kate says. "Correct me if I'm wrong, but didn't Eiden tell you when you first met that the reason he is keeping his eyes closed is because he got tired of seeing the ugliness of humanity? You've seen the way he acted around the earl and the ambassador of Ollendor. It's clear that he no longer holds anything other than disgust and disdain for the inhabitants of Varathia."

"Leaving Eiden aside," I say, "shouldn't we rather be discussing our plans for the arena?"

"Don't worry about the arena!" Hadrik says. "I alone should be more than enough to deal with whatever the ambassador can throw at us!"

"Oh, yeah?" I say. "And what if they separate us?"

"Barry makes a good point," Daren says. "The first thing we need to make sure of is that we can still communicate with each other, even if they decide to throw us in different cells."

Daren takes off his backpack, and then he takes three transceivers out of it.

"Kate, Hadrik, Flower, take these," he says, as he gives each one of them a transceiver. "Barry, you already have a transceiver. I don't think I've shown you this before, but you have a dial on the right side of your transceiver that you can use to change your calling frequency, in order to match the signature frequency of one of the other transceivers. Does everyone see the dial I'm talking about?"

"Yes," we all answer.

"Good," Daren says. "Each of the transceivers is assigned a number, which corresponds to its own unique signature frequency. Make sure you memorize everyone else's number so you'll know who to contact, when the need arises. The numbers are engraved on the back of the transceivers."

I look at the back of my transceiver and see that I am assigned the number 'two'. When we exchange our numbers, I learn that Kate was number three, Flower was four, and Hadrik was five.

"Alright," Daren says. "Now you all know your numbers. As an aside, if you ever need to communicate with transceivers that weren't enchanted by me, there's a small button next to the dial which you can use to switch to normal frequencies. I'll be using the transceiver with the number ‘six’.”

“What about number ‘one’?” I ask.

Daren pauses for a few seconds.

“That’s the number of the transceiver I was using originally,” Daren says, in a low voice. “The one I gave to Rose.”

“Oh,” I say, and then we all stay silent for a few moments.

“So, uh, do we know for sure that they’re going to allow us to keep our transceivers after we get sent to our cells?” Hadrik asks.

“You will be allowed to keep any items you wish,” the king’s servant says, having overheard our discussion. “You will each have your own personal cells in which you can store your belongings, but you will be allowed to carry items with you as well.”

“What about weapons?” Daren asks. “Are we allowed to use our own weapons and armor during the fights in the arena?”

“Yes, as long as your weapons don’t cast any spells, you are allowed to use any weapons you have at your disposal,” the servant says.

“What do you understand by ‘casting spells’?” I ask. “Would an item that enhances your physical abilities be considered ‘spell casting’?”

“It depends on the nature of the item,” the servant says. “Without knowing what item in particular you are referring to, I cannot give you a definitive answer to your question.”

I pull the stat device out of my pocket and show it to him.

“I’m talking about this item,” I say. “Do you know of it?”

The servant smiles.

“Yes, I am familiar with it,” he says. “Do not worry. The stat booster’s effect does not count as spell casting.

The magic detectors in the arenas will most definitely ignore it."

"Hey, Barry," Daren says, as both the king's servant and I turn our heads towards him.

"How long can we delay our trip to the arena?" Daren says, looking at the king's servant. "Can it wait half an hour? I was thinking that I could cast some basic sharpness and durability enchantments on my friends' daggers, if I find a shop that sells elven steel along the way."

"There is enough time," the king's servant says. "If you're looking for a shop that sells enchanting materials, there should be one in the marketplace we'll be reaching shortly."

"Why do you need elven steel, specifically?" I ask Daren.

"Elven steel is the best quality steel that money can buy," Daren says, "and basic enchantments like sharpness and durability are highly dependent on the quality of the materials used for enchantment."

"Is there any chance you could enchant my crossbow as well?" I ask.

"You are not allowed to use ranged weapons within the arenas of Varathia," the king's servant says.

"I'll be honest with you, Barry," Daren tells me, "even if ranged weapons were allowed, I would still not recommend getting your crossbow enchanted. It would be much better to buy a new one. Basic enchantment just isn't enough to compensate for poor craftsmanship. With daggers, it's different, because the quality of the metal is much more important than the way the blade was made."

"Why do you keep talking about basic enchantments?" Hadrik says. "Aren't you supposed to be one of the most skilled enchanters in the world? Why don't you just cast some of those crazy enchantments that you have on your sword on Barry and Kate's daggers?"

Daren frowns at him.

"The more advanced the enchantment, the more time and resources it requires," he says. "It would take me weeks to cast the enchantments I used on my sword, and it would cost a small fortune to acquire the needed materials. I doubt that I'll be doing anything other than basic enchantments for the duration of this tournament. Barry, Kate, give me your daggers. I will enchant them both as soon as we reach that shop."

Once he finds the shop, Daren goes in, and he doesn't come out until exactly half an hour later. After Daren gets out of the shop, he first gives Kate her dagger, and then he stops in front of me, with his hand held out, looking as if he were expecting some sort of payment.

"That will be ten gold coins," Daren says. "You can pay me with money from the Western Continent, if you want."

"You're charging me money?" I ask him, a little surprised.

"Well, what did you expect?" Daren says. "It's not like I was given all that elven steel for free, you know."

"But you didn't ask Kate for any money!" I say.

"That's because I didn't happen to see her pocketing a few dozen expensive gems in a certain ogre fortress a few days ago," Daren says. "You, on the other hand, should have money to spare."

"So, that's how it is," I say, with a grin.

"Cough it up," Daren says, with his hand still held out.

"Fine, fine," I say, as I place ten gold coins into Daren's palm, and then take back my dagger.

It took us about two more hours to get from the marketplace to the arenas. Once we reached our destination, we waved goodbye to the king's servant, and then we went inside a small building near the arena which we were told was the 'main office'. The room we entered looked more like the inside of a prison, than an office, but there was a man sitting at a desk in front of us, who seemed to be arranging some papers when we came in. The man paid us no mind until he finished what he was doing, and then he got up and greeted us with a curt nod.

"I was told that you'd be coming here tonight," he says, in a disinterested tone. "Only three of you will be participating, am I correct?"

"Four," Hadrik says, with a wide grin, as he hands his admission letter from the king to the desk worker.

"I see," the desk worker says, after he reads the letter. "Very well, then. Given that I am the only one who is still working at this late hour, I will have to ask you to wait patiently in this lobby, while I lead each one of you to your individual cells."

"Can't we just all go at once?" Hadrik asks.

"No," the desk worker says. "The ambassador of Ollendor insisted that none of you are to know the locations of each other's cells. He also made sure that you are each placed into separate divisions, so that you cannot work together during the arena events."

"Divisions?" Daren asks, confused.

"We'll start with the lessathi," the desk worker says, ignoring Daren.

He walks to a door behind him, and he turns to me.

"This way," he says.

I take one last look at everyone else, and then I go to follow the desk worker.

"Good luck, Barry!" Flower shouts, as I head through the door. "Petal and I will be cheering for you from the audience! And I'm sure Arraka will too!"

Once the door closes behind me, I start to walk slowly behind the desk worker, as we both begin to make our way down a very long flight of stairs. We don't exchange any words while we traverse the dark corridors beneath the arenas. With all of the twists and turns we're taking, it's hard to tell if I could still find my way back by myself. The torches inside the underground tunnels are dimly lit, and all of the doors look the same. After a long period of silence, the desk worker finally chooses to speak.

"There are currently two empty cells left in your division," he says. "Cell number three and cell number five. They are located on opposite sides of the recreational area. I haven't been ordered to place you in any specific cell of the two. Which one would you prefer?"

"I don't know," I say. "What's the difference between the two of them?"

"There is no difference," the desk worker says, bluntly.

"No difference at all?" I ask.

"None whatsoever."

"So, why are you asking me, then?"

"I'm asking you so you can make a decision. Now choose. Which will it be? Cell number three or cell number five?"

"I guess I'll go with cell number five, then," I say.

"Very well," the desk worker says. "Cell number five is located on the right side of the recreational area. Its number is written on the door."

He stops in front of a door, and he pulls a key out of his pocket.

"This is the key to your cell," he says, as he hands me the key. "You are advised to leave your belongings inside your cell and to lock the door when you are away. You can choose to spend most of your time locked inside your individual cell if you wish, but you will be required to spend at least two hours a day in the recreational area during the recreational period, in order to learn to get along with your new teammates."

The desk worker then pulls another key out of his pocket, and he uses it to open the door in front of him.

"This door will lead you to the recreational area of your division," he says. "I recommend that you go directly to sleep, because your next recreational period is scheduled for tomorrow morning."

I nod to him and then go through the open door.

"Farewell," the desk worker says, as he closes the door behind me.

The room I am now finding myself in is only being lit by a few candles. The recreational area appears to be empty, except for one particularly bulky man, wearing leather armor, who is now steadily approaching me.

"I've been waiting for you," the man says, in a menacing tone. "I heard that they'd be bringing you in tonight."

"Do I know you?" I ask him, confused.

"No, I don't see why you would," the bulky man says, as he stops a few feet in front of me. "I don't know who you are either."

"Then why were you waiting for me?" I say.

"Because I've heard the guards talking," the man says. "They were talking about a group of mages who killed the earl of Ollendor, and I heard them say that a member of that group would be sent to our division tonight. I'll have to admit that I wasn't expecting a stillwater."

I remain silent. There would be no point in correcting him. I'd much rather have everyone think I'm an all-powerful stillwater than give away the fact that I'm not a mage at all.

"It doesn't matter, though," the bulky man continues. "You may as well be one of the four sages, for all the good it will do you. Magic is not allowed in here. I could very well crush your puny head with my bare hands and you wouldn't be able to do anything about it."

"Now, why would you want to do that?" I ask him. "Aren't we supposed to be part of the same team?"

The man's face contorts into a snarl at the sound of my words.

"Do you have any idea what you've done, you little bastard?" the man shouts.

"Nope," I say. "No idea whatsoever. Why don't you explain it to me?"

"Oh, I'll explain it to you," the man says, grinding his teeth. "Your little stunt with that noble has sealed all of our fates. I heard the guards saying that the next arena event will be the greatest in all the history of Varathia. They're not expecting any of us to make it out alive. They are sending us all to our deaths, just to make sure that they also kill you in the process."

The man is now clenching his fist so hard that blood is starting to drip out of it. While the two of us were talking, the doors leading to the individual cells were opening one by one, and people who had been woken up by the sound of the bulky man's voice were now stepping out of their rooms, to watch the show.

"The only reason why I came to Thilias," the bulky man says, "was because I heard the gnome king would rarely let the arena events in his city endanger the lives of the gladiators. I came here because I thought there was some easy money to be made. But now?... Now I'm just sitting here, waiting for my execution. Cursing my fate. Cursing you!"

"Why don't you just leave, then?" I say.

"You think I didn't try?!" the man shouts, even louder than before. "The owner of the arena isn't letting any of us go. It's the first time in years when he's being allowed to make the show as deadly as he wants. Do you know that he's been collecting rare beasts and keeping them in the underground tunnels for the past ten years, waiting for a chance to parade them in front of an audience? Well, now that he's finally been given permission, the man is planning to make us fight every single one of them! He wants to make this the crowning moment of his career. He doesn't care about what the king of Thilias will do to him if he goes overboard. As long as this one show is successful, he may as well die, for all he cares, and so can we."

"Get a hold of yourself," I tell him. "You're acting as if we're being sent to the gallows, not to a gladiatorial event. I didn't come here to waste time, wallowing in self-pity. I came here to win."

After hearing what I had to say, the bulky man completely loses the little self-control he had left, and he swings his right fist at my face, with full force.

Knowing that I've recently upgraded my toughness stat, I make no attempt to dodge his strike, and the man's fist hits me in the bridge of my nose. The impact from the blow makes me feel almost no pain, and it doesn't even make me move an inch from my original position. As the bulky man retracts his arm, I look at him with the same disinterested expression in my eyes as the one that the desk worker had when he looked at me.

This makes the man even angrier, and he begins to put more strength behind his punches, but that doesn't help him much. After about twenty seconds of continuously hitting me in both my head and my stomach, during which I never even bothered to block a single one of his strikes, my attacker suddenly steps back, as if he's only just now understood the futility of his actions. The astonishment is clearly visible on his face, as he just stands there and looks at me, without saying anything.

"Are you done?" I ask him.

"Maybe I was wrong about you, stillwater," the bulky man says, in a tone suggesting that he's still trying to get over the shock of what he'd just witnessed.

He then puts both his hands on my shoulders, and he looks at me with the hope of a man who had not dared to hope any longer.

"Maybe you were right!" he says. "Maybe we can still win this… as long as we work together!"

"How about you apologize for attacking me, first?" I say.

The man starts to laugh, and he takes his hands off me.

"If it's an apology you want, stillwater, then you can have it!" he says. "I am not ashamed of admitting my mistake. I should not have assumed that you were weak, just because you were a mage, and I should not have attacked you without reason. Now, will you fight alongside me in the arena?"

"I guess so," I say. "We are part of the same team, after all."

"That we are!" the man says, with a wide grin on his face, as he gives me one long look, full of respect.

With these last words, the bulky man turns away from me, and he heads towards his cell. Of the four people that were spectating our fight, two are now going back to their cells, one is heading towards me, and the last one is still standing by the door, watching me intently. The one who is heading towards me is a man about my age, who is wearing his hair in a ponytail, and who has a way of smiling that reminds me of Eiden. The one that remained by the door, watching me is a girl with long silver hair, who appears to be no older than twenty.

The man with the ponytail stops in front of me and he smiles politely.

"I see that you were able to hold your own against Bruce even without your magic," he says. "Impressive! Not many would dare to face him head on like you did just now. May I ask you your name?"

"Yeah, it's Barry," I say.

"Barry?" the man asks, a little surprised. "That's an unusual name for a mage."

"So I've been told."

"Forgive me, I didn't mean to sound rude. It's just that most of the mages I've met in the past have had very unique names. Most parents who find out that they have a mage in the family feel the need to show it off in any way they can, so they usually give them pretentious sounding names like Zalnir or Vasiroth. It's almost like a tradition. But to give you such a common name as Barry..."

"My parents have never been the type to follow tradition."

"I see," the man says, smiling, as he extends his hand towards me. "My name is Wilhelm. Pleased to meet you!"

As I start to shake the man's hand, I suddenly get a vision of him stabbing me in the back with an orange hilted dagger, in the middle of an arena.

"Is something wrong?" Wilhelm asks me, as he sees the expression on my face.

"No, everything's fine," I tell him, as I quickly regain my composure.

"Listen," Wilhelm says. "I know that you haven't really gotten the best of receptions here in our division, but I personally think that there's nothing worse than having a fight with a teammate before a life-threatening event such as this. I just wanted to let you know that I'm on your side."

"It's good to know that you're watching my back, Wilhelm!" I say.

"Well, that's all I wanted to say for tonight," Wilhelm says. "We should both go to sleep. I hear that the recreation period is starting early tomorrow."

"Yes, I've heard that too," I say. "Have a good

night!"

"Same to you!" Wilhelm says, as he starts heading towards his cell.

An orange hilted dagger, huh? If my memory doesn't fail me, those are a special kind of enchanted daggers that are used by trained assassins to help conceal their presence. I'd better be careful around this guy.

After Wilhelm closes his door, the girl with the silver hair watches me for another few seconds, and then she also goes inside her room, shutting the door behind her. I decide that there's no use in lingering around any longer, so I head towards my room as well. When I get inside my cell, I see that the only piece of furniture available to me is a bed made entirely out of stone. I lock the door with the key I got from the desk worker, I throw my backpack on the ground, and then I go to sit down on the bed.

The only source of light in the room appears to be coming from a very small window above me, which gives me a direct view towards the corridor outside the recreation area. There doesn't seem to be any movement in the tunnels outside my cell. The guards must either be sleeping, or patrolling a different corridor. I take a sweater out of my backpack and I use it as a makeshift pillow to put on my cold stone bed. As soon as I place my head on it, I fall asleep, and I wake up about seven hours later, to the sound of a guard's voice, coming from outside my cell.

"Get up," the guard says. "It's recreation time. Go recreate. Come on, get out of here!"

I reluctantly get out of bed, put my sweater in my backpack and then head back towards the recreation area. I make sure to lock the door behind me on my way out, and then I head towards a corner of the room where there are no people around.

I take a quick look around the room to see who else

they placed in my division. Aside from Bruce and Wilhelm who I met yesterday, there's the silver haired girl that was staring at me, and then there are two more individuals that both look like the gladiator versions of Cutthroat Dave. The two thugs seem to be the only ones who are actually talking to each other. The other three are each standing somewhere as far as possible from everyone else, leaning with their backs against the walls, their arms crossed, waiting for the recreation period to be over.

What am I supposed to do now? I can't say that I feel like talking with any of these people. What is there to talk about? We weren't even told what the first round will be like. How are we supposed to make a strategy? Maybe I should just go back and get a book to read or something.

As I stand there and think about going back to my cell, Bruce suddenly moves away from the wall, and he starts to head towards me. When he stops in front of me, I see that he has an unusually serious look on his face.

"Listen," he says. "I saw that you were talking to Wilhelm yesterday, after your fight with me, so I wanted to give you a warning."

"A warning?" I say.

"Yeah," Bruce says. "About Wilhelm. He might seem like an ordinary guy to you, but in reality he's a trained assassin. I can tell by the way he moves and speaks. These assassin types can never be trusted. They're not real warriors like you and me. The only way they know how to fight is by stabbing people in the back. You should be careful around him. Don't believe anything he says!"

"Oh, yeah," I say. "I figured that he was an assassin. Don't worry, I'll look out for him."

"Just make sure that you don't get yourself killed before the arena," Bruce says. "You're the only one besides me who can actually put up a fight in this blasted division."

Bruce then pats me on the shoulder, and he goes back to where he was standing at the beginning. Just as I was about to go get that book, it is now Wilhelm who is approaching me, with a determined look on his face.

"Listen," Wilhelm says. "I'm not sure exactly what you were talking about with Bruce, but you should be careful around him."

"I should?" I ask him.

"Yes," Wilhelm says. "You already saw the way he treated you yesterday. He is the kind of person who likes to act before he thinks, and these types of individuals are always dangerous. He might act friendly towards you now, but who knows what he'll do tomorrow. When you're up against unpredictable brutes that prefer to rely on their fists instead of their reason, you can never know when they'll turn against you."

"That's nice," I tell him. "But I have a feeling that this isn't what you came here to talk to me about, is it?"

"No, it isn't," Wilhelm says. "What I wanted to tell you is that from what I've heard, in a few hours from now, the ambassador and the arena's owner should be discussing important matters about the organization of the arena events. The guards from this place have a habit of overhearing these types of conversations and they usually like to discuss them amongst themselves. Make sure you pay close attention to what they're saying when they're outside your cell. I will do the same. "

"I see," I say. "I'll keep that in mind."

"Alright," Wilhelm says. "That's all I wanted to tell you. I'll make sure to let you know if I hear anything. I hope you will do the same."

"Of course," I say.

I suddenly realize that the girl with the silver hair is staring at me again. In fact, I think she's been staring at me for a long time. Wilhelm notices me looking towards the girl, and he gives me a smirk.

"I wouldn't waste my time trying to talk to that one," Wilhelm says. "We've all tried, but she wouldn't say a word. I think that our little silver haired princess is either mute, or she's taken a vow of silence of some sort. Either way, I doubt that you'll get anything out of her."

He then bows politely, and he goes back towards his corner of the room. As Wilhelm walks past the girl on his way back, she pays him no mind, and she keeps looking directly at me.

Okay, now I'm certain that she's doing it on purpose. But what does she want from me? Does she want me to go talk to her? I guess there's only one way to find out.

I calmly start heading towards her, while paying close attention to her reactions. The girl seems unfazed by my decision to approach her, and she keeps looking me in the eyes, even after I stop in front of her.

Now that I take a better look at the girl, I see that she is at least one head shorter than me, and that she has a very frail constitution. I can see why Wilhelm would choose to call her a princess. She definitely doesn't look like a fighter. Her clothes, however, are nothing close to what a princess might wear. She is wearing a simple beige blouse, short leggings that seem comfortable to move in, and wooden sandals.

Despite her frail looking body, the girl is wearing two knives on her belt, and her arms and legs are full of bruises, which indicates that she's likely been in a fight, shortly before she was incarcerated. One other thing I'm noticing is that unlike all the rest of the gladiators, she is the only person without a warning sign above her head, which implies that she is either a tournament participant, or someone who is not a citizen of Varathia, and therefore not protected by their spell.

Seeing that the girl has no intention of saying

anything, I take it upon myself to initiate a conversation.

"So, are you going to tell me why you've been staring at me for the past five minutes?" I ask her, bluntly.

The girl gives me no sign of having heard me, and she keeps looking at me, without any change in her expression.

"Well?" I say. "Aren't you going to say anything?"

Still no response. Wilhelm was right. This is pointless.

I turn away to leave, but then I suddenly feel something pulling on my sleeve. When I turn back, I see that the girl is now holding me by my shirt's sleeve, and there is a blue colored writing, floating in mid-air, in front of her face. The writing is in the Common language, and it says simply: "Wait".

The writing then disappears, and it is replaced by a new text, this time saying: "Is it true, what they say about you?"

"What do you mean?" I ask, looking at the girl. "What do they say about me?"

Just like before, the previous phrase is now being replaced by a new text, which says: "They say that the reason why you were brought here is because you attacked a noble. Is that true?"

"Yeah, that would be the main gist of it," I say.

"But why would you do such a thing?" the blue writing in the air says. "Didn't you know how dangerous it would be to attack a noble in Varathia, let alone kill one?"

"We did," I say. "But we were trying to free a slave. And either way, that bastard had it coming."

The writing disappears again, but this time, there is a short pause before the next text appears.

"You don't seem to like our nobles very much, do you?" the writing says.

"Oh, I hate them with a passion," I say.

The girl smiles. It is the first time that I see an actual change in her facial expression.

"I see," the writing says. "Please, allow me to introduce myself. My name is Leila, and I have also been brought here because I tried to free a slave from a noble."

The girl then extends her hand towards me.

"I'm Barry," I say, as I shake her hand. "Pleased to meet you!"

"Barry, I have a favor to ask of you," the writing says. "Could we continue our conversation inside my cell? There's something else I want to ask you, and I'd rather do it in private."

"Alright, let's go," I say.

Leila nods, and she opens the door to her cell. As we both enter her room, I notice the fact that Wilhelm was watching us attentively, and there was a bit of disappointment on his face when he saw that I accepted the girl's request so easily.

It is only after Leila locks the door that I suddenly start to feel a sense of danger, and I jump back from her, watching her carefully.

"What are you doing?" Leila writes, looking at me, confused.

"I'm trying to tell if this is a trap or not," I tell her.

"A trap?" Leila writes, with a somewhat shocked expression on her face. "For what purpose? Aren't you aware that killing or critically injuring a member of your own division is against the rules?"

"Not really," I tell her. "Nobody bothered to tell me the rules of the arena before coming here."

"But it's one of the standard rules of all the arenas of Varathia!" Leila writes.

"I'm not from around here, remember?" I say.

Leila sighs, and she goes to sit on her bed.

"In that case," Leila writes, "you'd better take care to also not harm the organizers or any of the spectators. That is against the rules, as well."

"Are there any other standard arena rules that I should be aware of?" I ask.

"Yes," Leila writes. "Magic and ranged weapons are not allowed in the arena, and neither are items that can cast any spells. But don't worry, your stat booster doesn't count as a spell casting item. The magic detectors in the arena will ignore it."

The fact that the girl mentioned my stat device so casually took me completely by surprise. When she sees the look on my face, Leila laughs. Even her laughter is silent.

"Yes, I know about your stat device," Leila writes, while smiling.

"How?" I ask her.

Leila pulls a small trinket out of her pocket, and she shows it to me. It's a stat device, just like my own.

"You see, my stat booster is a little special," Leila writes. "Not only does it allow me to transform my thoughts into written words at will, but it also lets me know when there are other stat devices in my area. My father is the one who made these modifications. When you first came in here, I almost bought your stillwater story, but when I saw that you had a stat booster with you, I knew at once that you were a lessathi. There would have been no point in carrying such a device with you, unless you were part of the only race that it was designed to work for."

"But the same goes for you too, doesn't it?" I ask her, starting to finally understand what is going on. "Which means that you are also a lessathi."

Leila nods.

"Then how come you are here, in this arena?" I say. "I had the impression that lessathi have a higher status than nobility on this continent. Can't your father just pull some strings in order to have you released?"

Leila looks down at the ground for a few seconds, before her new text appears.

"My father and I are outcasts," she writes. "We aren't treated the same way as the other lessathi. We've been in hiding for years, but a few months ago my father was sold to a noble, and made into a slave. The reason why I'm here is because they caught me yesterday, shortly after I managed to rescue him."

Outcasts, huh?... I suppose that would explain why Leila doesn't have a warning sign above her head. From what I've heard, the tournament's spell was only cast on citizens of Varathia, and you can't exactly be considered a citizen, if you've been living for years as a fugitive, hiding outside of the cities.

"I see," I tell her.

"After they enslaved him, I never thought I'd see him again," Leila writes. "But a week ago, when the tournament began, and I started receiving my first stat points, I finally felt like I had a chance to free him. I waited until I could upgrade my speed, strength and combat technique stats to their maximum level of three, and then I singlehandedly defeated all of the guards holding my father prisoner. I only wish I'd waited until I could invest a little in toughness as well..."

Leila then shows me the bruises on her arms and legs.

"After I freed my father," Leila continues, "I made him promise that even if I got captured, he'd go to Ollendor without me, and wait for me there. Ollendor is the only remaining city of Varathia where the lessathi hold no power. In Ollendor, we would be safe from them. But the city's guards caught me before I could get out of the city. I held them off until my father could escape, but I was already weakened from the previous battle, and I couldn't beat them all. In the end, they tied me up and sent me here. I arrived in this cell yesterday in the afternoon, not long before you made your appearance."

"You mentioned that you had to wait until you could max your strength, speed and combat technique, and that your current maximum level is three," I say. "But wouldn't that mean that you only had nine available stat points until yesterday?"

"Yes, and I still do," Leila writes. "That is the reason why I wanted to talk to you in private. When I first saw how quickly I was gaining my stat points one week ago, I was amazed, but that was only because I did not know about the tournament. Apparently, it had been announced many times in the past few months, but it's easy to miss these kinds of announcements when you live mostly on the outskirts of the city, in order to avoid detection. It was yesterday in the afternoon, when the gnome king announced the first round's objectives that I first found out about the tournament. This made me realize how much magical energy there really is around us. I would have expected the stat booster to gather a lot more energy, given these circumstances. What I wanted to ask you was this: How many points did you get to spend on your stats until now?"

"Nineteen points," I answer her.

"Nineteen?" Leila writes, looking somewhat shocked.

She pauses.

"Then I suppose that my assumption was correct," Leila writes. "It really is harder for a stat booster to collect energy inside this city."

"I've been noticing that too," I tell her. "I've only gotten two points since I entered the city, but I used to get points a lot faster before, unless I was travelling through completely deserted areas. Maybe it's just because there aren't very many mages from the tournament who found their way to this city?"

"Perhaps," Leila writes. "Or perhaps it's because there are other stat device wielders in this city, and the energy is being split equally among us."

"You think there might be other lessathi using stat devices in this city?" I ask her.

"I don't know," Leila writes. "It's a possibility. Can I have a look at your stat booster, please?"

"Yeah, sure, I guess…" I say, as I take my stat device out of my pocket and show it to her.

The girl gives the device one long pondering look, before she writes again.

"Thank you," Leila writes. "I wanted to see how fast your stat booster is gathering energy, compared to mine. Yours is working a little better, but not enough to justify a ten points difference between us."

"You can tell all that just by looking at it?" I ask her.

"No, of course not," Leila writes. "Not by looking. I can tell by sensing the flow of the magical energy surrounding it. Can't you?"

"Well, I guess I can sort of feel the flow of it," I say, "but there's no way I could tell which one of our two devices is gathering more than the other."

"That's strange," Leila writes. "If you can't even tell the difference between our two devices, then how did you know that the stat booster was designed to work for lessathi before coming to this tournament? From what you've told me, it doesn't seem like you are acquainted with any of the other lessathi, so you must have discovered it on your own somehow. Unless…"

Leila pauses.

"Unless you had absolutely no idea how powerful the device would really be," Leila continues, "and you were planning to keep pretending that you are a stillwater until the end of the tournament, with your stat device only as a backup plan."

"What do you mean?" I say. "Of course I knew that

the device works better for lessathi!"

Leila starts to giggle silently, while covering her mouth with her hand.

"You are such a bad liar," Leila writes. "Your aura gets all spiky when you're not telling the truth."

"My aura gets… spiky?" I ask.

"I can't believe how crazy you are!" Leila writes, while smiling. "No one in their right mind would even think to try and bluff their way through a tournament like this! Now I understand why you seem so calm, even after you've heard what the arena's owner is preparing for us. This is just another regular day for you, isn't it?"

"Well, I don't know If I'd go so far as to call it regular," I say. "This is only the third time I've been thrown into a prison since I came to Varathia. There's still room for improvement."

"Hey, you two!" I hear a guard shouting to us from the window of Leila's cell. "You can have all the private conversations you want on your own free time. This is the recreation period. Get back outside!"

"Aye, aye, sir!" I say, and we both head back towards the recreation area.

Once we're out, Leila and I get back to our original positions, without saying another word to each other. We've already said what we needed to say, and there was no reason to give Wilhelm any more opportunities to spy on our conversations.

The rest of the recreation period was spent in silence. There was nothing for us to discuss about the upcoming fights, and nobody seemed to be in the mood for idle chatter. Since we couldn't just stand and do nothing for two hours, each of us tried to find something to occupy our time with. Bruce started doing push-ups, Wilhelm chose to sharpen his dagger, I spent my time reading from my notebook and the two thugs decided to play some dice. Leila seemed to be the only one content with simply standing there, gazing at an empty wall in front of her until the recreation period ended.

As soon as the recreation period was over, we all went quietly back to our cells. I continued to read from my notebook for a few more hours after leaving the recreation area. I've been reading through my notes about various creatures that I've come across in my studies, but there are so many of them that it's difficult to memorize all of the information by heart.

I still remember the day when I enchanted this notebook. It was the day when I decided to begin my journey around the world, in the hopes of finding a way to become a mage. The enchantment cost me a fortune, but it was still a lot cheaper than enchanting a backpack, and it was more than what I needed for my intents and purposes. A notepad with an endless number of pages. Was there any other tool that could have served me better in my quest for knowledge?

I skim through the pages again, trying to guess which creatures the arena's owner is more likely to throw at us. There are harpies, wargs, wyverns, three headed hounds, mammoths, giant spiders, giant eagles… The list is endless. And let's not forget that each type of creature has its own subcategories that cannot be ignored, because they are sometimes wildly different from each other. You can have red spiders, green spiders, white spotted black spiders and even ten-legged spiders, each of them with their own unique behaviors and weaknesses.

Now that I think about it, Bruce mentioned that the arena's owner was fond of dangerous creatures, but does that mean that he might be keeping monsters of the humanoid type in here as well? Monsters might be treated as if they are all mindless creatures by most people, but the reality is a little different. Monsters of the humanoid variety are generally much more intelligent than the average creature. Some of them are even organized in tribes, and they can communicate advanced information with each other through their own languages, even if most of them don't speak Common. The ogres from the fort were one such example. If they have any monsters here that are as strong as the ogre captain or the shaman, then we might be in for one hell of a fight.

As I sit on my bed and read, I suddenly hear a man's voice coming from my cell's window.

"Greetings," the voice says.

I turn around, to see if I can get a glimpse of the man's face, but he is hiding behind the wall outside my cell.

"Do I know you?" I ask him.

"No," the voice says. "But I heard that there was a fellow lessathi among the prisoners who were brought here yesterday evening, so I came to pay you a visit."

"A fellow lessathi, you say…" I tell him.

"Yes," the voice says. "I am here to offer you a deal. Normally we do not deal with criminals, but since you are a lessathi, I believe that it's only fair to give you a second chance."

He pauses.

"Go on…" I say.

"You see," the voice continues, "we couldn't help but notice that the king of Thilias seems to have placed an unusual amount of trust in you and your companions. Enough trust to invite you into his secret room below the throne. That is not the kind of invitation that is acquired easily."

He pauses again, to see if I have anything to say. He waits for a few more seconds, and then he continues from where he left off.

"The deal that we want to offer you is simple," the voice says. "All you need to do is convince the king to let you into his secret room again, while carrying one of our devices."

"Is this device of yours a bomb, by any chance?" I ask him.

The voice laughs softly.

"Of course not," he says. "If we wanted to assassinate the king, I assure you that there would be much easier, risk-free methods to use in order to get the job done."

"Then what is it that you are trying to do?"

"We are trying to subtly interfere with the way that one of the gnome's own devices works. One of the gnome king's inventions is currently making his secret room completely soundproof, which stops us from listening in on his private conversations. However, at the moment, we do not have any agents that the king trusts enough to allow them access to his secret room. This is why we turn to you. We are not asking you to do this for free, of course. There are ways in which we could make your fights here in the arena much easier for you. All you need to do is agree to help us, and we will take care of the rest."

"No, thanks," I say. "I like to keep things challenging."

There is a brief pause, during which none of us says anything.

"Is this your final answer?" the lessathi asks me.

"Sure," I say.

"While I did say that we could make things easier for you in the arena if you agreed to help us," the lessathi says, "what I omitted to say was that we can also make things more difficult for you if you refuse."

"In what way?" I ask.

"For example, we could have the guards confiscate your stat device, and leave you completely defenseless," the lessathi says.

"Okay, I don't know how you found out about my

stat device," I say, "but I'm pretty sure that it isn't illegal to use it, according to your arena rules."

"I never said that it's illegal," the lessathi says. "I only said that we would have the guards confiscate it. A little chat with the arena's owner should be enough to bend the rules for this one special occasion. Now, do we have an agreement, or not?"

He seems serious. But even so, I'm not planning to betray the king, just to save my own skin. Let's see if I can bluff my way out of this…

"Well, mister lessathi, sir, I guess you've got yourself a deal!" I lie to him.

"Excellent!" the lessathi says. "Here is the device that I told you about."

The lessathi throws a small piece of metal through the window of my room. It looks rather ordinary, except for a few engravings on it.

"Make sure that you don't lose it," the lessathi says. "It would be difficult to obtain a spare."

I can hear the lessathi moving to leave.

"Oh," he says. "And you should be expecting a last minute addition to your team before the arena event begins. He will take care of most of your problems."

Not long after the lessathi leaves, I start to hear some voices in a distant hallway outside my cell. I recognize one of the voices as that of the guard who woke me up this morning.

"Hey, did you hear about this morning's meeting?" the guard says.

"The one between the owner and the ambassador?" the other voice says.

"Yeah," the guard says. "I heard that they're bringing out the minotaur in round two."

"The minotaur?" the other voice asks, shocked. "You mean, the undefeated champion of the arena?"

"The one and only," the guard says. "And I heard that

they're also going to use the giant scorpions and the manticores for round one."

"What about round three?" the other voice says. "Will there still be duels between the gladiators?"

"Yeah, the survivors will have to fight each other in one on one duels at the end," the guard says. "But nobody is expecting any of them to make it past round one."

The last phrase was barely audible, as the guards were getting further and further away from me while they talked. The last thing I hear from them is the roaring of their laughter, as their voices fade away completely.

Scorpions and manticores, huh? It's a good thing that I've got extensive notes written about them in my notebook. At least we won't go in completely unprepared.

I spent the rest of the afternoon reading from my notes. When I felt like taking a break, I called Daren, Kate and Hadrik through the transceivers, to find out how they were doing. Daren told me that he couldn't stand any of his teammates, and that they were all cowardly mercenaries who had come here to make easy money. Kate said that she almost killed one of her teammates during the recreation period, and that she only stopped when she found out it was against the rules. No one had tried to pick a fight with her since.

Hadrik seemed to be doing a little better. From what he told me, he'd already made most of his teammates into his drinking buddies, and they were spending a lot more time in the recreation area than the two daily hours they were required to.

I also made sure to tell my friends everything that I heard from the two guards earlier, as well as the weaknesses and behaviors of each type of scorpions and manticores that I knew of. Hopefully, this information will help them out in some way.

After I finished talking to everyone, I got back to my reading, and I kept doing that until later in the evening, when I was interrupted by the creak of a door, and by the sound of a familiar voice.

"Farewell," I hear the disinterested voice of the desk worker coming from the recreation area, as a door slams shut.

I immediately realize what this means, and I open the door of my cell, to see who the newest member of our division is. The man who just entered the recreation area is simply radiating magical energy, and he makes no attempt at hiding it. However, he does not appear to be one of the tournament's participants, because I'm seeing a warning sign above his head, telling me not to hurt him. He must be one of the local mages. Judging by the look on his face, it's clear that he didn't come here of his own free will, so he's likely been sent here because he broke the Varathian law in some way. The mage notices me, but he doesn't bother to acknowledge my presence, and he goes directly to his room.

The rest of the day was mostly uneventful, except for a drunk call that I got from Hadrik on the transceiver, who insisted on passing me one of his teammates, because of the funny way in which he impersonated a famous noble from the Western Continent.

The next morning, I get woken up by the same guard from the previous day, telling me that the recreation period had started.

"Wakey-wakey!" the guard says. "It's recreation time!"

I open the door to my cell and start heading towards an empty area of the recreation room, just like yesterday. As I walk, I overhear the two thugs from my division talking loudly several feet away from me, and I turn around to see what's going on. It looks like they're talking to Leila, as she is casually leaning with her back against the wall, watching them silently.

"Hey, princess," one of the thugs says. "How about you take us both to your room, like you did with the stillwater, yesterday?"

"Yeah," the other thug says. "We have some very important tactical information that we'd like to discuss with you."

Leila continues to look at them, without saying anything. The first thug who spoke concludes that he wasn't being intimidating enough, so he now places both his hands on the wall behind her, as he leans closer to her face.

"Listen, princess," the thug says. "You can drop the silent act. I know you can understand me. So you'd better wise up and do what I say, or else I'm going to hurt you so bad, that you'll wish you—"

The thug didn't get to finish his sentence, because Leila decided she's had enough, and she punched him so hard in the stomach that the man fell down and started rolling on the floor from the pain.

"You bitch!" the other thug shouts, as he pulls out his knife, but he doesn't get a chance to use it, because a sudden kick from Leila sends him flying into a nearby wall.

"By the gods, that was amazing!" we hear Bruce shout from the other end of the room.

He rushes over to Leila and he grabs her by both her shoulders. Leila looks a bit shocked, but she quickly realizes that there is no ill-intent behind the man's actions, so she doesn't attack him.

"With strength like that, you could take out a small battalion by yourself!" Bruce says, enthusiastically. "How did they even manage to capture you?"

Suddenly, Bruce realizes that he got carried away too much, and he releases Leila from his grasp.

"I'm sorry," Bruce says. "I know that you don't like to talk. But I just want you to know that I've got your back. Whenever you feel like you're in a pinch in the arena, remember that you can count on me to help. That's all I wanted to say."

Leila looks a little confused, but she nods slowly, in acknowledgement of his words.

"Alright, then," Bruce says. "I'll be over there, if you need me."

He then turns away from her, and he goes back to his end of the room.

The thug that got punched in the stomach managed to get back on his feet, and he's now rushing towards his fallen comrade, who still hasn't woken up from his collision with the wall. Eventually, he manages to wake him up, and then they both walk towards their corner of the room, without even daring to glance towards Leila on their way back.

Nothing else happened during the two hour long recreation period. The mage from yesterday isolated himself, just like everyone else, and he hasn't exchanged a single word with anyone. I would have expected Wilhelm to welcome him to the division, like he did with me, but it seems that he didn't consider him worth the bother.

After we return to our cells, I go to sit on my bed, and I open my notebook. Not long after I start reading, I hear three light knocks on my door.

"Who is it?" I ask.

There is no answer. A few seconds later, there are three more knocks on the door which are a little louder than the last ones.

"If you're not going to answer me, then I won't open the door," I say.

Still no answer. After a brief pause, I can hear three more knocks on the door. I ignore them, and I go back to reading my notebook. Seeing that I'm no longer reacting, my visitor has now switched to knocking once every second, without stopping. After about a minute of constant knocking, I finally reach my limit, and I go open the door, leaving my notebook on the bed.

"What is it?" I shout, but I suddenly get silenced when I see that the person standing in front of me was none other than Leila.

"Oh…" I say, as I quickly understand why I wasn't getting an answer earlier.

Leila is staring straight at me, and she looks rather upset. Without a word, she grabs me by the arm, and she starts pulling me towards her room.

"Wait, I need to lock the room!" I say.

She stops, but she doesn't release my arm. She waits for me until I find my key and lock the door, and then she starts pulling me by the arm again, without looking at me.

"Look, I'm sorry!" I say. "I forgot that you couldn't talk."

Leila gives no sign of having heard me, and she keeps pulling on me until we get in front of her door. She then releases me, as she searches her pockets for her cell's key. Once she unlocks and opens the door, she gives me the same upset look as before, and she points towards her room.

"Okay, okay, I'm going," I say, as I enter her cell.

After she locks the door, Leila grabs me by the arm again, and she places my left hand on the wall behind her bed. She then looks me straight in the eyes, as if she's expecting some kind of reaction from me.

"Is there… something special about this wall?" I ask her, confused.

"Yes," Leila writes, with her usual blue text.

"Well, can you give me some sort of hint?" I say. "What am I looking for, exactly?"

"Don't try to look," Leila writes. "You need to feel it. Try concentrating your magical sense on your hand, as you are touching the wall, and you will understand what I mean."

As I do what Leila says, I suddenly realize that the wall is somehow resonating perfectly with my magical aura, and that it's reacting directly to my touch.

"Okay, you're right," I tell her. "There's definitely more to this wall than you can tell just by looking. But it's not doing anything. Even if it's reacting directly to my touch, I feel like it's still waiting for something to happen."

Leila nods.

"That's because the wall on the opposite side of the room is made in the same way," Leila writes. "I think that these walls react directly to our lessathi auras, and that they are supposed to act as switches that need to be pressed at the same time by two different lessathi."

"Switches for what?" I ask.

"For opening a passage to the underground caverns beneath these tunnels," Leila writes. "I've seen these kinds of switches before, in other buildings made by lessathi. They always open up secret passages. And I've heard that the caverns below us are where the arena's owner is keeping all the creatures locked up. If we could get a quick look, we would at least know what we'll be going up against. Or even better, we could sabotage the whole show, by killing the creatures one by one, while they are in their cages, instead of fighting them all at once in the arena."

"That does sound tempting," I say. "But what if they catch us? Won't they be able to disqualify us for cheating?"

"There are no rules saying that we can't kill the creatures before the arena event begins," Leila writes. "However…"

Leila pauses.

"However, what?" I ask.

"However," Leila continues, "the rules of the arena do state that the safety of the participants is not guaranteed outside of the area designated for their division."

"So, what you're saying is that if they catch us in the act, they can unleash all of their beasts upon us, without any restraint."

Leila nods.

"We can just go take a look," Leila writes, "and if we see that there are too many guards, we'll go back to our cells."

I pause a bit to think.

"Alright," I say. "We'll take one look, and we can decide after that."

Leila nods again. She then goes to the other end of the room, near the door, extending her hand towards the wall.

"Are you ready?" she writes.

"As ready as I'll ever be, I guess," I say.

Leila then places her hand on the wall, and at the same time, I can feel a sort of magical current flowing through my palm. Almost immediately afterwards, the floor beneath us opens up, and the next thing we know, we're both falling into a pit, while we can see the floor to our room slowly closing itself back up, above our heads. After what seemed like a hundred foot drop, we fall into an underground lake, with a big splash. As I tread water to keep myself afloat, I take a look above me, to see if there's any way we could go back the way we came.

The cavern's walls and ceiling around us seem to be littered with some sort of glowing blue crystals that are providing a fair bit of lighting throughout the area, but I see no obvious way to climb back up to our cell. The only things leading upwards are some ropes that are tied to a pulley which is hanging from the ceiling, but there's no way I could climb all the way up there on some rope.

Suddenly, I can hear the sound of repeated splashing water behind me, and as I turn to look, I see Leila desperately flinging her arms through the water, with her mouth wide open, looking as if she'd forgotten that she couldn't talk and was trying to scream. Realizing what's happening, I quickly swim towards her, and grab her by her shoulders, in order to stop her arms from flailing.

"Leila, it's okay!" I tell her, as she's looking at me, terrified. "Just grab onto me. I'll lead us to shore."

It takes her a few moments, but eventually she calms down, and she grabs onto me with both of her arms, holding me very tightly. Once I lead her safely to the shore, we take a break to catch our breaths. We are both soaked to the skin, and the air around here is definitely not as warm as it is on the surface. Ideally, I would make a fire in this situation, but is there any wood to be found in an underground cavern such as this?

My question gets immediately answered as I turn around and see a wooden cabin a few hundred feet from where we're standing. There's also a big pile of logs stacked up right in front of its door. How convenient.

As I look towards the cabin, Leila pulls on my shirt, to get my attention. When I turn to look at her, I see that she's lying on her knees, with her wet hair covering most of her face, and her head bowed down.

"I'm sorry," she writes, simply.

"About what?" I ask.

"About dragging you into this," she writes.

"Leila," I say, "If you hadn't dragged me into this, you would have ended up drowning in that lake."

Leila keeps staring at the ground, as her writing slowly disappears.

"Listen," I say, "there's nothing to be sorry about. I

didn't think this would be a trap either. I'm still not sure if it's a trap, actually. I mean, I'm sure that it was designed as a trap originally, but who knows if anyone even remembers that it exists. Either way, even if we've lost our way back, I don't think that we're in the wrong place. The only thing that's changed is that we now also have to look for a way back to our cells, while we look for the creatures."

As I talk to Leila, the ropes leading to the ceiling are starting to catch my attention. They're all coming out of the water, and the way they are distanced from each other makes me think that they are tied to some sort of platform at the bottom of the lake. Possibly an elevator. I wonder if there's a lever or something at the bottom of the lake that could activate the elevator and get us out of here.

"I just thought of something," I say. "Do you see those ropes?"

Leila nods.

"I think that they might be tied to a platform at the lower end," I say. "I want to check out the bottom of the lake, and see if there isn't a lever of some sort that I can use to activate the elevator. Can you wait for me here?"

"Okay," Leila writes.

I jump into the lake and I swim back towards the ropes. When I reach them, I take a deep breath, and I dive into the water. It seems that I was right. There really is a platform at the very bottom of the lake, tied to the ropes. However, there is no obvious mechanism that looks like it could be used to operate the elevator, as far as I can see. The only thing that looks like something of the sort is a stone pillar, next to the platform, with a hole at the top, shaped like a spider. If this elevator is requiring some kind of a spider shaped key in order to get activated, then I'm out of luck. After a few more unsuccessful rounds of circling the platform for signs of a lever, I finally run out of breath, and I go back to the surface to get some air in my lungs. This is pointless. Unless I find that spider key, there's no way I can operate this elevator. I might as well get back to shore.

"Did you find anything?" Leila writes, as she sees me get out of the water.

"I didn't see any levers," I say, as I squeeze the water out of my shirt. "The most I could find was a pillar with a spider shaped hole in it. Unless we find a spider shaped key of some sort, that elevator isn't going to be of much use to us. Let's head for the cabin. Maybe we'll find some flint or something to start a fire with."

Leila nods, and we both start to walk towards the cabin. There's something that's been bugging me about this wooden cabin since I first saw it. Unless there are some trees miraculously growing in these caverns somewhere, this cabin could not have been built by someone who got trapped in here before us. This means that it was most likely built by the same persons who designed the trap, or at least by people who know about it, and who can reach this place by some other means. The fact that there are a bunch of logs conveniently placed right next to the lake in which we fell makes me believe that this was done intentionally. Why would they go out of their way to make things more comfortable for us? Is this their way of granting us our last wish, before they send the beasts to kill us?

As we reach the cabin, I go inside carefully, making sure that there are no traps. The cabin doesn't have any fireplace or chimney, but there's some firewood inside, and also some flint. I take the firewood and the flint outside, and then I take some of the dried up moss from the cave's walls to provide a bit of kindling. Once we've set up the fire, Leila and I sit ourselves down next to it, trying to get as close to the heat as we can.

"Hey, this is not half bad," I tell Leila, as the two of

us do our best to warm ourselves up by the fire. "For a quick improvised fire that we lighted with flint and moss, I'd say we did pretty well!"

Leila nods.

"So…" I say. "Are you still upset about earlier?"

Leila looks at me confused.

"You know," I say. "When I refused to open the door of my cell for you."

"Oh," Leila writes. "No. I'd already forgotten about it…"

She then turns her back to the fire, trying to dry her hair without getting it burnt.

"You know, I've always meant to ask," I say, as I watch her dry her hair. "Is silver your natural hair color? I've never seen anyone with silver hair before, but then again, I can't say that I've met many lessathi in my life."

Leila doesn't answer me, and she just stares in front of her for a while. It's difficult to tell what expression she has on her face, because of the hair in her eyes.

"Is this something that you don't want to talk about?" I say.

"No, it's fine…" Leila writes.

She pauses.

"Have you ever heard of the Beacon of Hope?" she writes.

"If you're talking about the orphanage that was experimenting with creating artificial mages, then yes, I've heard of it," I say. "Were you one of the lessathi who worked there?"

Leila shakes her head.

"No," she writes. "I was one of the failed experiments. The reason why my hair is silver is because it lost its color gradually, as a side-effect of the several years in which they experimented on me, trying to make me into a mage. My hair used to be pitch black."

"Oh, gods," I say. "Is this also the reason why you

lost your voice?"

"No," Leila writes. "I was born this way. And I was given hell because of it. I don't remember much from when I was little, but I do remember what the other lessathi used to say about me. They said that I wasn't a real lessathi. They said that the lessathi are a pure race that cannot have any birth defects, and they suspected that the reason why I was born a mute was because I was in fact a half-lessathi. I think that even the person that I once used to call my father had doubts about me. He never seemed to consider me his real child, and he always used to blame my mother for dying, and for leaving him to care for her daughter. That's probably why he didn't think twice when they asked if any of the lessathi who worked at the Beacon were willing to volunteer their children for experimentation."

"Wait, you just said that you used to call him your father," I say. "But you said yesterday that the reason why you were brought here was because you saved your father from slavery. This person that you saved… is he someone other than your natural father?"

"The person I saved is the one that I've been calling father for the past eleven years," Leila writes. "He is the one who rescued me from the Beacon all those years ago, when I was almost about to give up all hope."

"Is this why the two of you became outcasts?" I ask her.

Leila nods.

"My father had been one of the caretakers at the Beacon," Leila writes. "When he couldn't bear to see us suffer any longer, he decided to help us escape, even if he knew that this meant he would be marked as an outcast for the rest of his life."

"Were there any others who escaped with you?" I ask her.

Leila shakes her head.

"My father tried to convince other children to follow him, but they were too afraid to trust him," Leila writes. "They must have thought that he was trying to trick them. He didn't have the time to talk to all of them, because one of the orphans ratted him out to the other lessathi, and he was forced to make a run for it. He made one last attempt to save the orphans, opening their cells before leaving the facility, but in the end, I was the only one who followed him."

"Didn't they try to capture you afterwards?" I say.

"They did," Leila writes. "That's why we were forced to live the next few years of our lives hiding in the woods of Varathia. At first, we would change our location once every few days, to make sure that they don't pick up our trail. But, after a few months, my father finally managed to obtain all the parts he needed to make a suggestion device. Suggestion spells are spells that can implant certain thoughts into the minds of people, and make them think that these thoughts are in fact their own. The device that my father made could cast a spell that would make people avoid an area, because every time they went near it, they would get a sudden urge to go around it."

"Oh, I know this spell!" I say. "I have a friend who uses it all the time."

"This spell allowed us to finally settle down in one place," Leila writes. "We built our own wooden cabin in the middle of the woods, near a river, and we even cultivated a garden. Some of the animals appeared to be immune to the suggestion spell, but they didn't seem to mind our presence. They even brought us food, on occasion."

"So, how did your father get captured, then?" I ask. "Did your suggestion spell malfunction?"

"No," Leila writes. "We moved out of the woods, eventually. We heard that the lessathi's leadership had changed while we were away, and that their new leader, Meridith, had prohibited the hunts for lessathi outcasts. My father insisted that we move into a city, because then he would have easier access to the parts he needed to work on his devices. At the time, I did not understand why he would want to risk his safety just to work on some devices. I only understood his true purpose a few years later, when he gifted me my stat booster on my sixteenth birthday. Back then, it could only write a few words, but he's been perfecting it over the years, and eventually, it got to a point where I could put almost all of my thoughts into words by using my device."

"Oh, no," I say. "I just remembered something!"

"What?" Leila writes.

"The device!" I say, as I quickly pull the stat booster out of my pocket. "I completely forgot about the stat device!"

I start to shake the stat booster, to make sure that it doesn't have any water in it, and then I test all of the buttons one by one, to see if everything still functions properly. When Leila understands what I'm doing, she begins to giggle silently.

"It will take more than a little water to make these devices stop working," Leila writes. "Don't worry, your stat booster is fine!"

"I'm sorry," I say, after I've made sure that the stat device still works, "I shouldn't have interrupted. You were about to tell me how your father got captured?"

"Yes," Leila writes. "You see, the thing is that even if the hunts for outcasts were prohibited, that did not mean that the old grudges had been forgotten. The lessathi who worked with my father at the Beacon had been meaning to punish him for a long time, but they couldn't do it openly. So what they did, eventually, was that they forged some documents, stating that my father had a huge debt to the owner of our house. They got the owner on their side, and he lied that we never paid our rent since we moved into his home. We didn't have any witnesses on our side, while the lessathi had all the witnesses and the fake documents that they needed to prove my father's guilt. Given that he couldn't pay his debt, my father was sold as a slave, to one of the nobles of Thilias. I escaped before they could sell me too, and I've been living on the outskirts of the city for months, trying to find a way to free him, but it wasn't until the beginning of the tournament that I got a chance to actually do it."

As Leila stops talking, I suddenly realize that I've been asking her all these questions, but I never even bothered to tell her that I'm currently travelling with one of her old colleagues from the Beacon. Should I tell her, though? Kate never told me anything about Leila before. She's only mentioned Diane. Was this because she thought Leila was dead, or because she considered her an enemy, for being a lessathi? Either way, I think it would be better if I told Leila the truth.

"I just realized that I never told you why I knew about the Beacon of Hope," I say. "Do you remember meeting a girl named Kate while you were at the orphanage?"

Leila nods.

"I remember her," Leila writes. "She always used to hang out with the elementalist siblings that were part of the lessathi's elite task force. I heard that she was sent off to die in a distant jungle along with all the other orphans, after the Beacon got shut down…"

"Well, your information isn't wrong, but I think that it might have led you to some wrong conclusions," I tell her. "Kate is not dead. She survived. She's the one who told me about the Beacon of Hope."

"She survived?" Leila writes, as her face suddenly lights up with joy.

"Yeah," I say. "I met Kate here, at the tournament, and I'm currently travelling with her. Would you like to see her?"

The joyful expression on Leila's face slowly gets replaced with one of sadness, as she looks away from me.

"I don't think that she'd want to see me," Leila writes. "I was being kept in a separate cell from the others at the orphanage, and we never got to talk much. Besides, I don't think that she'd want to meet a lessathi like me, after all she's been through at the hands of the lessathi from the orphanage."

"Hey, you can't know that until you ask her!" I say. "I'm a lessathi too, and I'm still friends with her, remember?"

Leila does not answer, and she keeps looking away from me, as before.

"Alright, then," I say, as I get up from the ground. "It's settled! As soon as we get out of here, I'll call her on the transceiver, and we'll arrange a meeting between the two of you. Let's get going! Your clothes should have dried up by now, right?"

Leila nods hesitantly, as she grabs my hand, and I help her up. We leave the fire behind, and we head towards the tunnels beyond the wooden cabin.

For the next twenty minutes or so, we walked in silence through the underground caverns, using a long stick that I'd gotten from the cabin to test the ground for traps. In the areas that were completely dark, we had to rely on our stat devices to light the way before us, but luckily the glowing blue crystals that we'd seen before were also scattered throughout these tunnels, imbedded into the walls, so we didn't have to worry about the lighting, most of the time.

As we advance through the caverns, we eventually reach a tunnel that has prison cells on either side of it, with doors made of rusted iron grating. Inside the cells, what we are seeing instead of prisoners are creatures of all shapes and sizes that are either growling at us menacingly, or studying us carefully, waiting to see what we'll do. There are dire wolves, gargoyles, giant rats, harpies, griffins, and sabre-toothed tigers, all kept in different cells of the same tunnel, and something tells me that this is only a small fraction of the vast array of creatures that the arena's owner has at his disposal.

"They're not guarded," Leila writes. "I think that they weren't expecting any intruders coming from this direction. This means that there's still a chance we can leave this place undetected."

Leila takes a rock from the ground, and she starts to toss it into the air and then catch it, repeatedly, while she looks towards one of the cells. I suddenly realize that the rock she's throwing in the air is just the right size to fit through the iron grating. With her maxed strength, she could probably easily smash one of those tigers' heads with a single throw.

"Now, the question is," Leila writes, "should we kill these creatures while we have the chance, or should we just concentrate on finding a way out of this place?"

"Forget the creatures," I say. "We don't want to risk alerting anyone of our presence, when we don't even have a way of escaping this place. Finding a way out of here is much more important, right now."

"All right," Leila writes, as she drops the stone from her hand. "Let's get going, then."

We make our way to the end of the tunnel, and we both ready our daggers, while we advance into the next area of the caverns. As we now enter a much narrower tunnel, we can't help but notice that there are two wooden chairs near the entrance which seem to have been knocked over in a hurry, and that there is a bowl of fresh stew lying on the ground, untouched.

"It looks like we've already been spotted," I say.

"Yes," Leila writes. "They're probably waiting to ambush us at the end of this tunnel. Get ready!"

Just as Leila anticipated, the moment we got out of the tunnel, we were greeted by six sharp lances pointing in our direction. The lances were being wielded not by humans, but by hideous monsters that were the size of humans, only with gray skin, long pointy noses, large fangs, and the appearance of savages. The monsters that were facing us were trolls.

Trolls are not as smart as goblins, but they're definitely smarter than ogres, and what is particularly dangerous about them is the fact that they have incredible regenerative powers. Unless you cut their head clean off or use fire to kill them, they can even grow back a limb if you give them enough time. These are not the kind of enemies that I was hoping to meet here.

"Throw down your weapons!" one of the trolls says in the Common language, with what is probably the most broken accent that I've ever heard in my life.

Leila and I exchange a look, but we hold on to our weapons, while the trolls seem to be growing impatient.

"Throw down your weapons now, or you will be executed on the spot!" the troll says.

Before we get the chance to answer the trolls, I suddenly hear Flower's voice coming from behind the trolls.

"Somehow, I had a feeling that you would be the source of all this commotion," the voice says.

"Flower?" I ask.

As soon as I stop talking, a water whip comes out of nowhere, and it beheads all of the six trolls in a single swipe. After the trolls' bodies fall to the ground, I get a good look at Flower, and I see that her eyes are bright blue.

“Flower is asleep,” Illuna says.

She gives Leila a quick glance, before she turns her gaze back to me.

“I see you’ve made a new friend,” Illuna says.

“Yes,” I say. “I met her in the holding cells below the arenas. She’s a fellow gladiator from my division.”

“My name is Leila,” Leila writes, as she extends her hand towards Illuna. “Pleased to meet you!”

“Charmed,” Illuna says, in her usual disinterested tone, without showing any surprise at the girl’s peculiar way of talking.

She then turns away, leaving Leila with her hand extended in the air, while she heads back towards the way she came.

“What are you waiting for?” Illuna says, when she sees that we’re not moving. “Follow me.”

“Wait, where are we going?” I ask her.

“There’s a ‘friend’ of mine who I’d like you to meet,” Illuna says. “I think you will find that his purpose in coming here is rather similar to yours.”

“What friend?” I say. “And what do you mean by ‘similar’? I don’t get it. What did you come here to do?”

“Why, Barry, I thought that much would have been obvious by now,” Illuna says. “We came here to sabotage the arena.”

Chapter 3

Illuna's friend was waiting for us in an area not far from the one where the trolls ambushed us. He was leaning on a wooden staff, with several dead trolls lying on the ground around him, and he was studying us closely, as we approached him.

His appearance shocked me at first, but when I saw Illuna nod to him, I immediately realized that he was the one that she brought us to meet. Illuna's friend was no taller than four feet, with fangs instead of teeth, a crooked nose, pointy ears, and green skin.

I must admit that I wasn't expecting this friend of hers to be a goblin, but given the fact that Illuna is a banshee, I suppose that I shouldn't find it too strange that she'd have a few monster allies in Varathia. I've heard before that goblins are supposed to be really smart, compared to other monsters, but this goblin in particular has a very shrewd look about him, and his cunning grin reminds me of those slimy merchants that are constantly looking for new ways to rip you off. And he's not trying to hide it, either.

His high intelligence is likely a result of his old age, which I've heard is not an easy feat to achieve if you live your life as a goblin. Most goblins die young, either because of starvation, or because they get killed, while trying to steal food, in order to survive. Since they are considered monsters by other civilized races, they are forced to live from scraps, and often need to resort to illegal activities such as smuggling and stealing in order to get the goods they require. But this goblin's skin is all wrinkly, which means that he must have lived well over two hundred years, given how slowly goblins are known to age, compared to humans. Living this long as a goblin, especially in a place like Varathia, is definitely not something that you can achieve through sheer luck.

"Is this the lessathi you were talking about, Illuna?" the goblin says, in the Common language, as he looks towards me.

"Yes," Illuna says.

"And the lessathi girl?" the goblin asks. "Is she from your group too?"

"The lessathi girl is apparently a teammate from his arena division," Illuna says. "I only just met her, myself."

"Hmm…" the goblin says. "If she's a gladiator, then I suppose I can safely assume that she has nothing to do with Meridith's group. I'll admit that I was a little worried, at first."

"Hold on!" I say. "I never told any of you that Leila is a lessathi. You're telling me you both realized that she isn't human from just one glance?"

"If your magical sense is sharp enough, you can tell the difference between a human and a lessathi with minimal effort, as long as you study their auras closely," Illuna says. "However, when you've dealt with as many lessathi as we have, it becomes second nature."

"Are you sure that these two can be trusted?" the goblin asks Illuna.

Illuna gives me one long look, before she answers the goblin.

"Barry is trustworthy enough," she says. "I don't know much about the girl, but I don't see any reason why she wouldn't agree with what we're planning to do. She is a gladiator, after all."

"Hey, wait a minute!" I tell Illuna. "If we're talking about trust, then the same question goes for him as well.

Just how much are you willing to trust this guy? To me, he looks just about as trustworthy as a swindler who would try to trick you into playing a rigged game of cards, on the main streets of Bagelberry."

The goblin laughs out loud, after hearing what I had to say about him.

"I like this one," the goblin says. "He speaks exactly what's on his mind without making any effort to sugar-coat his words."

"To answer your question, Barry," Illuna says, "I do not trust him at all. And he does not trust me, either. However, we are both smart enough to know that neither of us would benefit from betraying each other. The information he provides me with regarding the other monster races' activities is invaluable, and in return, I've been helping him from time to time, by ridding him of some of his enemies, or by joining him in covert missions such as this one."

"And what exactly is this covert mission that you are talking about?" I say.

"There is a minotaur being held here, in these tunnels," the goblin says. "They call him the undefeated champion of the arena. You are supposed to be fighting him in the second round, provided you survive the first one. I want to make him an offer."

"What offer?" I ask.

"I will offer him his freedom, if he agrees to join my goblin camp, and to be part of my army," the goblin says.

"You have an army?" I ask him, confused. "I thought you were just some random goblin that was acting as Illuna's informant."

The goblin laughs again.

"There really isn't any limit to your bluntness and disrespect, is there?" the goblin says.

"The goblin you are talking to is Fyron, the general

of all free goblins," Illuna says, in a bored tone. "He is at the top of the hierarchy of all the goblins from Varathia that are not under Tyrath's rule."

"Tyrath?" I ask. "You mean the dragon that I fought on my second day here?"

"The one and only," Illuna says.

"I am intrigued," Fyron says, as he strokes his chin, and he looks at me. "I can't say that I've heard of many beings that fought Tyrath and lived to tell the tale. How exactly did you manage to escape his wrath?"

"Who said that I escaped?" I say.

"So you managed to persuade him to let you go, then?" the goblin general says. "Or are you going to tell me that you defeated him all by yourself?"

"Not by himself," Illuna says. "He had help from a certain stillwater that I believe you are well acquainted with."

"You are talking about Eiden?" Fyron asks.

"Yes," Illuna says. "Eiden seems to have taken an odd interest in Barry and his group for whatever reason. I hear that the stillwater appeared out of nowhere in the middle of their battle with the dragon, and he powered up Barry's stat device in a way that allowed him to cast spells. This is the reason why Barry was able to fight Tyrath on equal terms."

"What you are telling me should be impossible," the goblin general says. "Unless the item itself is the one casting the spells, a lessathi should not be able to use magic by any means, because of the complete lack of magic in their aura. I did hear that the lessathi of old experimented with adding magical stats to the device a long time ago, but I am quite certain that they never managed to make it work. In order for someone to be able to cast spells by using those stats, they would need to have both the low magical frequency in their aura that is specific to the lessathi, and the potential to cast spells.

They'd practically need to be both a lessathi and a—"

The goblin stops talking suddenly, looking as if he'd just made a shocking realization. Seeing the look on his face, Arraka starts to laugh, from within her amulet.

"So you've finally figured it out, eh?" Arraka says.

"You knew?" Fyron asks her.

"I figured it out a while ago, after he started casting spells left and right, against a bunch of skeletons," Arraka says. "But I thought he was a regular lessathi too, at first. Eiden is probably the only one who knew it from the start."

"So that's why he's taken an interest in him…" Fyron says.

"What are you two talking about?" I say.

"They're saying that you're a half-lessathi," Illuna says. "A half human, half lessathi to be more exact."

Upon hearing Illuna's words, Leila suddenly turns her head towards her, and she watches her attentively. This is the first time I've seen her react in any way, since the beginning of our conversation.

"Oh, right…" I tell Illuna. "Now that I think about it, Arraka also called me a half-lessathi a while ago."

"It's the only possible explanation," Fyron says. "I don't know of any other races that look the way you do, and as long as you are also half human, your use of the magical stats makes sense."

"To be honest, I don't really care either way," I say. "Being a half-lessathi doesn't really make much of a difference to me. Besides, I have absolutely no idea how I'm supposed to use those magic stats that you are talking about. So far, I've only been able to use them for a very short period of time, and only after gaining access to a huge source of energy. That's not exactly ideal."

"There is a way to unlock those stats permanently," Fyron says. "However, doing so would require a code that is likely only known by a handful of lessathi, in the top brass of their organization. I wouldn't realistically expect you to get a use out of those stats any time soon."

"So, uh," I say, "it's not that I'm not enjoying our conversation and everything, but shouldn't we maybe get moving, before the trolls send more reinforcements our way?"

"Why would they send any reinforcements?" Fyron asks. "I already took care of all their scouts."

He then gestures towards all the dead trolls lying on the ground around him.

"Nobody else should know that we're here," Fyron continues.

"Speaking of the trolls," Arraka says, "are you guys going to hide these bodies any time soon, or are you planning on hanging them as decorations? Not that I'm against either of those ideas, of course."

"Can't you just wake up Flower, and have her incinerate the troll corpses?" I ask Illuna.

"I'd rather not wake up Flower unless it's absolutely necessary," Illuna says. "Stealth missions were never exactly her specialty, and she doesn't really get along with Fyron all that well, either."

"No need to worry," Fyron says. "I've got everything covered."

The goblin then smacks his staff into the ground, and all of the troll corpses get engulfed in flames, at the same time. After a few seconds, the flames disappear, and the dead bodies are replaced by ashes.

"Shall we proceed?" the goblin says.

"Arraka, are there any enemies in our way?" Illuna says.

"Nah," Arraka says. "You've already killed most of the guards from this area."

"And no one is hiding invisibly?" Illuna says.

"No one," Arraka says.

"Excuse me," Leila writes, as she looks at Illuna.

"Did you just say that the banshee from the amulet is named Arraka?"

"I did," Illuna says. "You've heard of her?"

"I've… heard a few things, yes…" Leila writes.

"What exactly have you heard about her?" I say.

"I've heard that she's a very evil and powerful spirit that played a major role in the still winter war," Leila writes. "Is this really the same Arraka as the one from six hundred years ago?"

"It is her," Illuna says. "I guarantee it."

"Who the hell are you two talking to?" Arraka says. "Have you both gone insane?"

"We were talking to Leila," I say.

"Who the hell is Leila?" Arraka says.

"The lessathi girl," Illuna says. "She's been communicating with us through written messages, floating in the air, in front of her."

"Oh, so that's what she was doing!" Arraka says.

"Can't you see the writing?" I ask her.

"No, I can't 'see' anything from inside here, are you stupid?" Arraka says. "I have no eyes. To me, it's all auras and magical particles. I sense the auras of objects in order to 'see' them, and I sense the sound vibrations in the air, in order to figure out what you people are saying. I can make out most things with my magical sense, so I don't really need my eyesight or my hearing for anything important, but to me, the girl's drawings in the air were just magical particles, floating around at random. Now that I know what they're supposed to be, I might be able to make a little more sense of them."

"Are you sure it's safe to carry her around like this?" Leila writes, looking concerned.

"Don't worry, she's not that tough!" I say. "Hell, I fought her with a dagger while she was in her best condition, and she still couldn't kill me!"

"You really like to play with fire, don't you, Barry-boy?" Arraka says.

"As long as she stays in that amulet, she's not a threat to us," Illuna tells Leila. "Come on, let's get going. We've been standing in one place for long enough."

She pauses.

"But before that," Illuna says, "I'm going to cast a few healing spells. Most of your wounds seem to be older than one day, and they're not severe, so I should have no trouble healing them completely. Barry, I have no idea if the blood on your clothes comes from your wounds, or from the trolls I killed earlier, but if you need healing, I'll tend to you afterwards."

"Thank you," Leila writes, as Illuna begins to cast her healing spells.

After Illuna is done with the healing, the goblin general takes the lead, and he guides us through an empty tunnel, on the opposite side of the tunnel we came in from.

"That is quite an interesting method of communication you are using, young girl," Fyron says. "Judging by the way the magical particles are forming in the air, I would venture a guess that you are using some kind of modified version of a stat booster to transmit your messages, am I correct?"

Leila does not answer the goblin immediately, and she takes a few moments to look him in the eyes before she writes her response.

"I see that you are very knowledgeable when it comes to magical devices," Leila writes.

"I've fiddled around with a few artifacts and devices, including my staff, yes," Fyron says. "But nothing as complex as your translator. It must have taken a very thorough understanding of the ins and outs of mind reading magic and years of hard work to make something this sophisticated. Whoever worked on your device must have been very talented."

"He is," Leila writes, with a solemn look on her face.

"So, uh," I say, "why are you looking to invite the minotaur into your army? Are you planning to go to war against the dragon?"

"How intriguing," the goblin general says. "You have absolutely nothing to gain from this information, yet you are casually asking me to divulge to you some of my most important military secrets without offering me anything in return. I know that you're not a spy, because no spy would be stupid enough to ask me something like this directly. So what is the reason behind this question, I wonder?"

"I believe this is what humans like to call 'small talk'," Illuna says, in her usual indifferent tone. "Empty words, with the sole purpose of engaging in a conversation, for no reason in particular. Barry is just particularly bad at being discrete, so he never stopped to think whether his question was appropriate or not, for this situation."

"Give me a break!" I say. "If you were so worried about me knowing your plans, then you would have never allowed me to find out about the minotaur in the first place. If you have any reason to think that I might somehow leak the information, then you can just tell me that you're looking to hire the minotaur as the army's accountant, and leave it at that. It's not like I can verify the information that you give me, anyway."

"Ah, so you are not completely stupid after all," Fyron says, with a smirk. "That is a relief. Well, in that case, as you've said, the minotaur will be joining our accounting team as soon as he completes his training program. I am expecting great things from him in the months to come."

Arraka laughs.

"If I were you," she says, "I'd make the minotaur do the accounting anyway, just to mess with him. I hear that jobs that do not involve physical labor are considered to be the most dishonorable, by minotaur standards."

"I'll keep that in mind," Fyron says, as he knocks on a wall with his staff, and a secret path opens up in front of us.

"You really know your way around these tunnels, huh?" I tell the goblin, as we all enter the hidden corridor.

"Fyron spends a lot of his time exploring hidden passages and underground ruins," Illuna says. "His hobbies are not much different from those of Flower, in that regard."

"Now, now, Illuna," Fyron says, "there is no need to insult me like this. After all, isn't it due to my so-called hobby that we have managed to remain undetected thus far? I would appreciate it if you refrained from comparing me to your dimwitted companion over a small similarity such as this."

"Oh?" Illuna says. "Did you forget perhaps that it is thanks to my dimwitted companion that you were able to build that staff of yours? We would have never met in that cave twenty years ago if not for Flower's unrivaled stupidity."

"Aha- Ahahahaha!" Arraka laughs. "I still remember your face when you woke up in the middle of that cave, surrounded by fire elementals! I can't believe that she actually fell for my bluff! Just thinking about it makes me burst into laughter!"

"Hello?" we hear a voice coming from a dark corridor to our right. "Is anyone there? Can you hear me?"

We all stop suddenly, and we look towards the corridor, in an attempt to find the source of the sound. The voice seems to have come from the end of the tunnel, but it's much too dark to see anything clearly.

"If you can hear me, please, help!" the voice says,

again. "I've been trapped here for months. I'll do anything you want! Please!"

"Hmm…" the goblin says, as he creates an orb of light with his staff, and then he makes it float all the way to the end of the tunnel.

Now that we get a clear look, we see that at the end of the corridor there is a locked cell, which holds only one prisoner: a tiger.

"Were you the one calling out to us earlier?" Fyron asks the tiger.

"Yes," the tiger answers him. "Please, let me out of here! I'll do whatever you ask!"

"Oh?" the goblin says, with a mocking smile. "Are you certain that it's a good idea to be addressing us in Common like this? I heard that the old fox is executing anyone who dares to speak in this language nowadays."

"The golden fox can go to hell and so can her rules!" the tiger shouts. "I'm never going back to that horrible place again!"

"You do not wish to return to the fox's domain?" Fyron says. "But what other place is there for animals like you? Who else is going to protect you, if not the spirit fox?"

"I don't need anyone's protection!" the tiger says.

The goblin grins.

"Is this why you are in this cell, alone, begging for our help, then?" he says. "Because you do not need anyone's protection?"

The tiger lowers his head, and he does not say anything.

"Let me see if I understand this fully," Fyron says. "From what you've hinted so far, I'm assuming that you'd abandoned the fox's domain long before you've been captured, am I correct?"

"Yes," the tiger says, with his head still lowered.

"Were there other animals captured alongside with

you?" Fyron asks.

"No," the tiger says. "I've been living by myself, ever since I left the sacred woods."

"I see," Fyron says.

He then makes his orb of light float inside the tiger's cell, and the light from the orb begins to fade. However, as soon as he moves the orb away from the cell again, its brightness immediately gets restored.

"Hmm," Fyron says. "As I suspected, the cell you have been placed into restricts the use of magic. Should I take it that you are a mage, then?"

"I am," the tiger says.

The goblin grins again, and he turns his gaze towards me.

"It appears that I'm in luck, Barry," Fyron says. "I may have just found myself the perfect candidate to lead my army's accounting team! What do you think? Does he look fit for the task?"

"I'm going to tell it to you straight," I say. "I don't see him holding a pen anytime soon."

"Fortunately, he will not be needing a pen in order to lead his team," Fyron says. "He just needs to be good at calculations."

"I'm sorry," the tiger says. "You want me to do what?..."

The goblin laughs.

"Pay us no mind," he says. "We were only jesting. Although, you did say that you'd do anything I ask, so you should not act so surprised, even if I made you arrange desk papers for a living."

"I suppose..." the tiger says.

"Illuna, could you take care of those iron bars for me?" the goblin general says. "The anti-magic properties of the cell do not seem to spread beyond those bars, so you should be able to slice them with your water whips from the outside."

"Very well," Illuna says.

She then conjures two whips made out of water that she appears to be holding with her hands, and she uses them to slice the iron bars into pieces.

"You are now free!" Fyron says, looking at the tiger that is now walking out of his cell. "And by this I mean that you are free to do my bidding. I really do hope that you are not planning to betray me and rejoin the fox immediately after we get out of this place."

"I assure you, that is not going to happen," the tiger says.

"Hmm?" the goblin says. "May I ask what it is that the fox has done in order to lose your loyalty to such a degree? Why would you still refuse to go back to your homeland, even after all this time has passed?"

"I have my reasons," the tiger says.

"See, that's not very reassuring," Fyron says, as he points towards the tiger with his staff. "If you're going to give me vague answers like that from the very beginning, what's to tell me that you didn't in fact make up that whole story about leaving the fox's domain, just to gain my sympathy?"

"The fact that I'm speaking to you in the Common language," the tiger says.

"Explain," Fyron says.

"Eleya, the great golden fox," the tiger says, "has a habit of interrogating all of the animals that return to her domain, after a long period of captivity. One question that is always asked is if you'd spoken to any humans in Common, while you were away. There is no way to hide the truth from the great fox. As long as she is studying your aura, she can easily tell if you are lying or not. Even if I weren't an exile, like I said, going back to my homeland now would be nothing short of suicide. She would execute me on the spot."

"I admit that I have heard of the fox's

interrogations," Fyron says. "But I assumed that she would make an exception for mages, and for other valuable members of her community."

"The fox does not make exceptions," the tiger says, with a look in his eyes that seems to show both anger and terror at the same time. "I used to think the same as you, before she murdered the leopard's son in cold blood."

"The leopard?" I say. "You mean Leo, the leopard?"

"Yes, that is who I was referring to," the tiger says. "He was her most loyal retainer. He still is. But that did not stop her from executing his cub, for the heinous crime of begging for his life in Common, to a couple of human hunters. The leopard may have accepted her judgment, but I never will."

The tiger pauses, for a few seconds, and then he repeats himself, in a lower voice.

"I never will," he says.

"Ah," Fyron says, "Now things are starting to make more sense. If the fox later also executed your family, in a similar manner to how she executed the leopard cub, I can see why you would choose to leave her domain forever. That would also explain why you left your homeland by yourself."

The tiger is looking pretty angry, after hearing the goblin's words, but he chooses to remain silent.

"You've said enough," Fyron tells the tiger. "At the very least, I would find it very unlikely that you would return to the golden fox after all you've just said. Regarding your debt to me, I ask only that you accompany me to my goblin camp on my way back. If the life there is not to your liking, then you may leave at any point, and consider your debt to me paid. I am, however, quite confident that you will choose to remain."

"And why is that?" the tiger asks.

"You will understand, once you get there," Fyron says. "Now, follow us. There is still another prisoner that we need to rescue before we can leave this place."

"Another prisoner?" the tiger asks, as he joins us, and we all resume our walk through the caves. "You don't mean the minotaur, do you?"

"Who else could I mean?" Fyron says. "Is there anyone else here that would be worth the effort of releasing?"

"I suppose not," the tiger says. "The minotaur is likely the only prisoner from this place aside from me who is not some mindless beast."

"I'm curious," I say. "You say that all the creatures trapped in these caverns are mindless beasts, but I've also seen some sabre-toothed tigers on my way here. Do you feel the same way about them, too?"

"Of course I do," the tiger says. "What kind of question is this?"

"Well, they are tigers…" I say.

"No, they aren't!" the tiger says, furiously. "They are sabre-toothed tigers, not tigers! How can you even compare the two?"

"Barry is not from Varathia," Illuna says. "Believe it or not, in the continents outside of Varathia there isn't much of a difference between animals and creatures. A tiger from the Western Continent is just as much of a mindless beast as a sabre-toothed tiger."

"You can't be serious!" the tiger says.

"On the contrary," Illuna says. "I am quite serious. I do not know if the high level of intelligence shown by the animals in Varathia is due to the golden fox's influence, or due to some other factors, but the fact of the matter is that Varathia is the only place in the world where animals can speak, and it is the only place where they live in civilized societies."

"Hah!" Arraka says. "How does it feel to know that

there are animals out there who are dumber than ogres? Did you think that you were anything special? I'm willing to bet that people from outside of Varathia would not even be able to tell the difference between you and a wild beast. To them, you're nothing but a mindless creature, no different from a harpy, or a giant slug. Isn't that right, Barry?"

"Well, it's a bit hard to treat him like a dumb beast, when he can speak Common," I say.

"Don't worry, I have an easy fix for that!" Arraka says. "Just ignore what he says. If you don't pay any attention to him, you'll find it much easier to treat him like an animal. Oh, I'm sorry, did I say animal? What I meant to say was creature. I always get the two mixed up! Aha- Ahahahahahaha!"

"Who the hell is that clown from the amulet?" the tiger says. "Some sort of prankster spirit?"

"That's rude, you know!" Arraka says. "You should not assume I'm a clown just because the girl wearing my amulet is dressed in clown clothes! Don't they teach you manners in animal school?"

"As unbelievable as it may sound," Illuna says, ignoring Arraka, "the banshee trapped in this amulet is the one responsible for the exile of all the banshees to the earthen plane. The gods didn't want to deal with her, so they banished her here, along with all her kind. Or so she claims."

"I can see why they'd want her out of the magical plane," the tiger says. "Even the gods would run out of patience when dealing with such idiocy."

"Oh, yeah?" Arraka says. "Well, I'll have you know that—"

She does not get to finish what she had to say, because Illuna snaps the amulet shut in the middle of her sentence.

"I've heard enough of this," Illuna says. "We have

more important matters to discuss right now."

She then turns to me.

"Barry, do you and Leila have a means of returning to your cells?" Illuna says. "I think I should warn you that Fyron and I will be teleporting out of here as soon as we free the minotaur, so we won't be there to escort you back."

"No, we don't have a means of returning to our cells," I say. "The way we came is sealed shut and a hundred feet above the ground. We need to find another way back."

"If you're looking to reach the main corridors below the arena," Fyron says, "there's a secret tunnel that I can open for you, not far from where the minotaur is located. You might have to get past several traps, in order to reach your destination, however."

"That's… awful nice of you," I say.

"Do not worry," Illuna says, seeing the mistrust on my face. "Fyron is not foolish enough to risk his alliance with me for no other reason than to amuse himself. He is not Arraka. If he says that there's a tunnel leading to the corridors below the arena, then he likely speaks the truth."

"I see," I say. "Well, in that case, thanks, I guess…"

"There's no need to thank me, Barry," Fyron says. "I never help people for free. There may come a time when I will be in need of your help as well. If that time ever comes, I'd rather have you owe me a favor, than the other way around. That's all there is to it."

"Fyron, is this the last tunnel before the labyrinth?" Illuna says.

"Yes," Fyron says. "The tunnel's exit should leave us very close to the maze's entrance."

"Wait, what maze?" I say.

"Do you know that old legend," Fyron says, "in which the gods worked together to build an elaborate maze for the sole purpose of trapping the king of the minotaurs? Well, it seems that the owner of the arena liked the story so much that he decided to build his own underground labyrinth, as soon as he got hold of a minotaur. Unfortunately, I did not have a chance to visit these tunnels since the maze was created, so once we reach it, I won't know my way around as well as I have so far."

"I don't think that will be a problem," Illuna says, "since there will likely be no need to hide ourselves anymore, once we reach the maze. They will surely have caught on to our presence by then. I think we should be able to handle their guards by ourselves easily, but if worst comes to worst, I'll wake up Flower as well."

"I'm sorry, who is Flower?" Leila writes, confused.

"Flower is the little girl inhabiting this body," Illuna says.

"You mean… she's still alive?" Leila writes, shocked. "But, aren't you a banshee? Didn't you consume her soul when you took over her body?"

Illuna laughs.

"If only it would have been that easy," she says. "Unfortunately, the two of us have been stuck together in this body for the past twenty years, and we'll likely continue living like this for years to come. Our souls are fused."

"I see…" Leila writes, simply.

She looks as if she'd still have some questions to ask, but ultimately she decides against it. As the tunnel's exit draws closer, Illuna reopens Arraka's amulet, and she asks her if she can spot any enemies nearby.

"Oh, so now you want me to talk?" Arraka says. "You're not going to close the amulet in my face anymore? Well, what if I don't want to talk? What do you say to that?"

"If you're not planning to talk, then I have no further

need of you," Illuna says, as she starts to close back the amulet. "Have a good nap."

"Wait, wait, wait!" Arraka says, just as Illuna was about to close the amulet completely. "Okay, fine! You win! There are some trolls much further down the next tunnel, but they're not in viewing range of the maze's entrance. The coast is clear."

"That doesn't sound right," Illuna says. "They should have at least some guards at the entrance of the labyrinth. I'm much more inclined to believe that they've become aware of our presence, and that they deliberately emptied the next tunnel, in order to lure us into the maze."

"That changes little," Fyron says. "The only way to reach the minotaur is through the maze. If the trolls choose to stand in our way, then we'll just have to make our way through them."

Once we reach the next corridor, we make sure that the coast is indeed clear, and then we proceed to enter the maze. The walls inside the labyrinth look a bit different from all the rocky walls that we've seen in the caverns so far. They are black as coal, and they appear to be made from a different material.

Fyron, who seems to have spotted the difference as well, gets closer to one of the walls, and he looks at it curiously. He swipes the wall briefly with his index finger, and then he brings the finger closer to his face, studying the black powder that has accumulated on the tip of it attentively.

"Tell me, Arraka," the goblin says, "are you sensing any trolls nearby?"

"What?" Arraka says. "No, I already told you that the coast is clear."

"Are you sure?" Fyron asks.

"What kind of question is that?" Arraka says. "Of course I'm sure!"

"Oh?" Fyron says. "Then could you perhaps describe to me what lies beyond this black wall?"

"Yeah, hold on a sec," Arraka says.

For about ten seconds, we all wait silently for Arraka's answer.

"Well?" Fyron says. "Weren't you going to describe to us what's on the other side?"

"There's… a bit of interference," Arraka says. "I'm still working on it."

"Oh, then by all means," Fyron says, "do not let this old goblin's ramblings interrupt you from your work. Please, take all the time you need."

It takes thirty more seconds of silence until Illuna finally snaps.

"Good gods!" she shouts. "How long is it going to take you to admit the obvious? This wall is clearly made from a material that blocks magical sense. We can wait here all day, and you're still not going to get through it. Are you really that stubborn?"

"Fine!" Arraka shouts. "I admit it! I can't get through it. I have no idea what's on the other side. Are you happy now?"

Fyron grins.

"Thank you, Arraka, I believe that will suffice," he says. "As Illuna noted, this wall is made from a material that does not allow magical sense to pass through. This type of black rock is not uncommon in underground caves such as this, and it is called 'seredium'. The owner of the arena must have chosen to build his labyrinth here specifically because of the existence of these rocks. There wouldn't be much point in making a labyrinth if people could just use their magical sense to see through walls, now would there?"

The goblin pauses for a few seconds, and when he sees that nobody is planning to answer his rhetorical question, he decides to continue his train of thought.

"So…" he says. "Now that we know what we're up against, I believe that our first priority should be the mapping of this maze. Arraka, I understand that you have the ability to generate holograms?"

"Yeah," Arraka says. "But I can't make a map of this place if my magical sense can't pass through the walls."

"It doesn't matter," Fyron says. "You can just draw the map as we walk. What's important is that we don't lose track of where we are. I will be marking the walls periodically, as we advance through the maze, for that same purpose."

"Alright, then," Arraka says. "Here goes."

She then conjures a hologram similar to the one she made in the ogre stronghold, where we are represented by colored dots, and the map is covered by a black fog, except for the corridor that we are currently in. In the meantime, Fyron uses his staff to imprint a complex symbol on the wall to our right, in magical green ink.

"We're good to go," Fyron says. "Follow me."

As we walk, the fog from Arraka's map is beginning to clear, little by little, getting replaced by the parts of the maze that we already know, while Fyron is making sure that he leaves no wall unmarked.

"Aren't you going to ask me what the complex symbol I'm marking the walls with means, Barry?" Fyron says, with a grin.

"No, thanks," I say. "It's not worth owing you another favor just to get an answer to that question."

"You are learning fast!" Fyron says, and then he marks yet another wall with his green inked symbol.

We walk through the maze for about fifteen minutes without encountering any resistance. Along the way, we reach a few dead-ends, but Arraka marks them all on the map, so there would be no risk of running into them again. As we continue our journey through the maze, however, we eventually manage to run into a situation that we had not predicted.

Even though we'd been carefully following Arraka's map the whole time, somehow we ended up in the middle of a corridor that had already been marked with Fyron's green symbol. Dumbfounded, we all look at Arraka's map, in an attempt to understand what we missed, while Fyron carefully inspects his symbol from the wall.

"How is this possible?" Illuna says. "I've been closely monitoring Arraka's map while she was drawing it, and I am certain that it's accurate. According to the map, this should be an unexplored area. Did the trolls manage to falsify the green symbol?"

"It's not a copy," Fyron says. "My mark cannot be so easily reproduced. And aside from that, I also recognize this corridor. I can tell you with a certainty that we've been here before. Although I'm not exactly sure how we—"

As he is talking, a certain rock formation in one of the walls catches his eye, and it makes him stop mid-sentence.

"Hmm…" he says, as he gets closer to the wall, and he taps it lightly with his staff.

"The goblin is not wrong," we hear a voice coming from a darker part of the corridor.

As the one who just spoke gets closer to us, we see that he is a particularly bulky troll, wearing anti-magic armor from head to toe, and holding two scimitars in his hands. He is grinning triumphantly.

"You've been running in circles ever since you entered this maze," the troll says. "I knew that you'd be coming back to this corridor, soon."

"Psst," I whisper to Illuna, while the troll is giving us his victory speech. "Why aren't you killing him?"

"He is wearing anti-magic armor, and he has a helmet," Illuna whispers back to me. "That means that I can't make my water sharp against him, so I won't be able to cut his head off with my water whips."

"Yeah, but isn't anti-magic armor basically just regular armor with some protections on it?" I whisper. "Can't you have Flower burn him alive?"

"There is no anti-magic armor in existence without protection from fire," Illuna whispers. "Casting fire magic on him would be pointless."

While the two of us were whispering, hiding behind Leila and the tiger, the troll seemed to have finished his gloating, and was now preparing to attack.

"There is no way for you to escape," the troll says. "Resign yourselves to your fate. Today is the last day of—"

Leila appears to have had enough, as she makes a dash towards the troll, shocking him with her speed, and slashing his head right off with her dagger in an instant. Instead of dropping to the ground, however, the troll's body attacks her with the two scimitars, which Leila barely manages to avoid, by making a quick jump backwards.

"That's not how you begin a battle, human," the troll's head says, from the ground. "Attacking an enemy out of the blue without giving them proper warning is a mark of cowardice. Did they not teach you proper gladiator etiquette when they brought you to the arena?"

His body then picks up his head from the ground, and it places it back on top of its neck. Within seconds, the head attaches itself back to its body, making it look as if there had never been a wound in the first place.

"A troll that doesn't die even when you cut his head off?" Fyron says. "This is not what I signed up for. Illuna, use the cage spell."

"I can only use that spell once per day," Illuna says. "If I use it now—"

"It doesn't matter," Fyron says. "You won't need to

use it later. I have a plan. Cage him, now!"

Illuna frowns at him, but she does as he asked. She stretches her arm towards the troll, and out of nowhere, a golden cage appears around him, trapping him inside. It is the same spell that she used to trap us when we were at the ogre fort. The golden fox's spell.

"Do you seriously think that a mere cage can stop me?" the troll says, as he begins slashing furiously at the cage's golden bars.

"Yes, we do," Fyron says, and he smacks his staff into the ground, generating a cloud of gray smoke that fills the entire corridor.

I then hear the sound of rocks moving to my right, and after that, I can see the outlines of my companions through the smoke, moving past me.

"Over here!" I hear Illuna's voice, as she grabs me by the arm and pulls me towards her.

I follow her through the smoke, and we both enter a narrow passage, leading to the other side of one of the walls. Once we are all through, Fyron smacks his staff into the cave's wall from the inside, and the hole in the wall closes itself back up. He then makes his way past us, to retake the lead, and he smacks his staff on the other end of the passage, opening another secret door, which leads us into an unexplored corridor, without any markings on the walls.

"That cage isn't going to hold him for long," Illuna says, as we all make our way out of the passage, and the secret door closes itself behind us. "Would you mind telling me what this plan of yours is?"

"He doesn't need to be held for long," Fyron says, "I very much doubt that he knows about the existence of that secret passage, so he's not going to find us anytime soon. More importantly, I recognized that corridor from earlier, and I recognize this one as well. It seems that they've kept some of the old corridors, and included them in the labyrinth, when they built this place. If that's the case, then I think I have a pretty good idea of where we are, and the minotaur's cell should not be far from here. Follow me."

"I've been meaning to ask," I tell Illuna. "Wasn't the golden cage from earlier one of the golden fox's spells? How did you manage to learn it?"

"It's not the fox's spell," Illuna says. "It is a complex spell that can only be used by beings that originate from the magical plane. I learned it from Arraka."

"I see…" I say.

"Hah, I was wondering why I didn't remember there being a wall on this side!" Fyron says.

As we turn to him, we see him walk straight through one of the walls, disappearing from our sights.

"Come over here!" Fyron shouts, from the other side. "The wall is an illusion. This is how they must have been fooling us for so long. If they've got illusions like this set up, then I wouldn't put it past them to also have a spell cast on this place that messes with our sense of direction. That would explain why Arraka's map didn't help. It doesn't matter, though. If my intuition is correct, we should be almost there."

We all walk through the illusory wall, and we continue our journey towards the minotaur. A few minutes later, when we are almost at our destination, we encounter a few more trolls, who are likely the ones that were chosen to guard the minotaur's cell. The monsters barely get the time to react to our presence, before Illuna slices their heads off, with her signature water whip.

"Aren't you going to burn the bodies?" I ask the goblin.

"I'm not wasting any more energy from my staff for something this trivial," Fyron says. "If you want, you can hide the bodies yourself. Not that it would make much of a difference at this point."

"Yeah," I say. "I guess there wouldn't be much point in hiding bodies if we're almost at the end of the maze. Let's keep going."

We make our way towards the end of the corridor, where we find a single cell, with a magical panel on the wall beside it. Inside the cell, there is only one prisoner, with the head of a bull, and the body of a man, laying on the floor, with his back against the wall. The minotaur is taller than Daren, and he has twice the muscles. When he hears us arrive, he does not move an inch, and he doesn't even turn his head to look at us.

"Who are you?" the minotaur asks.

"I guess I was right when I figured that they'd place you in the old paralysis cell," Fyron says. "The maze's only purpose was to keep the intruders out, not to keep you in."

"Who are you?" the minotaur asks again.

"I am Fyron, the general of all free goblins in Varathia," Fyron says. "I've come here to recruit you to join my army. What do you say?"

"A goblin army?" the minotaur says.

He laughs bitterly.

"I never thought I'd live to see the day," the minotaur says, "when I would actually seriously consider an offer like this."

"It's not as bad as you might think," Fyron says. "At the very least, in our goblin camp you should have access to more food than here, and you wouldn't have to spend your days locked up in a paralysis cell. Or would you rather spend the rest of your life entertaining these humans?"

"This goblin army of yours…" the minotaur says. "Is it made only of goblins? Or have you also recruited other warriors such as myself to join it before?"

"It is made mostly of goblins," Fyron says, "but our goblin camp accepts all races, as long as they follow our rules, and pay the yearly tribute."

"And how much is the yearly tribute?" the minotaur asks.

"It depends," Fyron says. "On average, it is about one copper piece for each goblin."

"Per year?" the minotaur asks, somewhat surprised.

"Per year," Fyron says.

"And why is it that you are recruiting?" the minotaur asks. "Are you preparing for war?"

"That remains to be seen," Fyron says. "For the moment, let's just say that I like being cautious."

The minotaur pauses for a bit, to consider the goblin's words.

"We can negotiate the terms of your employment later, if you wish," Fyron says. "The last thing I would want is to force you into this, by taking advantage of your current situation. All I want is your word that you will take my offer seriously, and that you will join me on my trip back to the goblin camp. I know how much minotaurs value honor, so as long as you give me your word, that is enough for me. We can discuss the details afterwards."

"You are clearly a skilled diplomat, goblin," the minotaur says. "You have a gift for finding the exact words that someone wants to hear, and you deliver them at just the right moment. Normally, my natural hatred for diplomats would make me not think twice before refusing your offer, but in this case, as you are well aware, I do not have much of a choice."

He pauses again.

"Very well, general Fyron," the minotaur says. "I give you my word. As long as you free me from here, I will accompany you to your goblin camp, and I will take your employment offer as seriously as I am able."

"That is all I wanted to hear," Fyron says, with a grin.

He then uses his staff to cast a spell on the panel

outside the cell, which deactivates the paralysis spell, and opens the gate.

"How are you planning to get me out of these caverns?" the minotaur says, as he gets up from the ground and walks out of his cell.

"By using magic," Fyron says. "It just so happens that Illuna and I are both rather adept at spell casting, and we both have the ability to teleport, within certain limitations."

He then turns to Illuna.

"Illuna," Fyron says. "Can you teleport the minotaur to the surface? As far as I know, your daily teleportation spell does not have a weight limit. Mine, on the other hand costs additional energy for every extra pound. I would rather you take the minotaur with you, since he is by far the heaviest of the group. I will be with you shortly, after I lead your friends to the secret passage I mentioned earlier."

Illuna nods, and the goblin now turns towards the minotaur.

"Once you are on the surface, Illuna won't be able to help you," Fyron says. "Everyone in this city knows your face from the arena, so she can't be seen fighting alongside you, unless she wants to get a criminal record. Don't wait for us. As soon as you are out of the caverns, make a rush towards the city gates, smash right through them, and don't stop until you reach the Mertram woods. We will meet you there."

"I will be waiting," the minotaur says.

"We should get going," Illuna says, and she grabs the minotaur's hand, in order to get ready for teleportation.

She gives us all one last look, stopping her gaze for a few seconds when her eyes meet mine.

"Don't die," she tells me, simply.

"I won't," I say.

She then casts her teleportation spell, and both her

and the minotaur disappear from our sight.

"This way!" Fyron says, as he goes back the way we came from.

He then stops by a wall, and he taps it lightly three times with his staff, causing a secret door to open up, and to reveal a hidden passage.

"This tunnel will lead you back to the upper levels," Fyron says. "I trust that you will be able to find your way back to your cells from there."

"We'll manage," I say.

"I think I should also mention that the tunnel can only be opened from this side," Fyron says. "Once you enter it, you won't be able to go back."

The goblin then turns to Leila.

"As far as I know," he says, "Barry is required to return to his cell, unless he wants to get disqualified from the mage tournament. You, however, are bound by no such rules. If you want, I could give you a lift. There is enough energy in my staff remaining to teleport one extra person."

"Thank you," Leila writes, "but I'm fine. I will take the tunnel."

"Are you sure?" the goblin asks. "I promise that I won't charge you… much."

"I'm positive," Leila writes.

"Very well, then," Fyron says, as he readies his staff, and he signals the tiger to come near him.

"Oh, there was one last thing I wanted to tell you," Fyron says, as he looks towards me. "A few days ago, four goblins that I'd exiled from my camp came back, with the two copper pieces that they required in order to pay the yearly tribute. When I asked them where they got the money from, they said that they got it from a scrawny human, who was travelling with a dark-skinned warrior dressed in heavy armor, and with two other women. They also said that the warrior had an 'X' shaped scar on his forehead. Since the warrior they were talking about is clearly the healer in armor, I can only assume that the scrawny human was you?"

"Yeah, that was me," I say.

"Hmm…" Fyron says, giving me a curious look for a few seconds. "Well, the four goblins said that they were very eager to meet you again, so if you ever find your way into our goblin camp, be sure to drop by their house. I'm certain that they will be of help to you in one way or another."

"Sure thing," I say. "If I ever have business there, I will pay them a visit."

Fyron nods, and he prepares to cast his teleportation spell.

"I wish you both luck," the goblin says. "Next time we meet, I hope it will be under better circumstances."

He then casts his spell, and he vanishes into thin air, alongside the tiger. Leila and I waste no time, and we enter the secret tunnel, as the door shuts itself behind us.

"You have some very… unique friends," Leila writes, smiling, as we walk through the dark corridor.

"You can say that again…" I tell her.

"I never thought that I'd ever travel in the company of so many monsters," Leila writes. "At least, not unless I'd been captured by them."

"To be fair," I say. "I wasn't expecting the goblin, either. But I guess that seeing a goblin is far less shocking than seeing two banshees on the same day."

I pause for a few seconds, and then I change the subject.

"So, uh… why didn't you accept the goblin's offer, earlier?" I ask her. "Is it because you didn't trust him?"

"Oh, no, it's not that," Leila writes. "It's just that I never intended to break out of here."

"Why not?" I say. "Couldn't you just run past all the guards in the city, now that your wounds are healed?"

Leila shakes her head.

"The lessathi that framed my father are watching me carefully," she writes. "As long as I survive the arena, the charges against me will be dropped, and they won't be able to touch me, but if I escape illegally, they will use all of the means at their disposal to hunt me down. I would never make it to the city gates alive."

"You are saying that you'd rather fight the creatures from the arena," I say, "than have a direct confrontation with the lessathi from this city?"

"Yes," Leila writes. "The lessathi have powerful artifacts that allow them to use magic, similar to the staff that the goblin general was using. At least in the arena nobody is allowed to use magic, so as long as I have my stat device, I can stand a chance."

"Yeah, I guess I see your point," I say. "Speaking of stat devices, I think we should pull them out to light this place up a bit. The goblin did say that there might be traps around here, so we should watch our step."

We walk down the dark tunnel for a few minutes, carefully checking every step of the way for traps, or enemy ambushes. As we step into a larger area, lit by the glowing blue crystals that we've seen before, we realize that all of our efforts to spot hidden ambushes have been wasted, because the enemy was waiting for us here, in this very room, without making any effort at hiding themselves.

A single troll stands between us and freedom. Unfortunately for us, it is the troll that we would have wanted to meet the least. It is the one that we managed to avoid earlier, thanks to Illuna's golden cage spell. However, Illuna is not here now, and our chances of survival are looking slim.

The bulky troll grins triumphantly at us, like before, and he announces his presence by speaking as loudly as possible.

"Did you really think that you could get away that easily, after all you've done?" the troll says. "Unfortunately for you, the existence of this passage was never a secret to us. As soon as you triggered the alarm by freeing the minotaur from his cell, I knew at once that you would try to use this tunnel to escape! Now tell me, where is the minotaur?"

"He's gone," I tell him. "He teleported away with our friends. I doubt you'll ever see him again."

"You are *lying*!" the troll shouts, furiously. "You would have never went through the trouble of navigating the maze, if you could have just teleported in and out at your leisure. And if your friends really did teleport out of here, then they would have surely taken you with them. If you're not going to tell me where the minotaur is, then I will just have to walk over your dead bodies, and search for him myself. You should know by now that you stand no chance against me. If you want this to be over quickly, then don't move. I will be sure to grant you a merciful death."

"That will not be necessary, Velgos," we hear a voice coming from behind the troll.

The man who spoke shows himself to us, and we see that he is rather plump, with short black hair and a goatee, wearing clothes that appear to be made entirely out of silk. The way he looks and dresses would normally make me peg him as a noble, if it weren't for the look in his eyes, which is similar to that of the goblin general's. That look makes him seem more like a war veteran that has seen many battles in his lifetime, than a pampered rich person who's lived his life in luxury.

"But, owner," Velgos, the troll says, "these are the intruders who came here to free the minotaur! We need to eliminate them quick, before they let him escape to the surface!"

"The minotaur is already gone," the man says. "I saw

him teleport out of here with my own eyes. There is nothing else for you to do here. Return to your post."

"I refuse!" Velgos says, baring his teeth at his master. "They are responsible for the deaths of many of my comrades. I am not going to let them go."

"I'm not telling you to let them go," the owner says. "I am only asking you to postpone your fight with them until the second round of the arena event. The minotaur is gone, and you are the only warrior we have who is on par with him, combat-wise. I will pay you handsomely if you join the fights in the arena, and you will also have your chance to avenge your fallen comrades, since these two will be participating in the fights. Wouldn't that be a better alternative for you than to lose your job needlessly because you lacked patience?"

The troll grumbles, but he does not seem like he wants to continue the argument.

"They'd better not get killed by the creatures in the first round," Velgos says, as he points towards us. "I want to kill them myself!"

"I wouldn't worry too much about that," the owner says. "I'd say that they have very good chances of making it to the second round alive, based on what I've seen so far. Now, get going. I need to lead our guests back to their cells."

"Fine," Velgos says. "We'll discuss my payment later."

With these final words, the troll walks away from us, and he disappears into the darkness of the caverns.

"You're going to lead us back to our cells?" I ask the owner. "Not that I'm complaining, but aren't you the arena's owner? Why would you let us go so easily?"

"I'm not letting you go," the owner says, as he knocks on one of the walls, and a secret door opens in front of him. "I simply think that it would be a great waste if the stars of the show got killed before the spectacle even started. Besides, it is well within your rights to come and sabotage the arena before the main event. In fact, I hear that this used to be something of a tradition before the still winter, when the lessathi were still in charge of this arena. It was even encouraged by the organizers. The secret trapdoor that led you from your cells to here is proof of that fact. Now, don't just stand there, follow me. This tunnel will lead us to where we need to go."

Leila and I exchange a look, and then we decide to follow the arena's owner into the newly revealed secret tunnel.

"You know," the owner says, as the door closes itself behind us, "I feel that I should thank you for the entertainment that you've provided me today."

"You do?" I say.

"Yes," the owner says. "It is not every day that you get to see Illuna of the sacred woods massacre, Arraka of the still winter and general Fyron of the free goblins wreak havoc through a monster filled dungeon. I realize that you weren't the ones who brought them here, but I would never have found out about them, if I hadn't followed the two of you since you fell into that lake."

"You've been following us from the very beginning?" I ask him, shocked.

"Yes," the owner says. "There is an ancient alarm system that has been set up since the age of the lessathi, meant to warn me if anyone triggers the trap from the arena cells. I found you while you were drying up by the fire, and I have been following you from afar ever since."

"But how did you manage to remain undetected?" I ask him. "We even had Arraka with us, who could detect invisible enemies."

"Your goblin friend is not the only one who knows about secret tunnels," the owner says. "Over the years, I have built many such hidden corridors throughout these caverns, and I've had them covered with seredium dust, in order to make sure that I cannot be detected while I walk through them. I've also had an illusionist cast a spell on all the walls, which makes it so that you can see through them from inside the hidden tunnels, but not from the outside. This allowed me to watch the events unfold, without giving myself away."

"So," I say, "you've just been watching all this time, instead of stopping us? Why?"

"Because the show has already started," the owner says. "I already told you, it is an old tradition of these arenas to have intruders attempting to sabotage the event, and I was not about to stop this from happening, when it was the first time that I'd seen any participants make it this far since I've inherited this arena from my late father. I only stopped the troll from killing you because I am expecting great things from you during the main event."

"Why from us?" I say. "Why not from any of the other gladiators?"

"Because the two of you are the only ones using stat devices," the owner says.

"Oh…" I say, not knowing exactly how to respond to this.

"Like I said, you are the stars of the show," the owner says. "I've even had one of the high ranking lessathi tell me that I would lose my job if I didn't confiscate the lessathi girl's device. But why would I? I've already decided that this is to be the crowning moment of my career. I do not care what happens afterwards. All I want is for this one show to be perfect. And you are both going to help me achieve my dream."

We make it out of the tunnel, and we find ourselves in a familiar setting, with a wooden cabin in front of us, and a lake further beyond.

"I don't know if you've noticed or not," the owner says, "but beneath the lake that the two of you fell in, there is an old elevator, built by the lessathi hundreds of years ago. The elevator can only be activated with a spider shaped key that has been passed throughout my family for generations, but has never been used until now."

He pulls a spider shaped statuette made from stone out of his pocket, and he hands it to me.

"The mechanism that requires this key is located at the bottom of the lake," the owner says. "Simply insert the statuette into the spider shaped slot, and rotate it twice, in a clockwise direction. That should get the elevator going. Expect it to move a little slowly, though. It has not been used for centuries."

I nod to him, and I jump into the water, with the statuette in my right hand. I tell Leila to wait for me by the shore, so I can come back for her once I've activated the elevator. After diving into the water, I head towards the spider shaped slot once more, and I do as the owner said, inserting the statuette into the hole and rotating it twice.

As I see the elevator start moving, I quickly swim back to the surface, and then all the way to Leila. She jumps into the water and grabs onto me, as I lead her right above the slowly elevating platform. Next, we wait in silence for a few minutes, while the platform gets out of the water and lifts us into the air, towards the ceiling. As we get close to the trapdoor that we initially fell through, the owner shouts his last words to us, from the lake's shore.

"Remember that I have very high expectations from you!" the owner says. "Make sure that you do not let me down."

Chapter 4

The trapdoor above us opens up, allowing the platform to slowly lift us through the thick layer of rock making up the cave's ceiling. Once we get close to the height level of our division's cells, a second trapdoor opens up, and the platform slows down to a halt, as we finally reach our destination. Almost immediately after it stops, the elevator changes its course, and it starts to descend back towards the lower levels. We jump off the platform and onto the cell's floor, while the trapdoor closes itself back up, blocking the elevator from our view.

"W-w-what's going on?" we hear a voice coming from behind us. "How did you get here? And how in the gods' names did you get so bloody wet?"

As both Leila and I turn around, we quickly realize that the elevator did not in fact lead us back to Leila's room. Instead, it led us to cell number three, which is one of the rooms that the desk worker offered me to choose from when I first got here, and also the room that is currently being inhabited by the mage who got locked up in this place yesterday.

The mage is looking at us with a somewhat frightened look, while a trickle of sweat is running down his forehead, and he appears to be hiding something behind his back.

"Sorry to bother you," I tell the mage. "We went out for a swim and we got lost on our way back. We'll be out of your hair as soon as you unlock that door for us."

"Out for a swim?" the mage asks, shocked. "You

were trying to escape, weren't you? Give me one good reason why I shouldn't call the guards right now, and tell them what you were doing."

"If you let us go, I won't ask anything about that thing you are hiding behind your back," I say.

"What thing?" the mage shouts. "I'm not hiding anything behind my back!"

"It's not going to work," Leila writes, while looking directly at the mage.

"What's with the writing?" the mage asks, confused, while looking at Leila. "Is this how you talk? What's not going to work?"

Leila reaches for the floor, in order to pick up an object that looks like it was made by gluing several pieces of scrap metal together in the most random way possible. The item is small enough to fit in her palm, so she grabs it with one hand, and she stretches her arm towards the mage, bringing the metal object several inches away from his face.

"This," Leila writes. "This is what's not going to work."

"I don't know what you're talking about," the mage says, feigning ignorance. "That's just a piece of scrap metal."

"No," Leila writes. "This is a device that's meant to enhance your physical abilities for a limited amount of time. And that thing you are hiding behind your back is likely meant to act as a bridge between you and your scrap metal device, allowing you to transfer your magical energy into it over a period of time."

"How did you—" the mage starts to say, but he stops when he sees a new text appear in front of him.

"You can't use this device in the arena," Leila writes, "It will be detected immediately. If you don't get it to somehow link itself directly to your magical aura, the magical energy that will burst from the device when you activate it will trigger all the magical detectors in a five mile radius. Either way, even if you do somehow get it to work, the device is so poorly made that you won't be able to use it for more than a few minutes, even if you spend the whole day charging it."

"A few minutes is more than enough in an arena!" the mage shouts. "A few minutes can mean the difference between life and death! You don't know how terrifying an arena can be! You have no idea! If I can get even the slightest advantage out of this device, then I will use it gladly!"

"Don't say I didn't warn you…" Leila writes, and she hands the mage his scrap metal device.

The mage takes the device and he looks at it for a few seconds, with a contemplative expression on his face.

"Link it directly to my magical aura, you say…" the mage tells Leila.

"It's the only way to avoid detection," Leila writes.

After spending a few more seconds to consider Leila's words, the mage finally pulls out a key from his pocket, and he walks past us, to unlock and then open the door.

"This meeting never took place," the mage says, as he looks towards each of us, in turn. "Do you understand? Now, go on. Get out of here."

"You don't need to tell us twice," I say, as I head out the door, and leave the room together with Leila.

As the mage closes the door behind us, the two of us start to head towards our rooms.

"I'm surprised that you could tell what that device was meant for from just one glance," I say.

"I used to spend a lot of time in my father's workshop, back when we were living in our forest cabin," Leila writes. "I learned a thing or two while watching him work."

"Do you think he'll be able to modify the device in

time for the arena?" I ask her.

"It's possible," Leila writes. "But he'll need to do it fast. He won't be able to charge it with energy while he's tinkering with it, and he'll need to charge it for at least ten hours to get any decent use out of it, given how inefficient it is."

"We should go get changed," I say. "I also want to take a look through my notebook, to see if I can find any useful information on the creatures we've seen in the caverns. I'll see you in a few hours, to tell you what I found."

Leila nods.

"See you later," Leila writes, and she heads towards her room.

I go back to my own room as well, and the first thing I do after I enter it is to search my backpack for a dry shirt and a new pair of pants. Once I get changed and leave my wet clothes to dry, I pick up my notebook, and I get back to studying.

About one hour after I started reading, I get a call on my transceiver from Flower.

"Barry, are you okay?" Flower asks me out of the blue, with a bit of panic in her voice.

I could immediately tell that it was her and not Illuna speaking, from the tone of her voice.

"Yes, I'm alive," I say. "We managed to get back to our cells about an hour ago."

"Thank the gods!" Flower says. "When I heard about what happened, I got really worried. Especially when I found out that you got left alone with that jerk Fyron. Petal's been worried sick, too!"

"Oh?" I ask her, surprised. "Did she say that?"

"Well, technically," Flower says, "what she said was that if you couldn't handle yourself in a situation like that after joining this tournament, then you deserved your fate, but I'm sure that's not what she really meant!"

"Oh, yeah?" I say. "Well, you tell her that her blue eyes make her look fat."

"I can hear you, you know..." Illuna tells me, with a menacing tone.

"Wait, do her blue eyes really make me look fat?" Flower asks.

"Hey, Barry!" Arraka says, cutting Flower off. "Something's been bothering me ever since we left the caverns. How in the hell did you manage to convince the troll to let you go? I thought for sure that you were done for when I sensed him come near you."

"You mean Velgos?" I ask her. "The troll that wouldn't die even if you cut off his head? He got stopped by the arena's owner. Apparently, he wants to make a show of our fight, and we'll be fighting the troll in the second round of the arena instead."

"Hah!" Arraka says. "I'll be looking forward to it!"

"Be careful, Barry!" Flower says. "We won't be able to help you while you're in the arena!"

"Yeah, I know," I say. "Don't worry, I'll be fine! But thanks for your concern."

After I was done talking to Flower and Illuna, I spent another hour studying my notebook, and then I started calling my friends from the other divisions, one by one, in order to tell them of my findings. When I got to Kate, I also decided to tell her about her old inmate from the Beacon, to see how she'd react.

"Hey, Kate," I say. "Do you remember having met a young lessathi girl with silver hair who couldn't talk, back when you were at the Beacon of Hope? Or maybe she had black hair back then, I'm not sure."

There's a brief pause after I finish my phrase, during which I can't even hear the sound of Kate's breathing.

"How do you know about Leila?" Kate asks me, after a few seconds.

"So you do remember her!" I say. "Were the two of

you on good terms, or…"

"Tell me how you know about her!" Kate shouts.

"Okay, okay!" I say. "I met her the other day. She is a member of my division. She's still alive."

There's another brief pause, during which Kate doesn't say anything.

"You are certain of this?" Kate says. "How do you know it's really her? She might be trying to trick you. Anyone can dye their hair white and pretend that they're not able to speak. The Leila I know should have been dead for a long time."

"Why?" I say. "Did you find her body?"

"…No," Kate says. "I did not."

"Well, then," I say, "I guess it wouldn't hurt you to meet her, would it? You'll be able to tell for yourself if it's really her when you see her up close."

"Alright, Barry," Kate says. "I'll agree to meet her. But be careful around her. You can't know for sure that it's really her. There were a lot of lessathi in that institution who knew about us. The information could have gotten out in any number of ways."

"Fine, I'll be careful," I say. "I'll see you at the arena, in two days. Don't get yourself into any more fights with your teammates until then!"

"See you at the arena," Kate says, simply, and then we both close the transmission.

Once I make sure that every one of my friends knows about the monsters from the arena and their weaknesses, I decide that it's time to get back to Leila, in order to finally formulate a plan for how to deal with them. When I reach her room, I knock three times, and she opens her door, dressed in the same clothes that she was wearing when we got back from the caverns. Her clothes are not as wet as they were when we returned, but they are definitely nowhere near dry yet.

"You didn't get changed?" I ask her, shocked.

"I don't have any change of clothes," Leila writes. "I wasn't carrying a backpack with me when I got captured."

"Well, why didn't you say something?" I say. "You could have asked me for some spare clothes until yours dried up!"

"I didn't want to be a bother," Leila writes.

"Wait a minute," I say. "If you don't have a backpack with you, then what about food? Don't tell me that you haven't eaten anything since you came here?"

"The guards have provided me with a minimum supply of food and water," Leila writes. "Just enough to get by. It's not a problem."

"Of course it's a problem," I say. "Wait here, I'm going to bring you a change of clothes and some food."

"No, you don't have to—" Leila starts to write, but I ignore her, and I go back to my room, in search for some clothes and some beef jerky from my backpack.

I then come back to Leila and I hand her a long sleeved shirt, a pair of pants, the jerky, and a bottle of water.

"Here you go," I tell Leila. "Now hurry up and get changed, will you? You wouldn't want to catch a cold right before the arena."

"Thank you…" Leila writes, as she takes what I've given her, and then closes the door, in order to get changed.

She opens the door a bit later, dressed in my clothes, with the long sleeves of the shirt hanging past her hands, and the pants trailing on the ground, behind her.

"These clothes are… a little big for me," Leila writes.

"You look fine!" I tell her. "It's not like you'll be fighting in these clothes at the arena event. It's just until your own clothes dry off. Come on, let's go inside. I want to tell you what I found out while reading my notebook."

We both enter her room, and I spend the next fifteen minutes telling her the most important parts about my findings. She listens closely to what I have to say, while taking a bite from the beef jerky I gave her, every so often. After I'm done talking, she puts the jerky on the bed, beside her, and she starts to write.

"From what you're telling me," Leila writes, "I understand that our biggest problem by far will be the troll, and his higher than average regeneration."

"Yeah," I tell her. "It is already known that a troll can regenerate fast enough to not die from a wound to the heart, but a troll being able to survive with its head cut off is something that I didn't think was possible. I guess it goes to show how little we really know about regeneration in general. According to all the books I've read, any living being that's had its head severed from its body should not be able to live any longer, regardless of how high its regeneration is. The fact that the body could even regenerate its head contradicts our most basic knowledge about how a troll's body is supposed to work."

"But the troll didn't regenerate his head," Leila writes. "The head kept talking from the ground, and the body had to pick it back up."

"You're right!" I say. "This means that the link between the body and the head is somehow not broken, even after the two of them get separated. Maybe we can use this. If the troll is still using his head to see and hear even after it's been severed from the body, then maybe we can cut his head off, pick it up, and then blindfold it, or something, leaving his body defenseless!"

"I don't think that the troll would leave himself open like that again, in the arena," Leila writes. "I used the element of surprise before, but now he knows how fast I am, and he won't let me cut his head off again so easily."

"Well, the only way you can kill a regular troll," I say, "is either by cutting its head off or by burning it alive. If cutting the head off is not an option, then the only alternative we have left is fire. That being said, getting access to any sort of flames will be next to impossible in the arena, and that troll is even wearing anti-magic armor, which gives him protection to fire. Even if we somehow manage to find a way to burn him, we'd first have to damage his armor badly enough that the magical protections on it would wear off."

"Do you think we should talk about all this with the other members of our division?" Leila writes. "Maybe they could come up with some ideas."

"I suppose it couldn't hurt to hear their opinions on the matter," I say.

Leila nods.

"Alright, then," I say. "Let's go knock on their doors, and we'll have a meet up in the recreation room."

I turn to leave the room, but Leila grabs me by the sleeve, and she stops me in my tracks. As I turn back towards her, I see that the blue writing in front of her says simply: "Wait."

The blue writing then quickly disappears, being replaced by a new text.

"Can we do this later?" Leila writes.

"Later?" I ask her, confused.

"After my clothes have dried…" Leila writes, with a pleading look in her eyes, as she shows me the long sleeves hanging from her wrists.

"Oh, right, right," I say. "Sorry, I forgot."

I pause for a few seconds.

"On second thought," I say, "maybe we should have this discussion tomorrow, during our final recreation period. The arena events won't start until the day after tomorrow, so we'll have plenty of time to make a strategy. I don't really feel like knocking on everyone's doors as if I were trying to distribute a bunch of pamphlets. Plus, some of them might not agree to a meeting, even if I call them. I think they'll be more inclined to hear me out tomorrow, when we're all in the same room."

Leila nods again.

"I think I'm going to return to my room and try to dig up some more information," I say. "I'll search for every note that I've written regarding regeneration, and I'll try to see if I can make some sense of this situation. Maybe if we properly understand the troll's ability, we can find a way to counter it. Let me know if you come up with any ideas in the meantime."

"I will," Leila writes.

"Well, then, I guess I'm off," I say. "I'll see you again, later!"

"See you later," Leila writes, and then I leave her room and go back to my own.

After I close the door to my room behind me, and I pick up my notebook once again, my thoughts race towards the lessathi who offered me the deal with the king. I still haven't told any of my friends about it. Should I tell them about it?

No, I shouldn't make them worry needlessly. If I am to tell them of this, then it will be after the arena, when everyone will be safe.

As I am lost in thought, while mechanically turning the pages of my notebook one by one, my eyes chance upon a paragraph that I seem to have skipped the last few times I was skimming through these texts. This paragraph mentions a theory that is not very popular among scholars, which states that the high regeneration of some creatures may be a result of an innate difference between their auras and ours.

I suddenly remember Eiden's lecture, before we entered the city, when he was telling me that if you mess enough with a person's aura, you can even stop them from aging. If what he told me is true, then it wouldn't be that far of a stretch to assume that a special type of aura could grant someone a high regeneration rate. If that is the case, then could this aura perhaps also help in keeping the limbs functional, even if they are severed from the body?

I'll admit that my knowledge about auras is limited, but from the little I know, a person's aura is not supposed to have unlimited range. What were to happen, then, if the troll's head would be taken too far away from the body after it's been cut off? Would his consciousness fade away? Would that make him die for good? If we ever manage to cut that troll's head off again, this is definitely something that's worth testing out.

I ended up spending the day trying to look for more information to confirm my theory. Unfortunately, not a lot of research has been done on this subject, since most people can barely even read the level of magic power in someone's aura, so the theory that an aura could influence a body's regeneration has been deemed as 'not grounded in facts' by most respectable groups of scholars, and the few who wanted to pursue this theory did not receive the appropriate funding to do so.

I spent my whole day researching this, and all I have to show for it is an outlandish theory, based on another outlandish theory whose validity hinges mostly on one of Eiden's offhanded remarks. Better than nothing, I guess…

I put my notebook back in my backpack, and I prepare to go to sleep. I'll have more time to study tomorrow.

Before falling asleep, Leila came to knock on my door, in order to bring me back my clothes. I asked her if she came up with any ideas, but she said that the only thing that came to her mind was that we could try to crush the troll's head, after we behead him, in the hopes that the head will no longer regenerate after it's been cut off from the body.

The next day, our recreation period was scheduled towards noon. As I stepped out of my cell to meet the others, I noticed, to my surprise, that everyone was gathered in the middle of the room, sitting on the floor, except for Wilhelm, who was standing up, shuffling a deck of cards.

"You're late!" Wilhelm says. "Have a seat. We were almost about to start without you."

"What's going on, here?" I ask Wilhelm.

"You are wondering," says Wilhelm, "why we are all suddenly on friendly terms after we've been mostly ignoring each other for the past few days? The answer is simple. It's because the owner of the arena just paid us a visit."

"The owner?" I ask him, surprised.

"Yes," Wilhelm says. "He was told by the guards in this place that we haven't really been using these recreation periods to get to know each other. He therefore decided to come here personally, in order to graciously inform us that if we aren't planning to act as a team, he will be sending us one by one to our deaths, instead of giving us the chance to work together. He also let us know that today's recreation period is the last time when we can prove that we are able to cooperate with each other."

"So, that's why you're all playing cards, then?" I say.

"Well, we had to start somewhere," Wilhelm says. "And I just happened to have a deck of cards with me, so I said, why not?"

"Fair enough," I say. "So, what exactly are we playing?"

"We're playing a game of shut your mouth, and pick

up the damn cards," one of the two thugs tells me, in a menacing tone.

"If the game is called 'shut your mouth', then why are your lips moving?" I say.

"What did you just say to me, you piece of sh—" the thug starts to say, while he gets up, but he gets interrupted by Wilhelm.

"Now, now," Wilhelm says, as he puts a hand on the thug's shoulder, in order to stop him from reaching me. "We're all supposed to act as a team here, remember?"

"Get your filthy hand off me, you lowborn scum," the thug tells Wilhelm.

I'm not sure if anyone else noticed, but for a second, there, I'm pretty sure that I could see Wilhelm's cheerful expression turn into one of pure bloodlust, as he heard the thug's words. I didn't get to see any more of his reaction, because Bruce suddenly began to laugh out loud, causing us all to turn our eyes to him, instead.

"Did you just call him a lowborn scum?" Bruce says. "And what are you supposed to be? The long lost prince of Olmnar?"

"No," says the mage that got locked up here, yesterday. "That makes him a disinherited noble. Take a good look at that filthy rag that he's wearing as a scarf. It bears the mark of the Tilirius family."

"The Tilirius family?" Bruce says. "Hah! So, I guess that makes him a highborn scum, then. My apologies!"

He laughs again.

"Can we please get back to our game of cards?" Wilhelm asks. "The guards are still listening."

"Nobody cares about your game of cards, Wilbert," Bruce says. "The owner said we have to talk, so we're talking. He didn't say anything about playing cards. Go do it by yourself, if you like playing cards so much."

"My name is Wilhelm, not Wilbert," Wilhelm says, in a calm but menacing tone.

As Wilhelm stops talking, a blue writing appears in the middle of us, with large characters, so that we can all see it clearly.

"Please excuse me," the text says, "but I would like to begin discussing our strategy for tomorrow, now, if you all don't mind."

We all turn towards Leila, who is staring at us with an upset look on her face.

"Oh, uh..." Bruce says. "Of course, of course... Maybe we should start doing that."

"I could not agree more," Wilhelm says.

"And just what are we supposed to talk about, exactly?" the mage says. "We still haven't been given any information in regards to tomorrow's events. The only thing we know so far is that we're likely going to be battling mythical creatures of some kind, in one of the rounds."

Leila gives me a look. I think she's trying to tell me that this would be the best moment for me to let everyone know about what we found out in the caverns. I nod to her shortly, as I begin to address the others.

"Actually there is some information that I would like to share with you all," I say. "But you'd better brace yourselves, because this is going to get long."

I then start telling everyone about our trip to the underground caverns, and what we discovered there.

During our conversation, I purposely omitted to tell them how exactly we reached the tunnels, and I did not tell them about our encounter with Flower and Illuna either, but I tried to describe the rest of our adventure to them in as much detail as possible, while simultaneously avoiding to tell them any information that might lead them to know that we are lessathi, and that we are using stat devices. After I was done with the story, I also gave them a quick summary of what I know about each of the creatures we've met, including their behaviors and their weaknesses, and I also told them my theory about the troll's unusual regeneration ability.

"This is all very useful information," Wilhelm says, after I'm done with the briefing. "I happened to overhear the guards last night saying that we'd be fighting a troll named Velgos in the second round, but I would have never imagined him to be so powerful. What I would like to add is that I've also heard them talk about manticores, which I don't believe you've met in the underground caverns. If your notebook has as much information in it as you've claimed, maybe you should do some research about them as well."

"I actually already did some research about them," I say. "I forgot to mention it before, but I also managed to overhear the guards talking about some of the monsters we might have to fight in the arena. In that discussion, they mentioned manticores and giant scorpions. I'll give you the briefing on them later."

"So, about that trapdoor which you triggered accidentally," Bruce says, "did you try to see if you could activate it again?"

"I've tried a few times after that," Leila writes, "but I didn't get it to work."

"Any chance we could have a look inside your room?" Bruce says. "Maybe one of us can figure it out."

"No," Leila writes. "I'm not letting either of you inside my room."

"Except for the stillwater?" the mage says.

"Except for the stillwater," Leila writes, simply.

"So our greatest problem remains the troll, then…" Wilhelm says. "I don't know what to say about that aura theory. I'm not really one to talk, because I've never studied magic, but it seems a little far-fetched to me."

"I like Leila's idea about crushing the head better," Bruce says. "I doubt he'll be able to regenerate it once it's been cut off."

"Either way," Wilhelm says, "what I think we can all agree on is that there's no way we could face these enemies alone. I know that we can't really stand each other, but we're going to have to call a truce until at least after the arena events. Our survival depends on it."

For once, everyone agreed with Wilhelm, even if some did so more begrudgingly than others, and we decided to spend the rest of the recreation period discussing various strategies that could work against the monsters that we knew about, but also against other monsters that I've read about in my notes. We even agreed to have a second meeting later, after we'd spend some time alone in our rooms, mulling over the information that we had at our disposal.

By the end of the day, we didn't manage to come up with better plans against the troll than our original ones, so all we could do was hope that at least one of them would work out alright. After going back to my room in the evening and lying down on my bed, my last thoughts before going to sleep went to the vision that I had about Wilhelm stabbing me in the back, during the arena event.

It's going to be fine. I already know what he's up to. As long as I never take my eyes off him, he won't be able to surprise me.

I decide to think no further about this, and I go to sleep. The next day, I get woken up in the morning by one of the guards, telling me to pack my bags, because we're leaving in twenty minutes. I put all my stuff back in my backpack, and then I walk out the door and into the recreation room, where the other members of my division were slowly starting to gather up. As soon as we're all set to go, we begin to leave our division's area one by one, and we stop outside the door, where we are greeted by an employee of the arena, who collects all of our keys, and tells us to follow him.

As we all walk through the dimly lit tunnels,

members from other divisions are slowly beginning to walk out of their division areas as well, and follow their guides through the corridors. When we finally reach the upper levels, we are told to line up in an orderly fashion, so that the guards who were sent to escort us to the arena will have an easier time keeping an eye on us. I didn't get to see any of my friends as we advanced towards the arena, but I did see a pretty big crowd of people making its way to the arena to see the show, and a very long line at the ticket booth.

The guards lead us through the gladiator entrance of the arena, and they show us to our locker rooms, where we get to store our belongings for the duration of the show. After we're done putting our backpacks in the lockers, the guards tell us that we're allowed to roam freely through the area designated for the gladiators until the events begin, but that we will need to gather up in the waiting area of our division after the sound of the first horn.

I figured that this would be the best moment to arrange a meeting between Leila and Kate, so I told Leila about my idea, and asked her to follow me. She seemed a bit hesitant at first, but in the end, she decided to come with me.

The area that we were given access to was the one right below the spectator seats, circling the area where the fighting is about to take place. The fighting area reserved for the gladiators looks much larger than those from the arenas that I've read about before, in history books. The amphitheater surrounding the arena seems big enough to host thirty thousand spectators, if not more, and yet, it does not seem that the seats are in any danger of not being filled. Even at this early hour in the morning, there are thousands of spectators pouring in through all the entrances, and then making their way through the rising tiers of seats, eager to reach their reserved spots, and to watch the event of the century.

It seems that three days were more than enough to spread the word throughout the city about today's event. We make our way through the lower level of the coliseum, while I look around, scanning the groups of gladiators to see if I can spot anyone I know.

Half an hour later, we are still nowhere close to finding any trace of them. I tried reaching them through Daren's transceiver as well, but I've had no luck. There must be too many people trying to use transceivers in the area to be able to lock onto the correct signals. Where could they all be? The horn that announces the start of the events could be sounding any minute now.

"Leila?" I hear Kate's voice behind me. "Leila, is that really you?"

Leila turns around, at the sound of Kate's voice, but when she sees her face, she hesitates to write anything, for a few moments.

"Kate, I…" Leila starts to write, but she gets interrupted by Kate rushing towards her, and hugging her as tightly as she can.

"Leila!" Kate says. "By the gods, I thought you were dead. They told us you died from the experiments. Oh gods, Leila, I'm so sorry! I shouldn't have believed them! I should have gone looking for you like I did for all the others."

"You don't need to apolo—" Leila writes, but she stops her text when she realizes that Kate is currently keeping her eyes closed, in an attempt to keep the tears from flowing out.

"I'm sorry," Kate says. "I shouldn't have abandoned you like this. Please forgive me! I was so focused on Diane that I—"

The rest of Kate's words get drowned out by the sound of a very loud horn. It seems that the arena event is about to start.

"Kate, we need to go," Daren says.

I only now notice that Daren and Hadrik were also there, standing behind Kate. They must have all met earlier, and came looking for me together.

"I know," Kate says, as she wipes her tears with her sleeve.

"Please… keep her safe…" Kate tells me, simply, as she walks past me, heading towards her division's side of the arena.

"I will," I tell her.

"Kate, wait, I…" Leila writes, with her mouth open, as if she'd forgotten that she can't talk, but Kate doesn't get to see the blue writing, and she keeps walking away from us.

"Hey, Kate!" I shout loudly, to make sure that she hears me.

Kate stops in her tracks, and she turns around, confused. Seeing that Leila doesn't do anything, I give her a nudge with my elbow. She finally understands what I was doing, and she quickly makes a message out of blue text, with very large letters, so that Kate can see them from a distance.

"Kate, I'm sorry too," the text says. "I'm sorry for having thought that you would never want to see me again because I was a lessathi! So, now that we're both sorry, let's win the arena and get out of here alive so we can continue being sorry together!"

At first, Kate had a bit of a shock when she saw the writing, but then she realized who it was coming from, and she managed to smile.

"It's a promise!" she shouts at Leila, and then she turns around, to hurry back towards her division.

"Knock 'em dead, Barry!" Hadrik says, with his usual grin, as he also heads towards his own designated area.

"Or better yet, don't get killed," Daren tells me. "We

only need to survive the arena, not win it. I'll see you again after the end of the event. Remember, no need to do anything crazy. Just stay alive. Got it?"

"Got it," I say.

Once Daren is also gone, Leila and I decide to head towards our division as well.

"So…" I say, as the two of us walk side by side. "Now are you glad that you decided to follow me to meet Kate after all?" I say.

Leila smiles, faintly.

"Yes…" she writes. "Yes, I am glad. Thank you…"

We make our way to our division area, where all of our other teammates were already gathered. We then take our places next to the iron gratings blocking our access to the fighting area, in order to have a better view of what's happening in the arena. Apparently, there are still some people who are making their way towards their seats, but most of the spectators seem to have found their places, and are now restlessly waiting for the show to begin. I take a look to see if I can spot Flower, but the seats are too far away from me to be able to make out any details. The announcer is now verifying his magical voice magnifier, in preparation for the event. He is situated on an elevated platform, above the spectator seats.

As we all wait for the events to begin, I suddenly hear a familiar beeping noise, coming from my pocket. At the same time, a similar beeping noise comes from the direction of Leila as well.

Finally. I've been waiting for this for a while. I quickly take the stat device out of my pocket, and I see that I have three extra points to spend on my stats.

Given that I'm about to fight in a deadly arena, my survival should take first priority. These three points are just what I need to raise my reflexes and toughness stat to their maximum level of four. I also still have my three points in speed and the four points I put into premonition, so hopefully, this will be enough to allow me to hold my own against the creatures that the arena owner is planning to throw at us.

Once I'm done with my stat device, I put it back in my pocket, and I see that Leila is just about done with hers as well. Knowing her, she must have placed all her points in toughness. I would ask her directly, but I wouldn't want to give away to the others the fact that we are lessathi.

"Found a way to send messages in private, have you?" Bruce asks us, after seeing us both use the same type of devices at the same time. "Well, I hope you've said what you needed, because the show's almost about to start."

Shortly after Bruce is done talking, we hear the sound of a second horn, now signaling the actual beginning of the event. The few spectators who came in late are now hurrying as fast as they can towards their seats, as the announcer is doing a few tests, to make sure that his voice magnifier is working properly. Soon, the constant murmur that could be heard throughout the arena slowly dies out, and the announcer takes a deep breath, preparing to officially announce the beginning of the arena event.

"Welcome," the announcer says. "Welcome to all! I don't think that there is any reason for me to make a lengthy introduction this time around. You all know why you're here. You came here because you were promised the event of the century, and we plan to deliver on that promise. Now, if it's alright with everyone, I would like to begin by announcing the rules."

The announcer waits for a few moments, in order to make sure that there are no objections, and then he continues to read from his notepad.

"By the request of the arena's owner himself, mister

Venard," the announcer says, "today's event will follow the traditional rules, which had been used by his father before him and by the lessathi of old, before the still winter. As most of you may already know, this also means that if a gladiator breaks one of the rules, they will not be disqualified from participating any further, but they will become an undesirable. By becoming an undesirable, a gladiator will be forced to participate in an additional round after the official event ends, where they will need to fight all of the other remaining gladiators at once, in one final battle. Any gladiator who manages to give the finishing blow to an undesirable will get rewarded either with his freedom, or with a large sum of money, depending on their status in this arena. Other gladiators can of course refuse to participate in this final round, and undesirables can also choose to no longer participate in the regular rounds, once they have been pegged as rule breakers."

The announcer coughs loudly, and he flips the page of his notepad.

"Of course," the announcer continues, "this does not mean that gladiators will now be exempt from following the general rules of the arena. If a gladiator is caught using magic, if they try to kill their teammates, or if they attack any of the spectators, they will be executed on the spot. The undesirable rule only applies for the rules of the actual event. Moving on, the traditional rules of the arena state that the arena events must be divided into exactly three rounds. The first round, as I'm sure you've already been told, will be fought against a variety of mythical creatures that have never been used before in this arena. We do have a surprise for the second round, however. For this special occasion, instead of our reigning champion, I think you will be happy to learn that the warrior who will be joining us is none other than the relentless mercenary Velgos!"

There is a loud murmur in the crowd when they hear the name of Velgos. From what I can tell, they seem excited about the prospect of watching him fight.

“In the third round,” the announcer says, “the gladiators that survived the first two rounds will need to fight in a series of duels, to decide who will be the victors of this event. Some of the duels will have to be fought to the death, while others will be fought only until one of the fighters surrenders. The exact duels will be decided after the end of round two, when we will know exactly which of the fighters have survived. And now that we got all of the introductions out of the way, I believe it is finally time to get this event started. Is everyone ready?”

The crowd bursts into loud cheers for a few seconds, and the announcer now raises his voice, in order to drown out all the loud noises.

“Then I will keep you waiting no longer,” the announcer says. “Let the event of the century commence!”

One of the iron gates from the lower level of the amphitheater is now slowly getting raised, while the crowds keep cheering as loud as they can.

“For the first round,” the announcer says, “divisions of fighters will be entering the arena one by one, in the order of their division’s number. Let us give a warm round of applause to this event’s first division!”

There is a mixed sound of applause and shouts coming from the spectator seats, as the gladiators from the first division make their way out of the gates, and towards the center of the arena. I do not recognize any of the warriors in this division, but judging by the continued cheers of the crowd, I’d say that most of the spectators have seen them perform at least once before. Some of the gladiators seem a little bit too confident. Former victors, perhaps? Either way, they’d better get their act together, and quick. From what Bruce said on my first day here, the events until now could not even begin to compare with what's coming.

A large iron gate on the opposite side of the arena makes a loud creaking noise as it opens. From beyond the gate, a lion with black wings, red eyes, two horns on its head and a scorpion's tail is making its way into the fighting area. This hideous creature, called a manticore, wastes no time and it soars directly into the sky. Two more manticores follow its lead, and they all start circling the skies above the arena, watching their prey intently. Seeing the beasts leave the fighting area with such ease, some of the spectators in the crowd are beginning to show signs of uneasiness.

"Do not worry," the announcer says, trying to calm down the crowd. "These beasts have been well trained. They would not dare to lay their claws on anyone other than the gladiators in the arena."

Several giant scorpions are now also joining the arena, coming from beyond the same gate that the manticores entered from. They are slowly advancing towards the warriors, in a straight line, without any attempt to surround them.

It's a good thing that I heard the guards talking about the scorpions while I was in my cell. I've had all the time in the world to prepare against them, and I've also told everyone else all the information they needed to know about them.

At least as far as the giant scorpions are concerned, we shouldn't have any… Hey, wait a minute! Those aren't giant scorpions… Those aren't giant scorpions at all. Those are desert marauders. Damn those idiot guards! Could they not tell the difference?

Okay… Calm down! Desert marauders are pretty much just giant scorpions with smaller heads. They should have more or less the same behaviors. But do they also have the same weaknesses? I think they do, but I'm not completely certain. If only I had my notebook with me now…

Should I go and get it? If they're going by order of the division number, then there should still be plenty of time until it's our turn to enter the arena. But if I leave now, I'm going to miss the fights. If I'm going to fight against these creatures, observing them in action may be crucial to my survival.

Hold on, I also have another choice! I could send Leila to go read my notebook, and rip the pages I need out of it, so she can bring them back to me. But would she be able to find the pages? I did make a page index at the beginning, but people have had trouble understanding my ugly handwriting in the past. I can't just tell her to bring me the notebook, because then she might not have the time to return it to my backpack before our round begins. Either way, I don't have much time. I'm going to need to decide what I want to do, and quick.

"Hey, Leila," I say, after taking a few more seconds to think. "Can I ask you a favor?"

Leila turns towards me, with a curious look in her eyes, waiting to see what I have to say.

"There was some information written about desert marauders in my notebook," I say, "but I don't remember some important details. Could you please go get the notebook out of my backpack, rip the pages about the marauders out and bring them to me? There's an index at the beginning of the notebook where you can find the numbers of the pages you're looking for. I'd go myself, but I'm the one who's studied about mythical creatures the most, and I'm afraid that I'll miss something important if I don't watch the fights."

"Okay, I'll go," Leila writes. "Give me the key."

I take the key of my locker out of my pocket, and I

hand it to Leila.

"The number of the locker is written on the key," I say. "You've seen what my notebook looks like, right? You'll need to have a clear image of it in your head if you want to retrieve it from the backpack."

"Yes, I've seen it," Leila writes. "I'll be right back."

She then leaves the area of our division and heads towards the locker room.

While I'd been talking with Leila, the marauders had gotten closer to the gladiators. The manticores are still flying in circles, waiting for the best opportunity to strike.

The warriors seem to be rather well organized, and they're not letting the monsters intimidate them. On their leader's signal, three of the men jump to attack the left-most marauder, while the rest of the gladiators try to distract the others. One of the warriors remains behind, and he watches the manticores attentively. He must have been tasked to observe the battlefield, so that he can warn his teammates if the situation changes.

The scorpion-like creatures are at least five times bigger than the gladiators, and they could probably crush any single one of them in their giant claws. The warriors seem to be experienced in battle, however, and they manage to remain unharmed, by anticipating the marauders' movements, and by covering for each other in their time of need. The group from the left in particular seems to be doing surprisingly well. They've managed to weaken the creature with a few well-timed strikes, and they're already moving in for the kill.

The most agile of the three jumps on the creature's back and he stabs it fiercely in the back of its head. The marauder screams in pain and it tries to attack the warrior with its tail, but the gladiator jumps off, while the other two make a rush for it and stab the monster in both its eyes with their swords, at the same time.

The crowd bursts into loud cheers and shouts, as the scorpion-like creature falls to the ground. The three warriors raise their swords for a few seconds, to signal their victory to the spectators, and then they head towards the other marauders, in order to help their team mates.

"Fall back!" we hear the desperate shout of the gladiator who was observing the battlefield. "Fall back *now*!"

The gladiators look up, but they have no time to react. It takes only a few seconds for the manticores that had been circling the skies all this time to dive down, to sink their claws into the warriors' chests, and then to soar back into the air, carrying their prey.

The screams of the gladiators silence the crowd completely, as the beasts fly higher and higher. Two of the gladiators dropped their swords from the pain, immediately after being attacked, but one of them managed to keep hold of his weapon, and he's now using it to stab his attacker in the underbelly. The manticore screams, and it drops the warrior, who falls to the ground and crushes his head against the hard soil. The other two gladiators are raised a bit higher by their attackers, but then they also get dropped to the ground, and they die on impact.

The remaining warriors are now finally starting to panic. Their leader was among the ones who died. Having lost the person who was giving them directions, the gladiators begin to break their formation, and the marauders take advantage of this by grabbing one of the warriors with their claws, while another marauder impales him with its tail.

As if all this wasn't enough, two more manticores are just now entering the fighting area from beyond the gate, and they're running fast towards the surviving gladiators. The observer gets killed first. He didn't seem to be very skilled in combat, and he got mauled in an instant. The other gladiators did not last much longer. The desert marauders and the manticores finally joined forces against them, and they couldn't stand a chance.

At the end of the fight, the arena falls completely silent, except for the sounds of the manticores, feasting greedily from the carcasses of their hard earned prey.

"By the gods..." Bruce says, as he watches the battle's aftermath in horror, from beyond our iron grating.

"It appears that not even our reigning champions could defeat these fearsome beasts," the announcer says. "This does not look good for the following divisions. Is this event going to end in a bloodbath?"

The iron gate for the second division is now getting raised. However, nobody seems to be coming out. After about ten seconds of silence, we hear a scream coming from their direction.

"I'm not going out there!" a man screams, at the top of his lungs. "If you want to kill me, then kill me now! You saw what happened to those gladiators! We don't stand a chance!"

"You're going to march in there and fight," another man's voice says, "or you'll be getting a death far worse than being eaten alive by a manticore."

"No, please, have mercy!" the other man shouts.

The discussion between what I presume is a gladiator from the second division and a guard of the arena is getting a lot of reactions from the spectators. Some of them seem to be getting scared, and others are fidgeting around nervously in their seats.

"We seem to be experiencing some technical difficulties," the announcer says. "There's no need to be alarmed. I'm certain that our guards will get the show up and running again in—"

The announcer stops mid-sentence, as a single dwarf

steps out of the second division's gate, carrying a bottle in his hand, and walking at a relaxed pace, towards the desert marauders. Both the crowd and the announcer fall completely silent, as they watch Hadrik walk calmly, and then stop in the middle of the arena, in order to chug down the last contents of his bottle.

"Ah!" Hadrik exclaims. "There's nothing like a fine bottle of dwarven ale to raise your appetite before a battle!"

He then starts turning his head around, as if he were looking for something.

"Say, you wouldn't happen to have something that I could throw this empty bottle away in, would you?" he shouts towards the announcer, as he shows him the empty bottle in his hand.

The announcer watches him, with a puzzled expression on his face, without saying anything.

"You know, like a trash can, or a paper bag, or something, so I don't make a mess?" Hadrik says.

The announcer and the crowd watch the dwarf silently, unable to decide whether he is being serious or not. While Hadrik was talking, one of the scorpion-like creatures was slowly creeping up behind him, and aiming to attack him with its claws.

"You know what, never mind!" Hadrik says. "I'll just use this as an improvised weapon, instead."

He then immediately turns around, and he clobbers the desert marauder in the head with his bottle, which breaks into shards of glass that stab the creature in its eyes. The monster starts screaming in pain, as Hadrik makes a quick jump, landing with his fist on top of the marauder, and smashing it against the ground, causing a loud shockwave while also forming a small crater below the creature, due to the force of the impact.

One of the manticores that was still up in the sky quickly dives down to grab Hadrik in its claws, but the dwarf steps away at the exact moment when the monster reaches him, and he grabs it by the tail. He then spins it around for about four seconds, building momentum, and then he throws it at a wall far away from him with all his might, causing the beast to smash right through it with a loud booming noise.

The crowd and the announcer are both speechless. They are looking at the dwarf with bemused expressions on their faces, not knowing how to react.

"Oh, you don't need to worry about that wall," Hadrik says, thinking that his reckless behavior is the reason for everyone's silence. "I checked that area out before the battle and there's nothing but an empty storage on that side, so there's no danger of anyone getting hur—"

A loud roar of cheering noises drowns out the rest of Hadrik's words, as the spectators finally regain their previous vigor, and start shouting and clapping like never before.

"See, now that's more like it!" Hadrik shouts, with a wide grin, as he sees the people cheering. "This is what an arena is all about! You all better hang on to your seats, because the fun is just starting!"

He then runs towards another marauder, and he headbutts it so fiercely that it drops to the ground in an instant.

"Release the second wave!" the announcer shouts, as a few more desert marauders come out of the large iron gates that had been opened previously.

Making their way from behind the marauders, a new species of creatures is now entering the fighting area. The creatures look like larger versions of porcupines, but from what I understand they should not be related to them in any way besides their looks. Unlike regular porcupines, the quills on their backs are deadly weapons, and they are sharp and durable enough to give elven steel a run for its money. The creatures have the ability to launch their quills as projectiles, with very high accuracy and speed. Due to their high regeneration rate, they also have the ability to regrow their quills almost instantly. This provides them with a near unlimited stock of ammunition to use against their foes. Their appearance and their behavior have led people to call these creatures 'archer porcupines'.

A few of the porcupines that have positioned themselves several dozen feet behind Hadrik are now turning their backs towards him, getting ready to attack. Hadrik is still fighting the marauders, and he doesn't seem to have noticed the porcupines. Should I shout a warning to him? I wouldn't want to distract him in the middle of his battle, but if those porcupines manage to aim their shots right, he might be in trouble.

"Hey, Hadrik!" I shout. "Behind you!"

Hadrik looks back, and he sees the porcupines getting ready to attack him. He waits for them to shoot, and he dodges at the last moment, causing the quills to hit a desert marauder instead. He then dashes towards his ranged attackers, not leaving them any time to ready up a second shot, and he pummels them repeatedly with his fists, until they're all either dead, or unable to move.

"Nice one, Barry!" Hadrik then says. "I owe you a beer."

The marauder who got hit by the quills was the last one standing, and the damage it took was enough to send it falling down.

The manticores have all abandoned their meals when Hadrik started his rampage, and they're now back to circling the skies, trying to find the right time to strike. One of the braver manticores dives down quickly, in an attempt to surprise the dwarf, but when it sees him react, the monster quickly soars back up into the sky, and out of his reach.

"Damn it!" Hadrik says. "Come back here, you coward! Come back here and fight!"

"Hey, dwarf!" I hear Arraka's voice coming from the crowd. "Why don't you try singing them a lullaby? Maybe they'll get sleepy and come back down. Ahahahahahahaha!"

Following the sound of Arraka's voice, I manage to identify Flower in the crowd of spectators. The people around her all have their heads turned towards her, and are watching her curiously. They must think that the amulet around her neck is some new type of transceiver.

"Shut up, you blasted old hag!" Hadrik shouts back at her. "When I get out of here, I swear I'm going to double your spinning sessions!"

"Yeah, I've got a better idea!" Arraka says. "How about you stop wasting everyone's time and get back to fighting? Do you have any idea how much this ticket cost?"

"I can't fight them, you moron!" Hadrik shouts, exasperated. "I'm not allowed to use ranged weapons in the arena."

"Then throw some spears!" Arraka shouts. "Do I really have to tell you everything? You've got spears mounted on the walls. Use them."

Now that Arraka mentions it, I see that there are indeed spears and various other weapons mounted on the walls of the arena. They must have been placed there to give people who didn't have any weapons when they got captured an equal chance in the fighting event. Hadrik mumbles something under his breath, and he goes to get one of the spears. He then tosses it at one of the manticores, and the spear lodges itself into its chest, causing blood to spray out while the creature falls towards the ground. Before the creature reaches the soil, the dwarf grabs two more spears, and he throws them in quick succession towards two of the other manticores, killing them as well.

The last remaining manticore decides that the skies are no longer safe, so it quickly dives down towards Hadrik, to end the fight with one big final clash. Hadrik does not wait for the creature to reach him, and he makes a jump, grabbing it from the air, and doing a spinning drop, crushing the beast's head into the ground.

He did it… The crazy bastard did it. He took both waves of monsters down all by himself, and he barely even got scratched.

The crowds are now cheering louder than ever before. Hadrik's teammates, who had been hiding this whole time, come running towards the dwarf, and they raise him in the air, while chanting his name repeatedly.

"Hadrik! Hadrik! Hadrik!" they keep saying, while the crowds are all cheering.

"Don't think that you're getting off that easy, you cowardly dogs," Hadrik says, with a grin, while his teammates are throwing him up and down. "When we get out of here, you're going to buy me a year's worth of drinks."

"What is the meaning of this?!" I hear the ambassador of Ollendor shout from above.

"Ambassador!" says Venard, the owner of the arena. "I see that you've decided to join us after all! Would you like some wine?"

The two of them seem to be talking from a private room above our division's area. Since my teammates are not reacting to their voices in any way, I'm assuming that I am the only one able to hear this conversation, thanks to my maxed hearing stat.

"Why is the dwarf here?" the ambassador says. "He wasn't supposed to be here! He's going to ruin everything!"

"Calm down, ambassador," Venard says. "The dwarf came here with a letter of admission signed by the king himself. We couldn't just turn him down."

"Just because you couldn't turn him down," the ambassador says, "it doesn't mean that you have to let him make a mockery of your entire arena!"

"But he hasn't done that at all, ambassador," the owner says. "Quite the contrary, in fact. He has provided us with a spectacle that this arena has not seen for ages, and the crowds love it. The show has only just started, and it's already exceeded all of my expectations!"

"I don't care about your expectations!" the ambassador shouts. "I want him out, do you understand? I do not want him to set foot in that arena ever again!"

"Hmm," Venard says. "Truth be told, I also think that allowing the dwarf to wreak havoc any longer than he already has would make the show too predictable and boring. Very well, ambassador. I will speak with the staff in charge of arranging the fights to make some modifications in the schedule. You will not be seeing him again."

After they've finished their discussion, the room above falls silent again. Meanwhile, on the outside, the crowds have still not stopped cheering, since the end of the previous fight. It takes about another minute for the cheering to finally die down, and for Hadrik and the others to step off the stage, so that the next division can enter the fighting area.

Shortly before the next division gets announced, Leila finally comes back from the locker room, with a few pages of my notebook in her hand.

"Sorry I'm late," Leila writes. "I got retained by a guard on my way to the lockers. He had to go and get me a pass from the owner before I could proceed."

"No problem," I tell her. "Are those all the pages?"

"This is all I could find," Leila writes. "Behaviors, weaknesses, and some diagrams."

"Perfect," I tell her. "That's all we need."

I take the notes from her hands and I study them closely. It doesn't take me long to realize that the desert marauders were indeed not much different from giant scorpions. Even their weaknesses are the same. I guess this whole trip that I sent Leila on turned out to be nothing but a huge waste of time.

The gate to the third division is now opening. The first one to come out of it is none other than Daren. His teammates also follow him after a short period of time, but they are looking a bit apprehensive.

"For your information," the announcer says, "the man with the scar who just entered the arena is known as Daren, the healer in armor. He is a well-known hero from outside of Varathia who has travelled the world and has saved countless lives throughout the years. You may have heard of him from various newspapers in the past. Today, he will be participating in our arena event as our special guest. Let us have a warm round of applause for the hero Daren!"

All of the spectators begin clapping, as Daren and his teammates get closer to the center of the arena and ready their weapons.

"Okay, listen up!" Bruce tells us, while the gladiators are still waiting to begin their fight. "After watching the two fights from before, I think that we need to change our battle strategy."

"Have you gone daft?" the disinherited noble thug says. "Why would we change our tactics a few minutes before the battle?"

"Because the way we are now, we're going to lose," Bruce says. "We don't have any teamwork. We should try being more like those gladiators in the first division. You saw how well they worked together."

"The gladiators from the first division are all dead," the mage says.

"Damn it, you know what I mean!" Bruce says. "I'm

talking about assigning roles to everyone. You all saw how they operated. One guy was the leader, another one was staying behind, to warn them of danger, some of them were decoys, and others were the main fighters. If we did that too, we'd be a lot more organized."

"I think that's a good idea," I say. "If we each have a role, and we know what we're doing, there will be less chance of panic."

"Oh yeah?" the mage asks. "That's probably what those guys from the first fight thought too. But when their leader died, all of their organization went down the drain."

"It's still better than fighting in complete chaos from the very beginning!" Bruce says.

"And who exactly is going to be our leader?" the disinherited thug asks Bruce. "You? Don't make me laugh. I'd rather get eaten by a manticore than have to listen to any of your orders."

"I never said that I would be leader," Bruce says. "We can vote on who gets to be leader."

"Forget it," the mage says. "I don't care who the leader is. I'm not leaving my survival in the hands of a person that I barely even know. It's not going to happen."

While Bruce and the others were fighting, the third division's first round was getting ready to start.

"Release the tramplers!" the announcer says.

Several creatures that look like a cross-breed between a bull and a rhinocerus are now slowly entering the fighting area. Each trampler has two horns on its forehead, one horn on its snout, and a tail that looks like it has a spiked mace attached to the end. I've also read that their skin is so tough that they may as well be wearing full plate armor. As their name suggests, tramplers will usually engage in battle by rushing towards their opponents and attempting to trample them to their deaths.

Sure enough, the tramplers do not wait for long, and they start rushing towards the gladiators at full speed.

"If you want to live, stay behind me," Daren tells the other gladiators.

Daren's teammates are looking terrified. It only takes them a few seconds of watching the beasts get closer and closer for them to completely forget Daren's warning and to start running for their lives.

Daren lets out a deep sigh, and he continues to stand his ground, with his sword at the ready. As soon as one of the tramplers comes within reach of his blade, he steps to the side, and he cuts off the beast's head in one single motion, causing the trampler's headless body to fall on the ground and to keep sliding forward on its belly for a few more feet, until its momentum is finally gone.

"Gods be damned," I hear Bruce shout behind me. "Why won't you listen to me? We're not going to stand a chance in the arena if we don't get our act together!"

"You don't need to be so negative, Bruce," Wilhelm says, with a calm tone. "I'm sure that we'll handle ourselves one way or another. The important thing is that we had that discussion yesterday about the creatures' weaknesses. As long as survival is the primary goal in all of our minds, we'll surely put that information to the best of uses."

The tramplers have finished their first tour of the arena, and they're now coming back towards Daren for a second round. Some of his teammates have managed to evade the stampede, but two of them were not so lucky, and they got trampled to death before they could get out of harm's way. Daren waits patiently until the last moment yet again, and then he runs his blade through the side of one of the creatures, slicing it in half. The crowds are going wild once more.

Seeing that the first wave of beasts is already being dealt with, the announcer signals the beginning of the second wave. Three giant cobras are now making their way towards Daren, while the tramplers decide to try chasing some of the easier prey. The cobras are both taller and wider than Daren, but their size is not the only dangerous thing about them. By the looks of the black spots on their necks, I'm almost certain that these are in fact acid-spitting cobras, and not regular ones.

Acid that comes from cobras is not as strong as the acid from mage spells, but it's definitely not something to be sneezed at. While it may not significantly damage weapons and armor that have been sufficiently enchanted, the acid from a cobra can still burn through most regular metals in a matter of minutes, and it can burn through human flesh in a matter of seconds.

Being now faced with ranged attackers, Daren decides that it is no longer safe to maintain his position, and he switches to the offensive. Advancing slowly, with his shield in front, Daren gradually closes the gap between himself and the cobras, until he gets near enough to be able to make a dash attack. The cobras have been spitting at him all this time, but judging by the impact it's had on Daren's shield, they may as well have been spraying water.

Daren makes a dash towards one of the cobras, and he slices its head off in one strike. Before the other two get to attack him, he bashes one with his shield, while stabbing the other through the mouth with his sword. He then makes sure that the third cobra is still dizzy, and he finishes it off as well, with one well-timed slash of his blade.

While Daren was busy with the cobras, the other gladiators had somehow managed to bring down one of the tramplers by themselves. Seeing that the other tramplers are not planning to attack him anymore, Daren decides to go help the others kill off the remaining creatures.

"If none of you are going to listen to reason, then I'll fight on my own!" Bruce shouts again, this time louder than before. "I don't plan on getting killed to save your sorry behinds!"

"I very much doubt that anyone was counting on your help to begin with," Wilhelm says. "Now could you please keep quiet? Our battle will begin shortly, and I would like to concentrate."

Great. Our fight didn't even start yet, and our team is already falling apart. I should have known from the beginning that these people couldn't be trusted.

There is a very loud burst of cheering coming from the outside. It appears that Daren and the other surviving gladiators have finally defeated all of the creatures. The announcer is signaling them to leave the fighting area, so that the show can proceed.

As Daren and the others are getting ready to leave, a man dressed in a dark blue robe with a hood on his head comes from behind me, and he joins my side by the iron grating.

"Who are you?" I ask him, even though I can probably already guess the answer.

"I am a last minute addition to your division," the man says. "I've been sent here to solve your troubles."

The man is carrying two scythes in his hands, that both have sapphires encrusted into their hilts.

"You were sent here by the lessathi?" I ask him in a low voice, in order to make sure that none of the others hear me. "What were they thinking? Don't tell me that you plan to fight all of the monsters by yourself?"

"I will uphold our end of the bargain," the lessathi says. "Make sure that you uphold yours when the time comes."

"Uh, yes," I say. "Yes, of course…"

The lessathi suddenly turns his head towards me, with an expression of shock and rage in his eyes.

"You are lying!" he says.

"What?" I ask him. "No, I was telling the truth!"

"You are a fool!" the lessathi shouts. "Any person with passable skills in reading auras could tell that you are lying from the way your aura is trembling right now. Don't you have any idea what happens to people that lie to us? I should kill you right now for your insolence."

"Hey, what's going on, here?" Bruce asks, after hearing the lessathi's shouts. "Who are you, and what are you doing in our division?"

The lessathi calms down, and he puts his scythes away when he sees Bruce confront him. It seems that despite his earlier remark, he would rather avoid a conflict that would draw too much attention to himself.

"The deal is off," the lessathi says, as he heads out of our division's area. "Enjoy your last fight."

He then walks out the door, without saying another word.

"Damn it, who was that?" Bruce says. "What did he want?"

"No idea," I say.

Leila looks at me suspiciously, but she says nothing. Meanwhile, the iron grating in front of us is finally being raised. We all make our way towards the center of the arena, like all the divisions before us.

"Ladies and gentlemen, I give you the fourth division!" the announcer says.

The crowd watches us in complete silence, as we make our way past all the animal carcasses, in order to reach our destination. It's clear that they do not recognize anyone from our division. They're probably already thinking that we're going to get butchered, like that first division from earlier. I hope we won't end up proving them right.

We hear a lion's roar coming from beyond the gates leading to the creatures' den. Two manticores walk out of the den, and then they immediately soar to the sky, just like the ones that fought the first division. Coming from behind them, three desert marauders are now making their way into the fighting area as well. But those aren't the only beasts that are coming our way. Two giant acid-spitting cobras are now also slithering their way out of the den, and if my ears are not failing me, I think I can also hear the sounds of a few tramplers, getting ready to charge towards us.

"For this fight, we are going to try something a little different," the announcer says. "The members of the fourth division will have to fight not two, not three, but four different types of our strongest creatures, and they'll have to kill them all if they want to advance to the next round. This change in our schedule was a personal request from our esteemed arena owner, mister Venard."

That bastard. Is this his way of telling me that in order to make it out of here alive, I'll need to outperform both Hadrik and Daren? You have got to be kidding me!

"Just make sure that you all follow my orders, and everything will be alright!" Bruce says.

"I knew it!" the ex-noble thug says. "I knew that you would start playing leader as soon as we'd get into the arena. I already told you, nobody is going to listen to you. So you can take your orders and shove them up your arse!"

"I completely agree," I say, in a sarcastic tone. "I should be the one to lead the team, not Bruce!"

"If you're so keen on leading the team," the thug says, "then why don't you go on ahead and attack those creatures over there. I promise we'll be right behind you."

"Or better yet," I say, "how about you shut the hell up and pay more attention to the battlefield. The creatures are already moving to surround us."

The cobras are now trying to get on our right side, while the marauders are coming from our left. Three tramplers are now also making their way into the fighting area, and they are pawing the ground with their hooves, getting ready to charge. The manticores are still circling the skies, biding their time.

"Everyone, hide behind the monster carcasses!" Bruce says. "That way, the tramplers won't be able to charge at us."

"Well, what do you know!" Wilhelm says. "The brute can actually say some sensible things every once in a while!"

We all hide behind some marauder corpses, and we keep watching the battlefield, to see what the creatures are doing. The tramplers are moving around, trying to find a way to charge towards us without any obstacles in their path. The cobras and the marauders have gotten much further away from each other now, and they are likely trying to flank us. The manticores are still flying around, waiting for the best opportunity to strike.

"If we just keep standing here, we're going to get surrounded!" the ex-noble thug's friend says. "We need to go and attack one of the groups now, while they're divided!"

"That will only encourage the tramplers to charge at us!" the mage says. "We should stay here, where we at least have some cover!"

"There are enough monster carcasses between us and the marauders to be able to make it there safely," I say. "We can make quick sprints and take cover behind each one of the corpses until we reach our targets. Then we'll just have to make sure that there's always a marauder between us and the tramplers, and we'll be fine."

"That… doesn't sound like a bad idea, actually," the mage says.

"Yes," Wilhelm says. "And if we travel as a group, we'll increase our chances of survival."

"Then let's get going," Bruce says. "And remember to keep a look out for the manticores in the sky. There's no telling when they'll take a dive for us."

We all start moving towards the desert marauders in short sprints, stopping behind a monster carcass every time, in order to make sure that the tramplers don't begin charging towards us. As soon as we reach our targets, we position ourselves in a way that blocks us from the tramplers' line of sight, and we begin our attack.

Bruce is the first one to engage the marauders, shouting loudly and swinging his large two handed sword towards them, in an attempt to intimidate them. Leila makes a rush at the marauder that's closer to Bruce, trying to get to its head, but the creature blocks her path with its claws, and it tries to attack her with its tail. She dashes out of the way, and she tries to attack it again, from the side.

One of the marauders charges towards the ex-noble thug, and it tries to impale him with its tail. The thug screams in shock, and he jumps back, but it doesn't look like he's going to get away in time. All of a sudden, Bruce jumps out of nowhere, and he deflects the marauder's tail with his sword, making the creature back up a bit, in order to measure up its new opponent carefully.

"The arena is no place for cowards!" Bruce shouts at the thug. "This is a place for real men! If you're planning to fight like a woman, then get out of my way!"

Bruce then quickly realizes the poor wording of his phrase, and he turns towards Leila, who is now frowning at him.

"Or you can… also fight like a woman if you want…" Bruce says. "Just don't be a coward. You get what I mean."

Bruce and Leila then resume their fight with the other marauder, while Wilhelm is providing support for them.

"Hey, you," I say. "Ex-noble thug!"

"What did you just call me?" the thug says, in a menacing tone.

"Never mind that!" I tell him. "Can you and your thug friend stand over here, and make some loud noises? I need someone to distract that marauder, so I can get behind it. The creature seems to have already taken a liking to you, so you'd make the perfect distraction!"

"Screw you and your distractions!" the thug says. "Do you take me for a fool?"

"If it's just a distraction, then I can handle it," the mage says. "Where do you want me to stand?"

"Over there would be perfect," I tell him, as I point him in the right direction.

The two thugs don't seem to want to be any part of my plan, so they're moving away from us, and joining the others. The mage gets into position, and he starts throwing rocks at the marauder, in order to make it come after him. As soon as he gets the desert marauder's attention, I walk behind the creature and quickly climb on its back.

Now let's see… If my notes are correct, then giant scorpion-like creatures should have a weak spot right around… here!

I stab the marauder between two of the scales on its back, and the creature starts to scream loudly, while rocking its body back and forth for a few seconds. As it drops to the ground, I seize the opportunity, and I move towards its head, delivering the finishing blow with one quick strike of my knife. I then get down from the marauder's back, and I get ready to join my teammates in dealing with the rest of the creatures.

No, wait… this isn't over, yet. From what I've seen in the past two battles, the manticores in the sky have always tried to dive for the gladiators right after they killed a marauder, in order to take advantage of their distraction. This means that if I look up right now—

Before I get to finish my train of thought, I suddenly see a premonition of a manticore diving straight for me and grabbing me in its claws. I look up, to confirm my suspicions, then I immediately jump backwards, and I slash at the manticore's wing with my knife, in order to cut off the feathers that it needs to fly properly. The creature tries flying away, but it no longer manages to gain altitude, and it crashes to the ground. I give the beast no time to recover, and I jump at it with my dagger, slitting its throat in one move.

Perfect! Two creatures are already down. But there's now a new problem that I need to deal with. Ever since we entered the arena, I've been keeping a close eye on Wilhelm, because my premonition did not tell me exactly when he would try to kill me. I tried to not let it show, but I've seen him getting closer to me ever since I jumped on that marauder. The fact that I can't see him now can only mean one thing.

I quickly turn around, and I see Wilhelm standing right there, holding his orange hilted dagger with both hands, looking as if he'd been only seconds away from delivering a lethal blow. However, in this very moment, the man seems almost frozen. He keeps holding onto his dagger with both hands as if he were still about to attack me, but now that I'm facing him directly, all of his assassin instincts must be telling him to retreat, instead.

"Wilhelm?" I say.

Wilhelm says nothing. He keeps staring at me, quietly, as a trickle of sweat runs down his forehead.

"Wilhelm, are you alright, my friend?" I tell him, with a concerned tone, as I put my left hand on his shoulder. "You look rather tense!"

Immediately after I stop talking, I use my right hand

to hit him very hard in his left temple with the hilt of my dagger, in order to make sure that I knock him out without killing him. He loses his consciousness almost instantly, and then he falls to the ground, with his dagger beside him.

"Idiot," I say to him, and then I begin heading towards the others.

"So, uh..." I hear the mage's voice coming from behind me, as he catches up to me. "Do you have any idea why mister smiley over there would want you dead?"

I completely forgot about this guy. I thought he already went to help the others, like the two thugs.

"No idea," I lie to him. "I'll figure it out later. Right now, we need to focus on killing the creatures."

By the time we reach the rest of our team, the two marauders they were fighting are already dead. It doesn't look like the second manticore had the guts to attack any of them while they were in such a large group, especially after what happened to its friend, earlier. Leaving the manticore aside, we've still got two tramplers and two cobras left to deal with. We should start making plans right away, before the creatures take the initiative.

"Hey, Leila," I say. "Could you go and kill those tramplers over there? With your level of strength, I'm sure that you'll be able to cut through their tough hides without much trouble."

"By herself?" Bruce asks, in a loud voice. "Are you insane? Why would we not attack them in a group, like we did with these scorpions?"

"Because I want her to bait that manticore in the sky, while she's at it," I say. "If she's alone, then the manticore will almost certainly try to attack her right after she kills one of the tramplers, but if we're in a group, the creature will be too scared to attack us. I would do this myself, but Leila is the only one of us who has enough strength to pass through the tramplers' tough hides."

"I'll do it," Leila writes. "You deal with the cobras in the meantime."

"Okay," I say. "You remember what the tramplers' weakness is, right?" I ask her.

"Yes, I remember," Leila writes, and then she turns away, heading for the tramplers.

"We can't just let her fight them alone like this!" Bruce says, as Leila gets further away from us. "What if she needs our help?"

"I guess we could wait here for a while, to see if she needs backup," I say. "She's probably going to be pissed about it, though. She told us to go deal with the giant cobras in the meantime, not to stand here and do nothing."

"We'll get going as soon as she kills all of the creatures," Bruce says. "We'll have plenty of time to deal with the cobras before she gets back."

We stand there and watch Leila run towards the tramplers for the next few seconds. Seeing her out in the open, the tramplers have also decided to target her, and they are now charging towards her. Neither of them are giving signs that they'll be stopping anytime soon.

Now, if what I've read in all my notes is correct, the tramplers are much easier to intimidate than one would suspect. Tramplers are not used to being challenged on their own turf, so if you keep running towards them at full speed while they are charging at you, they will eventually stop charging, and back down. Leila knows of this weakness, and that's the reason why she's not stopping. Hopefully, everything will turn out okay.

After a few more seconds of running at each other, the two tramplers finally stop, about a dozen feet away from her, and they begin to swing their spiked mace tails towards her, in an attempt to intimidate her.

Perfect! This is the best scenario that Leila could be hoping for. A trampler's strength lies in its charges. A few tail swipes are only good to scare off dumb beasts. They're not going to inconvenience her.

Leila jumps over one of the beasts and lands on its back, stabbing it in the back of its neck. Before the trampler even has time to fall to the ground, Leila already jumps off its back, in order to attack its companion. The second trampler barely has any time to react, before Leila gets below its head, running one of her knives straight through its lower jaw and all the way to its brain.

As soon as she gets away from the dying creature, the last remaining manticore makes a very fast dive towards her, in an attempt to surprise her. Leila feigns ignorance until the very last moment, and then she makes a powerful slash at the creature's chest, exactly when it reaches her. The manticore drops to the ground, and Leila finishes it off with one swift strike of her dagger.

"See?" I say to Bruce. "I told you we didn't have anything to worry about. Now let's hurry up and kill those cobras before she gets here!"

"Uh, actually," the ex-noble thug says. "I think I'd rather wait for the silver haired princess to get back until we go fight the cobras. The more the merrier!"

"Yeah, me too!" the other thug says.

"For once, I agree with these two," the mage says. "Why would we go fight the cobras by ourselves, when we could all go together? We'd just be taking risks for no reason."

Interesting. I've noticed this since we were fighting the marauder, but it looks like the mage is trying his hardest to avoid doing any actual fighting in this round. I don't think he's used his homemade stat device at all in this fight. He must be trying to save the little energy it has for a real emergency.

"Nobody was counting on any of you to begin with," Bruce says. "Come on, stillwater. There are two cobras, so there's one for each of us."

"Sure, whatever," I say, and then we both go on our way.

As we get closer to the giant cobras, the two creatures stop in their tracks, and they prepare to attack us.

"Make sure you never stop moving sideways," I tell Bruce, as we approach the snakes. "The cobras can only shoot their acid in a straight line, and it takes them a few seconds to take aim, so as long as you don't give them the time they need, they won't be able to hit you."

"Understood," Bruce says.

"You take the one on the left," I tell him, and I make a rush towards the cobra on the right.

I bait the cobra by standing in one place for two seconds, and then I jump out of the way, making the creature miss its shot, and waste its acid. While the snake is busy gathering up more acid in its glands, I make a dash towards it, and I stab it in the head, killing it in one strike.

I take a look to see if Bruce needs any help, but he seems to have handled himself just fine on his own. The other snake is already dead, with its severed head lying on the ground beside its body, and Bruce is now coming back towards me, holding his double handed sword by his side as he walks, while Leila seems to be heading our way as well.

This is it. It's over. The round is finally over. The crowds are going wild. They obviously weren't expecting us to make it. If I were Hadrik, I'd probably be making some sort of speech right now, but to be perfectly honest, all I want at this point is to go back to my division area, and get a little bit of rest, before the next round begins.

After a while, the announcer finally asks us to clear

the fighting area, and we prepare to go back to our division room.

"Wait, where's Wilhelm?" Bruce asks me, all of a sudden. "Wasn't he with you?

"Oh, he's over there," I say, as I point towards Wilhelm's unconscious body. "He said he was a little sleepy, and he decided to take a nap."

"Hold on, are you the one who knocked him out?" Bruce asks. "Did he try to attack you or something?"

"How did you guess?" I say.

"He was an assassin!" Bruce says. "I don't trust assassins. I've been watching my back for him ever since we entered the arena. Anyway, taking naps is all well and good, but the next division is waiting for us to leave the area. I'll go wake him up."

Bruce goes over to Wilhelm and he begins to slap his face, while he shouts at him.

"Wilhelm!" Bruce says. "Wilhelm, you no-good assassin, get up! Our first round is over. We need to clear the area."

After a few more slaps to the face, Wilhelm opens his eyes, grabs Bruce's hand, and then grips it hard, while looking at him as if he'd want to murder him here and now.

"I'm awake," Wilhelm says, forcing a calm tone in his voice. "Let's get out of here."

It takes us about a minute, but we eventually get back to our division area, and once we re-enter our room, the iron gate closes itself behind us.

"I need to go get something from my backpack," Wilhelm tells us, shortly after we enter the room. "I'll be right back."

"I hope you won't try to assassinate anyone else on your way to the locker room, Wilbert," Bruce says. "If you get knocked out again, I'm not coming to wake you up."

Wilhelm gives Bruce a scornful look before he opens the door, but he leaves the room without saying another word.

"Uh…" the announcer says, all of a sudden. "It appears that we need to take a small break, in order to do a little inventory of our remaining creatures. Please remain patient! This shouldn't take long!"

"Hah!" Bruce says. "They're already running out of creatures. I bet they weren't expecting so many of them to be taken out in the first few fights!"

"I don't think they're done," I say. "I haven't even seen any griffins, yet."

"Yeah, but griffins can't compare to manticores, in terms of deadliness," Bruce says. "They were probably saving them as their last reserve, in case they ran out of everything else."

As we wait for the announcer to resume the event, I start hearing some voices coming from further down the hallway outside. Yet again, it seems that I am the only one in the room who is able to hear the conversation. The two people talking appear to be Wilhelm and the ambassador of Ollendor.

"I paid you to get the job done, not to hear your excuses!" the ambassador shouts.

"You didn't pay me anything," Wilhelm says. "You just promised me that you'd get me out of this place, and that you'd make sure I don't get executed for killing a teammate, as long as I kept my end of the bargain. Well, I'm here to tell you that the deal's off. I'm not doing it anymore. It's too risky. I already tried to assassinate him once, and I failed. He'll be expecting it now. There's no point in trying to assassinate a target that's already onto you."

"If you can't backstab him anymore, then just attack him directly, you moron!" the ambassador says. "I don't care how you get the job done. I just want him dead!"

"I'm not doing any job anymore," Wilhelm says. "Stop bothering me. I've already said what I had to say."

Soon after their conversation ends, the announcer picks his voice magnifier back up, and he gets ready to make another announcement.

"Sorry for the delay, everyone," the announcer says. "After checking to see which creatures we have left, it would appear that we are down to our last reserves after that last fight. If this division will manage to kill all the creatures as well, then we will be forced to go back to our regular stock of creatures for the divisions that follow. Now, with all this said and done, I would like to introduce to you the fifth division!"

When the next iron gate gets raised, Kate is the first one to step out into the fighting area. As she proceeds to the middle of the arena, the other members of her division also start to follow in her footsteps. Once I get a good look at all of Kate's teammates, I get the sudden realization that Kate is likely the most capable fighter in her division, even without her magic. Most of the others look severely out of shape, and some of them don't even have weapons. These clearly aren't the types of gladiators that came here willingly.

As the unarmed fighters go to get their weapons of choice from the walls of the arena, the new creatures are slowly beginning to walk out of their den. I recognize the creatures immediately as being the ones that I encountered two days ago in the underground caverns. Or some of them at least. The giant rats are missing. I guess they may have only been there as food for the griffins. Either way, this is looking pretty bad. I don't see Kate dealing with those monsters all by herself, and her teammates likely won't be much help. Will she be forced to use her magic? Things could get really ugly if she does. I don't even want to think about what would happen in that scenario. Maybe she can make it somehow. There's always hope…

The harpies and the gargoyles are the first ones to make their way out of their den, and they immediately take to the air, studying their targets carefully.

Harpies are hideous creatures that have the appearance of women with scales, wings and claws. They might look almost human, but in reality, they couldn't be more different. They are just about as intelligent as the lowliest of reptiles, and they're twice as vicious. The gargoyles, on the other hand, could accurately be described as thinner ogres, with wings and horns, and with strength that is comparable to that of the ogres as well.

The dire wolves and the sabre-toothed tigers are next. They begin to walk slowly along the sides of the arena, trying to take measure of their opponents, and moving to surround them.

The last ones to come out of the den are the griffins. They are creatures that have the bodies, tails and legs of lions, while their heads, wings, and talons are those of eagles. Like the harpies and the gargoyles before them, the first thing that the griffins do is to soar to the air, in order to get a better view of their targets.

Damn it! I knew I should have killed them in the underground caves, where they couldn't use their wings to fly away. This is definitely not going to be an easy fight for Kate, even if I did tell her all these monsters' weaknesses.

The sabre-toothed tigers and the dire wolves are the first to attack. When Kate's teammates see the beasts charge towards them, some of them start screaming and running away as fast as they can, while others charge right back at the creatures, in a desperate attempt to intimidate them.

Kate is the only one who seems calm and collected, as her instincts take over again, just like in the ogre shaman's illusion, and she begins to move between one creature and another, slitting one's throat and then switching to the next target, without any wasted movements.

Even so, the enemies on the ground are by far the weakest of the group. The real threats are the gargoyles and the griffins. With the gargoyles' strength and the griffins' size, I can see very few ways in which Kate would be able to win a fight against them, especially while they've got the air advantage.

The griffins are now beginning to descend towards the gladiators, and they quickly make their first victim. One of the more frail looking gladiators in Kate's group gets grabbed in a griffin's claws, and the beast starts to peck at the man's chest with its beak, while he is still alive. Hearing the man's cries for help, and his terrible screams, the other men abandon all pretense of courage, and they run away as fast as they can, in all directions. One of the other griffins comes down, and it tries to attack Kate.

Knowing the creature's behavior and attack patterns, Kate manages to step out of the way, and to slash at one of the creature's claws with her dagger, but she doesn't get to hurt the beast much before it flies back up, preparing itself for another dive.

"Things aren't looking very good for Kate," Leila writes to me. "In the worst case scenario, she might even be forced to use her ice magic. You know what that means, right?"

"Yeah," I say. "The punishment for using magic in the arena is death. In order to get out of here alive after that, she'd have to fight every single guard in the place, and to make this entire kingdom into her enemy."

"And what would you do if that happened?" Leila writes, looking at me with a very serious expression on her face. "Would you join her, and make the kingdom into your enemy as well? Would you be willing to forsake the Magium tournament and your ambitions, in order to take her side on the battlefield?"

I open my mouth to answer Leila, but the words get stuck in my throat.

Would I be able to do it? Would I be able to give up this tournament, knowing full well that it may be the only way to fulfill my lifelong dream?

"I don't... I'm not..." I try to say, but I still don't manage to give her an answer.

While I was busy trying to formulate a coherent sentence, Kate was getting chased by one of the griffins all the way to the wall that is next to our division's gate, and then she got backed against said wall, with no place to escape.

"Time is running out, Barry..." Leila writes, with the same serious expression on her face. "What are you going to choose?"

This is it. It's over. It's all over.

There's no way I could just abandon Kate like this. Not after all we've been through together. I suppose it's finally time to say goodbye to this tournament. It was fun while it lasted. Maybe I will find another way to become a mage. Someday...

"Get ready," I tell Leila. "As soon as Kate casts her first spell, I'm going to need you to cut these iron bars for me. I'll be joining her in the arena soon enough."

"I was hoping you'd say that," Leila writes, with a relieved smile on her face. "Do not worry. When it will come down to it, you will not go there alone. Even if your other friends don't join you, I am prepared to take Kate's side, no matter the cost."

The griffin is now descending towards Kate, slowly, while still maintaining a bit of altitude, and it is preparing to go for the finishing move. Kate appears to have lost her dagger, and there are no weapons in sight. I can already feel the air around us getting chillier.

Just as Leila was preparing her daggers, one of the iron gates suddenly gets blown out of its hinges, and it drops to the ground, with a loud clang. Within seconds, Hadrik comes out of the gate, and he makes a dash towards the griffin attacking Kate, making a very high jump, and landing on the beast's back. The griffin doesn't appear to be too happy about what's happening, and it attempts to throw Hadrik off its back by doing sudden, violent movements, and by flapping its wings continuously.

"Hah!" Hadrik says, while he maintains his balance by holding onto the griffin's mane with one of his hands. "I always wanted to ride one of these!"

He then uses his other hand to wave towards the crowd, and he shouts as loud as he can:

"Did you miss me?"

The crowd explodes in an outburst of shouts and cheers, as the griffin keeps trying to shake Hadrik off its back with all its might. Seeing that the beast is not planning to settle down anytime soon, Hadrik grabs its head with both hands, and he snaps its neck with one quick movement of his arms.

"Down we go!" Hadrik says, as the griffin falls to the ground, along with him.

He then jumps off the creature, and he heads towards Kate.

"Are you alright, milady?" Hadrik says, with a bow.

"Hadrik, what are you doing here?" Kate says, shocked. "You're not allowed to help me! They'll ban you from the tournament!"

"No, they won't," Hadrik says. "There was never any such rule. Didn't you pay attention to the announcements at the beginning?"

He then lowers his voice, so that the announcer and the spectators can't hear him.

“And besides,” Hadrik says. “You were planning to use your ice magic just now, weren’t you?”

“I…” Kate starts to say, but she hesitates to continue.

“No need to worry about it!” Hadrik says, as he pats her on the side of her arm. “All I wanted was to make sure that this magnificent arena event can continue to run its course until the very end!”

He then walks away from her, and he looks towards the monsters, trying to decide which one to attack first.

“Attention, participant Hadrik!” the announcer says, loudly. “You will leave the fighting area immediately or you will face the consequences, do you understand?”

“And by these consequences,” Hadrik says. “do you mean to say that I’ll be invited to join a bonus round at the end of the event?”

“Well…” the announcer says. “Technically, yes. But you still can’t interfere with the fights of other participants!”

“Why not?” Hadrik asks. “Is that one of the standard arena rules?”

“Well, no, but—”

“Then I don’t see the problem!” Hadrik says.

“The problem is that you are ruining the show!” the announcer blurts out, all of a sudden.

“Oh, am I?” Hadrik says, with a grin.

He then turns towards the audience, and he raises his arms.

“What do you all think?” Hadrik shouts at the crowd. “Am I ruining the show?”

“Nooooo!” the spectators shout, in unison.

“Do you want me to stay?” Hadrik asks them.

In answer to Hadrik’s question, the crowd cheers louder than ever before.

“Well, I guess that’s settled, then!” Hadrik says, to the announcer, and then he rushes towards a griffin that’s flying at a lower altitude.

He jumps on the creature's back, just like he did with the previous one, and he holds onto its mane firmly, making sure to not get thrown down. The griffin tries to shake him off, just like the one before, but this time, the beast stops moving after a while, looking almost as if it were accepting Hadrik as its new master.

"I see you're smarter than the other one!" Hadrik says. "Alright then, let's see how well you cooperate. First, we'll go over there. If we're really doing this, then I'm going to need a weapon with long reach, before anything else."

To everyone's shock, the griffin obediently follows Hadrik's order, and it leads him all the way to the side of the arena, so that he can take a halberd off the wall. He then pulls on the griffin's mane, in order to show it the direction that he wants to go in, and the creature flies him all the way to one of the gargoyles, up in the sky. Hadrik cuts the head off the gargoyle's shoulders in one single movement of his halberd, and then he orders the griffin to move on to the next target. In the next few minutes, the dwarf travels from one monster to another, on the back of his trusty griffin, and he kills all of them in quick succession, without so much as breaking a sweat.

As the two of them finally descend to the ground, Hadrik sees that Kate had also taken care of the sabre-toothed tigers and the dire wolves on the ground in the meantime. This leaves Hadrik's griffin as the last remaining monster on the battlefield. As the crowds keep cheering, Hadrik lands on the ground, dismounts his griffin, and then he raises his arms in the air, to silence the crowd.

"All of the other beasts are dead," Hadrik says, to the announcer. "This last one has already surrendered itself to me. I request permission to spare its life, as a token of gratitude for its services! What say you?"

"Preposterous!" the announcer shouts. "Do you seriously expect—"

"Permission granted," we hear the arena owner's voice, as he makes his way on top of the elevated platform that the announcer is standing on. "If that is your wish, then we will take this griffin back to its cell, we will feed it, and then we will release it back into the wild. There will likely never be an event like this again in my lifetime, so there would be no reason to keep this beast shackled any longer."

"Much obliged!" Hadrik says.

"I hope," the arena owner says, "that you will continue to provide us with the same level of quality entertainment in the fourth round as in the previous two fights."

"I will do my best!" Hadrik says.

"Oh," the owner says. "And I will be expecting the same from you, Miss Kate, since you will also be joining your friend in the extra round as an undesirable. Given that his transgression of the rules was done specifically to save your life, I trust that there will be no objections?"

"No…" Kate says. "I have no objections."

"Very well!" the owner says. "Now, if you all don't mind, I would appreciate it if you cleared the fighting area as soon as possible. The next division's fight is about to start."

As the owner turns to leave, Kate and the others also head towards their respective division areas, while the warriors of the sixth division are preparing to enter the battlefield.

The next few battles weren't really anything special. A few gladiators died here and there, but most of them survived, and the number of creatures that were being thrown at them in each fight became gradually smaller, as the arena's stocks of regular creatures began to slowly deplete as well.

As I keep watching the fights, I'm starting to get a feeling of relief, because most, if not all of the warriors that we've seen since Kate's battle are nowhere near strong enough to deal with monsters such as manticores or desert marauders. This means that defeating them should be a piece of cake. Maybe this arena wasn't so scary after all!

"Don't get too relaxed," Leila writes, as she sees the expression on my face, while we watch the final battle of the round. "We still have no idea how we're going to defeat the troll, and to be frank, I think he's going to be much more dangerous than the monsters we've fought so far."

"Yes, but you are forgetting something!" I tell Leila. "We are the fourth division. This means that the troll will have to go through Hadrik and Daren before he reaches us. Regeneration or no, I honestly couldn't even imagine Hadrik losing a duel against him, after the way he's fought in this first round. The way I see it, they may as well be crowning us victors of this arena event right now, because there really isn't much of a point in dragging this any long—"

"Attention, all gladiators!" the announcer says in a very loud voice, all of a sudden.

While I was talking with Leila, it seems that the final battle had already ended, and the warriors were now returning to their division area.

"There has been a slight change in our fight schedule for the second round!" the announcer continues. "Unlike the first round, where the divisions have been fighting in the order of their division numbers, in this second round there will be one exception to the rule. By special request of our esteemed arena owner, mister Venard, the first division to fight Velgos in the second round will be none other than division number four! Gladiators of the fourth division, please make sure that you are ready! The fight will begin in the next few minutes."

"Humans!" we hear the voice of Velgos the troll, shouting from the other end of the arena, as soon as the announcer stops talking. "Your time is up! There is nowhere to run. Nowhere to hide. All that awaits you is death. Blame your fate for having been unlucky enough to cross paths with Velgos the mercenary!"

The crowds are going wild again, just like they did after Hadrik's first fight, and they're chanting the troll's name loudly over and over.

"Velgos! Velgos! Velgos!" they all keep chanting, as the troll waves to the crowd and makes intimidating gestures towards us, every once in a while.

"Huh," I tell Leila. "Well… damn."

Chapter 5

"Stillwater!" Bruce shouts. "Hey, stillwater, are you listening?"

I suddenly realize that I've been so lost in my own thoughts for the past minute, that I've been completely neglecting my surroundings. Wilhelm seems to have already returned to our room while I was spacing out, and judging by Bruce's tone of voice, I can only assume that he asked me a question, but I cannot for the life of me remember what it was.

"Sorry, I wasn't paying attention," I tell him. "Could you repeat that?"

"I was talking about Wilhelm," Bruce says. "We can't let him roam free throughout the arena after what he did last round. Who knows who he'll try to kill next? I say we tie him up, and leave him here. It's safer that way."

"He already tried and failed to assassinate me once," I say. "He's not foolish enough to try that again. I say we let him fight with us. We'll need all the help we can get against that troll."

"If you're worried about me backstabbing you," Wilhelm says, "then I'll make sure to always be in your line of sight during the battle, so you can keep your eyes on me without much effort. Would that be enough to put your worries to rest?"

"I suppose…" Bruce says. "As long as I can easily see where you are at all times, you're not much of a threat."

"Very well," Wilhelm says. "Fighting on the front

lines is not exactly ideal for me, but I'd rather do this than be forced to fight alone. I only hope that you won't take advantage of this situation to use me as a decoy."

Damn it! Now I've lost my train of thought. What was I thinking about, before I got interrupted? I'm sure it had something to do with the troll.

As I take another look towards the fighting area and see the troll still waving at the crowds, my previous thoughts suddenly come back to me.

"Hey, Leila," I say. "Is it just me or is the troll wearing different armor this time around?"

"Yes," Leila writes. "It's still anti-magic armor, but now he also has shoulder pads. He probably switched armors in order to make it harder for us to cut his head off again."

"Correct me if I'm wrong," I say, "but isn't this specific model of armor he's wearing vulnerable to regular fire?"

"The armor he is wearing does not protect him against regular fire at all," Leila writes. "Only against magical fire."

"That's what I thought," I say, and then I head towards the door leading to the corridors outside our room.

As I prepare to open the door, I turn towards Leila, to give her one final message before I go.

"Leila, could you do me a favor?" I tell her. "I need you to take one of the torches that are lighting the halls and to bring it with you in the arena when the round begins. Make sure that you don't let the troll see it, when you approach him. When we're both in the fighting area, I'll give you a signal, and then you can throw the torch at him. Got it?"

"Yes, but where are you going?" Leila writes. "What are you planning to do?"

"You'll find out soon enough," I say, and then I walk

out the door.

I make sure that the guards are nowhere in sight, and I start heading directly towards Hadrik's division area. If memory serves, his room should be very close to ours. I make my way down the hallway as fast as I can, and I try to figure out which one of the doors leads to the dwarf's room. When I hear Hadrik's laughter coming from behind one of the doors, I realize that I've reached my destination, and I knock on the door three times, calling out to him, to let him know who it is.

"Hadrik, are you in there?" I say.

"Yeah, yeah, give me a sec!" Hadrik says, and he opens the door for me a few seconds later.

Just as I was hoping, it looks like the dwarf brought more than a few bottles of ale with him, to keep him company. He likely tried to convince his teammates to drink with him before the battle, but it doesn't look like he's had much luck.

"Congratulations on winning your first round, Barry!" Hadrik says. "Did you come to make a toast, before your next battle?"

"Not exactly," I say. "But I did come here to ask you for one of your dwarven ale bottles, if it's not too much trouble."

"Not at all," Hadrik says. "I did say that I owed you a beer, after all. Well, dwarven ale isn't really anything like beer, but you get the idea! Take whichever bottle you like. I've got plenty!"

"Perfect!" I tell him, as I pick one of the dwarven ale bottles from the ground.

I then head towards the fighting area, through the hole in the wall where the iron gate used to be before Hadrik blew it out of its hinges.

"See you around!" I tell him, as I wave at him and walk out of his division area.

"Uh, see you, I guess..." Hadrik says, looking a bit

confused.

As I slowly make my way towards the troll, with the bottle of ale in my hand, the announcer starts shouting at me, from his elevated platform above.

"What do you think you're doing?" he says. "The round hasn't begun yet! Get back to your own division area right now! Do you hear me? Get back! Hey, are you listening to me?"

I ignore the announcer, and I look directly at the troll, while walking casually towards him. When he sees me, Velgos stops waving at the crowds, and he begins to grin maliciously at me.

"Did you come here to beg for your life, human?" the troll shouts at me. "It will do you no good! Your fate has already been sealed!"

I don't say anything and I keep walking forward.

"Damn it!" the announcer says. "Open the gates. Open them now!"

I hear a horn signaling the beginning of the second round, and the gate to my division starts to slowly get raised. As I keep walking, I make sure that I advance slowly enough to give Leila the time to catch up to me.

The troll is still taunting me. He must be thinking that I came here to offer him a drink. I don't think he's ever had the privilege of tasting dwarven ale before. Judging by the burning sensation that I got in my throat when I drank my first bottle with Hadrik, I'd wager that this is the strongest alcoholic beverage that money can buy. Maybe Velgos would be a little more worried if he knew what I had in this bottle.

"Are you trying to bribe me, human?" Velgos says, with a laugh. "It's going to take more than a bottle of ale to convince me to spare your life. How about you start by kneeling before me? I want every spectator in the crowd to see how pathetic you are, before I kill you!"

I stop right in front of the troll, and I smile at him,

while raising my bottle. Leila is now only a few dozen feet behind me, and she's closing in, with the other members of my division not far behind her. She is holding the torch behind her back, making sure that the troll doesn't notice it.

"Cheers!" I say to the troll, while I have my bottle raised in the air.

"What are you trying to—" Velgos starts to say, but I don't let him finish his sentence.

I quickly grab the bottle by its neck, and I smash it into the troll's skull, covering him in dwarven ale from head to toe. The troll seems shocked, unable to understand what is going on.

"Leila, now!" I shout, as I jump back from the troll.

As soon as I give the signal, Leila throws her torch at the troll, igniting the flammable liquid, and causing the troll to light up in flames. Velgos starts screaming loudly, as he attempts to extinguish the fire from his head with his bare hands. Leila makes full use of this opportunity, and she quickly dashes towards her enemy, slicing one of his shoulder pads right off his armor, with one of her enchanted daggers. The troll grabs both of his scimitars in his hands, and he tries to cut Leila in half, but she jumps back in time, avoiding his strike.

"I am going to destroy you," the troll shouts at us. "I will cut you into pieces so small that they won't even find enough of you to give you a proper burial!"

His eyes are red with rage, as the fire covering him is slowly dying out. The marks left from the burning flames are already starting to regenerate. I suppose I should have expected that regular fire would not be enough against an enemy with such high regenerative powers.

I decide to take advantage of the opportunity Leila gave me, by making a dash towards the troll and pretending that I'm trying to drive my blade through his chest. As the troll tries to attack me, I quickly step to the side, and I swing my arm towards his neck, from the side where his shoulder pad had been shattered. My strike is not powerful enough to cut his head off in a single movement, however, so my knife only slices through half of his throat. As Velgos attempts to chop my arm off with one of his scimitars, I am forced to step back before finishing the job, and the wound from the troll's neck heals itself back up in a matter of seconds.

Luckily for me, my distraction was enough for Leila to sneak up behind the troll, and to cut his head off in one strike. Immediately afterwards, Leila grabs the head by the hair, she throws it on the ground, and then she stomps on it as hard as she can, crushing it underneath her sandal.

The troll's body jumps away from us, but the head on the ground does not seem to be regenerating. Instead, a new head is now forming itself, starting from Velgos' neck. It only takes about five seconds until the head gets regenerated completely, although, judging by the expression on his face, this must have been a particularly painful process.

"I'm going to take my time killing you," Velgos says, looking as if he's still trying to hold back some of the pain. "I'll do it slowly, after I force you to watch all your friends die."

"Yeah, yeah," I say. "I've heard it all before."

"Watch out!" Bruce shouts at us, from behind.

Not long after his warning, two very large ogres make their way out of the gate behind Velgos, and they attempt to hit us with their oversized clubs. Both Leila and I jump back, and we join our teammates, who have now all arrived at our location.

"I knew it," our mage teammate says. "I knew that they wouldn't make it as easy for us as fighting a single troll. They just had to bring in the ogres too!"

"Stop complaining," Bruce says. "Ogres are easy to beat. They're dumb, and they're slow as snails. I can take them both on myself."

"I'd be careful, if I were you," I tell Bruce. "I've seen my fair share of regular ogres this past week, and I can tell you without a doubt that these two are a cut above the rest."

"Bah!" Bruce says. "Their size does not impress me. Big or no, I'm willing to bet that they bleed all the same."

The ogres do not leave us the chance to continue our conversation, and they start running towards us, roaring at the top of their lungs, while swinging their clubs.

"I'll handle the ogres," Bruce says, as we all dodge the ogres' attack. "You deal with the troll. Now, go. Go!"

As Leila goes to fight the troll, I take one long look at our enemy, trying to prepare a plan of attack. While I stand there, thinking, Leila manages to find an opening in the troll's defenses, and she cuts the troll's head off yet again. She then crushes Velgos' head under her sandal, like before, while a new head begins to form itself, starting from his neck. This time, however, it seems to be taking him longer to fully create it, and it looks like he's having a bit of trouble recreating the exact same facial features that he had before.

As soon as his head grows back, Leila begins putting pressure on the troll again, making sure that his focus is on her the whole time.

"Good gods," the mage says, exasperated, as he watches Leila fight. "Stop aiming for the head! Can't you see that it's doing you no good?"

"On the contrary!" I tell him. "I think that cutting his head off is exactly what we should be doing. You could clearly see that the troll was struggling to regenerate his head when it got cut off the second time. Even with his insane regenerative ability, there still has to be some kind of limit to how many times he can regrow his head in such a short period of time. My guess is that one or two more beheadings should do the trick!"

I take another look at Leila and the troll, while they are fighting, but they seem to be quite evenly matched. Even with Wilhelm helping her, Leila still can't seem to find another weakness to exploit in Velgos' defenses. It looks like we're going to need a few more people to flank the troll, in order for Leila to get another shot at him. The thugs are most definitely not going to be of any help. But maybe I can convince the mage to join in on the attack… If I play my cards right.

"So, anyway," I tell the mage, "I have a plan on how to attack the troll, but I'm going to need your help with something."

"What do you mean?" the mage says.

"I noticed that Velgos can't really keep up with Leila's attacks," I say, "and he keeps moving around, in order to compensate for his lack of skills at parrying her fast strikes. If the two of us close in from behind and attack him from both left and right, he won't have any place left to retreat, and Leila will be able to cut his head off easily. Better yet, we wouldn't even risk anything, since he'd be losing his head before he even gets the chance to strike back at us!"

"I… suppose that I could help out," the mage says. "If it's risk-free…"

"Perfect," I say, not giving him any more time to think it over. "Let's get going, then!"

I then make a rush towards the troll, and the mage is forced to follow soon afterwards, so he can catch up to me. I knew that he'd jump on the opportunity to join the fight, as soon as I'd offer him a plan without any risks. He's been acting with extreme caution ever since the first round started, but it's clear that he doesn't want to be seen as a coward. Of course he'd be more than happy to be able to prove his worth without endangering his life in any way. Let's just hope that my plan is indeed as foolproof as I made it out to be.

The mage and I both manage to get behind the troll, while Leila is keeping him busy, and when we are in attack range, I nod to the mage, as we each dash towards our enemy, from opposite sides. Just as we reach Velgos, we both stab him in his back, to which the troll instantly reacts by swinging his scimitars towards the two of us. Leila immediately takes advantage of the distraction, and she cuts the troll's head off in the blink of an eye, but this does not cause Velgos' attack to slow down at all. The mage and I are both forced to jump away from the troll, with superhuman speed, avoiding the fatal blow by mere inches.

That was way too close… If I didn't have such high levels in my speed and reflexes stats, I may well have been decapitated by that strike. But if the mage managed to get away as well, then does that mean he activated his own version of the stat device? That has to be it. I don't see how else he could have escaped that fast.

While the two of us were getting away, Leila crushed the troll's head under her foot, just like the last time, and the troll started regrowing his head from the neck again, except only slower than the last time.

Before the two of them start fighting again, a very loud high pitched noise begins to echo all around the arena, as the improvised stat device inside the mage's right pocket starts to shine with a bright red light. The mage panics, and he tries to hide the light by putting his hand on top of his pocket, but the harm has already been done. I guess that he didn't have the time to finish modifying his device, after all…

"Please excuse the noise, ladies and gentlemen," the announcer says. "That is the sound of our magic detectors being set off. Will the person with the red light in his pocket please remain still? Our guards will come to pick you up shortly."

Several guards from the arena are now making their way into the fighting area, with their swords at the ready.

"There's no need for any of the other gladiators to be alarmed!" the announcer says. "Just ignore the guards and continue your fights in an orderly fashion!"

Leila and the troll are standing still, looking at the mage intently, while they are also watching each other with the corner of their eyes, to make sure that neither one will try a surprise attack on the other, during this distraction. Meanwhile, Bruce and the ogres do not seem to be paying any attention to what's happening around them, and they are continuing their fight unhindered.

"No…" the mage says, in a scared voice, as he looks at the guards closing in on him.

Once the guards surround him, one of them attempts to grab the mage by the arm.

"You're coming with us," the guard says. "Come on, get moving!"

"No!" the mage shouts, as he pulls his arm away from the guard. "Get away from me!"

"There's no use fighting it, gladiator," the guard says, as he approaches him and tries to grab him again. "Your life is over, and you know it. Now you can either come with us peacefully, or we'll do this the hard way."

"I said *get away*!" the mage shouts, louder, and a jet of flames erupts from his hands, engulfing the guard, and burning him to a crisp.

All of the other guards quickly move to restrain the mage, but he raises both his arms in the air, blasting them all with a powerful wave of fire that leaves nothing but ashes in its wake.

"Guards!" the announcer shouts, starting to panic a bit. "Leave your posts and come to the fighting area immediately. We have a rogue fire elementalist on a rampage! I repeat! A rogue fire elementalist on a rampage!"

The mage looks around him, with a blank stare in his eyes, as if he were slowly starting to lose his sense of purpose. Then, as his eyes come in contact with mine, the look on his face changes, and he suddenly gains back his focus, while his eyes get filled with rage.

"You!" the mage shouts at me. "This is all your fault! You tricked me! You told me that there would be no risks… You traitorous son of a bitch, I'm going to kill you!"

"Wait, wait, hold on!" I tell him, but the mage is no longer listening.

He points his arms towards me, and a jet of flames comes out of his hands, making its way towards me at great speed. I manage to jump out of its way in time, but as soon as I land on the ground, I see a pillar of fire starting to form itself from beneath my feet. I dash out of the way just before the flames fill the area, but the mage does not allow me a moment's respite, and he keeps aiming pillars below me, just as my feet touch the ground.

"Crap, crap, crap!" I say, while I keep jumping between the columns of fire, looking as if I were performing some elaborate tribal dance.

How do I get out of this? Do I attack him? Am I allowed to attack him? Is he still being considered as my teammate after he broke the rules? Will they execute me too if I try to kill him? Should I just knock him out? Gods be damned, I can't think straight with all this jumping!

While the mage is keeping me busy, several more guards are now rushing towards him, trying to run their blades through his back, while he's not paying attention. The mage does not let himself get caught off guard, and he immediately begins to target his new attackers as well, while still making me dodge flame pillars.

"Velgos, do something!" the announcer says, in desperation. "Kill him! Kill him now, before it gets worse!"

The troll frowns at the announcer, and he starts walking slowly towards the mage, while still keeping Leila in his sight. The mage has already killed all of the guards, but when he sees the troll approach him, he forgets all about me, and he points both his hands at him, in an attempt to intimidate his new foe.

"Don't come closer!" the mage says, with a scared tone in his voice. "I'll burn you to a crisp!"

"Go ahead," Velgos says, as he keeps advancing towards the mage, while looking at Leila with the corner of his eye. "I'd love to see you try."

As Velgos gets even closer, the mage lets out a whimper, and the troll suddenly gets swallowed up by a newly formed column of fire, much larger than those from before. Velgos walks out of the flames completely unharmed, with a malicious grin on his face, and he keeps advancing slowly towards his target.

"Die, monster!" the mage shouts, when the troll reaches him, and he begins to stab him in the chest repeatedly with his dagger.

Seeing that it's not working, the mage attempts to go for the neck, like Leila, but Velgos easily blocks him with one of his scimitars, while bringing his other weapon down on the mage, slicing him in half. Almost immediately after the mage dies, Leila dashes behind the troll, giving him no time to react, and she cuts his head off in one strike, crushing it under her foot soon afterwards.

After his head gets crushed once more, the troll begins regrowing a new one from his neck, but this time, something is definitely off. The grotesque form that is emerging from his neck can no longer be called anything close to a head. The face is missing half of its skin, the eyes are coming out of their orbits, and the shape of it is nothing like before. More importantly, it would seem that his head has not been well enough regenerated to allow him to breathe.

The troll is now desperately trying to gasp for air, while looking at me and Leila with pure hatred in his eyes. He tries to speak, but he has no air left in his lungs. He only manages to make some unintelligible guttural sounds, while taking a few steps forward and stretching one of his arms towards us, in a futile attempt to reach us. Once he runs out of breath completely, he drops to his knees, and he starts clawing at his throat with his hands, as if he were trying to create a new pathway for the air to reach his lungs. Eventually, he stops moving altogether, and he drops face-first to the ground, lifeless.

"Hey, Velgos!" the announcer says. "What are you doing? Stop fooling around and fight seriously! What do you think we're paying you for?"

The spectators seem to be unsure of how to react. Velgos appeared to be something of a crowd favorite, so seeing him die in front of their eyes must be giving them mixed feelings about this whole thing. They can't really blame us for having killed him, but they don't seem very eager to cheer for us either. What we get instead are a few moments of awkward silence, while the announcer is still struggling to come to terms with reality.

"Velgos..." the announcer says, this time in a pleading voice. "Don't do this to me! Come on, I even bet good money on you! You can't just die on me like this! What about the rest of the second round? Who's going to fight the other divisions? Velgos, get up, damn you!"

Once the announcer finishes his rant, we hear Venard, the arena owner, clearing his throat from somewhere behind the announcer.

"Uh, please excuse me," the announcer says, to the spectators. "I'll be back shortly…"

He then heads in the direction of the arena owner, descending from his elevated platform and entering one of the upper levels of the main building surrounding the fighting area.

As the announcer was talking, I was barely paying any attention to him, because I was focusing on something else, entirely. After studying the scimitars that had fallen from the troll's hands for a while, I came to the conclusion that they were both in surprisingly good condition. I'm also quite certain that they both have at least the sharpness and durability enchantments cast on them, so they should be pretty comparable to my dagger, in terms of usefulness.

I've never really liked wielding two weapons at the same time when fighting, but maybe I could take one of these with me, so I can use it when I'm in need of a weapon with longer reach? Or maybe I should take the other one too, and sell it at a shop? I'm not exactly sure how much it would be worth, but if I could get Daren to identify all of the enchantments cast on it, I'm certain that I could negotiate a reasonable price at the local weapon shops.

After spending a few more seconds considering my options, I decide to take both of the scimitars, because it would be a waste to just leave them there. I put both of the weapons in their sheaths, and then I hook the two sheaths to my belt.

Not long after we kill Velgos, Bruce also finishes his fight with the ogres, and then he comes heading straight for us.

"You guys are already done with the troll?" Bruce asks, surprised, as he reaches us.

"Yeah, we killed him ages ago," I say. "What took

you so long?"

"Wait, how did the mage die?" Bruce asks, after noticing the mage's corpse on the ground.

"He got caught using magic," I say. "There were even loud alarms and everything. How did you manage to miss them?"

"Oh…" Bruce says. "I did hear some loud noises, but I was too focused on the fight to figure out what was what."

He pauses.

"So," Bruce continues. "Does this mean that the fight is over, then? What are we still standing around here, for?"

"We're waiting for the announcer to come back…" I say. "He's the one that's supposed to announce the end of the fight."

After a bit more time, the announcer finally returns to his platform, looking mildly upset.

"Sorry for the delay, ladies and gentlemen," the announcer says. "After a discussion with the arena's owner, mister Venard, we've reached the conclusion that the second round cannot continue after the death of Velgos, the mercenary. In other words, the end of this fight also marks the end of the round. The third and final round will commence shortly, as soon as the organizing team is done with the preparations. We apologize for the inconvenience."

He then turns towards us.

"All gladiators will have to wait in their division areas until the beginning of the next round," he says. "You will not be allowed to roam the halls any longer! Your rooms will be locked until the end of the third round. This time there will be no more… incidents."

I'm pretty sure that he was looking directly at me when he said those last words. He must still be upset because I entered the fighting area before the beginning of the round last time. Oh well, at least I don't need any more information from my notebook. Being unable to exit my division area shouldn't affect me that much.

As soon as we get back to our room, we hear a person shouting loudly from the hallway outside our door. It is the voice of the ambassador of Ollendor.

"What do you mean everything is going smoothly?" the ambassador shouts. "Are you mocking me?"

"Not at all, ambassador," Venard, the arena owner says. "There have been no problems with any part of our arena event, as far as I'm aware."

"No problems?" the ambassador says. "The earl of Ollendor's killers are all still alive, and you are telling me that there are no problems?!"

"I assure you," Venard says, "that our guests have been given no advantages over the other gladiators of the arena during these fights. Quite the opposite, in fact. Of course, if you have any doubts, you are free to talk with the organizing team in order to arrange the upcoming duels in any way you like. After all, you have always been the one to have the final say regarding the organization of these events."

"I've been a fool to leave things in your care until now!" the ambassador says, furiously. "If you are too incompetent to get the job done right, then I'll just have to do it myself."

We then hear the ambassador storming away from the hallway, presumably towards the room where the organizing team was making the preparations for the next round.

"Farewell, ambassador!" Venard says, calmly, and then we hear him leaving as well.

"It sounds like a certain someone really has it in for you," Leila writes, while looking at me.

"Who cares?" I say. "It's not like they can do anything anymore even if they try."

"I remember you saying something similar before our battle with the troll…" Leila writes.

"Yeah, but now it's different," I say. "The troll is dead. So are the creatures. I don't see what other tricks they could pull out of their sleeve this late in the game."

"Really?" Leila writes. "You don't see any way in which the organizers could guarantee your death in the next round?"

"Nope," I tell her. "None, whatsoever."

"Alright, then," Leila writes, simply.

A few minutes later, the announcer receives a written list from a member of the organizing team, and after glancing over it for a few seconds, he begins to read it aloud.

"I am now going to announce the names of the gladiators that will be fighting in the first duel," the announcer says. "This will be a fight to the death. The gladiators will need to battle until only one of them is left alive. No surrendering is allowed."

"Get ready," Leila writes to me.

"Ready for what?" I ask her.

"The name of the gladiators are—" the announcer says, as he gets ready to read the first line on the parchment.

"—Barry and Daren," the announcer continues.

"Oh," I tell Leila.

The iron gate in front of me gets raised, and so does the one from Daren's division.

"Will the two gladiators who just had their names called please enter the fighting area?" the announcer says, in a bored voice. "Thank you."

"Oh…" I tell Leila again, not knowing what else to say at this point.

"Good luck…" Leila writes, with a serious look on her face, as I slowly step out of my division area and into the arena.

Okay, calm down, there's no need to panic. I've gotten through every obstacle in my path so far. There's no reason why this should be any different. So there's no need to panic, okay? No reason. Just need to calm down. No panic. No panic…

While I'm busy thinking to myself, Daren is also slowly advancing towards me, only he seems to be unusually calm about all of this. Why is that? Is it because he knows he can beat me? No, no, that can't be the reason. Could it be that he already managed to figure a way out of this mess? What is he planning to do, exactly? Damn it, I'm sure that I could come up with a plan too, if only I could manage to calm down!

Once Daren and I both get to the center of the arena, facing each other, Daren gives me a wide grin, he drops his sword and shield on the ground, and then he throws his hands in the air.

"I surrender!" Daren shouts, as loud as he can. "I cannot fight this man. How could I?"

"This fight is to the death, healer," the announcer says. "Even if this man is your friend—"

"I mean, look at those muscles!" Daren shouts loudly, interrupting the announcer. "No sane man would ever dare fight such a beast!"

Suddenly all of the spectators in the crowd burst into laughter.

"Those arms look like he could smash my head like a watermelon between his bare hands!" Daren continues, with a mocking grin on his face. "And look at the size of his back! May the gods have mercy on my soul!"

Laugh it up, Daren…

Still, I have to give credit where credit is due. The idea to surrender was genius. Genius, and yet so obvious. How did I not think of this?

While the crowds are still laughing, the ambassador of Ollendor is making his way into the fighting area through one of the iron gates, and he is heading towards us.

"What is the meaning of this?" the ambassador shouts, and the crowds slowly fall silent. "Why aren't you fighting? This is a fight to the death! You can't just surrender!"

"Well, what are you going to do about it?" Daren tells him, with a smirk, when he reaches us.

The ambassador's face turns red with rage, and then he looks towards me.

"You there!" he says. "Peasant! Your opponent is disarmed. Finish him off now, or face the consequences!"

"Who are you calling a peasant? Peasant!" I say.

As I speak, I use a loud enough tone of voice to make sure that the spectators can hear me.

"I'm not the peasant, you lowborn scum!" the ambassador shouts. "You're the peasant!"

"No, you're the peasant!" I tell him.

"*You are the peasant*!" the ambassador shouts, with his face even redder than before.

The spectators cannot contain themselves any longer, and they all start laughing in unison.

"Hey, Daren," I say. "I think I finally found someone who is even easier to tease than Flower!"

"Are you incapable of comprehending the situation that you are in?" the ambassador says, while he is still fuming. "If you don't finish him off right now, you're going to regret—"

"Alright, fine, I'll finish him off," I tell him, without letting him end his sentence.

As the spectators grow silent once more, I slowly start walking towards Daren, with my dagger still in its sheath, and I stop within arm's reach of him. I then punch him lightly in the chest, and Daren throws himself to the ground, pretending to die in a very fake and dramatic way.

“It is done,” I tell the ambassador, in a very loud voice, in order to make sure that everyone in the crowd can hear me. “The healer is dead.”

The spectators once again burst into laughter, even louder than before.

“Are you mocking me?” the ambassador shouts.

“Of course we’re mocking you,” Daren says from the ground, as he slowly gets back up. “What did you expect? You didn’t really think that we’d change our minds and start killing each other just because you told us to, did you?”

“If you don’t kill each other, I’ll have you both executed!” the ambassador shouts.

“No, you won’t,” Daren says, loudly, so that everyone can hear him. “There is no standard arena rule that says we need to kill each other. We only broke one of this event’s rules. That means that you can’t execute us. You can only make us into undesirables, and force us to participate in the penalty round. Those are the rules.”

“I don’t care about the rules!” the ambassador shouts. “I make the rules! You will do as I say, or you are both going to die!”

There is a loud murmur coming from the spectator seats after the ambassador’s last outburst. The ambassador does not notice, and he continues his rant.

“Did you seriously think that those rules ever had any importance?” the ambassador shouts, even louder than before. “This whole arena’s only purpose was to have you killed! You were never meant to walk out of here alive! Do you hear me? This whole arena was nothing but a farce! Don’t make the mistake of thinking that you have any chance of survival just because you’ve won two measly rounds. I am the ambassador of Ollendor! If I wanted, I could have you both executed right now, in front of all these people, and nobody would bat an eye!

That is how much power I have! Now hurry up and kill each other like the dogs you are, or I will have your heads placed on spikes, along with all of your friends!"

While the ambassador was talking, the murmurs from the crowd started to slowly turn into booing that only intensified the more the ambassador spoke. By the time he finished his monologue, most of the spectators had picked up the booing, and they were getting louder by the second.

"Off with the ambassador's head!" shouts one of the spectators, loudly enough for everyone to hear him.

This one phrase seemed to have perfectly resonated with what everyone was thinking at that moment, because all the spectators in the crowd gradually picked it up and made a shorter version of it, in order to be able to chant it in unison, repeatedly.

"Off with his head! Off with his head! Off with his head!" the crowds keep chanting, as the ambassador's arrogant look on his face slowly gets replaced with a much darker and more fearful expression, while a trickle of sweat begins to run down his forehead.

"How does it feel, ambassador?" we suddenly hear Eiden's voice, coming from somewhere behind the ambassador, although the stillwater himself is nowhere to be seen.

"Damn it, not again!" Daren says, as soon as he hears Eiden's voice.

"Is that... Eiden?" the ambassador says, as he looks around, trying to identify the source of the sound.

"How does it feel to have so many people threatening to end your life at the same time?" Eiden says. "Take a good look at these people, ambassador. Do you think that they would care about your high rank if you met them now on the street? Do you think that they would hesitate to kill you, even for a moment, if they were given the chance to do so?"

He pauses.

"These are the people that you've shunned all of your life, ambassador," Eiden continues. "And you have done so due to your strict adherence to the belief that all of the people below your social rank were nothing but inferior creatures, unworthy of your attention. Do you still have what it takes to stick to your beliefs now, and face the direct consequences of your actions? What choice will you make, ambassador? Your time is running out."

I can almost imagine Eiden's smirk, with his closed eyes, as he watches the ambassador biting his nails, trying to find a solution that could help him both to calm down the crowds, and to have us killed on the spot. The solution, however, never came.

"I've changed my mind!" the ambassador says, finally, loudly enough so that the spectators can hear him. "We will follow the rules! These two gladiators have now become undesirables. If they survive the final round, then they will be set free, as promised. You may continue the rest of the round as you see fit."

He then storms out of the fighting area, and as far away from the booing noises as his legs can carry him. In the meantime, Daren has picked up his sword and shield from the ground, and he is now looking towards the place where we've heard Eiden's voice coming from.

"So, how's it going, Eiden?" Daren says. "Are you enjoying the show?"

The empty place that Daren is addressing gives him no answer.

"You know, I was thinking…" Daren says, ignoring the fact that Eiden never answered his question. "While I was travelling, I've often heard of these new types of circuses, where they involve their audience directly in some parts of their shows. I was thinking that since you're such a loyal spectator, maybe we could try some of that! What do you think?"

Daren pauses for a bit, as if he were actually waiting for Eiden to say something.

"Great!" Daren says. "Here goes!"

He then throws his sword with breathtaking speed, right at the spot where Eiden was standing invisibly a few minutes prior. The sword passes through the empty space where the stillwater had been standing, and it falls on the ground, a few dozen feet beyond that position. Looking a bit disappointed, Daren lets out a small sigh, and he goes to retrieve his sword.

Not long after the departure of the ambassador, the announcer officially ends the fight between me and Daren, and he declares me as the victor of the battle, due to Daren's surrender. As I am preparing to return to my division room, the announcer stops me, telling me that I was scheduled to fight to the death with a gladiator from the sixth division right after my battle with Daren. The announcer also reminds me that as an undesirable, I now have the right to refuse to fight until the penalty round, if I so desire.

After taking some time to think, I decide to accept the duel. I'd much rather fight this gladiator now, while he's alone, than be forced to face him later on in the penalty round, when we'll be fighting everyone at once.

I notify the announcer that I've decided to stay, and an iron gate opens up, clearing the way for my adversary to enter the battlefield. As the man enters the fighting area, I recognize him as being one of the more proficient fighters in his group. Actually, I'd even go as far as saying that he is comparable in terms of combat prowess to the fighters from the first division. His build is also quite impressive, being as tall as Daren and as bulky as Bruce. Just like most of the other gladiators, he seems to be wearing leather armor, but instead of a sword, his weapon of choice appears to be a large double-edged battle-axe, which he is now holding in both hands.

The beginning of the fight will likely be announced as soon as he reaches me. Now, then… How do I go about this? The fight is to the death, but as an undesirable, I am no longer bound by such rules. If I want him out of the way, killing him would be easier, but technically I could also just break one of his legs or something, and it should be enough for my intents and purposes. After all, I don't see any good reason why I should kill him. I have nothing against the guy. I just want to make sure that I won't need to fight him in the final round. All I need is to incapacitate him in some way, nothing more.

But how will I fight him? Do I try to disarm him first, or should I just focus on hitting him where he's undefended? Would it be a better idea to wait for him to make mistakes or to attack him head on and take him by surprise?

As I finish making my attack plan, the man reaches my position, and he stops about a dozen feet away from me, measuring me up with an arrogant smile on his face, while I take one of my newly acquired scimitars out of its sheath. He doesn't say anything, but it's pretty obvious what he's thinking. He clearly cannot picture himself losing this fight.

We both wait for the announcer to give us the signal, and once our battle officially begins, the gladiator charges at me directly, with his axe raised in the air, ready to strike.

I wait for him to reach me, and I begin dodging his attacks, trying to find the right opportunity to strike back at him. Evading the warrior's attacks is definitely not easy, due to the large size of his battle-axe, and there are more than a few times when I almost feel like I'm not going to make it. Fortunately, the long reach of my scimitar gives me a little bit more space to maneuver, and it also allows me to parry some of the strikes that might have hit me otherwise.

As soon as I catch my opponent on the wrong footing, I use my scimitar to stab him in an undefended area to the right side of his chest. Given the curved nature of my weapon, the cut does not go very deep, but it is enough for the gladiator to panic and to jump back, in order to get away from my blade. I quickly follow him, and I slash at him again, which makes him trip and fall on his back, while dropping the battle-axe from his hands. I then kick the weapon away from him, and I put my scimitar to his throat, to make sure that he won't try to get up anymore.

"Wait!" the gladiator screams, all of a sudden. "I surrender!"

"This is a fight to the death, warrior," the announcer says, coldly. "Surrendering is not allowed."

"Please…" the gladiator says, in a pleading voice, looking directly at me. "Have mercy… I don't want to die! Please!"

"Kill him! Kill him! Kill him!" the spectators start chanting, in unison.

I ignore the crowds completely, and I use my blade to stab the gladiator in his right leg. This should be enough to make sure that he won't be fighting me in the final round.

I then turn my back on him and start walking away.

"What do you think you are doing?" the announcer says.

"I'm going back to my division room," I say. "The fight is over. I won."

"No, the fight is not over until I say it is over," the announcer says, angrily. "Now, get back there and finish the job!"

"Nah," I say.

"What is your problem?" the announcer says. "This man isn't your friend! I bet you've never even seen him before this arena event. Why are you not killing him?"

"I refuse to kill a guy I've just met for the sole purpose of your entertainment," I say. "My only goal was to incapacitate him in order to not have to fight him in the final round. If you want to kill him, do it yourselves."

"I'm not going to announce your win until you kill this man," the announcer says.

"Then make him the winner," I say. "I don't care. I'm done, here."

As I take my leave, the crowds begin booing me. Their shouts and insults are only getting louder as I approach my division room.

"Shut up!" I shout at them, as I finally snap.

The noise from the crowd slowly dies down, as the spectators are all looking at me, curiously, to see what I have to say.

"What the hell is wrong with you?" I continue. "Is this what you consider entertainment? Watching people murder each other and get mauled by wild beasts? How sick in the head do you have to be to get enjoyment out of something like this? You're all pathetic! Does it make you feel good to know that some people have even worse lives than you? Is this why you're watching this crap? Well, I've got news for you! As soon as you walk out of here, it's going to be the same crappy lives waiting for you, outside! And you all deserve it! The way you are all treating these gladiators is the same way that the nobles are treating you. You have no right to complain about anything that is going on in your lives. How about you all take a small break and do a bit of self-reflection before you start booing me again like a bunch of mindless sheep? I'm going back to my cell. I'm done with you idiots."

Unsurprisingly, as soon as I finish my speech, the booing from the crowd gets louder than ever before, and the swearing is now a lot more diverse, as well. I ignore the sheep, and I return to my division area without as much as a single glance towards any of them.

"Wow," Leila writes, when the iron gate closes behind me. "That was… quite the speech."

"Yeah," I say, simply, and then we both watch the next fights in silence.

The rest of the battles went by without any particular incidents, and without any of the gladiators standing out in any way. However, there seemed to be something of a pattern forming with the scheduling of the duels. First of all, neither I, nor Daren, nor Hadrik were being called anymore for any of the fights. Kate was scheduled to fight a few times, but she refused every time, taking full advantage of her undesirable status. Secondly, there have been no more fights to the death whatsoever, after my last battle. Most of the battles ended with light scratches, or with gladiators surrendering before the fight even began, due to obvious differences in power levels.

By the time the third round ended, it was getting pretty obvious that these changes had been specifically requested by the ambassador, with the purpose of keeping as many of the gladiators alive as possible, in order to get us to fight them all in the penalty round.

The winner of the third round was some guy from the seventh division that didn't really do anything special, but had the luck of running into a lot of cowards who surrendered before their fights even began. Once the winner received his prize, the announcer called for all the gladiators to assemble in the fighting area one last time, so the penalty round could finally begin.

"Will the undesirables please form a line and face the rest of the gladiators?" the announcer says.

Daren, Hadrik, Kate and I all head towards the center of the arena, and we stand side by side, preparing our weapons.

"Now, who is ready to participate in the final—" the announcer starts to say, but he stops, when he sees Leila and Bruce both move at the same time, in order to join our side.

"What are you doing?" the announcer says. "You are on the wrong side! Neither of you are undesirables!"

"Yet!" Bruce says.

"You are saying," the announcer says, "that you are voluntarily turning yourselves into undesirables after the event has already ended, just to stand by these gladiators' side?"

"The true members of the fourth division shall stand united until the very last blow of the horn," Bruce says.

Wilhelm frowns at Bruce, who was looking straight at him when he said those last words. After a few seconds of silence, the assassin moves from his spot and then joins our side as well.

"Very well," the announcer says. "While we're at it, is there anyone else who would like to join the undesirables' side?"

"I will!" says the gladiator that I defeated in the third round, as he slowly limps over to our side as well. "I do not intend to leave this arena before settling my debt from the third round."

"Well, okay, then…" the announcer says, starting to get a bit annoyed. "Anyone else?"

The gladiators fall silent, and it seems that nobody else is planning to join us anymore.

"Great…" the announcer says, while mumbling under his breath. "Now that we have some new undesirables, you'll have to excuse me for a minute, while I add their names to a few important documents. You can use this extra time to decide whether you want to participate in the final round or not. I'll be with you again, shortly."

He then begins to descend from his platform, and into a small office in the upper levels of the arena, where he has all of his papers. While the announcer is still busy with his paperwork, Hadrik looks like he's suddenly remembered something important, and he addresses Daren and me in a low voice, making sure that the other gladiators can't hear him.

"Uh, guys…" Hadrik says. "I just realized something. I can't attack any of those gladiators. That blasted tournament's spell won't let me. It says they are citizens of Varathia!"

"You only realized that now?…" Daren says. "Isn't this something that you should have considered before specifically asking the king to write you that letter of admission?"

"Well, I figured that they'd make an exception for the gladiators!" Hadrik says. "Otherwise, why would they have let me join the arena in the first place?"

"The king and the arena owner probably assumed that you could bypass the spell, like the rest of us…" Daren says. "Look, it doesn't matter. Just say you'll forfeit, and wait for us outside. They can't force you to participate until the end, if you're not a prisoner."

"But then I'd end up looking like a coward!" Hadrik says. "I'm better off just dodging their attacks until you guys manage to finish them off!"

"Whatever…" Daren says.

"Finally!" the announcer says, after exiting his office and climbing back up on his platform. "Now that the paperwork's done, and sent to the organizers, I'd say it's about time that we get this round started, don't you think? Volunteers, please step forward, so that you may join this optional round."

One of the gladiators begins to move forward, but another one pulls him back, from behind.

"Do you have a death wish?" the gladiator from behind says. "Don't you see who you're up against? That dwarf pulverized half of the manticores and the scorpions all by himself! And that healer in armor pretty much fought all the monsters by himself too, and he doesn't even have a scratch. You'd have to be insane to want to fight them!"

Hearing the gladiator's speech, the few other warriors who were planning to join the final round are now all starting to have second thoughts.

"Really?" the announcer asks, shocked, as he sees that none of the gladiators are volunteering to fight. "No one? Do you people realize what you can gain if you kill either one of those warriors in front of you? You can be freed just like that, or get showered with riches!"

"Better to be poor than dead," one of the gladiators says, while many of the others nod in agreement.

"What do you all think you are doing?" the ambassador shouts furiously, as he comes running into the fighting area once more. "Why aren't you fighting them? There are dozens of you! Dozens!"

"Numbers don't mean anything when you're up against enemies of that caliber," one of the gladiators says.

"What caliber?" the ambassador shouts, furiously. "They are just a bunch of peasants! Do you think that fighting them is not worth the risk? Then I'll make it worth it! I can give you money beyond your wildest dreams. You will never have to work another day in your life! If you join this fight, I will free you all and give you a high enough status that you will never risk having to fight in a place like this ever again! Just tell me what you want, and I will provide it for you! All you have to do is fight! Fight, damn you!"

The gladiators are all looking at each other, with an uneasy look in their eyes, but it doesn't seem like any of them are seriously considering accepting the ambassador's offer.

"What is wrong with you?" the ambassador shouts,

with his face red from anger. "Do you have no ambitions? No goals? What is it going to take to make you fight them? What is it going to take? Tell me, you miserable excuses for human beings! What do you want? Tell me! Tell—"

The ambassador's last words get drowned out by a few very loud horns that seem to all be blowing in unison from different sides of the city. The crowds are starting to panic. It seems that they all know something we don't. Whatever it is that those horns were supposed to signify, I'm definitely not liking the sound of this.

"Oh, no…" the announcer says, trying to keep calm. "Will the spectators please evacuate the arena in a calm and orderly fashion? The show is cancelled. I repeat. The show is cancelled!"

The spectators are now rushing in droves towards the exits of the coliseum, and while they are not looking very calm and orderly to me, they are at least not knocking each other down, so they still have some sense of self-control left in them, despite their panic.

Now that he's done with the spectators, the announcer turns towards us.

"Gladiators," he says. "I'm afraid that I'm going to have to ask you to temporarily join the forces of our army until our current crisis gets averted. According to the laws of Thilias, during a city-wide state of emergency, gladiators are to be used as resources of the kingdom, until the state of emergency is officially declared to be over."

"Like hell, we will!" I say. "That wasn't the deal!"

"Listen, there's no time to argue!" the announcer says, with a little bit of panic in his voice. "Even if you don't want to join the army, you still don't have any time left to—"

The announcer interrupts himself, because a very powerful wind comes blowing towards us all, feeling as if it could lift us in the air any second, if we weren't on our guards.

This wind… I've only witnessed something like this once before. Oh gods, please, don't let this be—

"Half-lessathi," I hear a familiar voice calling me from above. "I've been looking for you."

As I hesitantly turn my head upwards, I see Tyrath, the king of all dragons, flapping his wings high above in the sky, while looking directly at me with a menacing stare.

"Gods have mercy…" Bruce says.

The announcer screams, and he falls on his back, as soon as he sees the dragon. The spectators look terrified. They are now screaming and pushing each other like madmen. At this rate, it won't take long until some of them get pushed to the ground and get trampled by the stampeding crowd.

The ambassador lets out a girly scream, and he runs away, as fast as his legs can carry him, outside of the fighting area.

"Did you think that you could hide from me forever, half-lessathi?" Tyrath says. "You should have realized that I would be able track down your smell as soon as you'd get out from your underground hole. All you managed to do was prolong the inevitable."

"Hey, Tyrath!" we hear Arraka's voice coming from our left. "Long time no see! Remember me? It's your old friend, Arraka!"

Flower is now jumping down from the spectator seats, using fire jets coming from her feet to slow down her fall. She then comes running to join the rest of us in the center of the arena.

"Arraka…" Tyrath says, taking his eyes off me to look towards her amulet.

"Is it just me or did you get a new look?" Arraka asks the dragon. "What happened to your scales made of molten lava? Where is that intimidating fiery aura that you used to have? Wait, is it because you got older? Aha- Ahahahaha! So much for being all-powerful, huh? I bet you must really hate yourself for having become such a weakling!"

"How did you break the seal?" Tyrath asks her.

"You mean the seal from the cave?" Arraka asks. "Seriously? You never even found out I escaped? How did you even manage to miss the still winter? Were you hibernating or something? Boy, do I have some stories to tell you!"

"The seal," Tyrath says again. "How did you break it?"

"Oh, that old thing had already started to crack after the first thousand years or so," Arraka says. "As soon as there were enough cracks in it, all I had to do was wait for someone to enter the cave, and BAM! I took over his body. Or at least I tried to. We ended up having to share it, eventually. But seriously, though, what did you think would happen? You had to ally yourself with all of those lessathi and mages just to stand a chance against me, and you thought that your half-assed seal would hold me there forever? Don't make me laugh! The only reason why you even managed to beat me was because I'd only just gotten myself banned from the magical plane, and I didn't really know the ins and outs of this world at the time. If we had a rematch now, I'd obliterate you."

"You would obliterate me from inside your amulet?" Tyrath says.

"Hey, you break this amulet for me, and we can have that rematch right now, if you want," Arraka says.

"You can stay there and rot," Tyrath says. "I didn't come here for you. I came here to get revenge, and to prove to an insignificant insect just how hopeless it is to oppose me."

"Wait, are you talking about me?" I say.

"Yes, I'm talking about you, you miserable wretch!" Tyrath shouts. "Now stop talking, and activate your magic stats again so I can prove to you how weak you truly are!"

"Uh, you see…" I tell the dragon. "The thing is that I can't really activate those stats anymore."

"So, you refuse to fight me at your full power, then?" Tyrath says.

"No, you don't understand," I say. "I'm saying that I really can't use those stats right now. Couldn't you come back later, after I've learned how to activate them?"

"If you're not planning to activate the stats," the dragon says, "then I'm going to start by slowly murdering all of your friends, one by one, until you finally come to your senses. And once I'm done with you, I will destroy this entire city, and then I will burn all the other human settlements from this continent to the ground. I will do today what I should have done ten thousand years ago. Your race was never meant to get out of the caves."

Immediately after he finishes his speech, a very large explosion envelops the dragon, and then a few smaller explosions start to fill the area around him. Flower, who is now high up in the sky, some two hundred feet away from the dragon, makes a victory gesture with her right fist, as soon as she sees the explosions.

"Nice job distracting him, Barry!" Flower says, as she gives me a thumbs up, while still floating in the sky, with the aid of the fire jets coming from her feet.

"Watch out!" I shout at her. "The dragon is immune to fire!"

"Even if he is immune to fire," Illuna says, "the impact from the explosions is still going to leave a mark."

"Well, you heard her!" Flower says, with a smirk. "One more fireball, coming up!"

The girl then creates a spinning ball of fire between her hands, and she sends it flying towards the dragon, making it explode on impact.

"So this is the dragon that you guys were talking about," Hadrik says, with half a grin, and with a look of both excitement and apprehension in his eyes. "Let's see what he's made of, then!"

Hadrik then turns into a giant eagle, and he soars into the sky, towards the dragon. Flower makes sure to stop her fireballs when she sees him, and as soon as Hadrik positions himself above Tyrath, he turns back into his usual dwarf form, making a dive towards the dragon and punching him in the back. Hadrik's punch was so strong that we heard it from all the way down here, and it sent the dragon flying a dozen feet towards the ground. The dwarf then turns back into an eagle, and he flies away, waiting to see what his opponent will do next.

The dragon looks furious. It seems that he's planning to go all out from the start, this time around. Before Flower gets to cast a new fireball, the dragon disappears from where he was previously, and he reappears right in front of her, slashing at her with one of his claws. Flower reacts immediately, and she uses a jet of fire from her left hand to propel her to the side, and out of the dragon's reach. Tyrath wastes no time, and he teleports again, right behind Flower. This time, it is Illuna who quickly turns around, and she uses two water jets from her hands to attack the dragon and also to push herself away from him at the same time. While the girl and the dragon repeat the same motions a few more times, Kate is preparing a very large cone of ice in the air above her, getting ready to send it flying towards Tyrath.

"Kate, this isn't going to work," Daren tells her, as he sees her preparing her ice cone. "Don't you remember how things went the last time we've fought him? Your ice cones didn't affect him at all. If you could use one of your ice platforms to fly me all the way into the sky, maybe I could manage to hurt him with my sword."

"This won't be like the last time," Kate says, with a determined look on her face. "Now that I know the full extent of my enemy's power, I no longer have the luxury to worry about conserving my magical energy. This time, I'm going to fight him with all I've got, even if I end up fainting from exhaustion."

"Damn it, listen to me!" Daren says, but Kate ignores him, and she surrounds herself in a cage made of ice that she then uses to lift her up in the sky, so she can get a better view of her target.

The cone of ice that she's creating is definitely looking a lot different from anything she's ever made before. It looks as sharp and durable as elven steel, and it is simply radiating magical energy. It feels like the whole area around it is trembling from the magical power that is being pumped into that one ice cone, and once the creation process is complete, the cone starts turning by itself, following the dragon's movements. After Tyrath teleports a few more times in order to attack Flower, Hadrik finally catches up to him again, in his eagle form, and he turns into a dwarf once more, punching him right in the face.

While the dragon gets briefly stunned by the dwarf's attack, Kate uses the opportunity to launch her ice cone at her target. There is an extremely powerful explosion of air behind the ice cone, as it gets sent straight into the dragon's chest at an incredible speed. The icicle penetrates Tyrath's tough hide, and he lets out a very loud roar, which almost makes everyone lose their consciousness, even while they are desperately trying to cover their ears. The dragon then yanks the ice cone out of his chest with his claw, and he teleports right next to Kate, who is now barely even able to stand on her feet, inside her floating ice cage, due to the dragon's roar from before. Just as the dragon is about to burn her alive with his fire breath, a golden cage appears out of nowhere, trapping him inside. This does not stop Tyrath from breathing his fire, but somehow, none of the flames manage to pass through the cage's bars, and they eventually die out by themselves.

"The fox's cage…" Tyrath says.

He then turns around, looking straight at Illuna.

"Is this your doing?" he asks her.

"I've had enough of your annoying teleporting," Illuna says. "You are going to stay put for the next few minutes. Do you understand?"

"How is this going to help you in any way?" Tyrath says. "I may not be able to attack you from inside here, but neither can you. All you are doing is wasting time."

"Not exactly," Illuna says.

Flower then starts to move around the dragon's cage with her fire jets, creating balls of fire with her hands, and then leaving them floating one by one, all around the cage.

"I'd like to see you handle all of these at once, king of dragons," Flower says, with a smirk.

The dragon scoffs, and he begins to cast a series of protection spells on himself, getting prepared for the moment when the cage disappears. Kate is now also creating as many of her newly designed ice cones as she can, although judging by the expression on her face, this process is definitely wearing her out much faster than her usual means of casting magic. I don't know if she can keep this up much longer.

Damn it, there has to be something I can do in this situation. Maybe I can find a way to get up there somehow.

As I look around, I see, to my surprise, that the empty spectator area is now slowly being filled with hundreds of people dressed in guard uniforms, and many of them are holding some very peculiar weapons in their hands. In the meantime, some other people are pushing several flying machines into the arena's fighting area. The machines look similar to the flying contraptions built by gnomes, with a large propeller on top, a long tail in the back, and two wings that help with gliding through the air. The propeller is usually powered by a spell cast by an air elementalist, but aside from that, there is no further need for magic in order to help these machines fly.

I used to know a gnome a few years ago who would keep making me do flight tests of his prototypes in exchange for the information I needed about mages. I remember one of those prototypes being so bad that the propeller actually stopped working while I was in mid-flight, and I had to glide all the way down. I still have nightmares about some of those flights even to this day.

One of the people that pushed the flying contraptions into the arena is now having an argument with a gnome, not very far from our position. As I look closer, I realize that the gnome is none other than king Golmyck.

"What do you mean the pilots and the gunners aren't here, yet?" Golmyck says. "I specifically asked for three pilots and gunners to be ready and waiting in case any of the manticores went berserk! Where are they now?"

"I apologize, your highness," says the man who helped push the machinery. "The manticores were all killed in the first round, so the pilots and gunners went out for a drink. I tried to contact them through their transceivers, but they wouldn't answer…"

"Damnations!" Golmyck says. "I'd pilot one of these myself, but I still need someone to man the guns!"

He then turns towards us.

"You there, gladiators!" he says. "You're all in the army now, am I correct? Do any of you have any experience piloting aircraft? Or are you at least any good at aiming from a moving vehicle? I could use some help, here!"

"I've piloted gnomish flying machines before," I say. "I could give it a try."

"Splendid!" Golmyck says. "Come over here, uh… Barry, was it? I'll teach you the basics."

"I'll go help the soldiers," Daren says. "They'll need all the protection they can get if they're planning to start shooting at the dragon."

He then rushes towards one of the gates, in order to reach the upper levels, where the soldiers are currently located.

"Now, Barry, listen closely," Golmyck says, once I reach him. "These are your flight controls."

He then points towards the cockpit.

"Over here you have the control stick," Golmyck continues. "The rudder pedals are down below. You should only change the rudder's direction for making minor adjustments, and not for actually turning the aircraft. Turning should only be done by using the control stick."

"Yes, I know," I tell him.

"This lever over here," Golmyck says, as he points towards a lever on the left side of the cockpit, "is used to adjust the pitch for the rotor blades. Increasing the pitch will make you gain altitude, but it will decrease your forward speed. Decreasing the pitch will make you lose altitude. Does this all look familiar to you?"

"Yeah," I say. "It's pretty similar to what I've piloted in the past. I can handle it."

"Perfect!" Golmyck says. "When I designed these machines, I tried to make the controls as intuitive as possible for people who have piloted other gnomish machines in the past. I'm glad to see that my efforts were not wasted!"

The gnome looks up at the dragon trapped in the golden cage, with a thoughtful expression on his face.

"Barry," Golmyck says, "you wouldn't happen to know how much longer that cage is going to last, would you?"

"Uh…" I say. "About two more minutes, I guess?…"

"Good," Golmyck says. "We have plenty of time. Hop in. I'll give you the rest of the instructions during our flight. Make sure to strap yourself in tight. Also, you should wear these goggles."

Golmyck gives me a pair of protective goggles, which I immediately put on, and then I enter the cockpit, strapping myself in. There are only two chairs in the cockpit, one for the gunner and one for the pilot, back to back. The gnome enters the cockpit as well, seating himself on the chair behind me and then putting on his straps.

"So, uh…" I say, as I see the gnome adjusting the turret that is located at the base of the machine's tail. "I may be stating the obvious, here, but you do realize that normal bullets will not work on this dragon, right?"

"Of course, of course," Golmyck says. "That's why we won't be using regular bullets. The bullets that I've loaded into this turret are made of a metal that is highly resistant to acid, and they have all been coated with acid, which we know for a fact that the dragon is weak against. We've had these prepared for a while, since Tyrath has been a looming threat for quite some time, now. Obviously, even with the acid coating, the bullets will likely only moderately inconvenience him, but that's fine, since they are only meant as a distraction."

The gnome then points towards a button on my control panel.

"You also have your own weaponry, by the way," Golmyck says. "Just press that button, and the bullets will shoot themselves. Both the front gun and the turret operate on a mechanism similar to cannons that are used on ships, except for the fact that they magically load themselves with black powder and bullets, so you only need to worry about aiming and shooting. Do try to use these bullets sparingly, though. Our ammunition is not unlimited, and these bullets cost a lot to make."

As soon as the two of us are ready to take off, the gnome signals an air elementalist nearby, and he casts a spell on the machine's propeller in order to make it rotate. I pull on the lever to my left side in order to increase the pitch, and the flying machine begins to slowly gain altitude.

"So, you were saying before that the bullets are only a distraction," I say, rather loudly, in order to compensate for the sound of the propeller. "What did you mean by that?"

"Oh, the real purpose of this machine is not to shoot down the dragon," Golmyck says. "What we are in fact aiming to do is to manage to place ourselves above him, and then to drop a spinning rope on him."

"A spinning rope?" I ask him, confused.

"Yes," the gnome says. "Our enchanters designed a magical rope that is made to unfurl itself and then to start spinning once it gets dropped from our small cargo hold below. The rope has been enchanted to be nearly unbreakable, and it is long enough to tie down the dragon's wings, in order to prevent him from flying. The only problem is that the dragon will need to hover in one place for quite a while and not be paying attention to us in order for this setup to work. We can't do it right after the cage is dismissed, because there will be too many explosions, and the dragon will try to get away from there as soon as possible. We only have one cargo hold, and only one rope, so we can't afford to miss our chance. We shouldn't use it unless we are absolutely certain that our plan will succeed. Until then, we'll only be using bullets to attack him, in order to provide assistance to your friends and my soldiers that will be attacking the dragon at the same time."

"And what if the dragon starts breathing fire at us?" I say.

"This aircraft is using lessathi technology," Golmyck says, "to provide us with some rather effective shielding against fire attacks. Of course, this does not make us invulnerable, and I'm not sure how long the shields can hold against flames that are as hot as the dragon's, so we should try evading his fire breath as much as possible."

As we reach a high enough level of altitude, the golden cage surrounding the dragon is slowly starting to fade.

"Get ready," the gnome tells me.

As soon as the cage disappears, all of Flower's fireballs explode at the same time, sending a very powerful gust of wind towards us, and Kate's ice cones also get launched into the dragon soon afterwards. The protections that Tyrath cast on himself during all this time help him to survive the damage, but it's clear that he didn't get out of that unscathed. What's more, the amount of damage that he needed to absorb with his magical shields also seems to have drained him of his magical energy for the time being, because he is no longer using teleportation to move around and has gone back to using his wings to fly.

Almost as soon as he gets away from all the explosions, the dragon uses his fire breath to attack Kate. He was rather far from her when he attacked, however, which gave Kate enough time to move her ice cage out of the way, before the flames reached her. Tyrath now attempts to make a dive towards her, but before he reaches his target, the king's soldiers activate their strange weapons in unison, and they release a very powerful bolt of lightning that hits him head on. Visibly upset, the dragon begins to rain down flames upon them, trying to dispose of them all at once. Luckily, Daren had already reached the spectator area a while ago, and as soon as he sees the flames, he uses his shield to create a large semi-transparent barrier, which defends all of the soldiers from the fire attack.

I think I'm finally starting to understand how the dragon's fire breathing works. It seems that he needs to inhale a great deal of air in his lungs before he attacks, and he also never exhales the fire right away afterwards. I'm guessing that this is because he first needs to ignite the fire, before breathing it out. This means that as long as you pay attention to his breathing, you should be able to tell when he'll attack you with fire, and you'll have all the time you need to dodge his flames, if you are fast enough. This information will really help me while I pilot the aircraft, because I don't think that I'd have time to maneuver out of the way otherwise.

Tyrath seems to have changed his mind again, and he's now chasing after Hadrik, who is currently in his eagle form. Even with Hadrik's speed, it still seems like the dragon is going to catch up to him soon. Maybe now would be a good time to make use of those acid coated bullets…

I use the control stick in order to maneuver the aircraft to align with the dragon, and then I turn my head towards the gnome.

"I'm going to attack Tyrath," I tell Golmyck. "Be ready."

"Understood," Golmyck says.

As soon as I make sure that I've got a clear shot at him, I press the button on my control panel, and I shoot about a dozen bullets into the dragon's right wing. The dragon screams in pain, and then he flies out of the way, preparing to make a charge at us. I decide that it's time to retreat, and I turn the plane around, in an attempt to get as far away from the dragon as possible.

I look back, towards Tyrath, and I see that he is inhaling a lot of air in his chest, preparing to attack us with his fire breath. I quickly change the direction of the aircraft in order to avoid the dragon's attack, and the flames miss us by a fair margin. The dragon is now right on our tail, but he seems to be having a bit of trouble with his wing that I shot earlier, which is causing him to fly a little slower than before.

In the meantime, Golmyck is using the turret to keep pressure on the dragon, but he doesn't get to hit him much, because Tyrath can easily tell where the bullets will be shot from the way the turret is facing, and he doesn't have much trouble dodging most of those shots.

As the dragon gets closer to us, Hadrik finally catches up to him in his eagle form, and he turns back into a dwarf in order to smack him in the back of the head. He then quickly turns into an eagle again, and he flies away, while one of Kate's ice cones penetrates the dragon's chest. Tyrath pulls the cone out with his claw, and then he starts inhaling air to prepare his fire breath, but just as he does that, the whole air around his head gets replaced with water, and he breathes that in, instead. Realizing his mistake, the dragon immediately attempts to cough out the water from his lungs, but the water around his head does not disappear, so all he manages to do is breathe more water in with every cough.

"This is it," Golmyck says. "This is our chance! See if you can fly us over the dragon while he's busy with the water, so I can drop the spinning rope on him."

"Alright," I say. "I'll try."

The dragon is now moving up and down, shaking his head violently, in an attempt to get rid of all the water above his neck.

"There's no use fighting it," Illuna tells the dragon, in a cold voice. "That water won't go away. And you can't burn it with your flame breath either, as long as you can't get rid of all that water in your lungs. Stop struggling and accept your fate."

"Hah!" Arraka says. "How do you like drowning in mid-air, Tyrath? I'm the one who taught this technique to Illuna, you know. You were blowing all that hot air just now, but in the end it turns out you can't even defeat one of my disciples! I guess you were never a match for me after all. Aha- Ahahahahaha!"

Tyrath's eyes start glowing bright red all of a sudden, and he looks more pissed off than ever. He now seems to be voluntarily increasing his body temperature to an alarming degree, because I'm beginning to see steam coming out from all over him. He must be trying to evaporate all the water from his body, in order to be able to breathe fire again.

While Tyrath is busy heating up his body, Golmyck and I manage to position ourselves right above the dragon, and we ready ourselves to drop the rope on him. As soon as the dragon achieves his purpose of evaporating all of the water inside him, he uses the last of his breath to exhale a large flame from his mouth, eliminating all of the water that was surrounding his head until now.

"I'm dropping the rope!" Golmyck says, as we watch the dragon gasp for air.

He then pulls on a lever to his right, and the cargo hold opens below us, dropping the rope. Just as the gnome said, the rope unfurls as it falls, and then it starts spinning by itself. The dragon is too busy catching his breath to look above him, and as soon as the rope reaches him, it ties itself around his wings, preventing him from flapping them any further. Tyrath looks shocked, as he starts falling towards the ground, and his first reaction is to try and break free from the rope by using the force of his wings. Failing that, he begins to chew on the rope with his fangs, while also attempting to cut it with his claws, but it's no use.

As he gets closer to the ground, the dragon tries using the last of his magic energy reserves to slow down his momentum by teleporting a few dozen feet above his position a few times in a row. This does not slow down his falling speed at all, however, and eventually he hits the ground, with an extremely loud noise, creating a crater in the middle of the arena's fighting area, and sending large clouds of dust all around him.

"The dragon is grounded!" Golmyck shouts, suddenly, to everyone in the area. "Finish him off, now!"

"*Enough*!" Tyrath shouts loudly, and a very powerful explosion of hot air originating from his position suddenly hits us all in the face.

Following the explosion, the dragon's body changes completely, and it starts looking like it is now covered by molten lava, and not by regular scales anymore. He is also now emanating an intimidating fiery aura that is completely different from the one he had before. But that is not all. The magic power that I am currently sensing from him is simply insane. If I were to compare it with anything I've felt before, I'd say that it's on a pretty similar level to the magical power of the golden fox. Is this seriously the true form of the red dragon, Tyrath? The one that Arraka was talking about earlier, before we began the fight? How are we even supposed to fight something like this?

The rope that was tying the dragon's wings has already been burned into ashes by the dragon's transformation. Tyrath now soars back into the sky, looking more menacing than ever before.

"This is all my fault," Tyrath says, in an unusually calm tone. "I alone am to blame for having given you the illusion that you could actually stand a chance against me. I am now going to fix that mistake. Instead of continuing to fight you individually, I will simply destroy this whole city and everyone in it with a single spell. This way, there will be no more misunderstandings."

"I'm afraid I can't let you do that, king of all dragons," says Eiden, who appeared out of nowhere again and is now floating right in front of the dragon, with his eyes closed, as usual.

"Eiden…" Tyrath says, in a mildly annoyed tone.

"See, if you'd kept fighting in your other, weaker form," Eiden says, "I might have been tempted to continue ignoring your gross violation of our pact, but now you've driven things to a point where even I can no longer gloss this over…"

"What are you babbling about?" Tyrath says. "What pact?"

"Why, the pact that you, I and the golden fox have signed several hundred years ago, of course," Eiden says. "Have you already forgotten? According to the pact, none of us are allowed to directly attack any of the other's followers. This is to avoid a fight breaking out between any of the three signing parties, because a fight between any two of us would have the potential of destroying the entire island before reaching its conclusion, and none of us would want that. As such, any and all conflicts between the three of us are to be resolved indirectly through our followers, and not through any direct means, whatsoever."

"Ridiculous," Tyrath says. "That old pact has long ago lost its meaning. The only reason why we signed the pact in the first place was because our powers used to be comparable. That has no longer been the case for more than a hundred years. Ever since you left the continent, you've only grown weaker, and now you are but an empty shell of your former self. If you didn't always resort to petty tricks, I would have killed you a century ago. You are no longer a threat, stillwater, and therefore, our pact is now void."

"Is it?" Eiden asks, with a wide smile. "Well, let us declare a new pact, then!"

All of a sudden, the air all around us starts to feel like it's weighing heavily on our shoulders, and the world itself seems like it is trembling. It's almost as if there was now an earthquake in the middle of the air, instead of the earth below, and the blue sky looks as if it is ready to crack any minute, under the pressure. I realize immediately that this is the direct result of Eiden unleashing his magical aura, and that this may well not even be the true extent of his power.

"Well, well," I hear Arraka talking from somewhere behind us. "I see that Eiden has finally decided to get a little bit serious."

"A little bit?" Illuna shouts at her, in disbelief.

"We never really got to name our old pact," Eiden tells Tyrath, "but we could call this new one 'The pact of the Creator's return'. What do you say, old friend? Will our words be enough this time, or should I get a pen and paper?"

Tyrath looks at Eiden for a while, measuring him up and down, with a thoughtful look on his face.

"Perhaps I was wrong," Tyrath says. "Perhaps your travels have not made you nearly as weak as I would have liked to believe..."

He pauses.

"I do not intend to destroy the whole continent while fighting with you, stillwater," Tyrath says. "I will honor the pact, and won't interfere any longer. But know that my purpose remains unchanged. If I cannot destroy all the human cities myself, then my armies will just have to do it for me. I will not rest until every single one of these cities is burned down, whether that takes me weeks or years to accomplish. The next time you will be seeing me will be after I've destroyed everything that you've once loved and cherished in this godforsaken world. Remember this."

As Tyrath turns to leave, Eiden calls out to him one last time.

"Oh, I forgot to mention," Eiden says, with a polite smile. "The mages that have joined the tournament will also temporarily be classified as my followers under the terms of our pact. They are our esteemed guests after all. Therefore, you are not to bring harm to any of them until the end of the tournament, unless, of course, they attack you first."

"Hmph," Tyrath says. "I will keep that in mind."

The dragon then soars higher into the skies, and he flies away from us, in the same direction that he came from when he first attacked us.

"Farewell, king of all dragons," Eiden says, as the dragon leaves.

"Eiden!" we hear a girl's voice coming from one of the empty sides of the spectator seats. "Hey, Eiden, do you hear me?"

I look towards the coliseum, and I see that there is a young girl in her late teens standing all alone in the middle of the deserted spectator seats, and she has been shouting Eiden's name for a while now.

"Damn it!" the girl says. "Don't you dare ignore me!"

Eiden makes a bored hand wave in the general direction of the girl, and suddenly, none of the words she is speaking are reaching us anymore, although the girl doesn't seem to have realized it herself, and she still appears to be shouting louder than ever. Did Eiden just cast a silencing spell?

The stillwater then turns towards the soldiers from the king's army, who are all looking at him as if they've seen a ghost. Eiden's smile widens when he sees them, and he decides to give them a parting message before he leaves.

"Well, what are you all standing there for?" Eiden asks the soldiers. "Go on, spread the news! Spread it far and wide. Rejoice, for your Creator has finally returned!"

He then disappears once more, leaving the soldiers just as confused as they were before.

"I think it's about time we descended back to the fighting area, Barry," Golmyck says. "Our job here is done."

"Hey, Arraka," I say. "Is Eiden still around, or is he gone for good, this time?"

"Nah, he's gone," Arraka says.

"Alright, let's get back down," I tell Golmyck, and then we make our way back to the fighting area of the arena.

Once we land our flying machine and get out of the cockpit, the king shakes my hand, and then he goes to meet his soldiers, telling me that we'll see each other again, back at the palace. Not long afterwards, Daren, Kate, Hadrik and Flower all gather one by one near my plane, so we can leave the arena together. I wave to Leila, who comes to join our group as well, and as we prepare to leave, Bruce comes to say his goodbyes.

"Good fight, stillwater," Bruce says, as he pats me hard on the shoulder. "Good fight! And the same goes for you, silver-haired princess. If we all ever get trapped in another deadly arena, I wouldn't mind having you again as my allies. Maybe we'll meet again, someday."

"Who knows?" I tell him. "It's a small continent, after all."

Both Leila and I bid him farewell, and then we join the rest of the group. Once we're all ready to go, the ones of us who participated in the arena go to grab our backpacks from the locker rooms, and then we meet back in the fighting area, in order to head towards one of the spectator exits.

"Come on," Daren tells us. "I think I saw Enrique spectating us from somewhere around here, and I'm pretty sure that he left through one of these gates when the evacuation started. He must be waiting for us outside."

We all exit through the gate, trying to find Enrique , but before we get to even look around, we are greeted by a young girl with a pleasant smile on her face. I recognize her immediately as being the same girl who was calling out to Eiden, earlier.

"Hello!" the girl says. "I hope I'm not bothering you. It's just that I watched you fighting during the arena event, and I was very impressed! I was wondering if you all could help me out with something."

"Sorry, kid," Daren says, as he pats the girl on the shoulder, briefly. "We're not giving autographs."

He then turns his back on her and heads towards Enrique, who was waiting for us not far from the gate. The girl looks mildly irritated by Daren's remark, but it does not seem like she's planning to give up just yet. Taking a better look at her, I notice that her clothes, while aesthetically pleasing, do not look much different from the pajamas that they sell on the Western Continent. They remind me quite a lot of the type of clothing that Eiden likes to wear.

Wait a minute… This girl knows Eiden… And she wears similar clothing to him… So, does this mean that… No, no, no, what am I even thinking about? It's just a coincidence. There's no way that this girl could be a—

"Hey, Barry, are you coming?" Daren tells me.

"Oh, yeah, yeah, I'll be right there," I say, as I throw the young girl one last hesitant look, and then I head towards Daren.

"My friends," Enrique says. "That was fantastic! Simply magnificent! I have no words! I thought I'd already seen everything when you were done battling those creatures in the arena, but then you went and defeated a dragon! And to top it all off, you've survived the encounter with barely any scratches. This calls for a celebration! Tonight, we will have a feast. I will not accept 'no' for an answer!"

"Um… excuse me, sir?" we hear the young girl from before, calling out to Daren from behind us.

"Listen, Enrique," Daren says, ignoring the girl behind him, "I really appreciate all of this, but this arena event already puts us three days behind all of the other participants in the mage tournament, so I really don't think it would be a good idea for us to be spending yet another night in Thilias."

"Umm, sir?…" the young girl asks again, but nobody pays attention to her.

"Come on, Daren," Hadrik says. "Don't be a stick in the mud! They never gave us a time limit for completing the first objectives. It's not like they're going to disqualify us if we don't start looking for the pine cones right away."

"Damn it, Hadrik!" Daren says. "You are the last person that I want to hear this from. You don't even care about winning the tournament! Didn't you say that you only came here for the challenge? I bet you're only trying to postpone this because you hate the idea of having to go search for pine cones."

All of a sudden, Kate, Daren and I slowly begin to get raised from the ground, and as we are floating, we all get turned around, simultaneously, to face the opposite way. Standing in front of us now is the young girl in pajamas from before, smiling pleasantly at us.

"Well, then!" the girl says, while clapping her hands together. "Now that I've got your attention, perhaps we could have a little chat? I promise you that this won't take any longer than a few minutes!"

Chapter 6

The girl dressed in pajamas is looking at us with a victorious smile on her face. She seems very pleased with herself for having managed to finally get our attention. Despite the fact that she is clearly the one who has magically suspended us into the air, her aura is showing no traces of magic whatsoever. Even when Kate and Flower hide their auras, you can still tell that they are mages if you inspect their auras very closely. The girl in front of us, however, seems no different from a regular human. This can mean one of two things. Either she is much better at hiding her aura than Flower and Kate, or…

"Hey, I know you!" Arraka blurts out all of a sudden. "You're that stillwater girl that kept trailing behind Eiden and the fox during the still winter! Uh… what was the name?… Melenda? Milandra?…"

"Melindra," the stillwater girl says, in a cold voice, and then she flicks one of her fingers, casting a wind spell that closes Arraka's amulet.

Arraka mumbles furiously from within her amulet, but nobody is paying any attention to her. Having silenced the banshee, the stillwater girl regains her smile, and she attempts to continue her speech from where she left off.

"So, as I was saying," Melindra says, "there is something that I would like to ask of you. The reason why I went to watch you in the arena was because I heard that you got convicted for killing a noble from Varathia, so I thought—"

"Hold on a second, there…" Hadrik interrupts her. "You're a stillwater?"

"Why, yes…" Melindra says, confused. "I thought that much would have been obvious by now. Even Arraka said earlier that—"

"But how did you become one?" Hadrik asks. "Did you get born this way? Can women be born as stillwaters?"

"No, of course not!" Melindra says, slightly irritated. "I didn't get born as a stillwater. I became a stillwater in the same way that everyone else did."

"Everyone?" I ask. "Even Eiden? Is Eiden an artificial mage too? Wasn't he born as a mage?"

"What is an artificial mage?" Melindra says, in a frustrated tone. "Eiden was born as a regular human mage. He just became a stillwater later, just like everyone else. How is this so difficult to understand?"

"But how?" I ask her. "How do you become a stillwater?"

"Listen," Melindra says. "If you think that I'm going to just stand here and answer every single one of your questions before you even listen to what I'm—"

"How do you know Eiden?" Daren asks her. "Are you working with him?"

"No, I'm not working with Eiden!" Melindra says, visibly upset. "If I were working with Eiden, do you think I'd need to come and ask you for help? Why can't you just shut up for ten seconds and let me finish one damn senten—"

"If you want our help, then how about letting us down first?" Kate asks her. "This is no way to treat someone whom you're trying to ask for a favor."

Melindra is now looking at Kate with a pouting expression on her face that could rival Flower's, when she's upset. After a few seconds of silence, the stillwater girl waves one of her hands, and we all slowly start to descend towards the ground.

It's funny. This girl may well have the power to crush us with a single flick of her fingers, but her demeanor makes her feel like one of the least threatening persons I've met in my life. Perhaps even less threatening than Flower, or the ambassador of Ollendor.

"There!" Melindra says, once her levitation spell gets completely cancelled. "You're all back on the ground. Now, can I continue from where I left off, or are you planning to interrupt me with even more questions?"

"Go on," I say. "We're all listening."

"Good!" Melindra says, smiling once again. "Now, as I've said before, if I would've managed to contact Eiden, I wouldn't be bothering you with this, but since he's been completely ignoring me ever since I came back to Varathia, I was thinking that maybe you, as his followers could—"

"What did you just call us?" Daren asks her, perplexed.

"Eiden's followers," Melindra says. "Aren't you his followers?"

"Hell no!" Daren shouts.

Melindra is looking at us confused.

"His friends, then?" she asks.

"Far from it," Kate says.

"Then how did you manage to attack that noble?" Melindra says. "Wasn't Eiden the one who gave you the power to do it?"

"It was indeed," Kate says.

"So, why did he do it, if you aren't his friends?" Melindra says.

"You seem to have known Eiden for a while," Kate says. "Do you really think that he needs a logical reason for everything that he does? Or for anything at all, really?"

"Well…" Melindra says. "I mean… not recently…

but if you really aren't his friends, I must say I am quite surprised that he left you alive..."

"Aren't we all?" Kate says.

"So, what was it that you wanted to ask of us?" Daren says.

"Oh, right!" Melindra says, as she regains her smile. "In short, I want you to kill someone for me!"

"Whoa, whoa, whoa!" Daren says. "I'm going to stop you right there, Melindra. Despite what you may have heard about us, none of us are assassins. We won't kill people unless we have very good reasons to do it. We're not going to kill someone just because you asked us to."

"Oh, but I'm not asking you to do it for free!" Melindra says. "I'm more than willing to compensate you for this task!"

"We're not looking for money," Daren says. "We're here to participate in a mage tournament, remember?"

"I know!" Melindra says. "When I was talking about compensation, I meant that I would help you with your objectives. Don't you want to know how to find the pinecones?"

"Why would we need your help for that?" Daren says. "It's just some pinecones. How hard could it be to find them?"

Melindra smirks at Daren, and she takes what appears to be a pinecone seed out of her pocket. She then puts the seed in her hand, and it immediately starts to glow with a bright yellow light, just like Golmyck said it would when he announced our first objectives. She then holds her hand out to Daren, inviting him to take the pinecone seed from her.

"Go on," Melindra says, with a smile. "Take it! You'll understand why you'll need my help soon enough."

As Daren takes the seed from the stillwater girl's hand, the bright yellow glow fades completely, and the seed does not light back up no matter how much Daren moves it between his palms.

"As you can see," Melindra says, with a victorious smile, "a glowing pinecone's seeds will not light up for just anyone. They only resonate with auras that have an extremely high amount of magical power in them. If we're talking about contestants from the mage tournament, I doubt that anyone other than the four sages would have enough magical power for a pinecone to start glowing in their hands. You'd need pure blind luck to discover a glowing pinecone if you can't even make them glow when you touch them. If you don't believe me, you can pass that pinecone seed between yourselves. I guarantee you that none of you will be able to make it glow."

We do as she says and we pass the pinecone seed between ourselves, to see if anyone is able to make it light up. Unfortunately, it seems that Melindra was right, and none of us have anywhere near the required level of magical power to make the seed glow.

"So," Daren says, as he hands Melindra back her pinecone seed, "am I to understand that what you will be offering us in exchange for the assassination will be one of these glowing pinecones?"

"Oh, no, no, no," Melindra says. "I never managed to get hold of a pinecone. I was lucky enough to find a few seeds on the ground near the border of a sacred forest, while I was on my way here. I wouldn't dare to venture any deeper into one of those forests in order to find an actual pinecone. The golden fox hates my guts!"

"But why would you need to go into a sacred forest to find a pinecone?" I say. "Couldn't you just get it from somewhere else?"

"You can't get glowing pinecones from anywhere else," Melindra says. "They only grow in the sacred forests, which are all territories of the golden fox."

"Oh, no!" Hadrik shouts. "No way! We only just got out of there a few days ago, and now we need to go back? What is wrong with these organizers? It's like they don't want anyone to actually win this damn tournament!"

"So," Kate says, "if you're not going to give us a pinecone, and you aren't volunteering to guide us through the sacred forests either, what is it that you are trying to offer us, exactly?"

"Information!" Melindra says, smiling. "There is a device that has been made specifically to resonate with these pinecones, and it can make them glow without requiring a high amount of magical power, as long as you are close enough to them. It is a very rare device, but I know someone who has it, and I can lead you to them, after you help me with my goal. I can't tell you who this person is, but I am quite certain that I can convince them to lend you the device for a few days, which should be more than enough for you to find a pinecone."

"Why can't you tell us who this person is?" I say. "Is it someone we know?"

"I very much doubt that any of you have met this person before," Melindra says. "The reason why I can't divulge their identity is because they've specifically asked me to keep it a secret, if I ever need to mention them in a discussion. I wouldn't read too much into it if I were you. They're just the more secretive type. That's all there is to it."

"Right…" I say.

"So, do we have a deal, then?" Melindra asks us.

"I'm sorry, Melindra," Daren says, "but I can't just go around murdering people for the sole purpose of furthering my own goals. Even if my goal is ultimately to help the entire world, I cannot just kill a man for the simple reason that you want him dead."

"So it is a moral justification that you seek?" Melindra asks, with a look of curiosity in her eyes. "Well what if I tell you, then, that the person I want assassinated is a tyrant that has killed thousands of innocent people, and who is ruling his kingdom through fear and intimidation? Would that help to change your mind?"

"Who are you talking about, exactly?" Kate asks.

"Why, it's the brother of the man that you've only just killed a few days ago!" Melindra says. "The king of Ollendor."

"You want us to assassinate one of the kings of Varathia?" Hadrik asks, shocked. "Are you out of your mind? We've been put in an arena just for killing a noble, and you now want us to kill a king?"

"Oh, don't worry," Melindra says. "Ollendor never participated in the organization of this tournament. Nobody wants to talk to them. Even Golmyck is less hated by the other kings than the king of Ollendor. I assure you that none of the organizers would bat an eye if you were to raise a ruckus in his kingdom. The only reason why they threatened you with your disqualification from the mage tournament after killing the earl of Ollendor was because you were within the borders of Thilias when you murdered him. If you were to start going on a rampage in Ollendor, I very much doubt that anyone would give a damn. Well, except for the local authorities, of course."

"I'm uh… not sure what to say about this," I say.

"She's telling the truth," Leila writes. "Ollendor is something of a rogue kingdom these days. Neither the lessathi nor the other kings have any influence anymore on what happens within their borders. Everyone pretty much ignores them, and many of the kingdoms have already kicked their ambassadors out of their territories. This is why my father went there, after he escaped from

Thilias. Because it's a kingdom where nobody would be able to find him."

"See?" Melindra tells us, after she's done reading Leila's text. "There's nothing to worry about!"

"But isn't Ollendor really far away?" Daren says. "And then you also have to lead us to your friend that has the pinecone detector. That sounds like a lot of time wasted, when we're already three days behind every other participant of the tournament."

"So, what?" Melindra says. "It's not like anyone's made any progress since the objectives were announced. Nobody has any idea that the pinecones can only be found in the sacred forests. In fact, they are avoiding the fox's territories like the plague, because they don't want to deal with her, so the chances of them finding even one pinecone in the following week are almost nonexistent. Even when they'll finally figure out what they need to do, they'll still need to go against the golden fox. Without using a detector, I can't even imagine how they'd be able to sneak by unnoticed long enough to manage to test every pinecone by hand, so they will need to engage the fox and her followers directly, and I think you can imagine how that will go for them."

"I'm sorry, but I'm still not buying this," Kate says. "You are a stillwater. Why would you need our help to assassinate a king?"

"Because I came to Varathia as a tournament participant!" Melindra says. "It was the only way I could think of to get back to this place after that blasted king of Ollendor exiled me! But now the tournament's spell is preventing me from hurting any of the locals, so I've been stuck here since day one, trying to find someone who can do the job in my place."

"And what guarantee do we have that you'll fulfill your promise, once we've completed our task?" Daren asks. "Hell, what guarantee do we even have that you won't start acting like Eiden, and try killing us off for fun, in the middle of our journey? We already know that you've worked with him in the past."

"Oh, for crying out loud!" Melindra shouts, exasperated. "If you're so worried about my motives, then why don't you force me to take an oath? You're an enchanter, aren't you? Just make me swear that I'll fulfill my end of the bargain and that I won't try to hurt you, and we can be done with this."

"An enchanter's oath?" Daren asks her. "Are you serious? You do know that you'll die if you break such an oath, right?"

"Yes, of course I know that!" Melindra says.

"And you would want us to also make an oath that we won't bring harm to you during our journey?" Daren asks.

"Oh, no, you don't need to do that," Melindra says. "It's not like you could do anything against me, anyway."

"Huh…" Daren says.

He then turns towards us.

"What do you guys think?" Daren asks us. "Leaving aside her mildly infuriating, condescending remark from earlier, I'd say her deal is actually beginning to not sound so bad, all things considered. At the very least, I'm not getting the feeling that she's trying to cheat us, and we'll also get to save a kingdom in the process."

"Well…" Hadrik says. "I can't say that toppling a kingdom is something I've had the opportunity of doing before, and it would also make for a pretty good story when I'm out drinking in taverns… It certainly sounds more fun than looking for pinecones, that's for sure!"

"I'll admit that if we take everything she said into consideration," Kate says, "her way of doing things may actually give us an advantage over the other participants, especially since the contest seems to have been rigged from the very beginning to only allow the four sages to move on to the next round."

"Yeah, what's up with that, anyway?" Hadrik says. "I can't say that I was aiming to win the tournament, but this is still making me pretty pissed. Why did they even invite the other mages, if they weren't planning to give them a fair chance? Was it all just for show?"

"You are forgetting," Illuna says, "that the condition for passing this round is to bring the pinecones to the city of Galamir. This means that the sages can still be attacked on their way to the city, and the pinecones can be stolen from them. So, if you are strong or resourceful enough to be able to take an item from a sage, you can still pass to the next round, even if you don't have sufficient power to make the pinecone glow. Plus, you also have the option to join the team of one of the sages, if they accept you. In other words, there's more than one way to pass this round, but they all require dealing with the sages somehow. If you want to avoid the sages, then the pinecone detector will likely be your best option."

"Well, I don't know about you guys," I say, "but I'm personally looking forward to causing a little mayhem in the homelands of the ambassador of Ollendor. It would feel pretty good to finally get some payback after all he's put us through in the arena. And besides, Ollendor is practically going to become Leila's new home, soon, so we may as well do some cleaning up before she moves in."

Leila looks a little taken aback by my last comment. I think this is the first time when she actually realizes that she won't need to part ways with us, now that the arena is over.

"You will be coming with us to Ollendor, right?" I ask her.

"Yes!" Leila writes, smiling happily. "Yes, of course!"

"Well, if everyone's on board with this," Daren says, "then we'll get started with the enchanter's oath right away. Does anyone have any suggestions for things that we should not forget to include in this oath? So far, Melindra has agreed to vow that she won't cause any harm to us, and that she won't back out of the deal after we've fulfilled our end of the bargain, but maybe there's something else we need to add, to make sure that the deal is made in good faith?"

"Yeah," I say. "Melindra should swear that her friend with the device won't try to hurt us, either."

"Good thinking!" Daren says. "The fact that she won't hurt us herself is meaningless if she's just planning to lead us into a trap."

"Uh…" Melindra says. "I'm not sure how much I can vouch for my 'friend', but what I could do is to guarantee that I won't let them bring any harm to you, and we could also make it so that our deal will not be considered done until I leave you somewhere safe, with the device in your arms."

"Sounds good," Daren says.

Once Daren makes sure that nobody else has any suggestions, he takes out his sword, and he lightly cuts one of the fingers from Melindra's left hand with it. Melindra then sprinkles some of the blood dripping from her finger on top of the sword, and the weapon begins to shine brightly, with a white light.

"Is it working?" Melindra says. "Can I say the oath?"

"Yes, the spell is working," Daren says. "You may begin."

"Okay," Melindra says. "So, first of all, I swear that I'm not going to harm any of you."

"You… do know how this works, right?…" Daren tells her. "If you don't specify a duration, the oath becomes life-binding. If I accept your vow like this, you won't be able to harm us for the rest of your life!"

"Listen," Melindra says, while pointing her finger at Daren. "If we're all just going to keep doubting each other, we won't get anywhere. Just accept the vow, will you?"

"Well… okay, I guess…" Daren says, as he puts one of his hands over the sword, and the white light begins to flicker.

"Wait, wait, hold on!" Melindra says.

"Seriously?" Daren says. "I barely managed to cancel the vow in time. What is it?"

"Can I change the word 'harm' to 'inflict serious injuries'?" Melindra says. "I wouldn't want to get killed for patting someone on the back."

"This is an enchanter's oath!" Daren says. "When you say harm, it's going to actually mean harm. Patting someone on the back or smacking them over the head is out of the question. And besides, you'll get ample warning if the spell considers that you are crossing the line. You won't be able to trigger it accidentally."

"Oh," Melindra says. "Well, in that case, carry on."

As soon as Daren is done confirming the first vow, he urges Melindra to continue with her second vow.

"Okay, uh…" Melindra says. "I swear that as soon as you kill the king of Ollendor, I will begin leading you towards the person who has the pinecone detector that I told you about earlier, and I will not take any breaks unless you specifically ask me to."

"That's not enough," Daren says. "You also need to swear that as soon as you're done leading us to this person, you will personally guarantee that they lend us the device, and that the deal will not be considered over until this device is actually in our hands."

"Fine," Melindra says. "I swear it."

Daren moves his hand over the sword again, confirming Melindra's second vow.

"For your third, and final vow," Daren says, "do you

swear that you will guarantee our safety from your friend with the device or any of their associates if they try to attack us, and that our deal will not be over until you've left us somewhere safe, with the pinecone detector in our arms?"

"Yes, I swear," Melindra says.

Daren moves his hand over the sword one last time, and then the light from the sword slowly begins to fade, until his weapon returns to normal.

"Is that it?" Melindra asks. "Are we done?"

"Yes," Daren says. "The oath is done."

"Perfect!" Melindra says, regaining her smile. "So I'm guessing that your team will consist of you, the ice mage, the girl with the banshee, the giant shapeshifting as a dwarf, and…"

Melindra stops suddenly, just as she was about to point towards me, and then she starts simply staring at me, without saying anything.

"The dwarf was a giant?…" Leila writes, surprised, but we are all too focused on the stillwater girl to pay attention to her writing.

Melindra starts heading towards me, with her eyebrows furrowed in concentration, and she stops less than one foot away from me, studying me closely.

"Hmm…" Melindra says, with a pondering look, as she studies me from head to toe.

Seeing the girl up-close, I can't help but notice that she has a rather cute face, which is nicely complemented by her light-brown hair that she wears in a high ponytail. The pajama-like clothes that she is wearing in broad daylight may look a bit ridiculous at first sight, but unlike Eiden's clothes, the ones that Melindra is wearing seem to have been chosen with a bit more care, from an aesthetical point of view. Also, unlike regular pajamas, while these clothes definitely look comfortable to move in, they also seem to have been designed to fit in a way that highlights the slim frame of her body and the shape of her breasts.

"Hmm…" Melindra says again, this time bringing her face much closer to mine, with the same pondering look in her eyes, as she strokes her chin with her right hand.

"Is there something you—" I start to say, but the girl interrupts me.

"Turn around!" she says.

Melindra does not wait for me to turn around, and she grabs me by the shoulders, turning me around by herself. After a few more seconds of silence, the stillwater girl finally seems to have found what she was looking for, and she gasps loudly, in astonishment.

"What?" I ask her, as I turn to face her. "What is it?"

"You're a half-lessathi, aren't you?" Melindra says, with a mixture of shock and excitement in her voice. "That's why your aura seemed so familiar! I'm a half-lessathi too! It's so nice to finally meet someone of my own race after all this time! There used to be thousands of us before the still winter, but the lessathi have gotten much stricter with their rules since then, and there aren't very many of them left either, so you barely get to see any half-lessathi these days."

She pauses.

"Wait," she says. "So that's why Eiden has taken an interest in your group!"

"What do you mean?" I say. "What's so special about me being a half-lessathi? Does it have anything to do with my stat device?"

"Oh, no," Melindra says. "Not with your stat device."

"Then with what?" I say.

"I'm sure you'll figure it out eventually!" Melindra says.

"You stillwaters sure like being cryptic, don't you?" I ask her.

Melindra smiles, but she does not answer my rhetorical question.

"Still, I'm surprised that you managed to get hold of a stat device," Melindra says. "I was also curious to see what effect a stat device would have in a tournament like this, given my half-lessathi aura, so I tried to buy one before coming here, but there weren't any for sale anywhere I looked!"

"On which continent?" I ask. "I bought mine in the Western Continent. Where I come from, you can pretty much find these on every corner of the street."

"I tried looking in the Western Continent as well," Melindra says. "In more than one city. All of the shop owners told me that they went out of stock several weeks before I tried to make my purchase."

"Actually, now that you mention it…" I say. "I also had a bit more trouble than I expected when I tried to buy my stat booster. I even had to visit several shops before I could find one, and that was more than a month ago. In fact, I remember many of the shop owners being very evasive when I asked them when they would replenish their stocks. It seemed almost as if they were afraid to talk about it. Do you think that these merchants might have been lying about their stock, because they'd been threatened by someone who did not want them to be selling the devices anymore?"

"Never mind, that!" Melindra says. "Could you lend me your stat device for a moment? I'm curious to see how well it resonates with my aura!"

"Sure, I guess…" I say. "But don't mess with it too much. I'm still not perfectly sure that there isn't a secret combination of buttons, capable of erasing all of my stats, if I'm not careful. "

"Of course!" Melindra says. "I only need to do one test, and then you can have it back."

I take the device out of my pocket and I hand it to

her. After she looks at it for a few seconds, Melindra begins to press the side buttons of the device, multiple times, in quick succession.

"Hey, what are you doing?" I ask her, as I panic a little. "You promised that you wouldn't—"

"Shhh!" Melindra tells me, with a very serious look on her face.

After a few seconds of silence, Melindra hands me back the device, looking rather displeased.

"It's not working," she says. "Or rather, it's working as badly as I'd expect it to work for someone of a non-lessathi race. I suppose that my aura has changed too much since I became a stillwater for the device to recognize me as a half-lessathi anymore. Too bad."

"What were you doing just now?" I ask Melindra. "I saw you fiddling with the stat device's buttons, but nothing seems to have changed."

"Oh," Melindra says. "I just used a code to increase the hearing stat temporarily by a few points, in order to see if my actual hearing sense improves or not. It's meant to be used as a test, to see how well the stat device reacts to your aura before you start using it. The code only works for the hearing stat, and it can only be activated once per day, for a few seconds."

"Can you give me the code?" I ask her.

"Sure," Melindra says. "It's three times left, three times right, two times left, four times right, then left right left right. Oh, and you need to do it within five seconds, or the code won't activate."

"Three left, three right, two left, four right, left right left right, got it!" I say. "Thanks a lot!"

"You're welcome!" Melindra says.

"Excuse me," Leila writes, as she pulls lightly on Melindra's sleeve.

"Yes?" Melindra says, looking at Leila, curiously.

"I have a question," Leila writes. "Are you able to

tell the difference between lessathi and half-lessathi just by the feel of their aura?"

"Yes," Melindra says. "I've met enough half-lessathi in my lifetime to be able to make the distinction. You need to have a pretty keen magical sense to notice the difference, though."

"Could you…" Leila starts to write, but she pauses for a few seconds.

"Could you tell me if I'm a half-lessathi as well?" Leila continues.

"A half-lessathi?" Melindra asks, surprised.

She gets closer to Leila and she furrows her eyebrows, like she did with me, earlier.

"Hmm…" Melindra says, while she studies her for a few seconds. "No, you're definitely not a half-lessathi. This is a regular lessathi aura any way I look at it."

"I see…" Leila writes, with a faint smile on her face. "Thank you for your answer!"

Seeing her relieved smile, I suddenly remember the story she told me about the lessathi from her youth that treated her like some kind of reject because she was mute, and who were accusing her of being a half-lessathi, due to her disability. It seems that those people's slander had in fact affected her a lot more than she let on until now.

"Well," Melindra says, as she turns to the rest of us, "I believe that we're done for the day! If nobody else has any objections, I would very much like it if we could begin our journey tomorrow, at the crack of dawn."

"Actually," Daren says, "we still need to get some papers from the king, before we can leave the city. We'll be visiting him later today, but it's not guaranteed that he'll have them ready by the time we get there. Hold on!"

Daren takes his backpack off, and he pulls a transceiver out of it, which he then hands over to

Melindra.

"We'll contact you through this transceiver in case our plans change," Daren says. "Don't worry about the range. It's been enchanted to cover very long distances, so we'll be able to contact you no matter where you are in the city."

"Okay, then," Melindra says, as she puts the transceiver in one of her pockets. "If nothing changes, then we'll meet at the city's northern gate, as soon as the sun rises. We'll need to head north to reach Ollendor anyway, so we might as well meet at the gate that's closest to our destination."

"Sounds good," Daren says.

"I'll see you all tomorrow!" Melindra says, with a smile, and then she goes on her way.

"Damn it!" I say, as I watch her leave. "She still didn't tell us how you can become a stillwater."

"You'll have all the time you need to ask her that question starting tomorrow," Daren says. "We'll be travelling together for a while, remember?"

"Oh, right…" I say.

"Anyway," Daren says, "we should probably be heading for the palace. The king seemed rather busy, and I'm not sure how long he'll be waiting for us."

"He told me that we should wait for about an hour before heading for the palace," I say, "because he still had to arrange a few things with his army. I suggest we do some shopping in the meantime. I've seen plenty of shops while we were walking between the palace and the arena, and we won't really get any other chance to buy stuff for a very long time after we leave Thilias."

"Yeah, that would probably be for the best," Daren says.

"Well," Enrique says, "since it's been settled that you'll be spending the night in Thilias, I believe that there will no longer be any objections to the celebration tonight, yes?"

Daren sighs.

"Do as you wish," he says.

"Perfect!" Enrique says. "I know some of the best cooks in Thilias, and there are still plenty of expensive wine bottles left in the cellar. Tonight, we shall have a feast that will put the king's royal banquets to shame!"

"Just make sure you don't overdo it," Daren says. "We'll be leaving before sunrise, so we can't afford to stay up until too late in the evening."

Once we wave goodbye to Enrique, we start heading towards the castle of Thilias, at a leisurely pace. As soon as we set out, Arraka starts making muffled noises again, from inside her amulet.

"What is it, Arraka?…" Flower says, as she opens the amulet.

"I can't believe the nerve on that girl!" Arraka shouts, with her voice sounding like three separate voices talking at the same time again. "Did you see what she did? She just closed my amulet without even so much as a 'hello'! Is that any way to act with someone that you've known for hundreds of years?"

"You know, I've always meant to ask," I say, to Arraka. "What's up with that voice of yours? Most of the time it sounds normal, but there are times when it sounds as if there are three of you talking at the same time. Is that what happens when banshees get old?"

"Oh, no, it has nothing to do with age," Arraka says. "Those two other voices are from the first two spirits that I absorbed, while I was still in the magical plane. Uh… Elkira and Rinaru, I think?… It's been too long. I don't remember their names that clearly anymore."

"The first two spirits?" I say. "You mean that you've absorbed more than two spirits while you were on the magical plane?"

"Oh, yeah, I've absorbed hundreds of them," Arraka

says. "The method that I used for absorbing other spirits was still experimental when I used it on Elkira and Rinaru, which is why their voices still pop up from time to time, even after all those thousands of years. I didn't have any more problems with absorbing all of the other spirits, though."

"But, didn't the other spirits try to stop you?" I ask her.

"Of course they did," Arraka says. "But I was only getting stronger with each spirit that I absorbed, and by the time the really strong spirits figured out what I was doing, I was already too much for them to handle."

"Is this the reason why you got banned from the magical plane?" I say.

"Eh…" Arraka says. "It was probably part of the reason. Mostly it was because of my murdering sprees, I think."

"Murdering sprees?…" I say.

"Yeah," Arraka says. "There isn't really much to do in the magical plane. Most of the spirits tend to just live for the sole purpose of maintaining their existence. It's pretty uncommon for a spirit from the magical plane to die of old age, so as long as you don't do anything too risky, you could theoretically go on living forever. That's why it's so hilarious to kill a spirit in the magical plane. On the earthen plane, most living beings will expect to die at some point, but the great majority of the spirits on the magical plane fancy themselves as immortals. The desperation with which they cling to life in their final moments cannot be compared with that of any being on this plane of existence, which is what makes it all the more satisfying when you do them in."

"So, what did the gods have to say about all of this?" I say. "Didn't you say that they live on the magical plane too? Why couldn't they just unite against you in order to kill you off?"

"Hah!" Arraka says. "You don't think they tried? The 'gods' are nothing special. They're just magical spirits like the rest of us. They only started calling themselves that after they found out that they could harness energy from the beings on the earthen plane, as long as they made them into their loyal followers. Once they gained enough followers, all of that worshipping went to their heads, and they began to call themselves gods, as if they were somehow more special than the rest of us. All of their 'godly' powers that they gained from their worshippers still didn't help them when I killed half of their kind by myself, though."

"You killed half of the gods on the magical plane?" I ask her.

"Yeah, but to be fair, it was mostly the weaker ones, who didn't have that many followers," Arraka says. "The stronger ones like the God of Death, the God of Fate and the God of Time managed to hold their own against me pretty well, so we went on a bit of a stalemate for some time, while I went to absorb more spirits, and they tried to gather more followers."

"Was this when they decided to ban you from the magical plane?" I ask her.

"No, that decision came a bit later," Arraka says. "When they realized that they couldn't amass their followers with the speed that I was absorbing other spirits, they eventually called some sort of a meeting, where they invited all of the powerful spirits in the realm, including the ones who did not call themselves gods, like the golden fox, who was still in the magical plane at the time. In that meeting, they decided to ban me from their realm, along with every other female spirit that belonged to what you people call 'civilized races' here on the earthen plane. You know, like humans, elves, gnomes and the like."

"Wait, you have different races in the magical

plane?" I say.

"Not just different races," Arraka says. "They're the exact same races that you have here on the earthen plane. Including the monster races and the animal races, of course. It's not like we have bodies or anything, but you can tell our races from our auras, just like you can on this plane of existence."

"So… does this mean that our spirits will go to the magical plane after we die?" I say.

"Nah," Arraka says. "You don't have spirits. You only have souls. When you die, the ethereal matter that makes up your soul gets decomposed and it melds with the rest of the ethereal plane. The same goes for the souls of us, magical spirits. It's possible that the souls which get decomposed after you die somehow get recycled and then they get linked with a newborn spirit from the magical plane, but that's just a theory. None of the spirits on the magical plane have any sort of memories from past lives on the earthen plane, or anything like that."

"You were saying earlier that the fox originated from the magical plane?" Hadrik says. "How did she end up here, then?"

"Why don't you ask her yourself?" Arraka says. "You're friends with her now, aren't you?"

" 'Friends' isn't exactly the word I'd use to describe our relationship with her," I say.

"Well, the only thing I know," Arraka says, "is that even before I got banned from the magical plane, the fox seemed to have taken a great interest in the animals that lived here, in Varathia. They were much more intelligent than the animals on the other continents, for some reason, and from what I've heard, the fox always talked about how unfairly these animals from Varathia were being treated on the earthen plane. I'm not sure when she decided to come here, but from what I could tell, she must have made a pact with all of the plants and animals from the region, so they would join together in some sort of a symbiotic relationship that would help her maintain a physical body, in exchange for her offering them protection. I don't really know more than that, since I've been trapped in a mountain while all of this happened."

"So, uh…" I say. "Getting back to your exile from the magical plane… do you know why the gods and the other powerful spirits decided to also ban the other female spirits and not just you?"

"Oh," Arraka says, "it's because I was only absorbing female spirits from the so-called 'civilized races', which made them think that there was something dangerous about the others too, and that they could turn out like me if left alone for too long. In reality, the only reason why I was absorbing just these types of spirits was because they were the only ones that had auras similar enough to mine for me to be able to absorb them, given that I'm an elf. There was nothing special about the spirits I was absorbing. The 'danger' of someone coming up with the same absorption technique as I did is still there, even after they threw us all out, but I wouldn't expect them to invent anything similar anytime soon, since they're way too stupid to come up with a spell that's so complex on their own."

"Wait, you're an elf?" I ask her.

"Of course I'm an elf!" Arraka says. "What did you think I was?"

"Well, I don't know," I say. "I always kind of figured that banshees were their own race, and I didn't really give it much thought until now."

"Banshees aren't a race!" Arraka says. "It's just a name that was given to us by the locals after we got banished to the earthen realm. You can clearly tell what our races are from our auras. Seriously, how bad is your magical sense, anyway? Illuna is an elf too, but I bet you didn't know that either, did you?"

"Petal's an elf?" Flower asks, shocked.

"Why are you acting so surprised?" Illuna says. "You have a clear image of how I look inside your own mind. Don't tell me that this is the first time you've noticed my pointy ears in the past two decades..."

"Oh, I've noticed them," Flower says, "but I always figured that this was just the way I imagined you, and that it didn't have anything to do with the way you really looked."

"So," I say, "you're telling me that we've been treating you two as if you were part of a monster race, but all this time you were in fact elven spirits?"

"Yes, that's what we are saying," Illuna says.

"It never ceases to amaze me just how bad these people can be at reading auras," Arraka says. "No wonder they still haven't figured out why their women can't be born as mages after all this time. If they can't even tell our races apart, then they have no chance of figuring it out by themselves."

"Did you..." I say, but I pause for a few moments to rearrange my thoughts. "Did you just imply that the reason why women cannot be born as mages on our earthen plane is directly related to your exile from the magical plane?"

After hearing my last sentence, Kate, who didn't seem to be paying very close attention to our conversation until now, has finally turned her head towards us, and she is now watching us intently.

"So you finally figured it out, eh, Barry-boy?" Arraka says. "What is it that tipped you off? Is it perhaps the fact that all of the banshees are practically humanoid female spirits? Or maybe the fact that female animals and monsters can still cast magic, while your women are completely unable to do it, unless their auras have been drastically altered? Oh... or maybe it's the fact that women only gain magic when they are possessed by banshees. That's a pretty big hint, if you ask me! Hell, you even had Flower as an example. Her element is fire, while Illuna's element is water. It's clear that she didn't just inherit the magic from Illuna, right? Didn't it ever occur to you that in order to channel that energy from the magical plane, you need to actually create a link with a magical spirit that is at least somewhat similar to you, in nature? You didn't seriously think that you could just pull that energy out on your own, without some magical spirit to act as a funnel for you, did you?"

"So," I say, "what you are saying is that every one of the mages on the earthen plane is in fact linked with a spirit from the magical plane?"

"Well, yeah, but it's not like either of them is doing it consciously," Arraka says. "Since they're on different planes of existence, the link does not need to be all close and personal. Most mages probably just link themselves to a spirit instinctively, and neither them, nor the spirits that they are linked to ever notice this for the rest of their lives. But you can't link yourself unconsciously with a spirit anymore if all of the spirits with similar auras to you are here, on the earthen plane instead. You can still try to cast magic through other means, sure, but then your aura would need to become something completely different. Like that of the stillwater girl, for example. Or that of your friend with the ice magic."

"But how did these spirits manage to exile you to a completely different plane of existence?" I say. "Surely, it can't have been as simple as just throwing you out and locking the door behind you!"

"Oh, the exile was Memphir's idea, from what I've heard," Arraka says. "He always did have the talent to come up with crazily elaborate plans like these, even though only half of them usually worked out in his favor in the end."

"Memphir is the God of Fate, right?" I say.

"Yeah, the one with the illusions," Arraka says. "I'm not sure how he came up with the idea, or how he managed to actually convince so many of the spirits to follow his plan, but what they basically did was to mess with the whole system that is in charge of assigning spirits to the magical plane, and they reprogrammed it in a way that assigns female spirits of the civilized races to the earthen plane instead."

"You can do that?" I say.

"Well, obviously it's not easy," Arraka says. "And you need a tremendous amount of energy to pull it off even if you figure out how to do it, but the bastards managed to rally enough of the spirits on their side to actually get the job done."

"So, why didn't you just change it back to how it was, after they sent you here?" I say. "Shouldn't you have more than enough energy to do it after absorbing all of those spirits?"

"I can't do it from here!" Arraka says. "That's why we're stuck. If I were to undo everything that Memphir and his crew did, I'd need to access the Magium directly, and I can't do that from the earthen plane."

"The Magium?..." I ask her.

"Well, not really the Magium," Arraka says. "You get what I mean..."

"No..." I say. "I don't, actually..."

"You know..." Arraka says. "I'm talking about the part of the Magium that specifically deals with the creation of magical spirits and then sends them to the magical plane. You know how it works, right? Spirits aren't made to reproduce, even if they are split into males and females like you are here on the earthen plane. That's why there's this sort of... nest, or whatever you want to call it within the Magium that makes sure to pump out new spirits and to send them to the magical plane after the old ones die, in order to have roughly the same amount of spirits on the magical plane at any given time. Except these bastards managed to change the way it works! As soon as they were done tampering with the nest, it even sent the ones of us who were already there to the earthen plane, not to mention all the new ones that were created after that. And even from Varathia, the only parts of the Magium that I can access are the ones that I don't need!"

"Other parts of the Magium?..." I say, confused. "I don't get it. Just how big is this Magium, exactly? Wasn't it supposed to be some sort of a powerful artifact that's only found here in Varathia?"

Arraka takes a long break before she speaks again, during which we all wait for her answer in silence.

"Did..." she says, struggling to find her words. "Did you just ask me how big the Magium is?"

"Yeah, that's what I said," I say.

After another short pause, Arraka suddenly begins to laugh, louder than she's ever laughed before, and she keeps on going for about ten seconds before she speaks again.

"Hey..." Arraka says, while she's almost out of breath from laughing, "Hey, Illuna, did you... Did you hear what he said? He asked how big the Magium is! Aha- Ahahahaha!"

"Stop laughing, damn it!" I say, as I finally snap. "Tell me what you know about the Magium!"

"Ahahahaha!" Arraka says. "You came here to fight for the Magium, but you don't even know what it is? Oh, man, that's rich! I'd be crying from laughter if I weren't living in an amulet without a body. I can't believe you people... You actually... You actually came here without even... Ahahahaha!"

"Knock it off!" I tell her. "Are you going to tell me what the Magium is or not?"

Arraka ignores me completely and she just keeps laughing and laughing, without giving signs of planning to stop anytime soon.

"Do you want me to spin your amulet until you give me my answer?" I say.

"Are you sure you want to do that, Barry-boy?" Arraka says, as she suddenly stops from her laughter and starts speaking in a much more serious tone. "Do you really think that you will never need my help anymore from now on? Do you really like being surprised by invisible enemies that much?"

"Let it go, Barry," Daren says, as he places a hand on my shoulder. "If she doesn't want to tell us, then no amount of spinning is going to make her change her mind. We'll just have to find out what the Magium is on our own."

"I know what the Magium is!" Flower says.

"You do?" I ask her.

"Yeah," Flower says.

"Well, what is it?" I say.

"Oh, I can't tell you that!" Flower says.

"Why the hell not?" I say.

"Because I'm not allowed to," Flower says, simply.

"Not allowed by whom?" I ask her. "The kings? Are the kings of Varathia prohibiting you from revealing the true nature of the Magium to the tournament participants?"

"I… can't answer that question," Flower says, looking a bit uncomfortable.

"But why?" I say. "What will happen if you tell us about the Magium?"

"We'll die," Illuna says, bluntly.

"You mean that they'll send someone to execute you?" I say.

"No, I mean we'll drop dead," Illuna says. "On the spot. Quite possibly even before we get to tell you what the Magium actually is."

"What do you mean?" Hadrik asks Illuna. "Why would you drop dead just from answering a question?"

"She's saying that they're under an enchanter's oath," Daren says. "They've probably been made to vow that they won't reveal the nature of the Magium to anyone. Either by the kings or by someone else. They're likely risking death even with what little they're already telling us. We should stop questioning them about this before Flower accidentally lets slip too much information and kills them both by accident."

"Damn it," Hadrik says. "I thought that we were actually onto something for a second there."

"Why are you acting so disappointed?" Daren says. "It's not like you were ever aiming to win the Magium. You've already told us that you're only in this for the challenge."

"Well, yeah," Hadrik says, "but imagine the stories we could tell if we managed to get our hands on the Magium before the end of the tournament!"

"It's not going to happen," Daren says. "Even if we find out what it is, it's probably too well guarded or too well hidden for us to be able to do anything about it. We should be focusing on our objectives, and not on trying to cheat the system. Come on, let's get moving. We still need to do some shopping before we go to the king."

As we continue to travel towards the castle, we notice that Leila and Kate are walking side by side, but they've hardly been exchanging any words since we left the arena. After a while, Daren pulls me to the back of the group, where he and Hadrik are walking at a slower pace, and he asks me a question, in a low voice.

"Hey, Barry," Daren says, "correct me if I'm wrong, but aren't Kate and the white haired girl supposed to be childhood friends or something?"

"Sort of," I say. "They both grew up at the Beacon,

but from what I've heard, Leila was more isolated from the rest of the group, due to her being a lessathi."

"Still," Daren says, "if they've known each other for so long, don't you think that they should have a little more to talk about? Maybe we could give them a push or something. You know, help them out a bit so they can get over the initial awkwardness."

"I say we wait a little more," I tell Daren. "Neither of them are exactly the talkative sort, and Leila is mute to boot. We should give them a bit more time to get comfortable around each other before we butt in."

"You know, I was thinking," Hadrik tells me, "if Leila is a lessathi, then shouldn't you be giving her Eiden's message? The one about the still winter?"

"Hey, you're right!" I tell him. "I'll tell her right now!"

"Barry…" Daren starts to say, but I ignore him and I call out to Leila.

"Hey, Leila!" I shout.

"Yes?…" Leila writes, as she turns around to face me.

"I've got a message from Eiden," I say.

"Eiden?" Leila writes. "You mean the stillwater who threatened the dragon in the arena?"

"Yeah, that's him!" I say. "He says to remember the still winter!"

"Uh… okay?" Leila writes, looking very confused.

"Ignore him, Leila," Kate says. "Barry's just being an idiot again."

Leila then turns around, and Kate starts filling her in on the details regarding Eiden, and what my message meant.

"Damn it, Barry!" Daren says, in a low voice. "Don't you think you should be taking this message thing a little more seriously? We almost died because of it the last time Eiden brought it up."

"Relax," I whisper to Daren. "My deal with Eiden is already off. I was supposed to deliver his message to the first lessathi I encountered, remember? The first lessathi I met were Diane's friends. The reason why Eiden almost killed us was exactly because I failed to uphold my end of the bargain. The fact that he got over it so quickly and that he never actually killed us, shows that he never really cared about that deal in the first place. If he really wanted that message delivered, he could have just teleported next to the lessathi and told them the message himself, given that he already recognized their auras from a distance when I met them. Realistically speaking, Eiden probably already forgot about that message, and he'll never mention it to us again."

"I hope you're right…" Daren says.

"At any rate," I say, "my joke from earlier was not made without a reason. Look!"

I then point towards Kate and Leila, who are still engaged in conversation, except the subject of their talk seems to have changed from Eiden and his plans to how much of an idiot I am.

"See?" I tell Daren, in a low voice. "Now they have something to talk about!"

Half an hour after our conversation, we reach the first marketplace on our way to the castle. We decide to split up into separate groups and to meet again in the center of the marketplace once we're each done with our shopping. While Kate goes together with Leila in order to help her buy some new clothes and a backpack, Daren and I head for the weapons shop, so I can buy myself a new crossbow and so that Daren can buy a new magical sharpening stone. In the meantime, Flower and Illuna went to buy some potions, while Hadrik, who did not need to buy anything in particular, went directly towards the center of the market, waiting for us to be done.

Before we enter the shop, I show Daren my scimitars,

while asking him if he could tell me what enchantments are cast on them, and if he could estimate the market value of the items.

"Hmm..." Daren says. "Both of these seem to have the same two enchantments. Sharpness and durability. However, the enchantments were done almost exclusively by using elven steel, and the craftsmanship of the weapons is also of high quality. If I were you, I wouldn't sell one of these for less than fifty western gold coins."

Once we are inside the weapons shop, the first thing I do is to approach the shopkeeper about my scimitars. It takes a bit of haggling, but in the end I manage to convince him to buy one of the two weapons for seventy gold coins, while keeping the other one for myself. As soon as I am done with the selling, I immediately move over to the crossbow section, to see if I can find anything that would fit my needs. What I am looking for in particular are repeating crossbows that can fire at least five bolts before being reloaded, like the one I'm currently using.

Two of the crossbows on display catch my eye, and they are both much better than the one I've got, but one of them is a lot more expensive than the other. With the amount of money I have right now, however, it honestly would not make much of a difference if I bought one or the other.

The advantage of the expensive one is that I can use it to shoot seven bolts before reloading, and it also has better power, range, and accuracy. The cheaper version is still better than the crossbow I have in every way, but it's not really comparable to the expensive one, and it can only fire six bolts before reloading.

After careful consideration, I decide to go with the expensive crossbow, even if I still can't shake the feeling that I'm getting slightly ripped off. Once we're done buying what we need, I put my new crossbow inside my backpack, and then Daren and I exit the shop, heading directly for the middle of the marketplace. As we walk, I suddenly remember that there was something else I needed to buy while I'm still in town, so I tell Daren to go ahead, and I go to enter the potions shop.

"Barry?" Flower asks, as she sees me enter the building. "Didn't you go to buy some weapons?"

"Yeah," I say. "But I remembered that I also had something to buy from here."

"What are you buying?" Flower asks.

"…An anti-poison elixir," I say, a little embarrassed.

Flower's eyes turn blue, and Illuna just stares at me for a few seconds, without saying anything.

"Remember to also get an anti-disease elixir while you're at it," Illuna says, finally. "They're more expensive than anti-poison ones, and they only work for certain, easily curable illnesses, but still, it would be rather pathetic if you were to die from some Varathian disease after having survived the tournament for so long."

I pay the shopkeeper ten copper pieces for the anti-poison elixir and a silver coin for the anti-disease elixir, and then I drink them both while I'm still inside the shop. Illuna does the same for all the potions she's bought, and then we both exit the building, heading towards the middle of the marketplace, where Hadrik and Daren were waiting for us. As we approach them, I notice that the two of them are in the middle of a rather heated debate about who would be the winner in a duel between Azarius, the Sage of the West, and Talmak, the Sage of the North.

"Listen," Hadrik tells Daren, as we get closer, "I know that Azarius can cast a lot of spells. That's not the point. What I'm saying is that in terms of raw power, Talmak is way above the Sage of the West. Plus, he's an earth elementalist! What use are a bunch of spells, when he's just going to crush you between two huge layers of rock?"

"Hadrik," Daren says, "I get that you're trying to take Talmak's side because he's a dwarf, but that's just not how things work in a magic duel. You can't win a fight through raw power alone. You need to have some versatility. As a generalist, Azarius can use spells of many different types, which makes his attacks a lot more unpredictable. Specialists will always be at a disadvantage when fighting against generalists for this reason. That's why I tried my best to master both enchantment and white magic, during my lifetime. Limiting myself to only one specialization would have given me far less options when fighting against other trained mages."

"Oh, come on!" Hadrik says. "It's not like Talmak can only cast earth magic. You've seen him at the last year's sage contest. He can cast lightning magic too. And a whole bunch of other spells!"

"Yes," Daren says. "Basic spells. I never saw him cast any complex spells outside of his own specialization."

"Does it matter if they're simple spells?" Hadrik says. "He can just use his huge energy to boost them and then they'll be just as strong as the more complex spells!"

"That would just be a waste of magical energy!" Daren says. "There's a reason why more complex versions of the basic spells were invented. It's because they're cost-effective."

"Why would Talmak care about cost?" Hadrik says. "He has plenty of energy to spare. It's not like we've ever seen him run out of energy in a duel before. Hell, as far as we know, his magical regeneration abilities may well be high enough that he can gain his energy back before he even has a chance to spend it!"

"Ugh!" Daren says. "Barry, can you believe this guy? He's actually trying to make a case that Azarius would lose in a fight against Talmak!"

"Yeah, I honestly couldn't imagine Azarius ever losing in a fair fight," I say.

"Bah!" Hadrik says. "Asking Barry is cheating. He's from the Western Continent. Of course he'd root for Azarius."

"That's just not true!" Daren says. "I come from the Southern Continent, but if someone were to ask me who would win in a fight between Azarius and the Sage of the South, I'd still pick Azarius, hands down."

"Fine, fine…" Hadrik says. "Okay, I've got another one for you, then! Who do you think would win in a duel between Eiden and Arraka?"

"Didn't this fight already happen, though?" I say. "During the still winter, I mean. I'm pretty sure that Eiden ripped Arraka to shreds the last time they fought."

"Well, from what I've heard," Hadrik says, "the last time they've fought it was Eiden and the fox against Arraka, so it was a two on one fight."

"Yeah," I say, "but you're forgetting that Arraka was also fused with some other stillwater at the time. So it wasn't a two on one fight, it was a two on two fight. That's close enough to a duel for me. Like I said, Eiden mopped the floor with Arraka the last time they fought."

"Hey!" Arraka says. "*Hey*! What the hell are you talking about? Nobody mopped the floor with anyone! And Therius doesn't count! He was a weakling! You can't even compare him with the golden fox, let alone Eiden!"

"Yeah, right," I say. "If he was such a weakling, then how come you weren't even able to take over his body properly, during your awakening?"

"That has nothing to do with power, you idiot!"

Arraka says. "Didn't your friend tell you about ethereals? The guy had an overwhelming advantage while we were fighting in his own mind. In a fair fight I would have annihilated him! And the same goes for Eiden!"

"Uh-huh," I say. "You say that, but you still lost against him in the still winter."

"That's because Eiden uses tricks!" Arraka says. "In terms of raw power, I'm way stronger than him!"

"Who cares if you're technically stronger than him?" I say. "Fighting isn't just about strength. You also need to know how to use it."

"This isn't about him being more skilled than me, you moron!" Arraka says. "I'm saying that he's cheating! He isn't using magic the way you're supposed to!"

"What's that supposed to mean?" I say.

"Forget it!" Arraka says. "I'm not going to sit here and waste time explaining to you how magic works. Tell you what. Why don't you ask Eiden directly what I meant? He's been standing there invisibly right next to you for the past twenty seconds, so I'm sure he doesn't have anything better to do, at this time."

As soon as Arraka is done talking, Eiden dismisses his invisibility spell, while wearing his usual polite smile on his face, with his eyes closed.

"You just won't let me have any fun, will you, Arraka?" Eiden says.

"Again?" Daren asks Eiden. "Good gods! What will it take for you to stop stalking us?"

"There's no need to be so rude," Eiden says. "Especially when I came all the way here only to congratulate you on your magnificent performance in the arena!"

"Uh-huh," Hadrik says, not looking very convinced. "You sure that's the only reason why you came here?"

"Now that you mention it, there was another reason!" Eiden says. "You see, I couldn't help but notice that the direction in which you've been heading since you left the arena leads directly to the castle of Thilias. You wouldn't happen to be going there because the king Golmyck gave you some sort of a mission, would you?"

"What are you talking about?" Daren says, feigning ignorance. "We're only going to the palace to get some papers."

"Oh?" Eiden says, in a tone suggesting that he doesn't believe Daren at all. "Well, in either case, I just wanted to let you know that if the king happens to give you a mission that is in some way tied to the well-being of the citizens of Thilias, you shouldn't really bother to complete it."

"Why not?" Daren says.

"Because the city of Thilias will not be around for much longer," Eiden says. "And neither will any of the other cities in Varathia, for that matter."

"Wait, what…" Daren says, but he is having trouble continuing his sentence. "What are you saying?…"

"I'm saying that shortly before the end of this tournament," Eiden says, "there will be a calamity of such proportions that it will completely eradicate every single city on this island, at the same time."

"And you're telling me that you're just going to stand idly by and watch it happen?" Daren asks, shocked. "What is wrong with you? Aren't you supposed to be the creator of this continent?"

"Actually, that's a common misconception," Eiden says. "While the people of this land may call me the Creator, the island of Varathia has been around for much longer than my lifespan. The only reason why people started to call me the Creator all those years ago was because they wanted someone to replace the old Creator, to symbolize the beginning of a new age, and they chose me to take this role because I was practically the founder of the new civilization that came after the still winter, together with the golden fox. Oh, and I think you might have slightly misunderstood what I said earlier. I will by no means stand idly by while this calamity occurs. In fact, the eradication of these cities will happen as a direct result of my own actions."

"You bastard!" Daren says, with his eyes full of hatred. "I'm not going to let you do this!"

"Why, Daren," Eiden says, "I thought that you of all people would have every reason to be happy due to this turn of events! Weren't you the one who told me that as long as you never give up, you can find a way to save everyone? Well, I've found a way! A way to save them all from their misery. I assure you that a quick death would be a much better fate than most of these people deserve, and as for the rest—"

"Oh, shut up," I interrupt Eiden.

"Pardon?" Eiden asks me.

"I've had it with your crap," I say. "You're acting like a spoiled child throwing a tantrum. Whenever something doesn't go your way, you break all of the toys and make a mess of the playground, leaving the adults to clean up after you. You did the same thing with Olmnar. Is blowing up a city your standard solution to everything?"

Every one of my friends, including Daren, are looking way too shocked at my sudden outburst to be able to say anything, and they're all just staring at me in disbelief. Eiden is also looking directly at me, with his eyes closed, but his smile is now gone from his face.

"What are you getting at?" Eiden asks me, calmly.

"I'm saying," I say, "that there's no way you can just build an entire civilization like that almost by yourself, and then in the span of only a few hundred years, you simply stop caring about what happens to any of these people and you kill them off like it's nothing. This is just you refusing to admit your mistakes. You failed. You had all the power in the world, but you still couldn't achieve what you wanted. And instead of manning up and trying to fix things, what do you do? You just sweep it all under the rug as if none of this was your fault, and then you decide to end everything by your own hand, as if that would somehow make it better. Stop this, already. You are only making a fool of yourself."

"I've heard just about enough of this," Eiden says, in a dismissive tone. "You speak without even knowing the situation in which the other cities are in. Do you think that slavery and arenas are the real problems in Varathia? You have no idea what's going on in the other kingdoms. The levels to which some of these people have stooped are much lower than what you could ever imagine."

"So, what?" I say. "Aren't you their leader? Isn't it the leader's job to make sure that his people don't go on the wrong path? How did you even manage to let it come to this? Did you just leave them all to organize themselves without even the least bit of intervention? Hell, even I would have done a better job at keeping things under control, and I know nothing about politics."

"You're saying you could have prevented this if you had my powers?" Eiden says. "You, who could not even deliver a simple message?"

"No," I say. "I'm saying that I could have prevented this even if I had no powers at all! You, on the other hand had all the power you needed, but all you managed to do was make things worse. What was the deal with Olmnar, anyway? Did you think that by destroying that city, the fox would forgive you? Is that what you thought? Don't make me laugh! If you're seeking forgiveness, then how about you start by fixing everything you broke and by not being such a damn coward!"

Once I finish my sentence, Eiden frowns, and all of a sudden, everything around me freezes, just like that time when I first fought the dragon. He then starts slowly walking towards me, while everyone except the two of us is frozen in place. He's looking pretty pissed.

I decide to stand my ground and to look Eiden straight in the eyes, as he approaches me. When he gets about a foot away from me, he stops and he opens his eyes, looking at me with a very dark expression on his face.

"You know..." Eiden says. "It has been a very long while since someone's made me this angry. I'll have to hand it to you, Barry. You have a very unique talent at pushing people's buttons. Tell me, do you enjoy risking death with every possible opportunity? Do you really want to die that much?"

"You're not going to kill me," I say.

"Why not?" Eiden says.

"Because deep down, you know I'm right," I say. "Everything I said about you was true. Otherwise you wouldn't have gotten so pissed off about it. Killing me now would only serve to prove my point, and that's the last thing you want."

"You really do like to play with fire, don't you?" Eiden says. "I think what makes me the angriest is the fact that you actually believe what you are saying. You actually believe that you would have been able to accomplish the impossible... to change human nature, without even having access to any of my powers. Just what exactly is it that you are basing these claims on, I wonder?"

"I'm basing them," I say, "on the fact that I've already been trying to accomplish the impossible for the better part of my life! And unlike you, I have never even thought about giving up. I mean, look at me, damn it!

Look at where I am! Who would be stupid or stubborn enough to go so far just for the sake of some childhood dream? And yet, here I am."

I pause for a few seconds before I continue, but I keep looking Eiden straight in the eyes, during this time.

"I don't care about human nature," I say, after a while. "After seeing how the people here are perfectly okay with other human beings getting treated like cattle, and after seeing how they consider people dying in an arena to be a form of entertainment, I think I've seen enough to know that things here need to change. And if you're no longer going to do it, then I will. I don't care if I have the power to do it or not. I will do it. I already told you this once before. I am going to do everything that you couldn't do, despite your immense power, and then I'm going to come back and shove it all in your face."

While I was talking, some of the anger has slowly vanished from Eiden's eyes, and he now looks a bit calmer than before. I also noticed that he's been stretching his right arm to the side every once in a while ever since he stopped in front of me, but I have no idea for what reason.

"One of the benefits of being very good at reading auras," Eiden says, "is that you can tell at every point during a conversation not only if a person is lying, but also if they are hesitating in some way, from the fluctuations in their aura. The fact that you were neither lying nor being hesitant at any point during your speech just now is something that I find truly fascinating."

Eiden takes a few moments to consider his next words, while he stretches his right arm to the side once more.

"Here's what we're going to do," he says, as he closes his eyes again, and he slowly starts to walk back and forth, over a distance of a few feet. "Whether you want to or not, this tournament is going to require you to visit a certain number of cities. You already know that you'll be visiting Galamir, and since you've met Melindra, I'm going to assume that you'll also be visiting Ollendor soon enough. There may also be other cities, depending on what the tournament's organizers prepare for the next rounds. I'm going to be monitoring your activity in these cities from afar, to see how much you can manage to change in the short time you'll have at your disposal. If you will stay true to your words from earlier, and you will indeed make radical changes through your own powers, then I will personally give you the power required to stop the calamity that is threatening these cities, and afterwards, I will leave you to shape the fate of these kingdoms in whatever way you see fit. If this unlikely scenario truly comes to pass, then I will—"

"By the gods!" I shout, interrupting him. "Arraka was right! I can't believe it. You really are cheating!"

"I beg your pardon?" Eiden says.

"I just realized why you've been stretching your right arm every so often since you cast the time freezing spell!" I say. "And also why you've been walking back and forth for the past thirty seconds. It's because of the warning message, isn't it? I also had access to that same time freezing spell back when you powered up my stat device, so I still remember how it works! You're not allowed to move more than a few feet from your original position, so if any part of your body goes over a certain boundary, you're going to get a warning message, telling you that if you don't retreat in the next ten seconds, your spell will get cancelled."

"And what makes you think that triggering this warning helps me in any way?" Eiden asks me.

"It helps you," I say, "because whoever designed that spell never bothered to take the actual warnings into account when calculating the duration! As long as you don't go too far beyond the boundary, and you retreat at the very end of the ten second countdown, you can practically add ten more seconds to the duration of the spell every time you do this. And since the time limit of the spell has been added by design, due to safety reasons, and not due to technical limitations, you could probably lengthen the duration of this spell almost indefinitely, if you're confident enough that you can keep it under control. So, that's what Arraka and Tyrath had been talking about all this time, when they said that you were using tricks. It's not that you don't need to obey the laws of magic because you're too powerful. You're just taking advantage of technicalities to get around the rules, and you make it seem as if it was thanks to your power all along. You're using loopholes!"

"While I do commend you for figuring this out all by yourself," Eiden says, "I really don't see how this could possibly help you with—"

"It was the same with Daren, wasn't it?" I say. "That time when you put him to sleep despite all of his protections was also because you exploited some technicality, and not because your spell ignored all the laws of magic!"

"Oh?" Eiden asks, while raising his eyebrows with his eyes closed. "And what technicality might that be?"

After pausing for a few seconds to think, the answer suddenly comes to me, as if it were as clear as the light of day.

"Protection overload…" I say, as I see Eiden's expression change a bit, even with his eyes closed. "That's it, isn't it? I heard that this only happens to very skilled mages that go overboard with casting protections on themselves, without taking into account that some of those spells might actually do more harm than good, because they are in conflict with each other. If you're not careful, you could end up generating small openings in your defenses that could easily be exploited by someone that is skilled at reading the flow of auras. I could totally see Daren making a mistake like this."

"Extraordinary!" Eiden says, with his smile back on his face. "I've used that trick countless times against many formidable foes in the past, and yet nobody managed to figure it out until now. However, I still do not see how this would help you and your group if you were ever to fight me seriously. Leaving aside the fact that I've had hundreds of years to learn these technicalities, even if you managed to learn them all, my level of magical power still dwarfs that of most beings on this island, with very few exceptions. I would say that you are not in a better situation now, than you were when you first met me on the second day of the tournament."

"Yes, I am," I say. "Because now I know that you're not invincible. If you needed to learn all these tricks, then it means that your power alone was not enough to help you win all of your battles. It means that you have weaknesses. And if you have weaknesses, you can be defeated."

Eiden laughs.

"So, you aim not only to achieve what I couldn't accomplish in a lifetime," he says, "but also to eventually defeat me in an actual battle. And here I was, thinking that I wouldn't have anything interesting to do until the end of this tournament."

He pauses.

"Very well!" Eiden says. "In that case, I'll be looking forward to your progress. And I will also be monitoring your activity within the cities, as I said earlier. Now then, would you happen to have any more questions, before I take my leave?"

"Just one," I say. "What is the Magium?"

Eiden grins.

"You weren't seriously expecting to get an answer to that question so easily, were you?" he says.

"No," I say, "but it was worth a shot."

Eiden gives me one last smile with his eyes closed, and then he teleports out of my sight. As soon as he disappears, the time-freezing spell gets cancelled, and my friends begin to look around them confused, trying to figure out where Eiden went.

"So, Eiden is gone…" Daren says, after a while. "And Barry is the only one that doesn't seem surprised by this sudden turn of events. Is there anything that you might want to tell us, Barry?"

"Daren…" I say. "I'm certain that you have many questions, and I'll be sure to answer them in a bit, but first I'm going to need you to do something for me."

"What's that?" Daren asks.

"Pull out a pen and some paper from your backpack," I say, "and write down all of the protection spells that you had cast on yourself on our second day in Varathia. We've got work to do."

Chapter 7

"Barry, how long are you planning to stare at that piece of paper?" Daren says. "I told you, there are no conflicts between my protection spells. No matter how many times you check, you can't find something that is not there."

I ignore Daren, and I continue to look at the piece of paper lying on the ground in front of me, while I cross-check the information on it with what I have written in my notebook. The paper has all of Daren's protections written on it, and I was able to find detailed information for most of these spells in my notebook, but I still haven't managed to find the loophole that Eiden used to put Daren to sleep. Hadrik is also sitting on the ground, beside me, looking at the list of spells and throwing wild guesses, but it's clear that he doesn't really know enough about white magic to be able to make any reasonable assessments.

Flower has also tried to look at the paper and at my notebook a few times, but she eventually gave up, after saying that she was getting a headache. Illuna, on the other hand, announced from the very beginning that she wouldn't participate in our brainstorming session, because her knowledge of white mage protection spells was too limited to be able to contribute in any meaningful way.

"Hey," Hadrik tells me. "Doesn't this protection from illusions have a similar chant to that protection from sleep over there? Couldn't that be what's causing the conflict?"

"No," I say. "There are plenty of spells with similar sounding chants, and that's never caused a conflict, as far as I know. It has to be something else. Something obvious I'm missing. I'm going to start again, from the beginning, to see if I didn't skip an important detail somewhere, or something."

"Oh, come on!" Daren says, exasperated. "Hasn't it crossed your mind that maybe Eiden was just pulling your leg back there? Why would he even tell you his weakness? What possible reason could he have to do such a thing?"

"Aren't you the one who told me your greatest weakness a few minutes after we met?" I ask him, while raising an eyebrow.

"Yeah, but that's different!" Daren says. "Anyone could tell that my shield spell is weak against enchanted weapons after seeing me fight for a while!"

"Wait, you were weak against enchanted weapons?" Hadrik says.

"Ugh…" Daren says.

"No, I'm serious," Hadrik says. "I never noticed. But, why enchanted weapons, specifically? Shouldn't the shield spell automatically defend you from most types of damage? What, are you cursed or something? And besides, why would it even matter? The shield spell is just a spell that they teach to beginner mages. Nobody really uses it in actual combat. It consumes too much energy, and it barely even absorbs enough damage to prevent you from dying, most of the time. The protections against specific types of damage should be much more effective. Not that I really bothered to learn any of those, what with my very durable giant skin and all."

"White mages have advanced versions of the shield spell," Daren says. "They are a lot more cost effective. And I'm not weak against enchanted weapons, specifically. I'm vulnerable against all types of physical damage. Remember that time when the captain from the ogre fort hit me with a club and threw me into a wall? I've tried many kinds of protection spells against physical damage, but none of them seem to work for me. The only one that kind of works is the shield spell, but it's barely even working against regular weapons, let alone enchanted ones. Enchanting my armor to be as durable as possible was the only way I found to give me some measure of protection against these types of attacks."

"Huh," Hadrik says. "That's odd. Do you suppose it could have anything to do with the spirit from the magical plane that Arraka said you are linked with? Like, maybe the spirit is allergic to earth matter, or something? Barry, what do you think?"

"I don't know what to say," I tell Hadrik, without raising my eyes from my notebook. "Honestly, I'd be more inclined to think that he linked himself to the spirit incorrectly."

"Yeah," Daren says. "Easy for you to say. You're not a mage. And the only way you've cast magic so far was through that trinket of yours. Even after hearing Arraka's explanation, I still don't have any idea how to see this connection between me and my spirit. I've tried every way I could think of to analyze my magical aura for traces of a link to the magical plane, but I don't even know what to look for."

"That armor of yours is probably better than a shield spell in most cases, anyway," I say. "It doesn't eat away at your energy, and you don't need to worry about it conflicting with all of your other— Hold on... did you just imply earlier that you are actually using a shield spell right now?"

"Well, yeah," Daren says. "It's the only protection spell I've got that offers me some measure of defense against physical attacks. I'd have to be a fool not to use it."

"Then why didn't you write it on this paper?!" I say. "Didn't I tell you to write all the protection spells that you had cast on yourself on our second day of the tournament, without exceptions?"

"I already told you on our first day that I was using a shield spell," Daren says. "And besides, why would it even matter? What does the shield spell have to do with conflicts between protection spells?"

"It has everything to do with them!" I say. "What the hell, man? Haven't you read any of the books in the 'Advanced Theory of Magic' series, written by Azarius?"

"Hey," Daren says, "some of us didn't spend the entirety of our lives nerding it up in libraries. Everything that I've learned about magic, I've learned from my teachers."

"Well, in that case, your teachers are all a bunch of idiots!" I say.

"You take that back!" Daren says. "My white magic teacher was an ex-sage. Do you have any idea how hard it is to become a sage when you only specialize in white magic, without any sort of combat training?"

"Not hard enough, apparently," I tell him.

"Gods be damned!" Daren says. "Do you have no respect at all for the work it takes to—"

"What's going on, here?" Kate asks us, as her and Leila are slowly approaching us, with some shopping bags in their hands. "What are you two arguing about again?"

"Barry is refusing to acknowledge the effort that is required to—" Daren starts to say, but I interrupt him.

"Never mind, that!" I say. "Daren, can you tell me which kind of shield spell you are using, exactly? Is it the newer one that gives an advantage against physical attacks?"

"What?..." Daren says. "Oh... Yeah, yeah, that's the one..."

"What's Barry doing?" Kate asks the others, when she sees me flipping my notebook's pages like crazy.

"He says he found out how Eiden managed to put Daren to sleep, despite his protections," Hadrik says. "Apparently, it's because of protection overload, and now he's trying to find the two protection spells that are conflicting with each other."

"Protection overload?" Kate says. "That does sound like something Daren would do..."

"I found it!" I say. "The sleep protection from Daren's shield spell has an almost identical aura flow to one of his individual sleep protection spells. Look at these two diagrams!"

I then show them my notebook, flipping the pages between the two diagrams, so they can see the resemblance.

"Are you sure that's not just because you suck at drawing?" Daren says. "If your ugly handwriting is anything to go by, I'm not sure how much I would trust your ability to accurately copy a diagram from a book."

I frown at Daren.

"Well, why don't we have a test, then?" I say. "Does anyone here know any sleep spells?"

"I know a sleep spell," Illuna says. "It takes a while to cast, and I need to touch him while I do it, but it should be more than enough for what we need."

"Perfect!" I say. "Here are the diagrams. You need to make sure to time your sleep spell just right, and to aim it at the exact point where the two aura flows intersect."

"Yes, I know how it works," Illuna says, as she takes one quick look at the diagrams, and then she heads towards Daren.

"Oh, this should be good," Daren says.

Once Illuna reaches Daren, she places the palm of her hand on his right arm, and she closes her eyes, trying to visualize the flows of the auras.

"See?" Daren says, after about five seconds of waiting for Illuna to cast her spell. "I told you that you're wasting your time by—"

Daren does not get to finish what he was saying, because his eyes suddenly roll to the back of his head, and he falls to the ground, like a log.

"That settles it," Illuna says. "The oaf was using conflicting protection spells."

"Well, what do you know!" Hadrik says. "Barry was right. I think someone should wake Daren up, though. That does not look like a comfortable position to be sleeping in."

"Allow me," Illuna says.

She then conjures a bucket's worth of water above Daren's head, which she immediately drops on his face.

"What the—" Daren says, as he quickly gets up from the ground, and then he coughs some water out of his lungs. "How did I end up on the ground?"

"Take a wild guess," Kate says.

"No..." Daren says. "It can't be..."

"Well, Daren," I say. "I guess this means that you will now officially be losing your last bit of protection against physical damage. Welcome to the club!"

"No!" Daren says. "I'm not letting go of the shield! I've worked too hard to learn it! I'd rather give up that other protection spell than stop using the shield."

"Suit yourself," I say. "The sleep protection from your shield is a little weaker than the individual one, though."

"I don't care!" Daren says.

"Well, as long as you make sure that there are no more conflicts..." I say.

I pause for a few seconds.

"So, I guess that now I am the only one left without proper protection against sleep spells, then…" I say.

"Well, technically, I don't have any magical protection against them, either," Hadrik says. "Giants are naturally immune to sleep spells."

"Lessathi are also immune to sleep spells," Kate says.

"They are?" I say. "What about half-lessathi?"

"No idea," Kate says. "Maybe you are only half immune."

"Half immune?" I say. "How would that even work? Hey, Illuna, could you try putting me to sleep too, so we can see what happens?"

Illuna sighs, and she approaches me, touching my arm with her right hand, just like she did with Daren. A few seconds later, I feel a strong dizziness, and everything around me is starting to get blurry.

"Damn it!" I say, as I feel the world spinning around me. "I may as well be put to sleep for all the difference this would make in a fight. I can't even tell up from down anymore. What's happening right now? Am I still standing up?"

"Nah," Hadrik says. "You're sitting with your arse on the ground, while grabbing your head with both your hands."

All of a sudden, I feel my mind become clear again, and as I raise my head, I see Illuna standing in front of me, with her hand on my forehead.

"What did you do?" I ask her.

"I cast a spell to cure your dizziness," Illuna says, as she takes her hand off my forehead. "I also have a 'protection from dizziness' spell that I can cast on you, if you want. Given your partial immunity to sleep spells, protection from dizziness should help you both against sleep spells and against spells that attempt to disorient you. There is also a downside, however. While you have this spell cast on yourself, you will be a lot more vulnerable to suggestion magic, since the clarity of your thoughts will make it easier for someone to magically insert ideas into your brain."

"Well, it's not like I had any protections against suggestion magic to begin with," I say. "A little more vulnerability to it couldn't do that much harm, right?… Besides, I think that it's much more important to have protection against sleep spells, given how many mages can cast them. Go ahead and cast the protection spell on me. It's probably safer that way."

Illuna nods, and she begins to say an incantation, while she has both her palms pointed towards me. Once she's done chanting, a white light surrounds me for a few seconds, which then disappears almost as quickly as it appeared.

"It's done," Illuna says. "The spell should last you for a few weeks, but there won't be any problem in recasting it earlier than that, if you want to be on the safe side."

"Great," I say, as I get up from the ground. "Of course, it would have been even greater if our team's white mage could actually cast any sort of protection spells on anyone but himself. You know, kind of like what every other white mage in existence is capable of doing?"

"Give me a break!" Daren says. "I already told you. Learning the versions of the spells that can only be cast on myself was easier. I was never planning to work in a team, during my travels, so it seemed like a waste of time to learn the more advanced versions of the spells, if I'd never get the chance to use them. The barrier that I can cast with my shield has always been more than enough to protect civilians from harm during monster attacks. And it's not like I can just make a few adjustments and change the spells I already know so they can be cast on other people. I'd have to learn entirely different spells for this to work, and we've got no time for that. Just let it go, already."

"Hey, I'm just saying," I say, "If you had actually decided to specialize in only one type of magic like everyone else instead of going for both enchantment and white magic, this wouldn't have been a problem."

"Drop it," Daren says.

"Fine, fine," I say. "I guess we're all done here, then? Should we get moving?"

"Not yet," Kate says. "Leila still needs to get her new backpack enchanted. We can't just walk with these bags in our hands, all the way to the palace."

"Alright," Daren says. "Give me the backpack. I'll enchant it right away."

As soon as Daren is done with the backpack and Leila puts all of her clothes inside it, we all leave the market area, and we make our way towards the castle of Thilias once more. As we walk, we begin to tell Kate and Leila about everything that happened with Eiden while they were shopping. I also take this opportunity to give everyone more details about my private discussion with Eiden, during his time-freezing spell.

"Eiden said he'd give you the power to stop the calamity threatening to destroy the cities?..." Daren says. "That doesn't make any sense. Didn't he tell us that he would be destroying the cities himself?"

"That's not what he said," I say. "His exact words were that the calamity would happen as a direct result of his own actions."

"Isn't that kind of the same thing, though?" Hadrik says.

"Not really," I say. "The way he phrased it, it didn't seem like the destruction of the cities would be his main purpose. More like a side effect of whatever he's planning to do. Let's say, for example, that Eiden knows for a fact that he will be forced to fight Tyrath personally before the end of this tournament. If the dragon is to be believed, then such a fight would completely raze the continent, which would most likely erase all of Varathia's cities from the map."

"Damn," Daren says. "You might be right. With the dragon declaring war against all of the cities, and Eiden announcing his return as the 'Creator', I wouldn't be too surprised if the two leaders of the armies ended up clashing before the end of the tournament."

"That's not all," I say. "Eiden specifically told us that this calamity would only happen 'shortly' before the end of the tournament. This means that he is expecting the tournament to play a part in triggering this calamity, somehow."

"Maybe the dragon will be waiting for most of the tournament participants to die out, before he begins his attack?" Hadrik says.

"That's definitely possible," I say. "I'm guessing that the cities of Varathia already have their own defenses against Tyrath's armies, and he's also got the animals to worry about. It would be a pretty bad idea for him to unleash his armies now, when there are mages wandering around the continent, capable of slaughtering hundreds of monsters without much effort."

"We should let the king know about this," Daren says. "He might want to make some preparations, in case these events really come to pass."

"Yeah," I say. "Although, I'm not sure if he could actually do anything to protect this city even if he knew about this stuff in advance. A few flying machines and some mages aren't exactly going to be a lot of help in breaking up the fight between a stillwater and a dragon."

I sigh, before I continue.

"I don't know why I'm getting the feeling that we're going to have to deal with that dragon in one way or another, if we want there to be any organizers left alive to hand us the prize at the end of the tournament."

"Ooh," Daren says. "And are you going to defeat the dragon by yourself too, just like you said you'd save all the cities? You've got a busy schedule ahead of you, I'll tell you that!"

"Shut up," I say. "I know I can't do it all by myself. I only said that on the spur of the moment, because Eiden was pissing me off with his defeatist attitude. Luckily, I've got a friend who's a well-known legendary mage that might be able to lend me a hand, if things get too rough. He can't cast a proper shield spell to save his life, and he sucks at magical theory, but at least he's decent enough with a sword and shield."

"Hey, now, is that any way to ask someone for a favor?" Daren says, with a grin. "Where's the head bow? Where's the pleading tone in your voice? Remember, you're speaking with one of the most renowned heroes in the world, here."

"Actually, you're right…" I tell Daren, in a more serious tone. "I should not be joking when discussing such matters. Allow me to ask you again, in a more proper way."

I then bow my head, and I use a much more humble tone in my voice, as I ask Daren my next question.

"Please, Daren," I say, "will you help me?"

"Whoa, whoa, whoa…" Daren says, as he takes a step back. "I was joking, Barry! It was a joke. I thought you'd have been familiar with my sense of humor by now. Listen, if saving the cities of Varathia is really that important to you, then we'll see what we can do, alright? Just stop bowing your head, already! It's making me uncomfortable…"

"In either case," Kate says, as I am now raising my head back up, "we shouldn't rely too much on Eiden's promise to give Barry powers if he succeeds in his task. The terms of their agreement are much too vague, and Eiden could very well change his mind at any moment."

"I agree," Daren says. "However, given the vague information we have about this so-called calamity, the only way we can be certain that it doesn't happen is by taking care of both Eiden and the dragon, and that is… definitely not going to be an easy task."

"Don't worry," I say. "I know what kind of tricks Eiden's using, now. I'm sure I'll have them all figured out in no time. I haven't been studying magic all my life for nothing."

"Hah!" Arraka says. "Now there's something I would love to see: Eiden getting beaten by his own tricks."

"Let's not be too hasty," Daren says. "Barry only figured out two of his tricks so far. I'm guessing Eiden would know hundreds of them after his long life as a stillwater. Anyway, I'd say we've talked enough about Eiden. Let's pick up our pace. We've spent quite a bit of time in that marketplace, so we'd better hurry up if we don't want to leave the king waiting."

It takes us about another hour to finally reach the front gate of the king's palace. The king's servant was waiting for us at the entrance, and as soon as we get within hearing range of him, he announces that Golmyck is currently waiting for us inside. As we make our way into the throne room, we see that the gnome is sitting on the floor, on all fours, with a wrench in his hand, trying to adjust the height of his throne.

"Just a minute," Golmyck says, as he tightens one last bolt at the base of his throne.

He then gets up from the ground, and he gives us each one quick look.

"I see that the young lessathi girl has decided to join your group," Golmyck says, and then he turns to Leila. "I'm very sorry about your father. He was a respectable inventor, and he did not deserve the fate that he got. Unfortunately, there was no way for me to intervene in his trial, even if I suspected the evidence to be forged.

For what it's worth, I made sure to cancel his pursuit as soon as he escaped the city, so he at least won't need to watch his back, on his way to Ollendor."

"…Thank you," Leila writes, not knowing exactly what else to say.

"You are here for the documents, yes?" Golmyck says, now turning to us. "Follow me to my private room. I will stamp the papers for you there."

He goes to pull the lever behind the throne, and the path towards his secret subterranean room opens up once more, just like the last time when we've visited the castle.

"Barry, as usual, the throne room is in your care until I return," Golmyck says.

"Yes, your highness," the king's servant says.

"Barry?" Leila writes, looking very confused.

"Yeah, that's what the king's servant is called," Hadrik says, while we go down the stairs towards the secret room. "Isn't that hilarious? We've been joking about it for hours after the last time we came here."

"I see…" Leila writes.

When we reach the subterranean chamber, the king lays out a few papers on his desk, and he begins to stamp them, one by one. While the gnome is busy with his papers, I suddenly remember the lessathi that came to visit me in my holding cell, below the arena, and the device that he gave me.

I panic for a few seconds, and I start feeling my pockets with both my hands, to see if the device is still there, but I calm down when I realize that I've already thrown it away while I was heading towards the castle, since I didn't see any reason to hold onto it anymore.

"So, uh…" Daren says, while looking at Golmyck. "I think there's something we should let you know about. We ran into Eiden on our way to the castle, and he told us that there will be a calamity shortly before the end of this tournament that will destroy all the cities in Varathia. A calamity that will be triggered by his actions. We are suspecting that he might get into a fight with the dragon Tyrath, which is what will cause all the damage."

"I see..." Golmyck says, as he takes a short pause from stamping the documents, to think about what Daren said. "Well, if this calamity is indeed of the magnitude that you describe, then it would serve no purpose to try fortifying our defenses. The only way we could survive such a thing is to make sure it doesn't happen at all. Did Eiden tell you that this calamity would involve the dragon?"

"No," Daren says. "But he implied that destroying the cities is not his actual purpose, even though their eradication would happen due to his actions. A fight between him and the dragon is the only thing we could think of that would make sense, given these circumstances."

"Hmm..." Golmyck says, as he rubs his chin. "There is something that I don't fully understand, here. Perhaps you could clarify it for me. What exactly is your affiliation with Eiden? He has personally intervened to save your lives before, and I see that you know him well enough to have private discussions with him, but I can't tell in what way you are connected to him. Have any of you been acquainted with him from before you came to Varathia?"

"No," Daren says. "We all met him here for the first time."

"Then why is he so fixated on you, and not on any of the other participants?" Golmyck says. "Surely you cannot be the only unique group that has joined this tournament?"

"Actually, for all we know, he may also be visiting other groups of mages," I say. "He has the ability to identify people by their auras from very long distances, and he can teleport anywhere he wants, so it wouldn't take him much effort to do it."

"I see..." Golmyck says. "Yes, I suppose you could be right. As long as we do not know his exact purpose, we cannot assume that your group is the only one he's interacted with so far."

He pauses.

"Now, then..." Golmyck says, as he gets a serious look in his eyes. "Leaving Eiden and the calamity aside, I believe there was a more pressing issue that we agreed we'd discuss once you'd be free from your imprisonment. Am I correct in assuming that you are all still on board with our plans concerning the lessathi?"

"Of course..." I say, as I take a quick glance towards the others, to make sure that none of them changed their minds in the meantime.

"What about your new friend?" Golmyck says. "Will she be joining you as well?"

"We haven't told her anything," Kate says, "since you said we shouldn't talk about any of this outside your room, but I think that she may want to come with us as well, given the circumstances."

"Ah, yes," Golmyck says. "Especially since some of the lessathi you are about to fight are the ones who imprisoned her, and also the ones who conspired with her landlord to sell her father into slavery..."

"Wait, what are you talking about?" Leila writes. "Why are you fighting the lessathi?"

"We've been told," Kate says, "that there is a select group of lessathi who reside in this city, and who have been tasked by the other kings of Varathia to keep the gnome king in check and to make sure that he does not overstep his boundaries. We intend to rid the king of this problem."

"You want to kill all the lessathi in this city?" Leila

writes, shocked. "You can't! If you kill any one of them, the others will find out, and they will send back word to their main headquarters. You will become one of their main targets!"

"I would be surprised if I weren't already one of the lessathi's main targets," Kate says. "They should know very well who I am."

"Actually, the lessathi will not have the time to contact their main headquarters," Golmyck says, as we all turn towards him. "When I accepted your help, it was because I already had an idea of how you could deal with this problem in a timely manner, without it affecting your tournament schedule. There would have been no use in requesting your aid if there wasn't a quick way to deal with all of the lessathi at the same time, before they get the chance to alert their allies."

"What do you mean?" Hadrik says.

"The lessathi will be holding a meeting in about two hours from now," Golmyck says, "in a subterranean chamber situated not far from this castle. The main purpose of this meeting is to discuss the political implications of the earl of Ollendor's murder, and how it will affect them and the city of Thilias in the coming weeks. At first, this gathering was supposed to be held after your trial and execution. However, as I suspected, Eiden's intervention forced them to postpone it until after the end of the arena fights. Since you all managed to survive, I am quite certain that they will have a lot to discuss, especially regarding the reaction that Ollendor will be having to this unexpected turn of events. The meeting is mandatory for all the four lessathi who reside in this city, so you will have the opportunity to attack them all at once, without fearing that any of them will find out what happened to their comrades, and go into hiding."

"But how will we get there without being noticed?"

Daren asks.

"This room that we are now standing in is connected to a large network of underground tunnels," Golmyck says. "One of these tunnels will lead you exactly where you need to go. I know this, because I've had one of my spies follow Barry through one of the underground corridors, and directly to the lessathi headquarters a few weeks ago. Luckily, none of them know that this room of mine also has a secret entrance to the tunnels, so they haven't bothered to post any guards at this particular entrance."

"Hold on, hold on," Hadrik says. "When you say Barry, you're talking about your servant, right?"

"Oh, that's right, I meant my servant!" Golmyck says. "I keep forgetting that I need to specify."

"Well, if it's your servant, then couldn't you have just asked him for the information directly?" Hadrik says. "Why would you go through the trouble of having him followed?"

"Oh," Golmyck says, smiling. "It's because my servant is a traitor. He's been working with the lessathi for years. That's why I never let him inside my private room."

"A traitor?" Hadrik asks, shocked. "What the hell, man? If you've known that he's a traitor for so long, then why do you still keep him around?"

"It's because Barry has never been very smart," Golmyck says. "He is extremely easy to read, and he also never manages to realize when he's being followed. I'd much rather have him as a plant, than someone who would be smart enough to actually fool me. And this way, I get to find out useful information about the lessathi, such as the exact hour and location of their meeting today. It's very convenient. All I need to do is let slip some seemingly sensitive, but ultimately useless information to him every once in a while, to avoid suspicion, and I get to have my own spy in the lessathi organization, with minimal effort on my part."

So the king's servant was a traitor… Now I understand why that lessathi who I met in the prison knew about my stat device. It's because I showed it to the servant on my way to the arena. Damn it, I should have been more careful.

"Does that mean that you will also have your servant killed once we're done with our job?" Daren asks.

"Oh, goodness, no!" Golmyck says. "Barry is harmless. There would be no reason to kill him. He does not know any lessathi other than the ones in this city, so as soon as those four are dealt with, he will revert to being just my servant, without any of the spying shenanigans."

"Do you have some sort of map of the underground tunnels that could help us reach our destination?" Kate asks.

"Yes, as a matter of fact, I do!" Golmyck says, as he takes a folded parchment from his pocket and then begins to unfold it.

He lays out the map on the workbench, so we can all see it clearly, and then he explains to us in detail which of the tunnels we'll need to take, and where the lessathi headquarters is located on the map.

"Arraka, can you—" Illuna starts to say, but she gets interrupted.

"Yeah, yeah, I've got it," Arraka says. "Hold on a sec."

She then conjures a detailed hologram of the underground tunnels, although the map seems to be a little different from how she usually draws it. The lines that represent the edges of the corridors are no longer all drawn in the same color. Some of them are blue, while others are green.

"Is there any reason why you decided to use a

different color for some of the corridors?" I say.

"Yeah, the green tunnels are the ones that I can't actually detect with my magical sense," Arraka says. "I only put them there because they're on the map. They probably have walls and ceilings made of seredium, which block my magical sense. I have no idea if there are people walking through them, or if they can even be accessed at all. The path to your destination doesn't have any seredium on it, though, so at the very least you can be sure that you won't encounter any guards on your way there."

"What about the meeting room?" I say. "Is there anyone inside it right now?"

"No," Arraka says. "Their headquarters is empty. I would have put some dots in there, if there were people in it."

"So, where are we going to wait for the next two hours?" Daren says. "Should we go outside, or?…"

"Oh, no, no, you should definitely not go outside," Golmyck says. "If you leave now and come back only a few minutes before the lessathi's meeting, my servant may get suspicious and contact them in some way. You can wait right here. I don't really have any chairs in this room, but I've only just cleaned the floor, so you can sit on the ground if you want."

He then stamps two more documents, and he hands them over to us, so we can each take a look at them.

"There you go," the king says. "These papers should be enough to absolve you of your crimes, no matter where you go in Varathia. Now, if there's nothing else you need from me, I will be resuming my work on the lessathi device that was supposed to send you the instructions related to the tournament's objectives, telepathically. I've been trying to get it fixed for more than a week, but I still can't figure out what's wrong with it, so you can imagine how frustrating this has been for me."

As Golmyck goes to work on his device, Hadrik puts down his backpack, and he reaches within it, to pull out a deck of playing cards.

"So…" Hadrik says. "Anyone up for a game of cards?"

We spend the next hour or so playing a card game that Hadrik learned from dwarven taverns. Apparently, one of the original rules of the game was that a player needed to take a sip of dwarven ale every time they lost a hand, but we had to scrap this rule for obvious reasons. The game involved a lot of bluffing, so it was no surprise that Leila was the one who came out on top, given that she could read auras, to tell if someone was lying. Since I was the one she could get a read on the easiest, due to the fact that for some reason, she can see my aura become 'spiky' every time I lie, I eventually got tired of losing every single match, and I decided to take a break to read my notebook some more, in the hopes of finding more loopholes that Eiden might be using.

"Hey, Daren," I say, after reading through the notebook for some time. "Remember that one time when Eiden paralyzed every one of you? Right before he teleported us in front of Thilias?"

"What?…" Daren says, as he's trying to focus on his cards while listening to me. "Oh, yeah, I remember. What about it?"

"How many spells do you have that protect you against paralysis?" I say.

"Just one," Daren says. "And the shield does not protect against paralysis, so it's not protection overload!"

"Okay, okay," I say. "Is anyone else using protection against paralysis?"

"Yes," Kate says. "I use the spell described in the latest 'Advanced Theory of Magic' book by Azarius."

"Alright," I say. "And you, Daren? Which protection are you using?"

"The golden one," Daren says. "The one that makes a spinning effect with sparkles when you cast it."

"Uh…" I say. "Okay… So, you mean the advanced version from the standard white mage spellbook. And Hadrik, I assume that you are relying on your partial resistance that comes from being a giant in order to defend yourself from such spells?"

"Yeah," Hadrik says. "But I got paralyzed completely, just like Kate and Daren, despite my resistance."

"Uh-huh," I say. "Well, do you guys know what these three defenses of yours have in common?"

"What?" Daren says.

"Absolutely nothing," I say, as I close my notebook. "Which means that Eiden was not using a loophole, this time around. In fact, I don't think he was using paralysis at all. He must have been using a completely different type of spell, which has the same effect. Remember that time when Kate's friend left us all unconscious on the ground? She didn't use a sleep spell to do it. She used electricity. I'm suspecting that Eiden used a similar method to temporarily paralyze you. Didn't you all feel a shock right before you fell to the ground? I'm pretty sure you must have also felt a few other electric shocks afterwards, which were meant to keep you paralyzed for a longer period of time."

"Come to think of it, yeah!" Daren says. "I did feel some electric shocks. But they didn't feel much different from the feeling you get from a normal paralysis, so I didn't really notice the difference at the time. But does this mean that Eiden can use electricity as an element, like Kate's friend?"

"I doubt it," I say. "The spell that he used seemed to have certain rules and limitations, which would not have been the case if he could have used electricity freely, as an element. The electric spell that he used to paralyze you felt extremely similar to a spell that I had access to, back when I had my stat device powered up, so it's likely the same one. I don't remember every single detail about it, but it was one of those spells that you could only cast once a day, and I know for sure that one major drawback of the spell was the fact that the area of effect was extremely small. I mean, you could pretty much just roll over to the side, and the following electrical currents would not target you anymore. The only reason why it worked against you was because you three happened to be standing very close together, and because you didn't know what kind of spell you were up against. If you knew how it worked, then you could have just gotten out of the way at the exact moment before a new electrical current hit you, since the effect of the paralysis wears off a bit, right before each new shock."

"Yeah, I very much doubt that I could have done that," Daren says, "since I was trying to break free of the spell's effect the whole time, and it didn't work."

"That's because the spell shocks you at faster intervals if it sees that you're trying to break free!" I say. "It doesn't work that way. You need to be relaxed, and to only try to escape at the very last second. Of course, you can't know how often it will shock you until you let yourself get shocked a few times, while counting the number of seconds for each interval. The intervals will not always be of the same length, but there will usually be a pattern that you can figure out. Once you're sure that you got the count right, you wait for the last moment, and only then you try to escape. Obviously, the easier way around this would be to use protection against electricity, but with the amount of energy it takes to keep that protection up and running, you'd have to be insane to use it at all times, on the off-chance that you'll get attacked by an electrical spell other than the standard ones."

"Uh," Hadrik says, "not that I want to interrupt you or anything, but we should really hurry up if we want to finish the game before we leave. We've only got about half an hour left before the lessathi meeting, and everyone except Leila is going to need at least three more rounds to gather all the points they need."

Once Hadrik and the others finish their game, we leave our backpacks in the care of king Golmyck, and we all get ready to descend into the tunnels below.

"Be careful," Golmyck says, before we leave. "The lessathi may not be mages, but their highly advanced magical devices make them into as big a threat as some of the most skilled participants that have joined this tournament. I would have given you more information about them, but unfortunately the only thing I know is that the one wielding two scythes is using electric attacks. The functions of the others' devices are still unknown to me."

"Well," I say, "at least we know who we'll be targeting first."

The king opens a trapdoor which leads to the underground corridors, and an extension ladder drops down, allowing us to reach the floor of the tunnel safely. We climb down one by one, and once we all reach the lower level, Golmyck wishes us luck, and he pulls the ladder back up, closing the trapdoor with a loud thump. Looking up, I can barely tell that there had been an open trapdoor on the ceiling above us, only seconds ago. The texture of the secret door blends perfectly with the rocky surface of the ceiling and walls, making it completely hidden, unless you know exactly where to look for it.

We travel through the corridors for a few minutes, making sure to carefully follow the directions that the king gave us, while periodically asking Arraka if she doesn't sense any guards on our way to the lessathi headquarters.

"Look, the lessathi are starting their meeting!" Flower says, as she points towards several green dots that are now moving inside the lessathi headquarters from Arraka's hologram.

"A little earlier than they were supposed to, but not by much," Daren says, as he also looks towards the hologram in front of Flower. "We should still make it there before they finish. It won't be long until we reach the last corridor, and then we should be able to see the entrance to their lair. I'm still feeling a little uneasy about all of these empty tunnels, though. I can't help but feel that we're walking into a trap of some kind."

"Don't be so pessimistic, Daren," Hadrik says. "The king said that the lessathi don't know about his hidden trapdoor, so it's normal that they wouldn't have anyone in charge of guarding these areas. Maybe they'll have some guards posted in front of their meeting hall, and that will put your worries to rest."

As we make our way further into the tunnel, I suddenly get a vision of our group walking straight into an explosion, not much farther from our current position.

"Stop!" I shout, as everyone turns towards me.

"What is it?" Kate says.

"That part of the corridor is rigged to explode if we go any further," I say.

"Did you see a premonition of this happening?" Kate asks.

"Yes," I say. "We can't go that way. We need to go back."

"But why would there be a trap on this corridor?" Hadrik asks. "Isn't this the path that the gnome's servant usually takes to reach their headquarters? Why would they risk it?"

"They're probably onto us," Daren says. "The king

already told us that the lessathi have listening devices inside the throne room, which means that they should be aware that we've visited Golmyck's secret room twice so far. Even if they don't know about the hidden trapdoor, they still have good reason to be cautious."

"Yeah, but to risk blowing up this whole corridor based on a simple hunch..." Hadrik says. "I don't know, I'm finding it a bit hard to believe. Barry, are you sure that your thingamajig isn't malfunctioning, somehow? I mean, you don't have any guarantee that those premonitions will always come true, do you?"

"Well, why don't you throw a rock, and see for yourself if it explodes, then?" I say.

"Don't mind if I do!" Hadrik says, and he picks up a rock from the ground, which he then throws further down the corridor.

As soon as the rock hits the ground, a big explosion covers the area around it, sending the whole ceiling above it crashing down, and blocking our path.

"Okay," Hadrik says. "You convinced me, Barry. Let's go back."

"You do realize that there's no way in hell the lessathi didn't hear that explosion from earlier, right?" Daren says.

"Even if they've heard it, they're not reacting to it," I say. "Look at the map. The four lessathi haven't moved from their original spots. Either they can't hear any noise from inside there, or they think we're dead. What we need now is to figure out a way to get around this cave-in. Arraka, you wouldn't happen to detect any other tunnels around here that aren't marked on the king's map, would you?"

"Huh?" Arraka asks. "Oh, I do, actually... Hold on, let me add them to the hologram."

A few seconds after she's done talking, three more blue corridors appear on the hologram that is floating in front of her amulet.

"Hey, look," I say, "one of those corridors seems to link the tunnel we're currently in with one of the seredium tunnels. And that tunnel also leads towards the lessathi headquarters."

"Yeah, but I can't guarantee that the seredium tunnel is currently functional," Arraka says. "Like I said before, I only put it there because it was on the gnome's map. I can't sense anything inside it. It may as well be filled with guards, for all I know."

"Well, it's better than nothing," I say. "Which wall leads to the secret tunnel? That one?"

I then point towards a specific area on the wall to our right, while waiting for Arraka's answer.

"Uh-huh," Arraka says.

"Alright," Hadrik says. "Well, in that case, I'll go open the path for us."

"Yes," Daren says, as Hadrik heads towards the wall that leads to the secret tunnel. "As long as we know which wall leads to the tunnel, finding the secret lever that opens it up shouldn't be that—"

Before Daren gets to finish his sentence, Hadrik reaches the wall, and he punches right through it, making it crumble into pieces.

"Seriously…" Daren says, as he smacks his forehead with the palm of his hand. "Do you have to do this every single time?"

"Relax!" Hadrik says. "The lessathi are too far away to hear a mere few rocks crumbling down, and if there really are guards on the other side, it's not like we'd have any way to sneak past them. It's a direct path to the lessathi headquarters from here. No way around."

"Fine, let's keep going," Daren says. "We'll see what happens, when it happens."

We travel through the secret tunnel without encountering any form of resistance. When we reach the end of it, Hadrik takes a quick glance towards the rest of us, and then he punches through the wall, clearing our way to the seredium corridor. As we look around us, we see that this tunnel is just as empty as the other ones.

"Arraka," Illuna says, "do you sense any guards?"

"Nope," Arraka says. "It's empty. No magical traps either. Don't know about regular traps, though."

"Well, regular traps tend to get triggered by stepping on the ground," Hadrik says, "so I'll just make sure to throw rocks ahead of us on a regular basis, to see if anything explodes. I'm the one with the tough giant skin here, so I'll go in front. If anything triggers, I should be able to handle it."

"Remember to suppress your auras as much as you can," Daren tells us, as we advance through the corridor. "We wouldn't want the lessathi to detect us before we reach them."

As we walk down the tunnel, I begin to hear a voice at the far end of the corridor. It doesn't take me long to recognize it as being the voice of the lessathi that came to visit me while I was in my cell below the arena. I also seem to be able to hear the other lessathi from the meeting, although it takes a bit of effort to focus on their words.

"That does indeed seem like our only alternative," says the soft-spoken lessathi who visited my cell, in the lessathi language, which I am able to understand thanks to my stat device. "Ollendor has already been isolated from most of Varathia, so the rest of the kingdoms will most likely not care if Thilias decides to cut all diplomatic ties with Ollendor as well. The gnome is probably going to do this either way, so there should be no reason for us to intervene."

"Ollendor is the least of our worries, right now," says another lessathi. "Do you have any idea how many mages have died since the beginning of this tournament?

This is why I've insisted from the very beginning that the tournament should have had a rule to prohibit the mages from killing each other unless the rules of the tournament explicitly required them to!"

"We've talked about this before," the soft-spoken lessathi says, in a calm tone. "The kings would not agree to it, remember? They said that it was against Varathian tradition to impose such a rule in a tournament, even if the participants are all outsiders."

"To hell with the kings and their outdated traditions!" the other lessathi says. "Don't you understand? They've ruined everything! Why did I even bother to sabotage the telepathic device meant to transmit the objectives, if the mages were going to kill each other before the first round anyway?"

"You've been complaining about this in every single meeting we've had since the beginning of the tournament," another lessathi says. "Give it a rest, already. What's done is done. Let's just focus on the present, shall we?"

"Barry!" Daren whispers. "Over here!"

As I take a look towards Daren, I realize that while I was listening to the lessathi conversation, we'd already reached our destination. The corridor that we are currently in and the corridor that we left from seem to both reunite in this point, and they lead to a much narrower hallway, which has a door at the end. On the other side of the door, the lessathi are still holding their meeting, and they don't seem to have noticed us. I join Daren and the others into the narrow hallway, and we prepare to storm the meeting room, on his signal.

Just as we're about to charge into their headquarters, I suddenly feel an electric shock all throughout my body, and I fall to the ground, unable to move. The same thing apparently happened to all of my friends, because they're now also lying on the ground beside me.

This spell… Could it be?…

As we all lie on the ground, unable to break free from the spell's effects, the door in front of us opens, and the four lessathi that were participating in the meeting are now slowly advancing towards us. They are all wearing their signature dark blue robes, with their hoods up, and each of them seems to be carrying a different type of weapon.

"Welcome, friends," says the soft-spoken lessathi, in the Common language. "I believe I've already had the pleasure of meeting some of you, but the others may not know who I am. It doesn't matter, because we will be the ones asking the questions, and you will be the ones answering. Do I make myself clear?"

"They can't answer you, you idiot," says another lessathi, in the lessathi language. "This spell paralyzes them completely. They are unable to talk."

"Where are your manners?" the soft-spoken lessathi says, in the Common language. "These are our guests! We should all speak in the Common language, so they can understand us."

"Is this supposed to be some sort of joke?" the lessathi from before says, still in the lessathi language. "You've always had a bad sense of humor."

"Well, it doesn't matter if you want to speak in Common or not," the soft-spoken lessathi says. "We don't need more than one person to interrogate them anyway."

"I told you that this would happen!" says another lessathi, also in the Common language. "That idiotic king's servant was never the type that could tell when he was being followed."

"Indeed," the soft-spoken lessathi says. "Your idea to leak the time and place of our meeting to the king's servant was definitely worth the effort. What I don't understand, however, is how they managed to not die in that explosion from earlier. Do you suppose that they somehow detected our trap before walking into it and used a decoy to activate it?"

"It doesn't really matter," says the lessathi from before. "What matters now is that we get as much information from them as possible. There's no use trying to interrogate the ones who can't talk due to the paralysis. Only the two lessathi should be able to speak right now. We'll just quickly find out what we need to know, and then we'll get rid of them."

These cocky bastards. They're using Eiden's paralysis spell. I'm sure of it. This narrow corridor is the perfect place to set up such a trap. And the periodic shocks I'm getting are definitely electric in nature. Due to my partial resistance to electricity that I get from being half-lessathi, it should be easy enough for me to find the right time window to spring out of the spell's area of effect, and I'm pretty sure that Leila is in a similar situation as well. The others might take a bit longer to get the timing right, though, since the windows they'll get will be extremely short.

As I lie there on the ground, a very small, barely noticeable, semi-transparent message appears right in front of my eyes, written in blue text.

"Don't free yourself yet," Leila's text says. "Wait for the others to get accustomed to the shocks. I'm also sending this message to everyone else. I'll give the signal, so we can all free ourselves together, at the exact same moment."

"Where the hell did you hide your trap?" Arraka shouts all of a sudden. "I've been searching for it since you came out of that door, and I'm not sensing any device that could cast this type of spell!"

It is unclear to me whether Arraka saw Leila's message and is now trying to buy us some time, or if she's just genuinely frustrated that her magical sense is not good enough to find the trap on her own. If I were to guess, then I'd say it's probably the latter reason.

"Well, it wouldn't be much of a trap if you could just detect it before you walked into it, now, would it?" the soft-spoken lessathi says.

"Wait, who are you talking to?" says the lessathi that agreed to speak in Common. "Where did that voice come from?"

"I'm talking to the banshee in the amulet, of course," the soft-spoken lessathi says. "Arraka, I believe, is her name. I heard that she was trapped in there by a rogue group of lessathi some twenty years ago. At any rate, the banshee is not the one that I'm interested in talking to."

He then walks towards me, getting within range of the electrical shock spell, but he doesn't seem to be affected by it. Could he be using some trinket that gives him protection against electricity?

"This is the one that I'm interested in talking to," the lessathi says, as he gets closer to me. "I honestly wasn't expecting to see you again, fellow lessathi. You are tenacious, I'll give you that. Well, no matter. This isn't important. What's important is how you managed to reach our location in one piece. Tell me, was it Golmyck that gave you the map of the underground tunnels? How were you able to avoid the explosion trap?"

"You know, I was thinking..." says the lessathi wielding the scythes, who has been notably silent until now. "We don't really need to have both of the lessathi alive for an interrogation, do we?"

As he talks, he slowly approaches Leila, who is lying on the ground, facing down, with her head towards him.

"What are you talking about?" the soft-spoken lessathi says, as he takes his eyes off me and turns to face his comrade. "Of course we need them both alive!"

"Yeah, but you see..." the scythes-wielding lessathi says, as he grabs Leila by the hair, and he lifts her head, so she can get a direct look at his face. “I’ve been itching to kill this little half-breed for a very long time. And I just don’t think I can restrain myself much longer.”

“Control yourself!” the soft-spoken lessathi says. “What’s gotten into you?”

“Control myself?” the scythes-wielding lessathi says. “That’s easy for you to say. You weren’t there, at the Beacon. The very thought that I had to share the same room for extended periods of time with this abomination makes me want to puke. And to make matters worse, there was also that idiot caretaker who used to treat her like she was an actual lessathi. Disgusting.”

He then turns towards Leila, when he sees the expression in her eyes change.

“Oh, I’m sorry, are you upset because I’m bad-mouthing your ‘father’?” the lessathi says. “Well, you know what? Your stupid father deserved much worse than the fate that he got. Parasites like him should be happy that they are even allowed to live as slaves. They have no place in our society. You may have freed him for now, but we’ll get him back, don’t worry. And when we do, we are going to give him the fate he truly deserves. The fate of a useless piece of trash.”

As Leila’s eyes fill with rage, she completely forgets about the signal, and she jumps on the lessathi in front of her, thrusting one of her knives directly into his heart. I quickly take advantage of this opportunity, and I also jump to my feet, aiming my dagger at the throat of the lessathi that was closest to me. The soft-spoken lessathi was not looking at me, and my attack takes him completely by surprise. He tries to jump backwards, but it’s too late, and I manage to slit his throat in one single movement.

“Damn it!” one of the other lessathi says, as he sticks a trident-like weapon into a wall.

About a second later, a very large hand made of stone

comes out of the wall behind me, and it closes its fist around me, attempting to crush me. I try to break free, but I simply do not have any room to move my arms. Luckily for me, my toughness stat is high enough that the stone hand does not manage to crush me, no matter how hard it tightens its grip.

While I am still unable to move, Kate manages to free herself from the paralysis spell, by jumping backwards, out of its range, and at a relatively safe distance from the lessathi. She then extends one of her arms towards the trident-wielding lessathi, with the palm of her hand facing him, and an ice cone shoots out of it, impaling him in the head. As soon as he dies, the stone hand that was gripping me quickly crumbles to dust.

All of a sudden, the last remaining lessathi raises the emerald encrusted shield he was holding in the air, and a powerful flash of light fills the room, blinding us all for a few seconds. As my eyes re-adjust, I see that there has been a clash between Leila and the lessathi while we were blinded, which has led to both of them dropping their weapons. Leila is on the ground, with her back against the wall, and the lessathi is now bending over to pick up one of her knives, in order to finish her off.

"Help me, Barry!" a big blue text appears in front of me, as Leila looks at the lessathi with a terrified look in her eyes.

As Leila is desperately calling for my help, I just stand there and look at her, trying to figure out why this whole situations seems completely off, to me. There's just something about what's happening here that feels very out of place, but I can't quite put my finger on it.

"Barry, please!" Leila writes, again, as the lessathi closes in on her with the dagger in his hand, while struggling to find his way towards her due to the lingering effects of the blinding flash from earlier.

Damn, it… I guess I'll go immobilize the lessathi for

now, and I'll figure out what's wrong later.

Just as I'm about to reach the lessathi, Kate suddenly shoots three ice cones into Leila's waist, causing her to scream in pain. Wait… Scream? Since when can Leila scream?

My question soon gets answered, as the Leila that was on the ground slowly fades into thin air, and she is replaced by the lessathi from before, who is clutching at his abdomen, trying desperately to stop the bleeding. At the same time, the lessathi that was in front of me turns into Leila, who is now staring at the screaming lessathi in front of her, with her dagger still in her hand.

An illusion? It was an illusion all along? How did I not figure this out sooner?

While I'm busy questioning myself, Kate wastes no time, and she finishes off the last remaining lessathi by sending an ice dagger flying into his head. She then turns to look at me, and she shakes her head in disapproval.

" 'Help me, Barry' ?" she says. "Seriously? When's the last time you've seen Leila play the damsel in distress? Especially against a weakling such as this?"

"Wait a minute," I say. "You're not going to tell me that Leila's call for help was the only thing that led you to believe that she was in fact the lessathi, are you?"

"Actually, that is exactly what I'm going to tell you," Kate says.

"But what if you were wrong?" I ask her, shocked.

"Then Daren would have had to cast an extra healing spell," Kate says. "I made sure to not hit any vital spots with my first few cones, just in case, so there would have been no lasting damage."

"Wow…" I say. "Uh… I'm not sure how to react to this."

"Just react like you always do," Kate says. "With a quip."

She pauses, as she sees Daren and the others starting to free themselves from the effects of the paralysis trap.

"Come on," Kate says. "We should search their headquarters and see if we can find anything useful. With a little luck, I might find some information about Diane."

"That was way too close!" Daren says, as we all begin to enter the headquarters. "We really need to do something about our vulnerability to electricity."

"Yeah," Hadrik says. "I don't think I've felt like having so little control of a situation since that time we got shocked by Kate's elementalist friend. If Barry hadn't figured out how this spell worked before we got here, we would have been goners."

"Well, I guess It's a good thing that you have a friend who spent his life nerding it up in libraries," I say. "Isn't that right, Daren?"

"Yeah, yeah..." Daren says, and we all begin to search the desks in the lessathi's room.

It takes us a few minutes of searching, but we eventually realize that every single drawer is completely empty.

"Damn..." Daren says. "Not even a single document. Do you think that they may have emptied out their headquarters before this meeting, as a precautionary measure, on the off-chance that they actually got defeated?"

"They may have done it way before that," I say. "If they were already suspecting that the king's servant got followed here, they probably considered this location to be compromised, so they made sure to not leave anything of value in this place."

"I guess you're right..." Daren says. "So, I suppose we should be getting back to the castle, then?"

"Yes," Kate says. "I'm definitely not going to find out any information about Diane from this place. Let's go back."

"You know…" I tell Kate, as we prepare to exit the headquarters. "You could have left that last lessathi alive, in order to interrogate him. You already had him more or less immobilized, with that first set of ice cones that you shot in his abdomen, so he shouldn't have been much of a threat."

"I didn't want to risk it," Kate says. "That lessathi was practically the illusionist of their group, and he may well have had other tricks up his sleeve. It's never a good idea to leave illusionists alive after a fight."

"What do you guys think… should we take these weapons with us?" Hadrik says, as we pass the lessathi's corpses.

"Oh, we definitely should be taking them," I say. "I could totally use one of these!"

I then take the emerald encrusted shield from the ground and I start swinging it up and down, in an attempt to cast a spell with it.

"Hmm…" I say. "I don't recall that lessathi uttering any incantations before he cast his illusion spell or before casting the flash of light that he used to hide the illusion from us. Maybe there's a hidden button or something I'm missing?"

"Let's take these to king Golmyck," Daren says. "He's a tinkerer. He should be able to make sense of how these weapons work."

"Whoa!" Hadrik says, and he jumps back three feet, after having taken only one step forward. "I almost forgot about that electric trap from earlier."

"Relax!" I say. "That spell deactivates automatically as soon as everyone in its range leaves the area."

I then go past the area where the trap had been activated before, and I turn around, to face Hadrik.

"See?" I say. "Nothing to worry about. Let's get out of here."

We grab the lessathi weapons, and we begin to head back, following the exact same route that we took on our way here. As soon as we reach the corridor below the king's basement, Hadrik starts throwing rocks at the trapdoor above us, in order to get the king's attention. A few seconds later, the trapdoor opens up, and the extensive ladder drops all the way down, just like before.

"It's going to be a bit difficult to climb this ladder while carrying these lessathi weapons," Daren says.

"Can't you somehow strap them to your back like you did with your shield?" I say.

"Well, the shield is made to be strapped to your back when you travel for extended periods of time," Daren says. "These weapons don't have any straps, and the shield strap is not designed to hold any other weapons on it."

"You're both making this sound way more complicated than it really is," Hadrik says, as he picks up the lessathi trident. "There's no need to carry these all the way up with us. I can just throw them through the hatch."

He then shouts loudly, to make sure that Golmyck can hear him.

"Hey, Golmyck!" Hadrik shouts. "I'm going to throw some things your way! Some of them have pointy ends. Make sure you stay away from the trapdoor!"

The gnome gives us an okay sign with his hand, and then Hadrik starts tossing all of the weapons through the hatch. As soon as he's done, we all climb the extensive ladder, one by one, and once we reach the king's basement, the trapdoor closes itself back up, behind us.

"Should I take it that the lessathi are all dead?" the king asks us.

"Yeah, we took them all out," I say.

"Extraordinary," Golmyck says. "And not a single scratch on any of you, either. I'll admit that I'm impressed."

"Just make sure to keep up your end of the bargain," Daren says. "We don't want to see any more slaves on the streets when we come back to this city."

"Of course!" Golmyck says. "I will begin making preparations for the abolition of slavery first thing tomorrow morning. I only wish there were something else I could repay you with, for your help. Given that the mission I've sent you on is a secret, I cannot give any official reason to the treasurer that would justify offering you a reward."

"Hey, there's no need," I say. "We're the ones who volunteered for the mission in the first place. If we wanted payment, we would have asked for it from the get-go."

"Still… I wouldn't want you to leave empty-handed," the king says. "Hold on, I think I've got something that might be of use to you."

He then disappears under his workbench, and he reappears ten seconds later with a small device in his hand, which only has a screen and a button.

"This device will help you find out if someone is a lessathi or a human," Golmyck says. "You simply need to press this button while aiming the device at someone, and the writing that will appear on the screen will tell you whether they are a lessathi or not. I made it a long time ago, back when I couldn't differentiate between the auras of humans and lessathi with my magical sense. I haven't really used it in years, so you can have it if you want it."

"We'll take it," I say. "I'm not sure how much use we'll get out of it, but you never know!"

"So, about these lessathi weapons that Hadrik threw into your room…" Daren says.

"Ah, yes," Golmyck says. "Let me have a look."

"I tried to get that shield to activate, but I just

couldn't find any switch on it," I say, as the gnome studies the lessathi weapons, closely.

"Well, it's no wonder," Golmyck says. "These weapons have clearly been designed to only work in the hands of the individuals that they were tailored for. If you don't have the exact aura signatures of the lessathi who were using these devices, I doubt that you could get any use out of them. This measure was probably taken in order to avoid having their enemies use their own weapons against them."

"So, they are completely useless, then?" I say.

"Not entirely," Golmyck says. "As weapons, they have no use, but if I disassemble them, I might just find some parts that I could use on some of my other devices."

"Oh," I say. "Speaking of your devices, I just remembered that I overheard the lessathi say something important about that telepathic device of yours, while they were still in the meeting. It turns out that they are the ones who sabotaged the device, in order to delay the first round of the tournament. From what I could understand, it sounded like they had some sort of a plan that they needed to carry out until the beginning of the first round, and they needed as much time as possible to get it done properly, but things didn't really seem to work out in the end, because a lot more mages died than they were expecting, which messed up their plan, somehow."

"Hmm," Golmyck says. "I definitely remember them trying to convince the other kings to insert a rule in the tournament where the participants couldn't kill each other unless the rules explicitly required them to. So, it was sabotage, that caused the malfunction… That would explain why the device was behaving so erratically, no matter how many times I tried to tinker with it. How interesting. This information will certainly help me to fix the device faster. Thank you for letting me know!"

"You heard what the lessathi were discussing during their meeting?" Daren asks me.

"Yeah, I could hear them from far away, thanks to my hearing stat," I tell Daren, offhandedly. "So, anyway, I guess we should be taking our backpacks, then. It's getting late, and we still have a feast we need to attend to."

"Alright," the king says. "Remember to not say anything about your secret mission while you are outside this room. The lessathi may be dead, but their spies are still alive and kicking. Many of them will probably leave the city as soon as they find out that they no longer have any employers to pay them, but some of the more loyal ones may seek revenge, and you wouldn't want to get yourself or your friends targeted by any of these assassins. I will have my own spies and assassins deal with these more loyal followers of the lessathi in due time, but for now, we should all be careful."

"Yeah, we'll be careful," Daren says.

"Good luck on your travels," Golmyck says. "And remember that you will always be welcome to Thilias, should you choose to visit this city again!"

We grab our backpacks, we wave goodbye to the king, and we go climb the stairs to the throne room. The king's servant was still there, and he had a rather uneasy look in his eyes, when he saw us finally exit the king's basement, after more than two hours, but he said nothing, and he led us outside, just like the last time when we came to the castle.

About an hour and a half later, we finally reach the mansion, where Enrique was waiting for us impatiently.

"Finally!" Enrique says. "I was almost beginning to think that you might not show up!"

"Yeah, sorry about that," Daren says. "Our meeting with the king took a bit longer than we anticipated."

"Well, what's important is that you are here," Enrique says. "The food is already done. I will tell the cooks to reheat it, and we will begin eating shortly."

He then goes into the kitchen, and he comes back out about fifteen minutes later, followed by five cooks, each carrying plates of food, and each of them bringing a completely different specialty dish to the table. I would not be surprised if these dishes actually tasted better than what Flower can magically conjure, given her relatively limited knowledge of the culinary arts. After the cooks are done placing all of the dishes on one of the bigger picnic tables from the yard, Ella and Rose's siblings also join us, and we all seat ourselves at the table, getting ready for the well-earned feast.

We spent the next few hours eating, drinking, and celebrating our long-awaited release from the arena. The food provided to us by the cooks actually did turn out to be on par with Flower's magically conceived delicacies, if not better. There were so many dishes on that table of which I'd never heard before, that it looked almost as if I were participating in a royal banquet of some kind. The cooks were initially all standing up in a line, in front of the table, waiting for us to order refills, but after a whole hour of Hadrik insisting that they join us for a drink, they eventually gave in, and began to slowly loosen up, as the effect of the dwarven ale was starting to set in. Towards the end of the celebration, Enrique made sure to supply us all with Rose's special herbs, so we could start fresh in the morning, without fear of any hangovers.

Since we needed to get up before sunrise the next day, we had to end the celebration early, in order to get at least a few hours of sleep, but the hours that we spent at that table were exactly what we needed, after what we'd been through in the past few days. The next morning, while it was still dark outside, we all lined up in the yard, to give Enrique our farewells.

"Well, I've only had the pleasure of talking to you for a few hours in total," Enrique says, "but they were hours well spent. I will never forget you, my friends. I hope you will all get to accomplish your goals, whether they be winning the tournament, or whatever else your hearts may desire!"

"Goodbye, Enrique," Daren says. "Remember to keep that transceiver that I gave you earlier with you at all times. You never know when we may need to contact each other again, especially while the tournament is still in progress."

We all wave goodbye to Enrique and we set out to find the northern gate. After losing our way a few times, and having to ask the locals for directions on numerous occasions, we finally manage to reach our destination, just as the sun rises, and as we get a good look at the city gates, we see that Melindra was already waiting for us there, with her back leaning against a wall.

As she waves at us, to make sure that we've spotted her, we quicken our pace, and we get ready to finally take our first step towards our original goal. After so much sidetracking, and so many delays, at long last, we can get back to what we came here to do. Participating in the Magium Tournament.

Chapter 8

"There you are!" Melindra says, once we all get within hearing range of her. "Just in time. Tell me, are you all ready to begin our adventure?"

"If by adventure, you mean waiting in line for an hour, then yes," Daren says, as he points towards the city's northern gate.

There seem to be at least a few dozen groups of people currently lined up on the main road leading to the northern gate. Some of them are just travellers, like us, but most of them appear to be merchants, with carts full of wares that need to be inspected one by one by the guards at the city's exit, before they are allowed to pass through the gate. Judging by how long it's taking the guards to inspect each cart, I'd say that Daren's estimation might actually be a bit optimistic. We're probably going to be stuck here for a lot longer than one hour.

"Ah, yes," Melindra says, as she takes a glance towards the very long line of carts in front of her. "I forgot that the northern gate is primarily used by merchants in this city. It would have been so much nicer if they actually made more than one gate on their northern wall, to solve their traffic problems."

"More gates means more vulnerable areas that need to be protected," Daren says. "It would not be a good idea in times such as these, when monster attacks are rampant. Let's just line up like all the others. The sun is barely up, so we'll have plenty of time to travel even if we waste another hour in this city."

"Actually, I have a better idea," Melindra says. "We'll be taking a shortcut!"

"A shortcut?" Hadrik asks, confused. "You mean, like an underground tunnel, or…"

"Oh, no, no…" Melindra says, with a smile. "I wasn't talking about a tunnel."

She then snaps her fingers, and we all begin to slowly get raised into the air, higher and higher, as I feel several currents of air moving around me, in a similar fashion to how they used to move when I was using air magic to fly, during my battle with the skeleton stillwaters.

"No way…" Daren says, as we keep getting raised higher into the air. "You're not seriously considering doing this, are you?"

"Doing what?" Melindra says, with a coy smile.

"Don't play dumb with me!" Daren says. "You're going to fly us over that whole damn wall! Are you out of your mind? This is against the law! Those guards stationed on the wall are going to start shooting at us the moment we go over them!"

"So, what?" Melindra says. "You're a white mage and an enchanter, aren't you? You can just use that shield of yours to create a barrier around us, and we'll be fine."

"I don't have any barrier spells that deflect regular arrows!" Daren shouts.

"Wait, seriously?" Melindra says, while raising an eyebrow.

"And besides, that's not the point!" Daren says. "We don't want to make this whole city into our enemy just because we were too lazy to wait in line!"

"You don't?" Melindra asks. "Why not? Are you planning to come back to this city afterwards?"

"Yes!" Daren shouts. "I mean, I think… I don't know!"

"Well, it's too late to go back now, anyway,"

Melindra says. "Look below us. We're already passing over their wall. And those archers are getting ready to attack us. I hope at least someone in this group can defend against arrows, because lifting so many people at once using only air magic requires a great deal of concentration, and I don't want to risk dropping any of you while trying to deflect incoming projectiles."

"Attention, to all the mages that are now flying over our wall," we hear a guard shouting through a magical voice magnifier, from the top of the city's wall. "You are to descend at once! I repeat. You are to descend at once! If you ignore this warning, we will treat you as an enemy of the kingdom, and we will open fire! I will not repeat this again!"

"Melindra, you heard the guy," I say. "Bring us down, so we can talk to them. Maybe we can still smooth things over with the guards, somehow."

"And wait three hours in some cell before they decide to let us go?" Melindra says. "No, thanks. I'd rather deal with the arrows."

"It's not just the arrows, damn it!" I say. "I don't want to become a lawbreaker in this city again, after we went through all that trouble to get absolved of our crimes!"

"Well, tough luck, then," Melindra says. "Because I'm not planning to stop, no matter what you say. But hey, if you think you can stop me yourself, then I invite you to try. I can't wait to see what you're planning to do against a stillwater of my caliber— AHAHAHA— Stop it! Stop it or I'll— Ahahaha!"

While Melindra was busy bragging, I decided I'd had enough, so I put both my hands to the sides of her waist, and began to tickle her from behind. As the girl laughs, I can feel the air currents around me become more unstable, and I start to wobble uncontrollably, in the air, along with everybody else.

"Damn it!" Melindra says, while struggling to control her laughter. "I can't— ahaha— I can't move away from you while I'm concentrating on levitating everyone! Ahahaha! Stop… *tickling me*!"

As Melindra is talking, the captain of the guards gives the order to attack, and now there are dozens of arrows heading in our direction, while our group is just floating in the air, not having moved an inch since I started tickling Melindra. As soon as she sees the arrows, Kate immediately conjures several shields made of ice, which begin to move in the air all around us, defending us from the enemy's projectiles.

"Barry, what the hell, man?" Daren asks, as he sees himself shaking up and down, while still floating. "Do you have a death wish?"

"Relax!" I tell Daren. "It's not like she's going to drop us."

"Yes, I will!" Melindra says, "I will drop you! Just you wait— Ahahaha! Quit it!"

"Yeah, right," I say. "You're going to tell me that you went through all this trouble to find someone who could kill that king of yours, and now you're just going to let us drop to our deaths? Just get us down, will you? Hopefully it's not too late, and we can still talk things over with the guards."

"I'm going to remember this!" Melindra says, as I stop tickling her, so she can finally start bringing us down, towards the ground.

When the captain of the guards sees us lowering our altitude, he signals his men to cease their fire, and then he hurries towards a ladder, in order to descend from the wall, on the outer side of the city. By the time we all make it to the ground, right outside the city walls, the captain of the guards is already waiting for us impatiently, with a few of the other guards accompanying him, as his escorts. The captain is a dwarf, of around the same size as Hadrik, wearing heavy armor, with a long brown beard covering the bottom half of his face, and a steel helmet covering much of the rest, aside from his eyes and his nose.

As soon as we reach his position, Daren and I quickly begin to explain to him what happened, while repeatedly reassuring him that we were not looking to start a fight, when we flew over their walls.

"Ugh…" the captain of the guards says with his eyes closed, as he rubs his forehead, while shaking his head in disapproval. "You know, if you really needed to leave the city in a hurry, you could have just asked one of the guards by the gate. We were all there when you people fought the dragon yesterday, together with king Golmyck, so it wouldn't have been a problem to do you a small favor in return for your service. Listen, I'm going to try my best to keep this incident off the records, but please, for the love of all the gods, don't do this kind of crap anymore. We guards are busy enough as it is. We don't have time to deal with your shenanigans."

"Of course…" Daren says. "Thank you for your understanding! And I apologize again, in the name of our group. I hope that the next time we meet, it will be under better circumstances."

Daren and I then turn back towards the others, and we signal to them that we're good to go. Melindra still has her pouting expression on her face after what happened earlier, but she doesn't say any more on the subject for the time being, and she takes the lead, as we all move to follow her.

"Why aren't we taking the main road?" Kate asks Melindra, as she leads us towards the woods. "I saw a sign that said it was leading directly to Ollendor."

"Oh, that road takes longer than going through the forest," Melindra says. "It's because it takes a more roundabout way, through safer territories, so that the merchants can better avoid monster attacks. There's no need for us to take such precautions, though. Most of you are powerful mages, right? Well, nowhere near as powerful as I am, but still…"

"Can you stop with the condescending remarks?" I tell her. "It's clear that your level of power cannot even compare to that of Eiden. And if we're talking regular stillwaters, then we already beat five of them at once without much trouble. They weren't anything special. Hell, I practically finished them all off by myself!"

"Stop bragging, you idiot!" Arraka says. "If it weren't for my advice, and your stupidly overpowered lessathi relic, those 'regular' stillwaters would have stomped you all into the ground!"

"Okay, fine, I admit it!" I say. "We may have gotten a bit lucky there, but still, there were five of them, and they were a squad! She's just one stillwater, and not a particularly impressive one, either. Judging by what spells I've seen her cast until now, I'd say she's an air elementalist. Isn't that right, Melindra?"

"And what if I am?" Melindra says.

"That's like… the single weakest type of elementalist in existence," I say. "Even if you take into account all the artificial mages with their non-traditional elements invented by the lessathi. Can you even cast anything other than wind spells?"

"Of course I can!" Melindra says, visibly upset.

"Oh, yeah?" I say. "Well, why don't you teleport us all to the city of Ollendor right now, then? Eiden could have done it."

"I am not Eiden," Melindra says.

"Okay, okay, my mistake," I say. "But surely, a powerful air elementalist such as yourself could easily fly us all the way there, right? Oh, wait… I just remembered that you could barely keep us afloat while we were going over that wall. So, I'm supposing that flying is off the table too, then? Huh… Well, I don't know about the rest of you guys, but to me, stillwaters are beginning to sound less like legendary mages, and more like regular mages with a little extra power and energy! Funny how this works, eh?"

Melindra is now furrowing her eyebrows and pursing her lips, making yet another pouting expression, as she looks at me.

"That's enough, Barry!" Daren says. "We only just began our journey. You don't want us to be fighting all the way to Ollendor, do you?"

"Hey, I'm just saying…" I say. "If she were to admit that she's not as powerful as she thinks she is, and that we could easily beat her if we were to all team up against her, then it would be much easier for all of us."

"Well, what if I were to prove you wrong, then?" Melindra says, smirking, as she cracks her knuckles. "All we need is for your white mage to temporarily cancel the effects of his enchanter's oath, and we can get down to business."

"Hey, now we're talking!" Hadrik says, with a grin.

"Sounds good to me," I say.

"Ahahaha!" Arraka says, as I see Kate smack herself hard in the face. "You're all going to get obliterated! That girl doesn't know how to hold back. Ahahahaha!"

"Shut up!" Daren shouts. "Nobody is fighting anyone! I am not going to undo the oath just because you people want a sparring match! We are outside city limits! We could be getting attacked by enemy mages at any moment. We don't have time to play games, here!"

"Fine!" Melindra says, frowning.

"What if we only ask her to demonstrate her powers, without fighting us?" I say.

"Hmm…" Daren says. "Well, I guess it couldn't hurt to know what she's capable of. Seeing as how we'll be working together for a while…"

"Perfect!" Melindra says, as her face lights up. "Hold on. Let me get really far away from you, because I wouldn't want to end up burying you under a ton of rocks by accident!"

"Uh…" Daren says. "What exactly are you planning to—"

He doesn't get to finish his sentence, because Melindra flies into the air right away, and she eventually gets far enough from us that we can barely even distinguish her shape anymore. She then stops very high up in the sky, and she appears to be raising her arms in the air, as she is channeling her spell. Not long afterwards, we feel a very powerful wind coming towards us, as we watch the air currents below Melindra spinning faster and faster, until they turn into a full-blown tornado.

Dozens of trees are now getting pulled from their roots and being lifted into the air by the giant twister in the distance, and even large rocks underneath the soil are starting to break off from the ground. As a large cloud of dust covers the whole area between us and the tornado, the merchants from Thilias are beginning to stop by the side of the road, in order to gaze at the terrifying spectacle that is unraveling before their eyes.

"Okay, Melindra, I think you've made your point!" Daren shouts, as loud as he can. "You should come down, now. You're scaring the locals."

As soon as she hears Daren call out to her, Melindra begins to cancel her spell, and all of the air currents forming the tornado slowly come to a halt, over the next thirty seconds, while the trees and the rocks that were caught in the tornado fall to the ground, one by one. Once the twister has dissipated into the air, Melindra comes flying back, and she lands in front of us, with a victorious smile on her face.

"How was that for a demonstration of my powers?"

she says.

"Okay, okay…" I say. "You win this round. Maybe the air element isn't as weak as I made it out to be earlier."

"Of course it isn't!" Melindra says. "Even wind by itself can do this much damage, but this is magic wind we're talking about! You can sharpen it like any other element. You can reinforce it. Do you have any idea how many possibilities—"

Melindra suddenly stops in the middle of her sentence, as she briefly falls from her feet, with her eyes closing, looking as if she were seconds away from fainting.

"Are… you alright?" Daren says, while he helps her regain her balance.

"I'm fine," Melindra says, simply, as she rubs her forehead, with her eyes still closed.

"Hah!" Arraka says. "I told you she doesn't know when to hold back. She used up all of her energy to make that tornado, and now she's so tired she can barely even stand up anymore!"

"Wait, are you serious?" Daren says, while he is still holding Melindra, to make sure that she won't faint again. "Should we take a break or something?"

"I said I'm fine!" Melindra says, as she pulls herself away from Daren. "Let's keep going."

We all exchange a few looks, but we don't say anything else, and we follow her in silence for the next few minutes. At the beginning, it was pretty obvious for everyone that Melindra was making an effort to even walk straight, but her situation gradually improved as we advanced through the forest, probably as a result of her magical energy getting slowly restored as she walked.

"So…" I say to Melindra, as we travel through the area filled with craters and fallen trees caused by the earlier tornado. "Do you still remember our discussion from yesterday? You were just about to tell us how stillwaters are created, but then we got sidetracked, and we never really got back to our initial conversation afterwards. Shall we continue where we left off?"

"That is a lie, and you know it," Melindra says. "I never said I would tell you anything about how you can become a stillwater."

"Okay, you never said you would… but you will tell us, right?" I say.

"No," Melindra says.

"Why not?" I say.

"Because Eiden decided after the still winter that we should keep what happened to us a secret," Melindra says. "He was worried that if people found out how we became stillwaters, certain individuals might try to exploit that knowledge for their own benefit."

"Wait," Hadrik says. "Are you saying that all the stillwaters got created during the still winter?"

"Sort of," Melindra says. "At any rate, I think it would be very unlikely for you to meet any stillwaters that are younger than six hundred years old."

"Does this mean that all stillwaters are immortal?" Kate asks.

"No, not immortal!" Melindra says. "We can be killed just fine. It's just that we stopped aging as soon as we turned into stillwaters. We also became sterile, and mostly immune to diseases, but that's beside the point."

"So, none of the stillwaters can have kids?" Hadrik says.

"Yes, that's what I just said," Melindra says.

"But where are all the other stillwaters?" Daren says.

"Dead, most likely," Melindra says. "Most of them got killed by Eiden, but there were also some of them that went wild and got hunted down by various mercenaries. I think there may have been others I don't remember, but either way, I haven't met other stillwaters aside from Eiden in ages. I heard he's been travelling around the world for a while, so I'm guessing that most legends you know about stillwaters were actually about him."

"Did you just say that Eiden killed most of the other stillwaters?" Daren says. "Why did he do that? And when?"

"Well…" Melindra says. "To be quite honest, I think I may have already said too much on this subject. If you want to know more, you'll have to ask Eiden directly."

"Could you at least tell us how you met Eiden, and what is your affiliation with him?" Kate asks. "Are you related by any chance?"

"Oh, no, we're not related," Melindra says.

"Ex-lovers, then?" Hadrik asks.

"Not really," Melindra says.

"Then why did Arraka say that you were trailing behind him and the fox during the still winter?" Kate says.

"Well," Melindra says, "we sort of became friends while he was being imprisoned. Actually, we were more like trading partners than friends, but I guess we also became friends, afterwards."

"Was this before the still winter?" I say. "What was he being imprisoned for?"

"Yes, it was before the still winter," Melindra says. "I don't know what he was being imprisoned for. He never told me."

"But how did he manage to get himself imprisoned when he has all these powers?" I say.

"He wasn't a stillwater back then," Melindra says.

"But he was still a mage, right?" Hadrik asks. "How were they keeping his powers in check? Were they using an anti-magic or paralysis cell?"

"No, it was a regular cell," Melindra says.

"Was Eiden wearing some sort of collar while he was

in his cell?" Kate says.

"Hmm…" Melindra says. "I'm pretty sure that he wasn't wearing any sort of collar back then."

"Then how did they manage to trap him?" Kate asks. "And who was it that captured him?"

"Uh…" Melindra says. "I really don't think I should be talking about this."

"Why not?" Kate says. "Did Eiden ask you not to talk about it?"

"Something of the sort, yes," Melindra says.

"What about that 'trading partners' thing you mentioned earlier?" Hadrik says. "Can you talk about that?"

"I suppose…" Melindra says. "See, when I was tasked with cleaning the prison corridors, I would often notice this large pile of rocks in one corner of Eiden's cell, and each of those rocks were so marvelously unique in their shapes, sizes and compositions that I could barely take my eyes off them. I wasn't sure how I could convince Eiden to give them to me, but once I saw those rocks, I knew that I needed to have them. So I kept coming back to Eiden's cell, and I kept starting conversations with him every day, in the hopes that I'd find out something that he needed from outside his cell, so that I could trade it to him in exchange for some of his rocks."

"You wanted to make a trade with him for some rocks?…" Daren asks. "Couldn't you just have asked him for them?"

"Well, obviously, I could have just asked him for them!" Melindra says. "But who would be stupid enough to give them away for free?"

"But they're—" Daren starts to say, but he interrupts himself mid-sentence. "Ugh… you know what? You're right. My mistake. Please, continue."

"Thank you!" Melindra says. "So, anyway, after

several conversations with Eiden, I found out that the food they were serving him was of extremely poor quality. Since I was also in charge of serving dishes, and I had access to the kitchen, I offered to sneak some better food into his cell, every once in a while, in exchange for certain rocks from the pile in his corner. At first, he thought that I wasn't being serious, and he accepted the trade, somewhat in jest. But when he actually saw me bring him the food, while holding out my hand, waiting for my hard earned prize, he looked rather shocked. I had to point several times towards the rock that I wanted before he actually gave it to me. He also seemed to be amused every time I referred to our bargains as even trades, but I'm not sure exactly why. He never told me the reason."

As Melindra talks, I suddenly remember my first conversation with Eiden, when I also offered him my own version of an 'even trade'. After hearing this story, I think I'm starting to understand a bit better why he burst out laughing like that when I made my proposition to him.

"You collect rocks?" Flower says, all of a sudden. "Do you still have them with you?"

"Why, of course!" Melindra says. "I always carry them with me. My collection has gotten a lot larger in the past six hundred years, but I still have those original rocks that I started my collection with here in my backpack. Do you want to see them?"

"Yes!" Flower says, excited. "I'd love to!"

"Well, okay, but just so you know, I won't be slowing down my pace," Melindra says. "If you want to see them, you'll have to join my side, and I'll show them to you as we walk."

"Of course!" Flower says, as she rushes by Melindra's side.

The stillwater girl then takes off her backpack, and

she begins to take out her rocks one by one, handing them over to Flower so she can get a good look at them, and then putting them back inside when she's done. As I was suspecting, none of the rocks seem to have any real marketable value, and they would look completely worthless to anyone else, but that still doesn't seem to stop Flower from marveling at every one of the rocks, while Melindra proudly explains to her the features that made her consider the stones to be worthy of her collection, making sure to also give her a brief summary of where she found each of them.

While Melindra and Flower are having their discussion, Daren gives the rest of us a signal, and we all slow down a bit to have a talk, outside of Melindra's hearing range, while still following her.

"So, what do you all think about Melindra so far?" Daren whispers, while making sure that Melindra isn't paying attention to us. "Do you think that she might be working with Eiden?"

"You mean, like an informant?" I say. "I don't know… I'd say the chances of that are pretty slim."

"Yeah, Daren, I think you're overreacting," Hadrik says. "We already knew that she was friends with Eiden when we took her deal. There's no need to doubt her every step of the way."

"You're all looking at this the wrong way," Kate says. "It doesn't matter if she's trustworthy or not. As long as we don't discuss any crucial information while she's around, we'll be fine."

"It does matter, damn it!" Daren says. "If we're all just going to lag behind like this every time we need to discuss something important, it will look suspicious as hell!"

"So what?" Kate says. "Why would we care if she thinks we're suspicious?"

"Because she's a member of the team!" Daren says.

"Is she?" Kate says, raising an eyebrow.

"Listen," Daren says. "My question was whether we should trust her or not. If you're just going to say we should keep everything hidden from her, then it's the same as saying that—"

"You know," Melindra says, as she sees us all huddled up together, far behind her and Flower, "if you're going to talk about me behind my back, you could at least *try* to do it in a less obvious way…"

"What?" Daren says, in a painfully obvious fake tone. "No, you've got it all wrong! We weren't talking about you! We were talking about… err… Flower!"

"You were?" Flower says, looking worried.

"Hey, nice save, Daren!" I say, as I pat him hard on the back. "I don't see how anyone could still think that we're being suspicious after a well thought-out explanation like that!"

"Shut up," Daren mumbles, but he doesn't say anything else.

"Listen," Melindra says, "if you all want to have your own private conversations about strategies and whatnot, it's fine, but could you at least wait until we make camp or take a break somewhere? It's annoying to have to keep a lookout for you, so you don't get lost, while I'm also monitoring the monsters that are trying to ambush us."

"There are monsters trying to ambush us?" I say, while I quickly take off my backpack, and pull out my crossbow. "Damn it, Arraka, you had *one* job!"

"My 'job' was to tell you about invisible enemies, jackass," Arraka says. "None of these enemies are invisible. What kind of morons are you that you can't even tell when monsters are laying an ambush for you, anyway?"

"What type of monsters are we talking about?" Kate says. "And how many? They're too far away for me to be able to get a read on them with my magical sense."

"Oh, they're actually not that far away," Melindra says. "But they are all suppressing their magical auras, so it's understandable that you can't sense them approaching. I think there are about five orcs, two ogres, and two goblins. The goblins are both mages, but the others seem to be just warriors. You should be able to take them out without much trouble."

" 'You' ?" Daren asks. "Don't you mean 'we'? As in 'we', the group of people that are all travelling together, who will also be fighting these monsters together, as a team?"

"What?" Melindra says. "Of course not! Don't be ridiculous. What would be the use of bringing you all the way to Ollendor with me if you can't even beat a few monsters by yourselves? Do you have any idea what good defenses they have in that city? How else do you think their king could afford to piss off every other kingdom in Varathia without getting killed off by now?"

"But what if the monsters kill us before we get there?" Daren says.

"Then I'd have to find somebody else to help me," Melindra says. "Someone who could kill off a few orcs without complaining so much. Listen, it's just a few monsters. It's not the end of the world. The ice mage could probably take them all out by herself. The little girl too. Even the half-lessathi could probably handle them if he invested in the right stats."

"We have names, you know…" Daren says.

"I don't know your names," Melindra says. "And besides, why would I need to know them? You're all distinguishable enough by your races and specializations that I don't need to bother to learn them."

"You're trying really hard to get on our nerves, aren't you?" Daren says.

"Why do you say that?" Melindra asks, with a

genuinely puzzled expression on her face.

"Be quiet!" Kate says. "I can hear the ogres approaching from behind us. I think the orcs started advancing as well. We should be seeing them in front of us soon."

"Wow, that's impressive!" Melindra says. "You can tell all that just from the sound of their footsteps? How can you tell the difference? Is it because ogres are bigger and heavier than orcs?"

"I said be quiet!" Kate says. "If you're not going to be useful, then at least stay out of our way, and don't distract us with your talking."

"How cold!" Melindra says. "I'm starting to wonder if there isn't actually some truth behind those myths which claim that there is a direct correlation between a mage's personality and their elemental affinity!"

"Do you ever shut up?" Kate says.

She then suddenly conjures a shield made of ice in her hand, and she places it in front of her, just in time to block an arrow that came shooting straight for her.

"For Tyrath!" shouts an orc from behind the trees, in the Common language, as he and four of his companions come rushing towards us, while roaring loudly, in unison.

All of them are green-skinned, tall as Daren, with muscular physiques, pig-like faces and fangs coming out of their mouths, just as one would expect most orcs to look like, but these ones are armed to the teeth. One of them is wielding two flaming double-edged battleaxes in his hands, another one is wielding a two-handed broadsword that is almost as big as him, and the other three are all using maces and shields that appear to be made from high quality metal.

The orc with the flaming axes seems to be the leader of the group. He is the one that shouted the first battle cry, and all of the other orcs followed his directions, as he led the charge towards us, and as he clashed directly with Daren.

"Watch out!" we see Leila's writing, in large blue letters, in front of us. "They're one of the dragon's elite squads! Do not take them lightly!"

She then dashes behind one of the orcs that is less heavily armored, and she stabs him in the back with both her daggers. The orc roars, and he turns around, swinging his mace at her. His movements are much too slow for Leila, however, so she quickly dashes back, out of his reach, and tries to attack him again.

"Leila, behind you!" Kate shouts, as another one of the orcs tries to position himself behind Leila, in order to strike.

Kate then attempts to impale the monster with a spike made of ice that appears from the ground, in front of him. The orc manages to smash the icy spike with his enchanted mace, but he loses his momentum, and doesn't get to attack Leila anymore, who quickly slides out of his reach.

"I'll take the ogres," Hadrik says, as he rushes towards the two ogres that were trying to jump us from behind.

In the meantime, Flower engulfs one of the orcs in a pillar of fire, but he walks out of it completely unscathed, thanks to his anti-magic armor, and he starts running towards her, with his broadsword at the ready.

"Damn it!" Flower says, as she jumps out of the orc's way and rolls on the ground.

Once I get a clear shot of the orc that attacked Flower, I aim my crossbow for the narrow slit in his helm, and I pull the trigger. My aim was a little off, and the crossbow bolt didn't go exactly where I wanted, but it still hit the monster's head, and due to the power behind the shot, it passed right through the orc's helmet and through his skull, making him stop his movements and drop to the ground like a log.

As I make sure that the orc is dead, I suddenly realize that the two goblin mages that Melindra talked about earlier have still not made their appearance. Should I go look for them?

If I stay here, I'm probably not going to get much use out of this crossbow against those three orcs using shields, and I'd rather not risk hitting Daren and Hadrik by trying to attack the monsters that they're already busy fighting.

I could fight the orcs at close range, but would it be a good idea to let those mages unchecked? I'm going to have to think carefully about this.

As I place the crossbow in my backpack, I take a quick look at the battlefield to assess the current situation. Daren seems to have his hands full, fighting the orc captain with the flaming axes. The orc appears to have completely thrown away his defense, and he is focusing on delivering relentless attacks, one after the other, in order to not give Daren the chance to retaliate. Hadrik is still fighting the ogres behind us, and from what I can see, they are giving him just as much trouble as the ogre captain from the fort, so he'll probably still be busy with them for a while.

In the meantime, Leila is fighting three orcs at once, in an attempt to keep them away from our spell casters, while Kate, Flower and Illuna are all struggling to find ways to penetrate the orcs' anti-magic armor.

"I can't believe you people!" Arraka shouts, from her amulet, as Flower tries to aim a fireball in a way that would not hit Leila, along with the orcs. "You were fighting the dragon head-on, yesterday, but now you can't deal with a few of his lowly mooks? Are a bunch of anti-magic armors really all it takes to throw you into disarray?"

"Yeah, I'll have to admit that I'm a bit disappointed,

here," Melindra says, as she calmly looks around her, at all the people who are fighting for their lives. "If this is how these people handle a well-organized team of reasonably-skilled combatants, I shudder to think how they will handle Ollendor's numerous teams of mercenaries."

Melindra's monologue appears to have caught the attention of one of the orcs that was fighting Leila, because he is now heading directly for the stillwater girl, with his mace at the ready. As soon as he reaches her, the orc swings his mace hard towards her, in an attempt to bash her head in, but the girl evades his strike by floating a few inches above the ground, while pushing herself away from him with a small burst of air from the palms of her hands.

"Quit it!" Melindra shouts at the orc. "Fight them, not me! What are you, stupid?"

The orc ignores her completely, and he tries to hit her again, this time with his shield.

"I said, *cut it out*!" Melindra shouts at him, as she makes another jump backwards.

She then props herself into the ground with her feet, assuming a rather peculiar stance, as she bends her knees and keeps her elbows close to her body, while she faces her palms towards her attacker.

A very powerful burst of air then comes out of her hands, as the orc gets blown away, and thrown directly towards Kate, who was just about to launch an ice cone at one of Leila's opponents. Seeing the orc flying in her direction, Kate is forced to cancel her spell and to jump out of the way, in order to avoid getting knocked off her feet.

"Are you trying to get us all killed?!" Kate shouts furiously at Melindra, as she gets back up from the ground.

"Hey, it wasn't my fault!" Melindra says. "That orc

attacked me out of nowhere, when I was just minding my own business!"

"This is the middle of a battlefield, you fool!" Kate says. "If you want to mind your own business, then fly away from here and stop sabotaging us at every step!"

"Well, there's no need to be so rude about it," Melindra says, as she casts a spell, and she flies high into the air, out of the orcs' reach, while the orc that she blew away earlier goes back to fighting Leila.

"Flower! Illuna!" I say. "I want to go check why the two goblin mages haven't attacked us yet. Could you come with me? We should be able to find where they're hiding, with a little help from Arraka."

"Oh, right, the goblins!" Flower says. "I completely forgot about them. I think I may have actually sensed one of them cast a spell when the orcs attacked us. Follow me, it's this way!"

She then heads into the woods, and I rush to follow her, leaving the others behind, for now. After about twenty seconds of running, for some reason, I'm feeling that we aren't making a lot of progress, and some of the trees we are passing look oddly familiar.

"What the hell are you doing?" Arraka asks us, after a while. "Are you completely incapable of running in a straight line for more than five seconds? How many times are you going to keep circling around this area before you decide to finally head towards those goblins?"

"What are you talking about?" I say. "We've been heading in the same direction this whole time."

"You've been running in circles, you moron!" Arraka says. "Do I need to draw you a map? Hold on, let me show you."

She then conjures one of her map holograms into the air, and she starts drawing a line on it, showing us the direction in which we've been going since we began heading for the goblins. The line goes into one direction for a while, but after that, the trajectory changes completely, going through the same area over and over again.

"See?" Arraka says. "This is you. This is how stupid you looked. And do you see those two dots over there? That's where the goblins are. Now stop wasting time and get going. I'm getting second-hand embarrassment just from watching you people."

I try to head into the exact direction where the goblins are drawn on Arraka's map, but for some reason, I simply can't advance further than a few steps. Every time I get too close to the goblins, I instinctively turn away from them, without realizing, and then I see myself going in the opposite direction on the map. Even worse than that is the fact that my mind gets almost completely clouded every time this happens, and it feels as if the only thing that I can think of is how I need to get away from that area, even if I don't have any actual reason to do it.

"There is a suggestion spell cast on this area," Illuna says, as she studies the area in front of us closely. "Arraka is probably not as affected by it as we are because she's inside the amulet, but the spell seems to have a similar effect to the one that Kate is using to protect our camp."

"Wow…" I say. "I guess you weren't kidding when you said that your protection from dizziness would make me vulnerable to suggestion spells. The spell's effect on me was so strong that I could barely manage to think of anything other than getting away from that area, until I was at a far enough distance from it."

"Yes," Illuna says. "But sleep spells and dizziness spells are far more widely used than suggestion spells, so it's not that bad of a trade. Either way, we're not going to get past this area unless we get a very detailed description of the environment that those two goblins are situated in, so we can imagine that location as we move forward. Arraka, what can you tell us about the area around these goblins?"

Before Arraka gets to answer, we hear the sound of a very loud horn, coming from the area where all of our friends were fighting, and only a few seconds afterwards, the two dots representing the goblins disappear from Arraka's map, along with the auras of all the orcs and the ogres from the battlefield.

"Well," Illuna says, "at least now we know what the goblins were there for. One of them was maintaining the suggestion spell, while the other one laid in wait, in a secluded place where he could not be disturbed, in case he needed to concentrate on casting the teleportation spell, after receiving the signal to retreat."

"Let's get back to the others," I say. "Hopefully, everyone is alright."

As we get back to the area where all the fighting took place, we soon find out that not everyone had managed to walk out of the conflict completely unscathed. Leila is now lying on the ground, with her left ankle red and swollen, as Daren is kneeling beside her, while holding his hands slightly above her wound, with a bright white light coming out of them.

"You just need to bear with this for a little longer," Daren says, as he sees Leila grimacing from the pain, without making any sounds. "The healing spell is almost done."

"Gods, what happened here?" Flower says.

"Leila managed to kill two of the orcs she was fighting by herself," Daren says, "but the third one crushed her leg with his mace before she got the time to retreat. At least this gave Kate the opening she needed to aim one of her ice cones through the open slit in his helm, in order to finish him off, but the wound that Leila took was no joke. It looks much better now than it did before. Anyway, after the three orcs got killed, their captain jumped away from me and he blew in his horn, to sound the retreat. What happened to the goblins? Did they get away along with the other monsters?"

"Yes," Illuna says. "We didn't manage to reach them in time because they had a suggestion spell that was keeping us away from them. They got the signal to retreat before we could find a way to get around the spell's effects."

"But where did they go?" Hadrik says. "Are they planning to ambush us again?"

"Nah," Arraka says. "They're gone. If I can't sense them, then they've probably retreated back to their main headquarters. Wherever that is."

"There, it's healed," Daren says, as Leila's ankle goes back to its normal color and size. "But not completely. You shouldn't try any more acrobatic stunts for at least a day, until you fully recover. You should be able to walk without much trouble, though."

"Thank you…" Leila writes, as she gets up from the ground.

"Man, those ogres that I fought earlier were quite something!" Hadrik says. "I had almost as much trouble with them as I had with that ogre captain from the fort. It's a shame that they got away, though. That orc captain seemed to know his stuff too, judging by how long he could hold a stalemate with Daren."

"Yeah," I say. "This is the first time when we ran into monsters that were so strong and so well-organized. Leila, you said earlier that these were one of Tyrath's elite squads?"

"Yes," Leila writes. "He usually only dispatches these teams for special missions. I'm guessing that this particular group was sent here specifically to target you guys, since he could no longer kill you personally, due to his pact with Eiden. He must have sent at least one elite group to guard each of the city's exits, but they couldn't stay too close to the city gates, without being detected, so they made their ambush here, in the forest."

"Does Tyrath have any teams that are stronger than these elite squads?" I say.

"He used to," Leila writes. "But I don't think he has them anymore. I heard that there was a time when he actually had teams of dragons under his rule. But this was likely before he became unable to maintain his molten lava form at all times. From what I understand, the dragons in Varathia now live isolated, somewhere in the mountains, and they don't want to have anything to do with Tyrath, despite his claims of being the 'king of all dragons'."

"Regardless of what team Tyrath decides to send after us next," Illuna says, "what is most important is that we detect them before they actually have us surrounded. Arraka, from now on, you will also let us know when there are groups of monsters trying to ambush us, not just invisible enemies. Do you understand?"

"Hey, if you want my help, then how about you fight seriously, next time, huh?" Arraka says. "What was with that ridiculous performance of yours in the fight from earlier? Why didn't you use that drowning technique that I taught you on them, like you did yesterday on the dragon? It's not like their anti-magic helmets would have prevented them from breathing water into their lungs."

"I've already told you countless times," Illuna says. "I never managed to fully control that technique. What I did yesterday was a gamble, and I only did it because we were running out of options. And even so, I had to time my spell perfectly, so I'd cast it exactly as the dragon inhaled, when he was preparing to breathe his fire. This way, Tyrath's lungs were already full of water before he could react. If he had any air left in his lungs, he could have simply blown some air out of his mouth, and my water bubble would have dispersed into thin air. That's how little control I have over this spell. And aside from this, I can only cast it on one person at a time, and if someone breaks my concentration while I cast it, the spell will be undone in an instant."

"Well then, why don't you master it?" Arraka says. "Why did I waste my time teaching you such a useful technique if you're not even going to practice using it? Do you really hate me so much that you are willing to limit your spell arsenal just to spite me?"

"Fine!" Illuna says. "If it will make you shut up, then I will start practicing the spell! Now, will you agree to warn us about monster attacks, or not?"

"Of course, of course…" Arraka says. "After all, it's also in my best interest that you two remain alive… at least until I manage to take control of your body."

"Say, Daren…" I say, as I look at one of the dead orcs in front of me. "The armor that you're wearing right now is anti-magic armor, correct?"

"Among other things, yes," Daren says.

"So, why aren't you also wearing a helmet to go with the set?" I say. "You saw how useful these anti-magic helmets were for the orcs just now. And if you're already willing to wear full heavy armor, a helmet isn't exactly going to weigh you down a lot more, is it?"

"It's not about the weight," Daren says. "It's about being aware of my surroundings. These mindless brutes might be okay with losing their peripheral vision over some extra defense, but when you're on a battlefield with enemies coming from every side, limiting your vision is the last thing any sane person would want to do! And it's not like there's any way to properly enchant the types of helmets that don't cover most of your face.

The anti-magic barrier, for example, cannot be maintained unless the metal covers your head from all sides, and it's the same for many other enchantments. Then there's also the fact that this scar I have on my forehead makes me easily recognizable to most people nowadays, as long as I keep it visible, and when people recognize me, they usually tend to get intimidated, and not engage me in battle, which helps avoid some unnecessary bloodshed."

"How did you get that scar, anyway?" Hadrik says. "I've never asked. And why is it shaped like an 'x'? Is there like a monster with an 'x' shaped tail that I don't know about, or something?"

"No," Daren says. "The 'x' is actually formed from two separate scars that I got during the same battle."

"Oh?" Hadrik asks, suddenly getting more interested. "Someone was actually strong enough to scar the great hero Daren twice during the same battle? May I ask who this was?"

"It was my martial arts and enchanting master," Daren says. "An ex-sage from the Southern Continent. Well, he wasn't a sage back when he was training me, but he became one afterwards, and he lost the title in the next year. He was an extremely harsh teacher, especially when it came to martial arts, and he was the type that always tried to make you learn lessons from your own experience, rather than just giving you the answer himself. As his final lesson, he told me to fight him with all my strength, by using everything he's ever taught me. This is when I got my two scars. The first time he wounded me, I did not understand his lesson, so he decided to cut me a second time, in the exact same spot, from the opposite side, in order to properly get his point across. Only then, did I realize that the whole purpose of that battle was to show me a huge weakness in my fighting style that I'd ignored for years, without giving it much thought. The third time when he attacked me in the same spot, I was ready for him, and I quickly disarmed him, which concluded my last lesson. Now, every time I see my reflection in the water, it reminds me to always remain vigilant, and to always look out for even the tiniest of weaknesses, because in a real battle, they can mean the difference between life and death."

"Huh..." Hadrik says. "That's actually oddly inspiring. I think I may also have some of these small weaknesses that I never really bothered to correct because I didn't consider them to be that big of a problem, due to my durable giant skin, but after hearing your story, I'm thinking that maybe I should get off my arse and actually do something about it, before it's too late. After all, you never know what might happen!"

"Hey!" Melindra suddenly shouts, from high above us. "So... are you guys done with your secret strategy meeting, yet? You think maybe I can come back down so we can continue our trip? No pressure, though. Take as long as you like."

"What are you—" Daren starts to say, as he looks towards Melindra, but he interrupts himself. "Ugh... Yes, Melindra, you can come down, now."

"Splendid," Melindra says, as she dives down towards us, reaching the ground level in a few seconds. "Just so you know, the battle you had just now with the monsters was far below my expectations. You're going to have to clean up your act if you actually plan to be of any use to me when we get to Ollendor."

"Listen, Melindra..." Daren says. "You may have taken an oath to uphold your end of the bargain, but none of us took an oath to fulfill ours. You may have forgotten about this, but we can still cancel this deal at any time, if we don't want to work with you anymore. And with the way you've been acting so far, you've given us some pretty good reasons to reconsider our arrangement. So, I'll tell you what we'll do. If you still want us to help you with Ollendor, then you can stop complaining and lead us to where we need to go. If you don't, then I'm afraid you might have to go looking for some other group to do your dirty work."

"Fine!" Melindra says, frowning. "If that's how it's going to be, then you won't hear another word from me."

She then storms in front of us, and we all begin to follow her, one by one, into the depths of the forest.

"So, uh..." I say, as we all walk behind Melindra. "Illuna, do you think those two goblins might have been part of Fyron's army? Could the goblin general be working with the dragon, now?"

"I highly doubt it," Illuna says. "The dragon already has plenty of goblins under his rule. He shouldn't have any need for Fyron and his 'free' goblins. In fact, the only reason why Fyron and his group have survived for so long is most likely because the dragon doesn't really care about them. There is no pact protecting goblins, so Tyrath could very well destroy their whole camp by himself if he deemed it worthy of his time, and nobody would be able to stop him."

"Did Fyron ever serve under the dragon, before he joined the free goblins?" I say.

"Yes, he did," Illuna says. "A long time ago. From what I understood, he left because of the very poor way in which the goblins were being treated by the dragon, and by the other monster races. They may be the most resourceful of the monster races, but physically, they are by far the weakest, and there aren't many mages born in their race either. As such, the goblins were always being forced to perform menial tasks, they were ridiculed by the other monster races, and they were almost always on the verge of starvation. When Fyron left Tyrath's army and took his goblins with him, the dragon never bothered to stop them, because they were mostly irrelevant to him, and so, the goblins formed a new faction, calling themselves the 'free goblins'. Only a fraction of the goblins actually followed Fyron, though. Most of them preferred to stay behind, because at least the dragon would ensure their protection against animals and humans, and he would give them enough food to scrape by. Even some of the goblins that left with Fyron decided later to return to the dragon, due to the even poorer conditions that they were getting in Fyron's camp. However, those who decided to stay, eventually managed to make a better life for themselves than they used to have, after a few long years of hard work and effort, and in time, they managed to get other goblins, and even other types of monsters to willingly join their camp."

"Speaking of other types of monsters," I say, "do you know how many types Tyrath has under his rule?"

"I do not know all the details," Illuna says, "but as far as I'm aware, the monsters that are by far the most loyal to the dragon are the orcs. They are not as strong as the ogres, but they're not dumb like them, either, and they are generally more powerful than most humans. The orcs are the main force of the dragon's army, but he also has other monsters of the humanoid variety like ogres, trolls and goblins, alongside various creatures such as wyverns and hydras. While it would be pretty unlikely to meet an orc in Varathia that does not serve Tyrath, there are plenty of ogres that have nothing to do with the dragon, like the ones we fought in the fort, and the trolls are mostly a race of mercenaries, so their allegiance to the dragon is fickle. As far as the goblins go, I'd wager that most of the goblins in Varathia still follow Tyrath, although Fyron has also been getting some new recruits in his camp, lately."

"Hold on a minute, there," Daren says. "Who exactly

is this Fyron, and why are you both acting like you've met him before?"

"Fyron is the general of the free goblins of Varathia," Illuna says.

"Okay, and how do you guys know him?" Daren says.

"Illuna has known him since before she met us, I think," I say. "I met him while I was walking around the underground tunnels of the arena with Leila, trying to sabotage the event."

"You were trying to sabotage the—" Daren says, shocked, but he stops mid-sentence, and he shakes his head. "Oh, boy… Nothing is ever simple with you, is it, Barry?"

"So…" Hadrik says. "I don't mean to interrupt your discussion or anything, but shouldn't we be getting a little worried about these well-trained groups of monsters going after our heads? I mean, even I was having trouble with those ogres, and from what I've seen, our elementalists had almost no effect on the orcs that were wearing anti-magic armor. Maybe we need to rethink our strategies, a bit?"

"Well," Kate says, "maybe the battle would have gone better if a certain member of the group didn't ignore the fight completely…"

"Drop it, Kate," Daren says. "This discussion won't get us anywhere. And besides, Melindra won't be part of our group forever. Hadrik is right. We need new plans. I was way too focused on my fight with the orc captain to be able to pay attention to my surroundings, so I can't say for certain, but I think that one of the main problems in the way we organized ourselves was the fact that Leila jumped in to attack all those orcs by herself, which forced all of our elementalists to concentrate only on the orcs that were fighting her, instead of say… dealing with the ogres, who did not appear to be wearing anti-magic armor, and who would have been easier targets for them."

"Sorry…" Leila writes.

"Oh, there's no need for you to apologize!" Daren says. "I know that you were trying to act as a decoy, in order to keep the attention off our elementalists, and that's a great tactic, but it just didn't work well for this situation. That's why we're having this discussion, in order to learn from our mistakes, and to improve our tactics for later battles. For example, maybe the next time you want to act as a decoy, you could try to keep your distance from your enemies, instead of actually engaging them in battle, so that you wouldn't put yourself into any immediate danger, which would allow our elementalists to also pay attention to the rest of the battlefield, without feeling obligated to jump to your aid."

"Okay, I'll try…" Leila writes.

"Also," Daren says, "the next time Hadrik says he'll 'handle the ogres', it doesn't mean that you need to let him handle them all by himself. He may be strong enough to not get himself killed, but if either one of you helped him kill those ogres, he could have made mincemeat out of the orcs, without breaking a sweat. And when I say either one of you, I'm talking especially about you, Kate. A few well-placed ice cones should have been enough to finish off those ogres, given how busy they were with fighting Hadrik. I know that Leila is your friend, but you can't just completely ignore your surroundings every time she is in danger. If we're going to fight as a team from now on, you're going to need to put a little more faith in her fighting capabilities."

"I understand…" Kate says.

"Hmm?…" Melindra says, as she turns around, suddenly appearing to gain an interest in our conversation. "That is some very good advice coming from someone who hasn't been paying attention to his surroundings. Maybe I've been underestimating you a little bit…"

"Of course it's good advice," Daren says. "I haven't spent the last twenty years fighting monsters for nothing. Also, didn't you say earlier that we wouldn't hear another word from you? Why are you talking to us all of a sudden?"

"Hmph!" Melindra says, as she turns around. "I wasn't talking to you. I was just thinking out loud. There's no reason for me to talk to any of you people."

"Does this mean that you won't show me your rock collection anymore?" Flower says, with a disappointed tone in her voice.

"Well…" Melindra says. "I suppose I could make an exception. Just this once. Come here, and we'll pick up from where we left off."

As Flower rushes again to Melindra's side, we all continue our journey through the forest, and for the next few hours, we do not get any more interruptions.

For the duration of our journey, Melindra has not spoken again to anyone other than Flower, and the rest of us mostly ignored her as well. While we walked, we sort of split ourselves into little groups, with Kate and Leila in the back, Hadrik, Daren and I in the middle, and Flower and Melindra in the front. It seemed that Kate and Leila had a lot of catching up to do, so we decided to not bother them, and to let them have a little privacy.

On the opposite side of the group, once Melindra had finished showing Flower the rocks, she began to ask her a lot of technical details about how her fusion with Illuna actually works. Some of the questions were more personal than others, but it didn't seem like Flower was being bothered by them in any way, and she answered them all without hesitation, while Melindra was eying her with a look of sincere and eager curiosity.

When it got past noon, we decided to have a break near a river, in order to eat our meals, fill our gourds with fresh water and gather some fruits, so that Flower could conserve some of her magical energy by not creating food every time we needed to eat something. It would have been nice if the water that Illuna conjures were actually drinkable, because then we wouldn't have to worry about finding sources of fresh water, but from what she told me, the water that she creates with her spells disappears by itself after a while, so we might as well be drinking empty air.

After I finished eating, I sat down on a rock, and I pulled out my notebook, to see if I could find any more of Eiden's loopholes while we were resting. While I was calmly flipping the pages of my notebook, I could see with the tail of my eye how Melindra was slowly closing in on me, although she seemed to have conflicting feelings about whether she wanted to talk to me or not, and she went back and forth a few times, before she finally decided to stop in front of me.

"So, uhm… Barry… was it?" Melindra says, with an obviously forced smile, while attempting to appear cute and approachable. "How are you this fine day?"

"I see that you've finally bothered to learn my name," I say, as I casually flip a page from my notebook, without raising my eyes to look at her.

"Yes, your name is easier to remember than the others," Melindra says.

"That's funny… Because you were calling me 'half-lessathi' just a few hours ago…" I say, still not taking my eyes off my notebook.

"Oh," Melindra says. "Well, back then it was harder for me to remember it, but now it isn't."

"Because now you need to ask a favor of me, but back then you didn't?" I ask her.

"Yes, exactly!" Melindra says. "I'm glad to know

that we're both on the same page, here!"

"You and I both," I say, as I flip another page of my notebook.

"So, anyway," Melindra says, "I was curious about something. I know that you're a half-lessathi, and I also know that you came here as a participant in the tournament, but as far as I'm aware, lessathi can normally only be found in the continent of Varathia. So, I was wondering who your parents are, exactly, and why did they leave this continent?"

"If you're talking about my real parents, then I most likely never met them," I say. "I'm pretty sure that the parents who actually raised me were both regular humans."

"They 'were' regular humans?" Melindra says, intrigued. "Not 'are'?"

"No," I say, simply. "They're dead now. They were killed by a banshee."

As I say these words, Daren, who was sitting on a rock not far from me, sharpening his sword, now seems to be paying a little more attention to our discussion. I suddenly realize that I never really told him how I met my first banshee.

"Killed by a banshee?" Melindra says. "And you weren't there when this happened?"

"I was there," I say. "I'm the one who killed her."

"You killed a banshee by yourself?" Melindra says. "But the only way someone as powerless as you could ever hope to defeat a banshee would be to attack her in her most vulnerable state, right after the awakening. Which means…"

She pauses for a second, as realization dawns upon her.

"Which means that the person who turned into a banshee was also part of your family, wasn't she?" Melindra says. "Your sister, perhaps? Cousin?"

"Sister," I say.

"And you killed her with your own hands?" Melindra asks, with a look of morbid curiosity in her eyes. "How did the banshee look when she awakened? Did she really look like a genuine monster, like they say in the legends? What about your sister? Did it seem like she was still retaining a part of her consciousness, before the awakening process was over, or was she completely gone?"

"Listen, Melindra," I say, as I close my notebook and finally look her in the eyes. "If we're going to be delving into subjects that we're uncomfortable to talk about, then I also have a few questions for you…"

I then lower my voice, in order to make sure that Daren can no longer hear me talking.

"For starters," I say, "why did you lie to us when you said that the reason why you weren't helping us fight the orcs earlier was because you wanted to test us?"

"I don't know what you're talking about," Melindra says, feigning ignorance. "I didn't lie about anything."

"Oh?" I say. "So you're saying that after spending more than a week in search of someone who could help you kill the king of Ollendor, you were going to waste your only chance, just like that, because we weren't able to hold our own against one of Tyrath's strongest teams of combatants?"

"I already told you," Melindra says. "Olmnar's defenses are no joke! If you think that some 'elite' team of monsters can compare with what is to come, then you are sorely mistaken!"

"Okay…" I say. "Then let me ask you something else. Why exactly did you need to bend your knees and to keep your elbows close to your body when you cast the spell that blew away the orc who was attacking you? Because as far as I'm aware, that stance is what they teach novice elementalists at the very beginning of their training, in order to help them better control their powers, when they are still getting accustomed to them. Are you still getting accustomed to your powers, after six hundred years, Melindra?"

"I…" Melindra starts to say, but she hesitates, and I interrupt her.

"Or is it perhaps that Arraka was speaking literally, when she said that you don't know how to hold back?…" I say. "Those crazy stillwater powers must surely come with some sort of drawbacks, no? I would expect someone like Eiden, who knows all the ins and outs of magic to find a way around such a problem, but you don't seem like the type. You still haven't learned how to control your stillwater powers properly, have you? It's too much for you to handle, and you're afraid that you'll accidentally put too much power behind one of your spells, and blow us all away, while also killing yourself in the process because of that oath you made."

"No, you're wrong!" Melindra says. "The only reason why I used that stance was because I was still tired after casting that tornado earlier, and I wanted to be extra safe!"

"Yeah, I'm not buying it," I say. "I know how elemental magic works. Being tired should only affect your concentration, and there is no need to concentrate on how powerful your spells are, once you've mastered the basics. Admit it, there would have been no reason for you to use that stance, if you didn't have trouble controlling your powers."

Melindra frowns at me, but she doesn't say anything.

"What I don't understand is why you would purposely avoid telling us about it," I say. "Do you really care about your image that much? Is it really so important for you to be known as this perfect and all-powerful stillwater that can do no wrong, that you'd be willing to risk this entire mission?"

"I swear…" Melindra says, with a menacing look in her eyes. "If you plan on telling anyone about this…"

"You'll what?" I ask her. "Pat me lightly on the back? Caress me softly? Because that's about the most you can do to me after that vow you made. I bet you must be regretting your decision to make that oath life-binding now, huh?"

"A little…" Melindra says.

"Relax," I tell her. "I don't have any reason to tell anyone about this. It's not like you could help us if you wanted to. If you want to appear as even more unlikeable than you already are, then who am I to stop you?"

"Oh?" Melindra says, with the smile of a child who's just found a new toy to play with. "So you find me unlikeable, do you?"

"Quite unlikeable, yes," I say.

"And you don't enjoy talking to me?" Melindra says.

"Not really, no," I say.

"Well, in that case, I see no other alternative than to keep pestering you until you'll begin to find me likeable," Melindra says, with a coy smile.

"That's not how these things work," I say.

"What are you talking about?" Melindra says, still smiling. "Of course that's how it works. You're a half-lessathi, I'm a half-lessathi, we're both half-lessathi. What possible reason could you have to dislike me?"

"Oh, I don't know…" I say. "Maybe your personality?"

"Hey, Melindra," Daren says, as he closes in on us. "We're all ready to go. Can you show us the way?"

"Oh, sure," Melindra says. "Just follow the river in that direction for a while, and you'll be fine. We'll catch up to you in a second."

"Uh… okay, I guess?…" Daren says, and then he turns to the others. "Well, you all heard her. Let's follow the river."

Daren and the rest of the group then grab their backpacks, preparing to leave, and as they go past us, I can see Kate glancing at us a little suspiciously.

"So, about your parents—" Melindra starts to say, but I don't wait for her to finish her sentence, and I go to follow the others, while I put my notebook back in my backpack.

"Hey, I wasn't done talking, yet!" Melindra says, as she hurries to my side.

"Oh, you weren't?" I say, in a dry tone. "Sorry, I wasn't listening."

"Well, in that case, I accept your apology," Melindra says, seemingly oblivious to the sarcastic undertone of my previous remark. "So, anyway, I think that one of your parents might have been part of the lessathi top brass, or at least related to them in some way."

"What makes you say that?" I say.

"Well, marrying a non-lessathi is strictly prohibited in today's lessathi society," Melindra says. "So it stands to reason that any such relationships will remain hidden from the eyes of the other lessathi. This is the reason why you don't really see any more half-lessathi nowadays. However, if a lessathi woman were to become pregnant with the child of a non-lessathi, such a relationship would become much more difficult to hide. I'm thinking that the reason why your parents left this continent was because they considered it would have been too difficult to keep hiding after your mother became pregnant with you."

"Okay, but why would they be related to the top brass?" I say.

"Because the only people that have access to teleporting devices on this continent are the kings and the lessathi," Melindra says. "And those teleporters are the only way to leave the continent. Since only the highest ranked lessathi have access to the lessathi teleporters, it means that your mother needed to ask help from one of them, if she wanted to leave, and they would need to do it secretly. Maybe you're even related to the leader of the lessathi! I'm guessing you were born around thirty years or so ago, so the leader back then would have been… Heksol. Yeah, that was the name. I think he might have died since then, though. Or was he killed? I'm not sure. I don't really follow lessathi politics that much anymore."

"Can you two stop talking and focus for a second, here?" Daren says. "I can sense a group of mages approaching us. And I'm not sure if they're friendly. Keep your guards up."

It takes a while before the mages show themselves, but it would appear that they are yet another group of weapon enchanters. They don't really look like thugs, so who knows, maybe this time we can just say hello and then be on our way, like civilized people. I know that I'm being optimistic here, but still…

"Hey, look at that!" one of the weapon enchanters says. "These bozos have brought whores with them to the tournament."

"Wow, you're right," says a second mage. "They even made sure to bring at least one for each of them."

"Do you think that the little girl was brought by the dwarf?" says a third mage. "That sick bastard."

All of a sudden, Melindra grabs my arm with both her hands, and she presses herself against me.

"Darling, are you going to just let them talk about me like that?" Melindra says, with pleading eyes, but with a mocking smile. "You're not going to let them walk away after calling me a whore, are you?"

When I turn my head around, I notice that Kate is currently staring at Melindra, with a shocked expression on her face.

"Hmm?…" Melindra says, with an intrigued look in

her eyes, as soon as she sees Kate staring at her.

She then squeezes my arm even harder, while she's still looking at Kate, to see her reaction. Once Kate realizes what Melindra is doing, she turns her face away, in disgust.

"Hmm…" Melindra says, this time with a smile.

"Don't worry, love," the first mage tells Melindra. "We're not walking away anywhere. At least not until you guys empty your pockets and your backpacks, to show us if you have any pinecones with you…"

"Are you serious?" Daren says, almost breaking into a laugh while saying that last word.

"Heh," Hadrik says. "I guess not every mage in the world can recognize you by your scar, eh, Daren?"

"That or they don't care," Illuna says. "They were mad enough to join this tournament, after all."

"We don't have time for this," Kate says, as she stops hiding her aura, and she shoots three ice daggers in front of the first mage's feet.

"Aaah!" the mage screams like a little girl, with a terrified look in his eyes, as he finally understands the situation he's in. "A banshee! It's a banshee! What are you guys still standing here for? Run for your lives, you idiots! Run as fast as your feet can carry you!"

He then jumps over the small river, and he heads into the forest, as all of his companions hurry to follow their leader.

"Are you going to let go of my arm, now?" I ask Melindra.

"Of course, of course!" Melindra says, as she casually releases my arm. "There's no need to be so upset. It was only a joke!"

"That's lovely," I say. "Now how about you take the lead, like before, and leave me alone?"

"Will you come and walk by my side if I go take the lead?" Melindra says.

"I will do no such thing," I say.

"Then I'll stay here, thank you very much," Melindra says.

"Woah…" Hadrik says, with a grin, as he looks towards us. "Did something happen during that break we took earlier, Barry? Do you have anything that you might want to tell us?"

"Shut up," I tell him.

"Leave them alone," Daren tells Hadrik. "I'm sure that Melindra will get bored eventually, and then things will go back to normal. We already know the direction that we need to go in, so we don't need a guide for now. Come on, follow me."

Just like Daren said, after about an hour or two of walking, Melindra finally got bored of pestering me, and she went to talk with Flower, who appears to be the only member of the team that she actually gets along with, so far. We spent the rest of the day travelling, without getting into any more fights, although we did run into several groups of mages, who seemed to be very busy gathering pinecones from trees, and stuffing them into their backpacks.

When we decided that it was finally time to make camp, we started placing our tents not too far away from the river that we'd been following since noon. Melindra didn't really seem to want to spend time with our group any longer than she needed to, so as soon as she was done leading us, she went to the river bank, to see if she could find some more rocks to add to her collection.

As soon as we were done setting up the tents, I immediately pulled out my notebook, because there were a few things that I wanted to check before going to sleep.

While I flip through the pages, I suddenly notice an old page where I wrote some notes about the stat device, and one particular phrase catches my attention. According to my old data, the stat booster was supposed to gather more energy from the air, if powerful spells were cast around it, but I've never actually seen this happen since I came to Varathia. Realizing that I may need more info on the subject, I decide to go ask some questions to the only other person in the camp that has more knowledge of stat devices than me.

As I go over to Leila, I notice that she was still in the middle of a conversation with Kate.

"Hey, Leila," I say. "Got a minute? There was something I wanted to ask you about your stat device."

"Of course..." Leila writes.

"Since when were you the studious type?" Kate asks me, while raising an eyebrow, after seeing the notebook that I'm still holding in my hands. "I've never seen you use that notebook before, but now you seem to be reading from it all the time."

"Oh, I used to write in this notebook every day before coming to Varathia," I say. "It's just that I kind of had to put that hobby to the side, for a while, because I was too busy fighting for my life in this godforsaken place."

"You were going to ask me something about the stats?" Leila writes.

"Yeah," I say. "I wanted to know if you've ever felt like your stat device was receiving more energy from the air after a big mage fight had occurred in your vicinity."

"Not in particular, no," Leila writes. "I mean, we just had that big fight with the dragon, yesterday, and neither of us got any stat points."

"Yes, exactly!" I say. "But according to the data I'd gathered before coming here, the stat device should not be gathering the energy selectively. And yet, I don't remember ever getting stat points after participating in a mage battle. Do you know why this might be happening?"

"I don't know," Leila writes. "I haven't really thought about it that much..."

"Well, I have a theory," I say, "but I'm not exactly sure how accurate it is. You see, there was a time when I got to temporarily activate my hidden magical stats, but I only got the option to do it because there was a great amount of magical energy in the air around me at that time. The fact that the makers of the stat device included an option to quickly burn through the available energy makes me think that the energy would have been wasted otherwise, because the device wouldn't have been able to convert it all into stat points fast enough. Do you understand what I'm getting at?"

"Yes," Leila writes. "The energy residue from spells does not stay in the air very long after they've been cast. So, if the stat device cannot convert the energy fast enough, and if it does not have enough capacity to store it for later use, this would mean that in reality, most of the energy that the device is getting is not from spells, but from mage auras."

"That's what I was thinking," I say. "But since the device can only extract a very low amount of energy from each person's aura at a time, this means that what really matters is not how powerful the people are, but how many mages there are within the stat booster's radius, which, if I'm not mistaken, should be around thirty miles, give or take. There would likely need to be hundreds of mages within the device's range, for the conversion to stat points to have any noticeable effect. That would sort of explain why the number of points I've been receiving have slowed down, lately, because a lot of mages have died since the beginning of this tournament, but it still wouldn't explain why we've been receiving fewer points while we were in the city."

"Maybe it's because there were other people with stat devices gathered in Thilias," Kate says. "Surely, you couldn't have been the only person to come up with the idea of bringing one with you to this place. And if you didn't know that stat devices would be mostly useless to people without lessathi blood running through their veins, then there were likely others like you, who didn't know that either."

"Don't forget that there were also lessathi in the city," I say.

"The lessathi we fought did not have any stat devices with them," Leila writes. "Even if they were hiding them somewhere, I should have still been able to detect them with the help of my own device. Also, one of those lessathi came to threaten me while I was still in my cell, and he wasn't carrying a stat device back then either."

"A lessathi threatened you?" Kate asks.

"Yes," Leila writes. "He was trying to convince me to hand over my stat booster to him, but I refused to do it. He later ordered the arena owner to confiscate it from me, but the owner decided to not listen to him, because he wanted me to keep my stat device, in order to make the fight more interesting."

"I just remembered that there was also something else I wanted to ask about the stat device," I say. "Leila, you told me that you had level three in speed, but when you were fighting in the arena, you seemed to be moving a lot slower than me, even if we both have the same level. Is your device defective by any chance?"

"No," Leila writes. "My father once told me that the physical stats from the device enhance the physical abilities that you already have, and that the more fit you are, physically, the more effect those stats will have on you. Given that I've always had a very frail constitution, this is the most I can get out of my stat device, at my current level."

"Huh…" I say. "Well, then, I guess that all those months I've spent doing physical training in preparation for this tournament were not wasted after all."

"You did physical training?" Kate says, shocked.

"And this is the result? I bet I could beat you in an arm-wrestling match if I tried hard enough."

"I said that I only did it for a few months," I tell Kate. "And it's not like that was the only thing that I did during that time. I also needed to do my research. The research that I'm now using to figure out Eiden's weaknesses so we can finally— hold on a second… Where is Melindra? I could swear that I saw her by the river bank just a minute ago."

"Who cares about Melindra?" Kate says.

"Well, I didn't see her set up her tent," I say. "Do you think that she's not planning to spend the night at our camp?"

"Melindra can go sleep in the river, for all I care," Kate says. "It's not like she's going to help guard the camp in any way. Which reminds me that I should be preparing to take the first shift. You guys should go get some sleep. Neither of you are scheduled to take any shifts tonight, so you might as well enjoy your rest."

We decide to take Kate's advice, and we each head towards our tents. Once I get inside, I place my notebook in my backpack and I prepare to go to bed. I still have some stuff that I'd want to read, but I can do that in the morning.

It only takes me about a minute to fall asleep after I put my head on the pillow. I am, however, woken up barely an hour later, by the feeling of a pair of breasts slowly pressing themselves against my chest.

As I quickly open my eyes to find out what's going on, I see that Melindra is currently trying to squeeze herself inside my tent, right next to me, but due to the relatively small area available inside, she's having a bit of trouble fitting in.

"What the—" I start to say, but I get interrupted by Melindra quickly shushing me, and putting her index finger on my mouth.

"Shhhh!" Melindra whispers. "You're going to wake up the others! Hold on, let me cast a silencing spell on the area around us."

She then quickly whispers an incantation, and the sound of the crickets that I've been hearing until now suddenly stops, along with every other sound that is coming from outside the tent.

"There!" Melindra says, in a louder voice, with a triumphant look on her face. "Now we can talk normally. Nobody outside the tent should be able to hear us."

"What are you doing here?" I ask her, as I slide myself to the opposite end of the tent, in the little space that is available to me. "How did you even get here? Isn't Kate the one keeping watch right now?"

"Oh, getting inside unnoticed was easy," Melindra says. "I just had to cast an invisibility spell, and then I opened and closed the tent at a moment when the ice mage wasn't looking."

"An invisibility spell?" I say. "You mean the one that also masks your aura?"

"Yeah, that's the one!" Melindra says. "Eiden is the one who taught it to me."

"Okay," I say. "So I've learned how you are here, but you still haven't told me why you are here. What do you want? And why couldn't this wait until morning?"

"Well, you see," Melindra says, "when I checked the inside of my backpack this evening, I found out, to my dismay, that I'd forgotten to pack a tent before I left Thilias."

"You've got to be kidding me," I say. "And you couldn't just ask Daren or Hadrik to loan you a tent?"

"I don't know if you've noticed," Melindra says, "but I haven't really been getting along very well with most of the members of your group since we left the city."

"And your solution was to come and wake me up in the middle of the night?" I say.

"I wasn't trying to wake you up!" Melindra says, frustrated. "Your tent is just so damn small! I only wanted to sleep inside your tent for a few hours, and to get out before you woke up. Hell, I even tried to sleep outside for a while, but there were just so many bugs trying to crawl on me, and the only protection spells I have that work while I sleep aren't made to guard me against insects!"

"But why my tent?" I say. "Why not Flower's? Or Kate's?"

"Because I couldn't stand sleeping next to Arraka for more than two seconds," Melindra says. "And your girlfriend hates my guts."

"Kate is not my girlfriend," I say, simply.

"She may as well be, judging by that ice cold look she gave me when I grabbed you by the arm," Melindra says.

"Is that what you're basing your assumption on?" I say. "Kate gives ice cold looks to everyone. Except maybe Leila."

"If you're under the impression that the ice mage doesn't have any feelings for you, whatsoever, then you are clearly in denial."

"Listen," I say. "Kate has lived most of her adult life in the wilderness, fighting for her life. The only contact she's had with humans for the past ten years was either banshee hunters trying to kill her, or regular people running away from her, scared for their lives. She probably doesn't even know what feelings are, anymore. Kate didn't come here to have fun, and neither did I. She came here to look for her friend, and I came here to fight in a deadly tournament, in the hopes of achieving an impossible dream. Whatever it is you are seeing, it's not there."

"Well, whatever helps you sleep at night!" Melindra says. "And speaking of sleeping, I think I'm ready to hit the sack. If you need anything else from me, just whistle. Nighty-night!"

"Are you serious?" I tell Melindra, as I see her laying her head on the tent's floor, and closing her eyes. "You can't sleep here!"

"How about this, then?" Melindra says, as she opens her eyes and looks at me again. "If you let me sleep in your tent tonight, I promise that I will forget all about that tickling incident from this morning!"

"Really?" I say. "You're going to bring that up now?"

"Why not?" Melindra says. "It seemed like the most opportune moment."

"Get out," I say. "Go sleep with Flower, go sleep with the bugs, I don't care."

"You're not seriously going to kick me out of your tent, are you?" Melindra says, this time in a more serious tone. "I'm only asking for a few hours of uninterrupted sleep. I'm not going to bother you. I'll wake up long before anyone gets out of their tent, and I will do my best to get out undetected. It will be as if I was never here."

"Actually, I think I have another idea," I say, after spending a few seconds to consider her words.

I then struggle to crawl over her on all fours, in order to reach the entrance of the tent.

"Hey, what are you doing?" Melindra says, as I accidentally hit her chin with one of my elbows. "Cut it out!"

"I'm going to let you sleep in here for a few hours, while I'll be joining Kate on her night shift," I say.

"Wait... what?" Melindra says. "No, hold on! There's no need for you to leave your own—"

"After the first shift is done," I interrupt her, "I'll see if I can convince Hadrik or Daren to lend you a tent, since I'm pretty sure that they're the ones who will be taking the next shift. I'll come wake you up when your new tent is ready."

I then open the tent's zipper, and I begin to crawl outside.

"Wait, listen to me!" Melindra says. "You don't have to—"

"Good night, Melindra," I tell her, once I'm outside the tent, and then I close the zipper.

Chapter 9

"Barry?" Kate says, as she sees me head towards her. "What are you doing? Didn't you go to sleep?"

"Oh, I couldn't sleep," I say. "So I decided to go for a little night stroll, to get some fresh air."

"Why couldn't you sleep?" Kate says.

"Because I got a visitor in the middle of the night," I say. "And it was getting a little too crowded in there for my liking."

"A visitor?" Kate asks, shocked. "But how is that possible? I was keeping watch the whole time! Nobody even came close to your tent."

"Remember that spell that Eiden keeps using to mask his presence?" I tell her. "Melindra also knows that spell."

"Melindra?" Kate says. "She's the one that visited you? And she kicked you out of your own tent?"

"Wait, wait, no, you've got it all wrong," I tell her. "She didn't kick me out of the tent. I chose to leave by myself."

"But why would you do such a thing?" Kate says. "Why not just tell her to get out and be done with her?"

"Because I didn't want to kick her out like a dog, when she didn't have a place to sleep," I say.

"No place to sleep?" Kate asks. "What do you mean? Didn't she bring a tent?"

"She forgot to pack one," I say.

"Is this what it's all about?" Kate says. "Couldn't she have just asked Daren or Hadrik for a tent?"

"She didn't want to ask them, because she doesn't get

along with them very well," I say.

"Wow..." Kate says. "So, that's how you got stuck with her, then. And what is your plan? Spend the rest of your night doing night shifts so the stillwater can sleep comfortably in your tent?"

"I'm not planning to stay here all night," I say. "As soon as Hadrik and Daren's shift begins, I'll ask them to set up a tent for her, so she can leave me in peace. But I figured that I may as well come here and chat with you, given that I was already up."

"Oh?" Kate asks. "And what was it that you wanted to talk with me about?"

"I don't know," I say. "Lots of things. It feels like it's been ages since we've had a chance to talk, in private."

"You're right..." Kate says. "It has been a while. I think the last time we've had a private conversation was that time when we were celebrating our release from the golden fox's collars. Back when... Rose was still alive..."

Kate's words hit me like a dagger through my chest. I suddenly realize that I've been completely avoiding thinking about Rose ever since that day when we held a toast with Enrique in her memory. Even when I promised myself that I would not avoid thinking about her because of her death, I still managed to do it. I guess some things are easier said than done, after all.

"Yes... back when Rose was alive..." I say, and then we both stay silent for a few moments.

"So... how have things been going with Leila?" I say, trying to change the subject.

"They've been going... great," Kate says, with a faint smile. "We've been talking a lot about what our lives have been like since we left the Beacon. It's been a long time. We both had many stories to tell..."

"So, you're back to being friends again, then?" I ask her.

"What do you mean?" Kate says.

"Well, at the beginning, you weren't really talking to each other," I say. "So, I thought that maybe you might have had an argument or something, before she left the Beacon, which made it difficult for you to begin a conversation."

"Oh, no, it's not that…" Kate says. "It was just that…"

She pauses.

"You see," she says, "Leila and I were never exactly friends back when we were at the Beacon… I spent most of my time with Diane and her brother, and Leila wasn't really allowed to socialize much with the rest of us, because she was a lessathi. But even so, the first time when I found out that she died, I was devastated. Gods, why did I have to believe the lies of those lessathi, who said that she was dead? Why did I not try to look for her?"

"Hey, even if you did, it's not like you would have made any progress, right?" I say. "Leila's lived all of her life here in Varathia with her adoptive father, so you wouldn't have had any more luck in finding her than you've had in trying to reach Diane. Don't beat yourself up over it too much. The important thing is that she was kept safe all this time, thanks to that lessathi caretaker that she calls her father."

"Yes, you're right," Kate says. "I really owe a lot to her father. I hope we'll meet him when we reach Ollendor, so I can express my gratitude to him."

She pauses again.

"What about you, Barry?" Kate says. "How's it going with your notebook? Have you found anything useful?"

"It's hard to tell," I say. "I have a lot of information in my notebook, but there's also a lot of stuff missing. If only I could somehow figure out how to activate these magic stats from the stat device, it would be a lot easier to fill in the notes with the details I need, but I don't think I'll ever be able to unlock those hidden stats by myself."

"Do you think that Leila's father might be able to help?" Kate says.

"It's a possibility," I say. "But I won't get my hopes up for now. From what the goblin general told me, in order to activate these hidden stats, I'd need some secret codes that should only be accessible to the top brass of the lessathi, and I doubt that Leila's father would have any reason to know them."

As Kate and I take another short break from talking, I suddenly remember what Melindra told me in the tent, about Kate having feelings for me. Should I discuss this with her? No, no, no, it would only end up placing us in an awkward situation. But then again, if I never talk to Kate about this, things will never get cleared up.

Maybe I could find a way to bring up the subject in a subtle manner, without shocking her too much. I should try to let the conversation flow naturally, and when I find the right opportunity, I will introduce the idea as an afterthought, just to see how she reacts. Yeah, that could work! That's what I'll do.

"So, Kate…" I say. "I was just wondering about something…"

"Yes?" Kate says.

"You wouldn't by any chance happen to have any feelings for me, would you?" I say.

Damn it, that wasn't subtle at all, was it?

"…Have you lost your mind?" Kate says, as she's looking straight at me, unsure what to make of me.

"No, wait!" I say. "I know that it looks as if I'm just asking you this completely out of the blue, but the truth is that there was something that Melindra said to me earlier that drove me to ask you this question."

"Melindra again…" Kate says. "What did she say to

you?"

"Well…" I say. "She told me that you might have feelings for me… because of that look you gave her when she grabbed me by the arm, yesterday, while she was pretending that we were a couple."

"Oh…" Kate says, as she gets a thoughtful look on her face, and turns her gaze to the side. "I see…"

After a few seconds of contemplation, Kate once again looks me straight in the eye, and she continues to speak.

"It's true that I was a bit shocked when I first saw that scene between the two of you," Kate says. "I'd seen you having a private conversation with her only a few minutes prior, and I was worried that you might have done something that you would later come to regret. Obviously, I realized soon afterwards that it was all only a joke, but I still think you should be careful around Melindra. There is no telling what goes through that woman's mind. And, regarding any feelings that she claims I may have for you… rest assured that my main reason for looking out for you is because I care for you as a friend, and I wouldn't want you to make a mistake that would be very hard to fix later on."

"Hold on, did you just say this was your *main* reason for looking out for me?" I say, with half a grin. "So you are implying that there might also have been other reasons?"

Kate frowns at me, when she hears my question.

"You can be impossible sometimes, do you know that?" Kate says.

"Hey, you're the one who chose to phrase your words that way, not me!" I say.

"Well, regardless of how you may choose to interpret my words," Kate says, "I think we can both agree that what's important right now is to focus on the tournament, and on our objectives."

"Oh, yes, totally," I say.

"If you're still not satisfied with the answers I've given you," Kate says, "then we can continue our discussion at a later time, after we've all managed to survive this tournament to its very end."

"Don't you mean, after I win the tournament?" I tell her, with a smirk.

"Of course," Kate says, and then she smiles faintly. "After you win."

She then conjures an ice dagger out of thin air, and she starts flinging it upwards, and catching it with her hand, repeatedly, as she continues to speak to me.

"You know," Kate says, "you should consider yourself very lucky that I'm not actually planning to compete against you in this tournament. With your non-existent protection spells, and your unreliable ranged attacks, you would have no way of even touching me, while I'd be floating high above in an ice cage, raining down icicles upon you."

"I don't know," I say. "I wouldn't be so sure about that."

"Why not?" Kate asks.

"Well, the winner of the fight would still depend on a number of factors," I say. "For example, if the fight were to happen underground, or inside a building, you wouldn't be able to fly away to safety. And even if we were to fight on an open field, I could still get the upper hand if we were to start our fight relatively close to each other. From what I've seen in the past, you are particularly vulnerable to surprise attacks, so if I were to get close to you faster than you could react to defend yourself, then I think I'd stand a fair chance at— Hold on a sec! This discussion that we're having right now… it's only hypothetical, right? You wouldn't actually try to kill me if the tournament pinned us against each other… would you?"

"I would not," Kate says. "Would you?"

"I… don't think I could, no…" I say.

"Well, then," Kate says, as she makes her ice dagger vanish into thin air, "In that case, I suppose we should both be feeling lucky that we won't be competing against each other."

She pauses.

"But I think you already know that things will not go as smoothly with Daren," Kate continues. "The two of you are practically the only members of our group who are actually aiming to win this tournament, so if you both continue on your current path, you will eventually have no other choice than to fight each other. There can be only one winner of the Magium tournament."

"Yeah… I know," I say.

As the two of us remain silent for a while, we eventually see Daren's tent getting opened from all the way across the camp, and soon afterwards, Daren also comes out, and he starts heading towards us.

"Barry?" Daren asks, when he gets closer to us. "What are you doing here? I was pretty sure that Kate was the only one who took the first shift."

"I could ask you the same question," I say. "Wasn't your shift supposed to begin in an hour or so?"

"An hour and a half," Daren says. "But I couldn't sleep. I kept thinking about that fight we had today, and trying to think of ways in which we could have handled ourselves better. So, I figured that I may as well come here and relieve Kate of her shift early, so at least she could get some rest."

"Oh, well my story is a little longer than that," I say.

I then begin to tell him about how Melindra came into my tent because she forgot to pack her own, and how I eventually let her sleep inside, while I left to join Kate on her shift.

"So that's what happened, then," Daren says.

"Alright… Barry, you come with me and we'll set up Melindra's new tent. Kate, you should go to sleep. I'll take the rest of your shift."

"I will take you up on that offer," Kate says, as she gets up from the ground. "Good luck with… Melindra's tent."

She then starts heading towards her own tent, as Daren and I head towards his, in order to get a spare tent from his backpack. Once we are done setting it up, I go back to my own tent to wake up Melindra.

"Hey, Melindra, wake up!" I tell her.

"Mmmnnn…" Melindra says, with her eyes half-closed, in a sleepy voice. "Let me sleep a little longer…"

"You can sleep as much as you want in your own tent, but not here," I say.

"But I don't… have a tent…" Melindra says, in the same sleepy voice. "I told you that I forgot to—"

"I'm talking about one of Daren's tents," I say. "I spoke to him, and he agreed to lend you one for the night."

"He did?" Melindra says, this time actually opening her eyes.

"Yes, now go sleep over there," I say. "Daren will show you where it is."

"Alright, alright…" Melindra says, as she gets up and prepares to exit the tent. "I'm going."

As soon as Melindra walks out, I enter my tent once more, I close the zipper behind me, and I fall asleep almost as soon as I put my head on the pillow.

When I wake up the next morning from the sound of people dismantling their tents, I see that there is barely any light coming through my tent from outside. As I open the tent's zipper, I realize that this is because of the fact that the sky is currently filled with dark clouds, and there isn't even a small glimpse of the sun, even though it must have risen for at least an hour. It appears that most of the others have already woken up, and presumably, have already had their breakfast.

Not long after I walk out of my tent, Melindra comes rushing towards me, with an unusually serious expression on her face.

"Listen," Melindra says, as she stops in front of me. "I didn't mean to kick you out of your own tent last night."

"Yes, I know that," I say. "It's fine."

"No, it's not fine!" Melindra says. "All I wanted to do was to sneak silently into your tent, doze off for a few hours and then walk away unnoticed. I didn't mean to cause all this ruckus!"

"So what?" I ask her, confused. "You got your tent, didn't you?"

"Yes, but that's not the point!" Melindra says. "The point is that I didn't mean to cause you that much trouble, when you were the one helping me!"

"Huh…" I say, as I give her a long, pondering look. "So, you *are* capable of giving a damn about other people, then…"

I pause for a second before I continue.

"But why would you choose to act the way you do, if that is the case?" I say.

"What are you talking about?" Melindra says.

"Well," I say, "from what I've seen of your behavior yesterday, you never really seem to care about what people think of you. You don't make an effort to remember anyone's names, you don't stop to think whether speaking your mind bluntly would annoy the people around you or not, and you didn't give me the impression that you'd care much if your habit of provoking reactions from people would cause the others to become upset at you."

"And why would I care if the others become upset at me?" Melindra says. "I don't need them to be my friends. I just need them to get the job done."

"But do you need them to be your enemies?" I say.

"Eiden did not become my enemy when I acted like this with him," Melindra says.

"Well, most people are not Eiden!" I say.

"But that doesn't mean that I need to change how I live my life just to accommodate others!" Melindra says.

"I'm not telling you to change your entire lifestyle," I say. "I'm just telling you to not piss off everyone that you meet on purpose. Can't you at least do that much? Or would you rather spend the rest of our days on this journey without even being able to ask someone the simple favor of lending you a tent for the night?"

Melindra is now looking at me with her eyebrows furrowed, and with another pouting expression on her face.

"Fine," she says. "Maybe I could change my behavior a little. But *only* a little."

"Well, it's a start," I say. "Anyway, I think we should be getting ready to leave, soon. I see that the others are almost done with dismantling their tents, so I'm guessing that they've already eaten their breakfast."

"Yeah, we're already done eating," Melindra says. "You should talk to Flower about making you some food. She remembered some new recipes after watching the arena, which are supposedly rare dishes, meant for kings. Archer porcupine pie and trampler stew, I think they were called. Now, if you'll excuse me, I'm going to grab my backpack from inside your tent."

"Wait, when did you leave your backpack in there?" I say, as Melindra crawls into my tent.

"I flew it over you with my wind magic while you were still asleep," Melindra says. "Okay, I found it."

She then exits my tent with her backpack in her hand, and she heads towards the river bank, to collect more of her rocks. Once I'm done dismantling my tent and handing it back to Hadrik, I go to Flower, in order to ask her to magically create some food for me. I spend the next twenty minutes or so savoring my meal, and then I go join the others, who seem to be preparing for our departure. Once we're all ready to go, Melindra takes the lead, and we all begin to follow her, as we walk along the river's bank, just like yesterday.

We travel in a straight line for the next hour or so, and every once in a while, we see one or two mages, who are too busy to take notice of us, while filling their backpacks with pinecones as if their life depended on it.

"What do you guys suppose they're doing?" Hadrik asks us, as we walk past two mages that were busy collecting pinecones. "Shouldn't they just be checking to see if the pinecones light up in their hands? Why would they go out of their way to actually collect them?"

"Maybe they found a detector, and they're taking the pinecones to it," I say.

"I doubt it," Melindra says. "If they really had access to a detector, they would have taken it with them. It can be easily carried in one hand."

"It's possible that they know a person who has a detector, but won't give it to them," I say. "We can't know for sure."

"I suppose…" Melindra says.

"Well, whatever the reason," Daren says, "there's at least one thing that we can be certain of. And it's the fact that in some way or another, these people managed to figure out the fact that they can't make the pinecones light up by themselves."

"But they still don't know that the glowing pinecones can only be found in the sacred forests," Melindra says. "Otherwise, they wouldn't be wasting their time around these parts. As long as they don't know this crucial piece of information, they still have a long way to go until they can complete their objective."

"To be honest, what worries me the most right now has nothing to do with those mages gathering pinecones," Daren says. "Look at the sky. It's only been getting darker since we woke up this morning. I have a feeling that there will be a storm coming soon."

"Do you get storms often in Varathia?" Hadrik asks Flower.

"No, they're pretty rare," Flower says. "But when we do get one, it tends to be rather nasty. Especially in the summer."

"In that case, we'd better watch out for falling trees," Daren says. "Also, we should expect to get soaked to the bone once it starts pouring, so we're probably going to have to take a break to dry up near a fire afterwards."

"I could make an ice dome to protect us from the storm," Kate says.

"And I could make little balls of fire to spin around us and make us dry!" Flower says. "There's no need to light an actual fire for that."

"Yes, but I think it might be better for you two to conserve your magical energy," Daren says. "There's no telling when we'll be meeting another one of Tyrath's elite monster groups, so we should always be ready for them."

"I really doubt that we'll be meeting another one of Tyrath's elite groups anytime soon," Melindra says. "It's not like they grow on trees or anything. He can't afford to send all his finest warriors after just one group of mages. By the time we'll be seeing them again, we're probably already going to— Whoa…"

Melindra suddenly stops in her tracks, as if she were just about to hit something, and then she begins to study an empty area in front of her very carefully, while the rest of us gather around her, trying to understand what she's doing.

"Are you seeing something there?…" Hadrik says,

confused, as he tries to touch the empty area with one of his hands.

"No, don't touch it!" Melindra shouts, as she continues to inspect the area. "I still don't know what the spell actually does, yet."

"A spell?" Daren asks. "Here, in this area? But I can't sense anything."

"It's one of Eiden's spells," Melindra says. "It's designed to remain hidden from people without a keen enough magical sense. I can tell that it's been cast by him from the aura signature, but I can't tell what it's supposed to do. It must be some sort of spell that he designed himself, although I'm not familiar with it."

"Oh, yeah, I remember seeing this spell in plenty of other places in the past week," Arraka says. "Eiden must have been casting it all over the continent since he came back here. And he's probably still doing it, as we speak. Casting complicated spells like these takes a lot of time and concentration."

"But what does it do?" Kate asks.

"How should I know that?" Arraka says. "It's not like I'm some spell researcher. I can't tell what a spell as complex as this does just by looking at it. But there's one thing that I can tell for sure, and it's that the spell is waiting to get triggered by something. Whatever that is."

"Could this have anything to do with that calamity that Eiden spoke of?" Hadrik asks. "Or maybe with the lessathi? Maybe they're all bombs, and they're meant to explode when they detect a lessathi nearby."

When she hears this, Leila suddenly takes a few steps back from the area that Melindra is inspecting.

"I mean," Hadrik continues, "I'd say it's pretty clear by now that Eiden and the lessathi aren't exactly best buddies. He told Barry to deliver that threatening message to them, and from what I can understand, he's killed a bunch of them in the still winter, so it's not like he'd need any special reason to kill more of them now."

"What are you babbling about?..." Melindra says, as she's still concentrating on analyzing the hidden spell. "Eiden never killed any lessathi during the still winter. He took their side..."

"He did what?..." Hadrik asks.

"Oh..." Melindra says, as she suddenly realizes what she's done. "I don't think I should have told you that."

"Wait, so Eiden fought against the stillwaters in the still winter?" Daren says.

"Oh, yeah, he killed plenty of them during that time," Arraka says. "Almost as much as me!"

"What do you mean?" Kate asks. "Weren't you the leader of the stillwaters during the still winter war?..."

"Oh, no, no, no," Arraka says. "Therius was their leader. I was just fused with him. And the two of us weren't exactly friends. We tried to take over the body from each other constantly. But the most hilarious thing happened when he had to go to sleep for the first time. There was no way for him to stop me from taking over his body anymore, so I wreaked havoc all throughout his camp. Those idiots tried to kill me along with him, but I squashed them like bugs. I still left half of them alive, though, so that I could play some fun games with them. You should have seen Therius' face when he woke up to see the dead bodies of his friends. And the funniest part was that none of his friends would ever follow him of their own free will after that, so he had to lead them through fear and intimidation from that moment onwards. Oh, man, those were the days!"

"But what triggered the still winter?" Kate asks. "Why were the lessathi and the stillwaters at war with each other? And why wasn't Eiden on the side of the stillwaters?"

"Do you seriously think I was paying attention?" Arraka says. "I only just told you that I massacred half of my own army in one night. It's not like I cared to hear their reasons for going to war."

"And I'm guessing that Melindra won't be revealing this information to us, either," Daren says.

"I've said too much, already," Melindra says. "I've promised Eiden long ago that I wouldn't give anyone any important details about the still winter, and I intend to stick to that promise."

"Right..." Daren says.

"Anyway, since I can't really tell what this spell is supposed to do, I recommend avoiding it for now," Melindra says. "There's no telling what could trigger it, so we shouldn't take any unnecessary risks. Come on, let's move."

For the next few hours or so, we kept following Melindra, as she led us away from the river, and through the thick of the forest, once more. As time passed, the wind that was only a small breeze this morning began to slowly intensify, while the sky was still as dark as ever. We spent most of these hours listening to some of Hadrik's and Daren's stories from their various adventures, and not much else, although one thing that I've noticed was that Melindra and Flower often seemed to be more preoccupied with their own discussions rather than paying attention to our group chats. For some odd reason, the more these two talked with each other, the more things they found that they had in common, which only sparked new topics of conversation between them that seemed to never end.

Once it got past noon, we decided to take a small break to eat some lunch. This time around, we didn't ask Flower to make any food, so she could preserve her magical energy, in case of an attack. Since I wasn't particularly hungry, I sat myself down on a tree stump, and I pulled a pack of biscuits out of my backpack, to serve as a little afternoon snack.

"Barry, I thought you had some food with you," Flower says, when she sees me opening up the pack of biscuits. "If you've only got those biscuits to eat, then I could make some proper lunch for you with magic. It's not that big of a problem."

"No, I've got plenty of food with me," I say. "It's just that I'm not very hungry right now. And besides, I really do love these biscuits. I got them from a shop near my house back in the Western Continent, and no other biscuits that I've tried tasted quite like this."

"Oh," Flower tells me. "Well, there was also something else that I wanted to talk to you about."

"Go ahead," I tell her, as I take a bite from one of my biscuits.

"Remember when we found that puzzle piece inside the castle of Thilias?" Flower says.

"Yeah, I remember," I say.

"Well, Melindra told me earlier that she knows where we can get another one of the puzzle pieces!" Flower says. "She said that she had a puzzle piece herself a few hundred years ago, but she didn't feel like wasting time looking for the others, so she eventually threw it away. But she knows where she took it from. She found it in an abandoned building in one of the poorer districts of Ollendor."

"I see…" I say.

"Anyway," Flower continues, "so when Daren overheard our discussion, he said that you guys also found a puzzle piece in the ruins where we first met, and that you're the one holding onto it. Would you mind giving it to me, or are you also trying to collect all the pieces?"

"You can have it, if you want," I say.

"I can?" Flower says, with hopeful anticipation.

"Yeah," I say. "I wasn't really planning to do anything with it, anyway. Hold on, let me get it out of my backpack."

I then finish one of my biscuits, and I reach over to the side of the tree stump, to get the puzzle piece out of my backpack. Once I give it to Flower, she stares at it for a while, and then she squeals with excitement.

"Thanks a lot, Barry!" Flower says. "I'll make sure not to waste this!"

"Sure," I say. "Go crazy."

"Alright, that's all I wanted to ask of you," Flower says. "I'll let you eat in peace, now. Enjoy your biscuits!"

I take a bite from one biscuit, and with my free hand I do a military salute, as Flower turns around, and she heads towards the others. I continue to eat for a few more minutes, and once I'm done, I open up my backpack and I place the pack of biscuits back inside.

Before deciding whether I should be taking my notebook out of my backpack to read some more, I take a quick look towards the others, to see what each of them is doing. Kate is currently eating alone, while sitting on the grass, with her back against a tree. Meanwhile, Leila seems to have been coaxed by Hadrik and Daren to act as referee in a rock throwing contest between them. As with most contests that I've seen between Hadrik and Daren in the past, the rules appear to be a convoluted mess, and it's very hard to tell what the actual goal of their game is. And lastly, Flower and Melindra appear to be continuing their discussions about random topics that they started this morning.

Since I don't really have anything to discuss with anyone in particular, I decide to take out my notebook, and to start reading from it. After a while, I notice that the others are slowly gathering up and preparing to leave, so I put the notebook back inside my backpack, and I get ready to join them as well.

"Prepare yourselves," Daren says. "The rain could

start pouring any minute now, judging by the intensity of the wind. Remember to stick together, and to watch out for falling trees."

"We're going this way," Melindra says, as she takes the lead. "Follow me."

We follow Melindra for half an hour or so, and during this time, the wind intensifies considerably. After a while, we start seeing lightning, and shortly afterwards, we get to experience a downpour of rain of the likes we've never seen before. It takes less than a minute for all of us to get completely soaked, and the powerful wind spraying the rain drops in our faces makes it feel almost like we're under a waterfall, instead of simply walking through some rain. As we move forward, the wind starts to blow even harder, and now it really does look like the trees are about to be pulled from their roots.

"Stay close together!" Daren shouts, in order to make sure that we can hear him through the sound of the wind. "And watch out for lightning. We should always be careful to have tall trees surrounding us, so the lightning will strike them instead of us. Make sure to avoid flying at all costs. Come on, keep moving!"

As we advance through the storm, the wind finally manages to blow a few trees out of their roots, but we all manage to avoid sustaining any injuries by being alert and by paying attention to our surroundings.

We keep pressing forward for another twenty minutes, but the storm still doesn't look like it will be stopping anytime soon. In fact, it's been getting worse by the minute. Every time we hear a thunder, it feels almost as if someone set off a powerful explosion spell in our vicinity. The wind is now almost powerful enough to push us back while we're walking, and the number of rain drops has greatly increased as well. Will this storm never end?

"I've had enough of this," Kate says, all of a sudden, and then a large dome of ice quickly begins to form itself around us, until it covers us completely, shielding us from the wind and rain.

"Kate, what are you doing?" Daren says.

"We're taking a break," Kate says. "As it stands, we're only getting ourselves tired for no reason. We're barely moving forward with this wind pushing us back, and at this rate, half of us will wear ourselves out before we even get into a fight."

"Even I am forced to agree with the ice mage," Melindra says. "Trying to walk through this storm is a complete waste of our time. We're better off just resting for a while, and resuming our journey afterwards."

"Well, if everyone else is also okay with this…" Daren says.

"Yeah, I think we all could use a little break, right about now," Hadrik says.

"I'll dry everyone up, then!" Flower says.

She then conjures a few dozen small flying balls of fire, and she sends several of them towards each of us. The balls of fire quickly begin to circle around us, coming very close to our clothes, in order to evaporate all of the water.

"Whoa… watch out, there…" Hadrik says, as he sees one ball of fire approaching his face.

"Don't worry," Flower says. "I've been drying up like this since forever. You're not going to get burned."

"I most certainly hope so…" Daren says, as he looks suspiciously at one of the balls of fire circling him.

Once we're all dried up, Flower dismisses her spell, and the balls of fire each fade away, into the air.

"Alright!" Hadrik says, as he claps his hands together, loudly. "Well, it looks like we're going to be here for a while, so how about we find something to talk about, before we all get bored out of our skulls?"

"Like what?" Daren says.

"Like… for example Barry could tell us his progress on finding Eiden's loopholes," Hadrik says. "That's something that everyone is interested in, right?"

"Or maybe we could avoid giving away our strategies in front of someone who has openly admitted to being Eiden's friend," Kate says, with a cold tone in her voice.

"Come on," Hadrik says. "It's not like she's going to tell on us. Didn't you see how Eiden was ignoring her two days ago? "

"And yet she still considers him her friend," Kate says. "She said so herself. What is to stop her from telling Eiden all of our strategies the first time she meets him again?"

"Really?…" Melindra says. "Would you like me to take an enchanter's oath for that too? Because I'll do it, you know. Maybe at least then you won't feel the need to lower your voice for every little thing you say when you are within hearing range of me."

"There's no need for you to take another enchanter's oath, Melindra," I say.

"Oh?" Melindra says. "So what would you rather have me do, then? Plug my ears?"

"Nothing," I say. "Because I haven't really discovered anything new about Eiden's loopholes, yet."

"Damn…" Hadrik says. "So, I guess we still don't know any of Eiden's weaknesses, then."

"Well, I wouldn't say that we don't know *any* of Eiden's weaknesses," I say. "It just depends on what you'd be willing to call a weakness. For example, do you remember that time when Eiden teleported us all to your location, after you turned into a giant and challenged everyone to a brawl?"

"Oh, yeah, I remember!" Hadrik says. "It was on the second day of the tournament."

"Well," I say, "the thing is that Eiden teleported

every tournament participant in the vicinity, including me, Daren and Kate, but he didn't notice the three of us until later. This means that even if he has the ability to monitor everyone on the island with his magic sense, he still can't concentrate on everyone at once. Which shows that even with all his power, he still has some weaknesses that a normal person would have. He can still be distracted."

"Well, as far as weaknesses go, this one isn't really all that useful," Hadrik says.

I shrug.

"It's a start," I say. "When you're up against an enemy of this caliber, I'd argue that every little bit of information helps."

"Fair enough," Hadrik says. "So, what if we tried to uncover stuff about his past, instead? Or his motivations. Maybe that could help us fight him somehow. Like, for example, maybe we could find out the reason why he's filling the whole continent with those weird invisible spells."

"Good luck finding that out," Melindra says. "I've known him for most of my life, and even I have no idea what he's trying to pull."

"Maybe he's trying to win back the fox's heart," Arraka says, in a mocking tone. "I heard they had a bit of a falling out after that stunt he pulled in Olmnar. And I don't think they were exactly on the best of terms before that, either."

"Their relationship had been slowly degrading for a long time," Melindra says. "I think it all started when the cities in Eiden's care began to introduce the concept of slavery, and it all went downhill from there. The fox had always blamed Eiden for all the messed up things that ended up happening in his cities. She kept saying that if he would have reined them in and imposed stricter rules on them, it wouldn't have gotten to this point. But back then, Eiden had this naive belief that all humans are inherently good, and that as long as they'd be left to their own devices long enough, they would find the right path. He thought that as long as people were given everything they needed, without having to work for it, and as long as they were given no reason to fight each other, they'd all live like one happy family. Well, we can all see how that turned out."

"So, are you telling me that he just gave up?!" Daren shouts, all of a sudden.

"Oh, no, he didn't 'just' give up," Melindra says. "He tried to reason with them for a long time. Much longer than your lifespan. And he did manage to lead them back on the right path a few times. But the more his expectations got betrayed, the more he stopped caring. I think it was when the people he trusted the most betrayed him that he finally lost it. I don't even remember their names. The king and queen of one of the cities. They seemed like such nice folk too… until it was uncovered that they were secretly running an underground show where people were getting eaten alive by dogs. I remember that after Eiden found out what they were doing, he organized a whole arena event just to have the king and queen eaten alive by the very dogs that they were using in their own events. It was shortly after this whole episode that Eiden told me he was finally giving up, and it was also around that time that he began closing his eyes."

"So he was just going to let those bastards do what they wanted?" Daren says, furiously. "What about all the innocent people in those cities that had nothing to do with all the atrocities?"

"He stopped caring about them," Melindra says. "He started calling them all sheep, and he said that they deserved everything that was happening to them. He even started to encourage some of the more messed up things that were happening in those cities, saying that it was 'what the people wanted'. It was around that time that the fox started to really lose her faith in him, and also when she began to impose all those ridiculously strict rules in her own kingdom, in order to avoid what happened in Eiden's cities at any cost. Eventually, Eiden just left the continent without a word, on a journey of self-discovery, or whatever the hell it was, and when he came back for the first time, twenty years ago, he heard about the animal hunting going on in Olmnar and… well I think you all know what happened then. That's when he had his official falling out with the fox, and then he left the continent again, soon afterwards."

"Yeah," Arraka says. "He probably tried to tell her that he solved the problem by destroying Olmnar, when it was in fact his departure that caused the animal hunts to begin in the first place. What a moron!"

"Uh…" Hadrik says. "I'm not trying to interrupt or anything, but weren't Eiden and the fox just two old allies from the still winter? Why was Arraka joking about Eiden trying to win her heart back, earlier? Why does it matter if they had a falling out or not?"

"Oh, they were a lot more than just two allies," Melindra says. "Why, six hundred years ago, they were nearly inseparable. You would have almost thought that they were a couple by looking at them, except for the fact that one of them was a human, and the other was a spirit fox from the magical plane."

Inseparable, huh? Well, I guess this explains why Eiden got so angry when I suggested that he destroyed the city of Olmnar because he was seeking the fox's forgiveness…

"Huh…" Hadrik says. "Well, the more you know…"

"Hey, Melindra, you still haven't told them the funniest part!" Arraka says.

"What are you talking about?" Melindra asks Arraka,

in a cold tone.

"I'm talking about how the fox has been confined to her sacred forests for decades, because of her spat with Eiden!" Arraka says.

"Why?" Daren asks. "Did Eiden lock her inside with a spell?"

"It's not because of Eiden," Melindra says. "It's because of the dragon, Tyrath. Whenever she leaves her sacred forests, the fox loses most of her powers. The dragon knows this, and he would immediately seize the opportunity to kill her, as soon as she stepped out of her realm."

"Yeah," Arraka says, "but back when the fox and Eiden were still buddies, Tyrath would not dare to attack the fox, even when she left the sacred forests, because he knew that Eiden would immediately teleport to her aid, since he could sense them both from all the way across the continent."

"Wait," I say. "That's the only reason why the dragon hasn't attacked the fox while she was outside her sacred forests? Because of Eiden? Couldn't he just… send some of his elite squads to fight Eiden, and kill the fox while he was distracted, or something?"

"No," Melindra says. "Definitely not. Eiden would never get distracted from watching over the fox by a few mooks. She's much too important to him. If you wanted to distract Eiden from the fox, you'd need to bring a whole army to fight him. Or a god."

"Hold on a sec," Hadrik says. "Didn't the fox, the dragon and Eiden all have some pact which prevented them from fighting each other? Why would the dragon try to break that pact by killing the fox, when he'd know that it would lead to a direct confrontation with Eiden?"

"Because it would be too good of an opportunity to pass up!" Arraka says. "And one of the main reasons why the dragon agreed to make this pact in the first place was because he knew that Eiden and the fox were allies, and he didn't want to risk fighting them both at once. Starting a fight with Eiden would be a small price to pay for ridding himself of the fox, especially since he is under the delusion that he could defeat Eiden without destroying the whole continent in the process, if he tried hard enough."

"And you don't think he could?" Daren asks.

"Of course he couldn't," Arraka says. "Tyrath would not stand a chance against Eiden if he went all out. Do you remember when Eiden revealed his aura in the arena, and I said that he was finally getting a little bit serious? Well, I wasn't joking that time. Eiden is much more powerful than he lets on. I would know. I fought him in the still winter. He could probably fight the dragon on equal terms even without his tricks. But with his tricks? He would probably destroy him without blinking."

"If he really is that powerful, then why didn't he just kill Tyrath until now?" I say.

"Well, the first time when they made this pact, they also negotiated a truce between the three armies," Melindra says. "And it's not like Eiden's always been at odds with the dragon. We even used to have monthly councils where Eiden, the fox, and the dragon would meet and talk about the common problems that affected all their kingdoms. I also participated in a few of those, and while the discussions between Eiden and Tyrath were not much different from what they are today, they gave off a much friendlier vibe, back then. I think that even if he won't admit it, Eiden would be sad to see the dragon killed."

"Hah!" Arraka says. "As if! Eiden's probably just keeping the dragon alive because he amuses him."

"Who knows?" Melindra says, shrugging. "It's been a long time since I've actually had a discussion with

Eiden, so I don't really know what's going on in his head anymore."

"You've been sharing quite a lot of things with us about Eiden's past today, Melindra…" Illuna says, all of a sudden. "May I ask to what do we owe this sudden change of heart on your part?"

"Well, since I am obviously Eiden's spy," Melindra says, with a sarcastic tone in her voice, "I can't just keep everything a secret from you. I need to reveal some sensitive information here and there, to make sure that you people actually start to trust me."

She then looks straight at Kate, with a mocking smile.

"Wouldn't you agree?" she asks her.

Kate frowns at her, but she doesn't say anything.

"Uh… maybe it's about time we changed the subject," Hadrik says, in an attempt to avoid another argument breaking out between Kate and Melindra. "Like for instance, did you guys also notice that we haven't really encountered a lot of animals while we've been walking through these forests? I would have expected these places to be teeming with wildlife, but we've mostly only run into monsters and other mages."

"Most of the animals have likely already gone to the sacred forests by now," Flower says, "where they can get the direct protection of the golden fox until this tournament is over. It would be too dangerous for them to wander around these parts when there are so many mages roaming throughout the lands. Remember that the tournament's spell is only made to protect the citizens of Varathia, not the animals as well."

"There are still some idiots who stayed behind, though," Arraka says. "For example, do you see that forest fire over there? I've been watching a bear and two wolves running in circles for the past two minutes, trying to find a way out to safety, but they're pretty much surrounded by burning trees. They're probably going to get engulfed in flames soon enough."

"What?" Flower asks, shocked. "That's horrible!"

"I know, right?" Arraka says. "Nothing beats free entertainment. Anyone want to make a bet on how long they've still got to live?"

"*No*!" Flower shouts.

"Wow, you really don't like gambling, do you?" Arraka says.

"Hold on, there's a forest fire?" Daren says, as he tries to look through the semi-transparent ice dome for traces of smoke. "How close is it to us? Is there any risk of the fire spreading any more than it already has?"

"Well," Arraka says, "it's barely raining anymore, the lightning hasn't stopped yet, and the wind is still blowing hard, so I'd say that's all the conditions you need for the fire to keep spreading. But judging by the direction in which the wind is blowing, I'd say it shouldn't reach us, unless the lightning will strike some tree right next to us or something."

"Oh," Daren says. "Well, in that case, we should be able to wait here until the storm ends."

"What do you mean?" Flower asks. "What about those animals trapped between the burning trees? We have to help them!"

"Why would we risk our lives to help some animals?" Daren says. "They're the fox's problems, not ours."

"I agree with Daren," Kate says. "We shouldn't be taking any unnecessary risks in a situation like this."

"I can't believe you guys!" Flower says. "Well, Petal and I are going. Even without your help!"

"Actually, I'll be coming too," I say.

"Oh, come on!" Daren says. "They're animals!"

"Animals that can talk, though," I say. "It's not like they're some dumb beasts."

"But they're still animals!" Daren says.

"Barry, let's go!" Flower says to me, after using her fire magic to melt a hole into Kate's ice dome.

"Alright," I say. "Lead the way."

"Barry, wait!" Daren says.

"Relax," I tell him, as I step out of the dome. "It's not like I'm going to just die in some forest fire after having survived in this tournament for so long. We've got Illuna with us, who can extinguish the flames with her water magic. We'll be fine."

"Melindra, what are you doing?" Flower says, when she sees that Melindra has remained in the dome. "We need to hurry!"

"Who, me?" Melindra says, with a surprised look on her face.

"Yes, you!" Flower says. "Now, come on! We have no time to waste!"

"Ugh, fine…" Melindra says, as she also walks out of Kate's ice dome, in order to follow Flower. "Let's go save some animals, I guess…"

"Damn it!" Daren says, as Kate is slowly closing up the hole in her dome. "Watch out for lightning! And for flaming branches falling from the trees!"

"Yeah, yeah, we'll be careful," I tell Daren, and then we all head towards the black smoke coming out of the burning trees in the distance.

We run in the same direction for about a minute, with Flower leading the way. The downpour of rain from before has turned into a drizzle while we were inside the dome, but the wind is still as powerful as ever. At the speed we're currently going, we're probably going to make it to the flaming trees in less than a minute.

"I'm surprised that you came with us," I tell Melindra, as we run side by side behind Flower. "I was under the impression that you didn't really like the golden fox and her animals."

"I don't care about the animals," Melindra says. "I only came because Flower asked me to."

"I see…" I say.

"Guys, focus!" Flower says. "We're getting close to the fire. Arraka, can you show us exactly where the animals are right now?"

"Well, I could, but where would the fun in that be?" Arraka says.

"Of course you would say that…" Flower says. "Fine, we'll find them on our own, then. We should be able to sense their auras once we get close enough."

"Uhm…" Melindra says. "If you're looking for the bear and the wolves, then they're in that direction. I can sense auras from a distance too, remember?"

"Oh, right, I completely forgot!" Flower says. "Thanks a lot, Melindra! Come on, let's get closer."

When we begin to approach the forest fire, we quickly find out that there is a thick layer of black smoke between us and the burning trees, and we're going to need to traverse it before we can reach our destination.

"Melindra, could you blow this smoke away with your wind magic?" Flower says.

Melindra just stands there without saying anything, and she appears to be very focused on the smoke in front of her. As I look at her, I suddenly remember how she was unable to fully control her powers, which would explain why she's simply staring at the smoke, unable to make a decision.

"Melindra?…" Flower asks again, in a lower voice.

"She's probably thinking that she'll need a big blast of air to clear out this whole area of smoke," I tell Flower. "Come over here. We should give her some space."

"Oh, okay…" Flower says, as she starts to follow me.

When Melindra understands what I'm doing, she gives me a curt nod, and then she prepares to cast her spell. Once Flower and I are far enough, Melindra unleashes a very powerful blast of air that scatters away all of the smoke, giving us a clear view of the flaming forest ahead of us. As soon as she gets within range, Illuna shoots a very powerful jet of water out of her hands, and she uses it to extinguish the flames from the trees in front of us, one by one.

"The fires are out," Flower says. "Let's move!"

After we move past the flaming trees, it does not take us long until we manage to find the three animals, by detecting their auras. As soon as we reach them, the two wolves both turn to face us, while growling and baring their fangs at us menacingly, and the bear is raising himself upright on his hind legs, in order to look more intimidating.

"Wait," I tell them, in the ancient language of the animals. "We're here to help!"

"How did you get in here?" one of the wolves asks me, in the animals' language. "We've been circling around this area for more than five minutes, and we haven't found a single way out."

"We have a water elementalist on our team," I tell them. "What were you three doing here? Shouldn't you be waiting in the sacred forests until this mage tournament is over?"

"We were sent on a mission by the golden fox," says the other wolf.

"Don't tell them about the mission!" the first wolf says.

"They came here to rescue us," the second wolf says. "At the very least, we could show them some sincerity."

"What is this mission that she sent you on?" I say. "Maybe we could help. Unless it's a secret, of course."

"We were told that the stillwater, Eiden, may have cast a peculiar spell somewhere in this area," the second wolf says. "My brother and I were sent here to investigate it, because we both have very keen magical sense. The bear is our bodyguard. You wouldn't have happened to run into a barely detectable spell with Eiden's signature on it while you were on your travels, would you?"

"We actually did run into such a spell," I say. "In order to find it, you'll need to walk in that direction for a few hours, until you reach a river. Then, you'll need to follow that river downstream for about another hour, and you should be able to detect the spell, as long as your magic sense is good enough."

"Your help is much appreciated," the second wolf says. "Unfortunately, we do not have anything to reward you with, right now, but if you ever come near one of the sacred forests in the future, you should not hesitate to send word to us. We wolves do not forget our debts easily."

"Right," I say. "But I think you should hurry and escape from here, before the fire spreads even more. The exit is that way."

"You have our sincerest gratitude, human," the second wolf says. "I hope we'll meet again. Come, brother, let's get out of this infernal place."

"Wow, I didn't know that you spoke the language of the animals so well, Barry!" Flower says, as the three animals all head towards the exit. "I only managed to understand certain parts of what you said. What was that mission that the wolf was speaking of, earlier?"

"The fox sent them to investigate that hidden spell of Eiden's that we found this morning," I say. "I told them where they could find it, and so they went to look for it."

"Oh, I see…" Flower says. "Alright, well, let's leave them a little time to get out of here, and then we can go back to Kate's ice dome."

We do as Flower says, and wait for a while, until the wolves and the bear go past the burning trees. Once we can no longer see them, we make our way out as well, and we head back towards our friends. While we walk back towards the dome, we notice that the storm is slowly coming to a halt, although the sky is not quite clear of dark clouds just yet. The wind is much more bearable right now, and the lightning has almost stopped. A few minutes later, we finally reach our teammates, who were all waiting impatiently for us inside the ice dome.

"You can come out of the dome, now!" Flower shouts at them. "The storm is almost over."

"Oh, good, you're all unharmed," Daren says, as the ice dome gets dismissed, and he gets to have a good look at the three of us. "I was getting worried that I might have to heal some serious burn wounds, with how long you took to come back. Did you find who you were looking for?"

"Yes," Flower says. "The animals are all safe. We can be on our way, now."

"Alright," Daren says. "Let's get going, then. Preferably in a direction that leads us away from the forest fire."

With the storm gone, the rest of our journey for the day turned out to be relatively uneventful, except for a few more run-ins with mages that were gathering pinecones from trees. After a few hours of walking, we decided to set up camp earlier today, because the sky still hadn't cleared up entirely, and we wanted to make sure that we'd catch some sleep before a new storm would rear its ugly head to blow away all of our tents.

Before going to sleep, Hadrik insisted that we all join him in another card game that he learned from dwarven taverns. While I managed to use my notebook research as an excuse to not participate, the others weren't so lucky. It seemed that the ones he wanted the most to participate in the game were Kate and Melindra, because they both tried to refuse him several times, but Hadrik would have none of it.

It was pretty obvious what he was trying to do. His true purpose was likely to create a scenario in which Kate and Melindra would be forced to interact with each other, in the hopes that they would start to get along better. Everyone probably knew this fact as well as I did, but Hadrik is pretty hard to refuse once he sets his mind to do something, so they all had to reluctantly agree to join his game, eventually.

After about fifteen minutes of sitting on the grass, reading from my notebook, I suddenly see a blue message floating in front of my eyes.

"Still busy with your notebook?" Leila writes.

"Yeah," I say, as I raise my eyes to look at her. "Those loopholes aren't going to find themselves. Weren't you playing Hadrik's card game just now?"

"I was," Leila writes, "but the game requires us to call out the names of the cards as fast as we can, and my written messages don't form themselves instantly, so I had too much of a disadvantage, compared to the others. May I have a seat?"

"Of course," I tell her, as Leila sits herself on the grass, next to me.

"So, how do you like our little group, so far?" I say.

"It's not bad," Leila writes, while smiling. "Hadrik's cheerfulness can get a little exhausting at times, and Daren can be a little too stern in certain situations, but they're all good folk, and I'm enjoying their company."

"Yeah, they can be pretty fun to hang around with," I say. "Don't worry, you'll get used to their quirks after a while. Hell, I even managed to get used to Arraka, and you've seen what she's like. I guess this is what happens when you travel with the same people for a longer period of time, and face many hardships together with them. Before you know it, you become a part of a tight-knit group, and you almost start to think of them as family. By the way, how have things been going with Kate, lately? I saw that you two have been talking a lot these past two days."

"They've been going… better than I expected," Leila writes. "Kate and I didn't really talk much during our time at the Beacon, so I didn't think she'd actually consider me her friend. I'm glad to know that I was mistaken."

"Yeah, I was also surprised to see how much she's opened up to you these past two days," I say. "Kate is usually the silent type, and she rarely comes out of her shell, so it was nice to see this other side of her, for a change."

"She wasn't always like this…" Leila writes. "She used to talk a lot more while we were at the Beacon, especially with her friend, Diane. Maybe she's starting to go back to the way she used to be, now that she finally has some people she can trust."

"You're right," I say. "I think that this is the first time in at least ten years when she managed to become part of a group that she can actually rely on, without fearing that she'll get stabbed in the back."

"Do you think I could do it too, someday?" Leila writes.

"Do what?" I say.

"Become a part of your group…" Leila writes.

"What are you talking about?" I say. "You're already a part of our group!"

Leila shakes her head.

"Only temporarily," Leila writes. "Once you'll all be done with your business in Ollendor, I will stay behind with my father, and the rest of you will be leaving the city, to go on your next adventure."

"Yes, but it's not like we'll be doing this forever, either," I say. "Eventually, the tournament will be over, and our group will disband, but that doesn't mean that we won't be meeting each other again, later. And when we do, you'll be welcome to join us."

"I'm… not sure how easy it will be for us to meet again, after you leave Varathia," Leila writes.

"Well, I heard that citizens of Varathia can invite outsiders," I say, "so I don't think it should be that much of a problem, if you write an official invitation for us."

"I'm not sure how well that would work," Leila writes, "given that my father and I are both wanted criminals. There's also the fact that Ollendor is a rogue kingdom, so the other kingdoms would never approve such an invitation, even if I weren't considered a criminal."

"Yes, but you are forgetting that our goal in Ollendor is to assassinate their king," I say. "Things will most certainly not stay the same after this happens. And your criminal record might get erased in the future, with a little help from Golmyck. I think he made it pretty clear that he's on your side, so I'm certain that he'll find a way to aid you once he's gained a little more influence in his city. Think positive!"

"Perhaps you are right…" Leila writes. "At the very least, something tells me that Hadrik would never leave Varathia without having a final celebration, regardless of who will actually win the tournament in the end, so we'll be sure to meet at least one more time before you leave."

"See? What did I tell you?" I say. "You already understand how our group works, and you've barely travelled with us for more than two days. You're practically an official member of the team, by now!"

"Then I will make sure to work hard to be worthy of this title," Leila writes, smiling.

"Hey, Leila!" Hadrik shouts. "I know that I'm asking for a lot, here, but could you please come and help us keep the scores with those handy floating texts of yours?

Maybe we could change the rules a bit, so you can play with us on equal terms."

"It appears that my talents are needed elsewhere," Leila writes to me, as she gets up from the grass. "Good luck with your notebook, Barry. It was fun chatting with you!"

"Likewise," I say. "Make sure to work hard, so you can earn your permanent group membership!"

"I will," Leila writes to me.

She then turns away from me, and she starts heading towards the others.

"I'm coming!" she writes in big blue letters, as she hurries to join the card game once more.

For the next thirty minutes or so, I focus only on my notebook, trying to ignore the sounds in the background made by Hadrik and the others while playing their game. Unfortunately, simply focusing very hard is not enough for me to make another major breakthrough. Maybe I'm going to need to start taking a different approach than simply going through all of the information that I have available and hoping that I'll figure something out eventually. But what other approach is there?...

As I sit there and think, I suddenly hear a familiar voice, speaking loudly through my transceiver.

"Hello?" I hear Rose's voice say. "Is this channel still open?"

Hearing Rose's voice out of the blue like this makes my heart skip a beat. Seeing that there is no response from my side, the voice calls out to me once more.

"Are you hearing this?" Rose's voice says again.

Calm down, Barry. This isn't Rose. You know very well who it is. It's the revenant. The fact that she has access to this channel means that she's using Daren's old transceiver. The one that he gave to Rose on the second day of the tournament. I tap the transceiver once, so she can hear me, and then I try to answer her as calmly as possible.

"What do you want?" I say.

"So you can hear me, then," the revenant says. "Good. Make sure to leave this channel open. I will be contacting you again soon. Don't try to call me. I will be keeping this channel closed on my side until I'll have a reason to call you. Goodbye."

"Damn it, wait!" I say, but it's no use trying to contact her anymore.

The channel of communication on her side is now closed.

After careful consideration, I decide to do as the revenant asked, and to keep the channel open on my side. I have no idea what the revenant might be planning, but it couldn't hurt to at least hear her out.

"Was that… who I think it was?" Daren asks me, as he and all the others are approaching me.

"Yes," I say. "It was the revenant. Apparently she's still holding on to your old transceiver."

"What did she want?" Daren says.

"She was checking to see if the channel was still open," I say. "She also said that she'd be contacting me again, later, and that I should keep the channel open, but she didn't tell me why. I tried to ask her for more details, but she closed the channel on her side."

"Huh…" Hadrik says. "Well, I don't know about the rest of you guys, but this whole thing kind of killed the mood for me. I think I'm going to gather up the cards for now, and we'll finish the game some other time."

After Hadrik and the others were done with their card game, we all went to sleep in our tents, except for Illuna, who took the first shift. This time around, Daren made sure to lend Melindra a tent, so I could get a good night's sleep, without any more interruptions. It didn't take me long to fall asleep, and I woke up several hours later, at the sound of Hadrik's voice, who came to tell me that our night shift was about to begin.

"Come on, Barry," Hadrik says. "We're up next. I hope you're in the mood for drinking tonight, because I've got these dwarven ale bottles with me that are just begging to be emptied."

"Sure, I'll have a few sips," I say. "But I won't be drinking a whole bottle. I get drunk too quickly from dwarven ale, and I'd rather stay relatively sober, in case we actually need to fight someone."

"Good enough for me," Hadrik says. "Let's get going!"

After getting dressed and grabbing my weapons, I follow Hadrik outside of my tent, and then we both head towards a spot that gives us a good view of all the tents, without being close enough to wake up the others when we talk. The sky is now mostly clear of clouds, so it would seem that we won't need to worry about another storm today. We both seat ourselves on the trunks of two fallen trees that are facing each other, and then we clink our bottles of dwarven ale.

"Cheers, Barry!" Hadrik says.

"Cheers!" I say, as we both start to drink from our bottles.

"You know," Hadrik says, "since we're both drinking tonight, I was thinking that maybe we could play a game or two of Met-Zek, with the original rules, this time around."

"You mean the card game that involved bluffing, which required you to drink a sip of ale every time you lost a hand?" I say.

"That's the one!" Hadrik says.

"Sure thing," I say. "Let's go for it."

We spend the next few minutes arranging the cards, and then we start to play the game. The rules are just as complicated as I remembered them to be. I don't really understand how this can be a game that's usually played in taverns. Normally, you'd think that after a certain point, the players would become too drunk to be able to play the game correctly. Or maybe that's supposed to be part of the game's charm. Who knows?

At any rate, there is at least one thing I know for sure, and it's the fact that I'm not very good at this game. Ever since we started playing, Hadrik has barely lost any hands, and my score is rather terrible. The good news, however, is that Hadrik eventually got bored of waiting to lose a hand in order to take a sip from his bottle, and he began to drink at random time intervals. The drunker he got, the less attention he started paying to his hands, and this has led to a somewhat more even matchup between us, although, with the number of times I've had to drink from the ale bottle, it was getting a bit difficult for me to concentrate as well, even if I've only been taking small sips, in order to avoid getting too drunk.

"So, Barry," Hadrik says, as he places a card on the ground, facing up. "I've been meaning to ask… What is your opinion on Melindra so far? You've had that little episode with her in your tent, and aside from Flower, you seem to be the only other person that she's talked with, in private. Be honest, do you think that she'll ever manage to fit in the group?"

"It's hard to say," I tell him, as I place a card on the ground, facing up, as well. "I've had a little discussion with her this morning, and she promised me that she would try to antagonize people less from now on, but a lot of harm has already been done. Kate, at least, doesn't seem to trust her at all. I'm not sure about the others, but it's pretty clear that aside from Flower, nobody is really trying to be her friend."

"I know," Hadrik says. "That's why I tried to arrange that card game before we went to sleep. I was hoping that maybe if they all got to talk to each other more, they'd reach some kind of understanding. I haven't had any luck so far, though."

He then looks at his cards, and he gets a confident grin on his face, as he places one of his cards on the ground, facing down. Now, the rules of this game state that you can interrupt any round, at any moment, to ask your adversary to turn all his cards face up. In case his card is bad, his round would be immediately forfeited, and I would gain five times more points than I would have gained, if I waited for the round to be over. However, if I do this, and the card facing down was actually a good card, I would be losing five times the points that I'd lose normally.

So, the question here is… Did he place down a good card? Or a bad card?

"Flip your card, Hadrik," I tell him, eventually.

Hadrik grins at me, and he turns his card face up. Apparently, the card he placed down was one of the worst cards he could have had in this situation. Not only did he lose the round, but he did so in a spectacular fashion. I'm almost wondering if he wasn't just looking for an excuse to have another drink from his bottle.

"Nice call, Barry!" Hadrik says. "I almost thought I had you there, for a second."

He then takes another sip from his ale bottle, before shuffling the deck again, and dealing our new cards.

"So, anyway," Hadrik says, as we both start to place our cards on the ground, in order to begin a new round. "I was thinking that maybe we could have a discussion with the others about Melindra. I'm not sure if it's a good idea to leave things like this until we get to Ollendor. It's bad enough that we'll need to infiltrate a heavily fortified city on our own. I'd rather not also have us fighting each other every step of the way."

"If we'll have another private conversation without Melindra, we'll just piss her off even more," I say. "She's made it pretty clear today that she has been bothered by all those times when we were excluding her from conversations, because we didn't trust her. There's no need for us to twist the knife in the wound even more."

"But how are we going to convince them to get along with Melindra otherwise?" Hadrik says.

"I don't know," I say. "But it most certainly won't be through talking. Let's be serious, here. If simply having a conversation would have been enough to get this whole situation fixed, we wouldn't be where we are now. It's through her actions that Melindra needs to earn the team's trust, not through words. I doubt that anything you and I could say at this point would make much of a difference."

As I finish talking, I take a look towards the cards that I have on the ground, and I suddenly realize that the round was already over, and that I had won it by a fair margin.

"Congratulations on winning the round, Barry!" Hadrik says, as I can see the sun slowly rising behind him. "Now, I think we should be taking a bit of a break, in order to greet our new guest properly. He will be reaching us shortly."

Hadrik is right. I can sense a mage slowly approaching us, and he is making no effort to hide his presence. By the feel of his aura, I'd say that he is most definitely one of the stronger mages that have joined this tournament. Once we get a good look at him, we see that he is a dark-skinned man, in his late fifties, with short, gray hair, a muscular physique, and a stern, unforgiving look in his eyes. He is wielding two large swords in his hands, and he is wearing leather armor that appears to be heavily enchanted. The man walks slowly until he reaches Hadrik and me, and then he stops right in front of us, with a rather calm expression on his face.

"May I ask if this is the camp where Daren, the

healer in armor resides?" the man says. "If so, then I would very much like to meet him."

"I think you already know the answer to that question," Hadrik says. "But before we let you go any further, I'm afraid that you're first going to have to introduce yourself. Tell us… who are you and how do you know Daren?"

"I am surprised that Daren hasn't told you about me," the man says. "We've known each other for a long time. We are very old friends."

"That still doesn't answer the question," Hadrik says.

The man smiles.

"Very well," he says. "In that case, I will introduce myself. My name is Nolderan. I am an ex-sage, a renowned enchanter, and a martial arts master. And also, I am the man who gave Daren his scar."

Chapter 10

"Hey, Kate," Hadrik says. "Come over here, for a second! We have someone that we'd like you to meet!"

Kate had only just gotten out of her tent when Hadrik called out to her. It's now been almost an hour since Daren's old enchanting master made his appearance before us. As soon as we established that he did not come here with the intention to start a fight, we told him that Daren would wake up shortly, and we invited him to join us in a game of Met-Zek.

We spent the last hour playing cards, while Nolderan told us various stories from the years that he's spent teaching Daren martial arts and enchanting magic. The ex-sage agreed to play the game with its original rules, so he's already managed to empty a bottle of dwarven ale in the short time since he joined us. However, he appears to be holding his liquor about as well as Hadrik, since I'm not yet seeing any signs of him being drunk.

"Who is this?" Kate asks, as she approaches us cautiously.

"Remember how Daren told us that his old master gave him his scar during a sparring session?" Hadrik says. "Well, this is the old master that he was talking about. His name is Nolderan, and he apparently came here to greet Daren, since he hasn't seen him in a long time."

"Pleased to meet you, my lady," Nolderan says, as he takes a polite bow.

"Save your pleasantries," Kate says. "Why don't you say what you really mean? It's not like I'm making any effort to suppress my magical aura at this point. If you are indeed Daren's master, then you must also be the one who taught him to fight against banshees."

"You must be thinking of Daren's other master," Nolderan says. "The white mage. We were both ex-sages, so I can see how you might make the confusion. I assure you that I have no qualms with any banshee. As long as you are trusted by these people, I see no reason why I should consider you my enemy."

"She's not a real banshee, just so you know," Hadrik tells Nolderan. "She's a woman mage."

"Oh?" Nolderan says, while raising his eyebrows. "Now, that is certainly something that you don't see every day."

"How did you know that Daren would be here?" Kate asks him.

"I didn't know that he'd be in this general area," Nolderan says. "I just happened to be close enough to sense his aura, so I decided to come and say 'Hello'."

"You just 'happened' to be close enough?" Kate says. "So you were just wandering alone, by yourself, in the middle of the night?"

"Actually, my camp is not that far from here," Nolderan says. "I volunteered to do some scouting of the surrounding areas, during my night shift, which is why I was doing a patrol around these parts. I do understand how this could look a little suspicious from your point of view, however."

"Of course I'm suspicious of you," Kate says. "We don't even have any guarantee that you actually know Daren. What proof do you have that you are really one of his teachers, and not just some assassin, who was paid to kill him?"

"Well, if you want proof, then you can ask Daren himself," Nolderan says. "He is heading our way right now."

"Master Nolderan?" Daren says, shocked, as he approaches us. "Is that really you? You look so old!"

"The first time we meet in more than ten years, and this is what you tell me?" Nolderan says, with a grin, as he puts down his cards, and he gets up from the tree trunk, in order to greet his old pupil. "Maybe if you paid me a visit every once in a while, you wouldn't have been so surprised at the sight of my gray hair."

"I'm sorry…" Daren says. "It's just that I've been so busy with—"

"With saving the world, yes, yes, I know," Nolderan says. "You don't need to take everything so seriously all the time, boy. I was only joking. I know all about your adventures. Now stop being such a killjoy, and come give your old teacher a hug!"

Nolderan then hugs Daren for a few seconds, while patting him hard on the back.

"I see that you're still wearing that heavy plate armor of yours," Nolderan says, as he releases Daren. "Don't you get tired of walking around like this? What's the use of all those fancy moves I taught you if you can't even do half of them due to the weight of your armor?"

"I already told you," Daren says. "The armor is the only reliable protection against physical damage that I have. I'm not throwing it away."

"Who needs to have protection when you can just dodge your enemies' attacks?" Nolderan says. "Do I really need to give you a third scar before you learn your lesson for good?"

"Ugh…" Daren says. "Let's not start this discussion again. We only just got reunited after I don't even know how many years. Should we not be celebrating, instead of having a fight?"

"You're absolutely right, Daren!" Nolderan says. "Hold on, let me get another bottle of dwarven ale, so we can have a toast."

"Dwarven ale?..." Daren says. "At this hour? You can't be serious! What if we get attacked?"

"Of course you would say that..." Nolderan says. "Well, in that case, I'll just clink these two bottles, and imagine that you're also drinking with me. Cheers, Daren!"

He then clinks two dwarven ale bottles, like he said he would, and he takes a long sip from one of them.

"You're all welcome to join me in this toast, of course, if you want," Nolderan says, as he looks towards Hadrik, Kate and me. "It's a celebration, after all!"

"Sure, I'll join," I say. "Give me the bottle."

"Good, good," Nolderan says, as he hands me the bottle that he didn't drink from. "Anyone else?"

"Well, I'm already holding a dwarven ale bottle, so why not?" Hadrik says, as he joins us, and prepares for the toast.

"I'll pass," Kate says, simply.

"Let us toast, then!" Nolderan says, as he raises his bottle, while Hadrik and I do the same. "Cheers, my friends! Thank you all for keeping my old pupil safe, during this tournament. I know that he can be a little hard-headed at times, but he has a good heart."

"Cheers!" Hadrik and I say, as we all clink our bottles together and start to drink.

As I put down the bottle, I suddenly realize that I may have went a little overboard with the drinking, considering that I also had to take a lot of sips of dwarven ale while I was playing cards with Hadrik. I can already feel my head spinning a little from all the alcohol. Hopefully, this drunken sensation will pass soon.

"What's going on?" Flower asks, as she and Leila are both coming towards us, after having been woken up from the noise. "Are we having a visitor?"

"Yeah, this is Daren's old enchanting master,"

Hadrik says. “It’s the first time that they’re seeing each other in over ten years, so we’re holding a toast to celebrate their reunion.”

“Another female mage?…” Nolderan asks, as he senses the magic in Flower’s aura.

“Uh… sort of,” Hadrik says. “The girl is a mage, but there’s also a banshee that lives in the same body. Their names are Flower and Illuna. You can tell when the banshee is talking because the girl’s eyes will turn blue. It’s a little confusing at first, but you’ll get used to it soon enough.”

“Right, right…” Nolderan says.

“Pleased to meet you!” Flower says, smiling.

“And this over here is Leila,” Hadrik says. “She’s a lessathi.”

“A what?…” Nolderan asks.

“Uh…” Hadrik says. “I think the locals call them ‘the ancients’. Does that name sound familiar?”

“Oh, yes, yes…” Nolderan says. “The name does ring a bell. I think they were some old forgotten race that used to be very good at making magical devices.”

“Yes, exactly,” Hadrik says. “Leila is a descendant of that race.”

“Charmed,” Leila writes.

“Err…” Nolderan says, not exactly sure how to interpret the floating text in front of him.

“Oh, I forgot to tell you,” Hadrik says. “Leila can’t talk. She can only communicate through writing.”

“Ah, so that’s what the blue text was about,” Nolderan says, as he then turns his gaze towards Leila. “I’m pleased to meet you as well.”

“Master… it’s not that I’m not glad to see you, but may I ask what you are doing here, in Varathia?” Daren says. “I thought that you were done competing in mage tournaments after… well, you know…”

“After I lost my sage title, you mean?” Nolderan

says. "You can say it out loud, boy. It's not like I'm going to sulk. It's been fourteen years since then. I've moved on by now. Sure, I haven't really been competing as much, since then, but this time it's different. This Magium tournament has given me an opportunity of a lifetime, so I couldn't just ignore it."

"I'm sorry for interrupting," Flower says, "but why didn't you try to reclaim your sage title after you lost it if it meant so much to you? Don't they hold a competition for it every year, in each of your continents?"

"Are you by any chance from Varathia, little girl?" Nolderan asks.

"Yes, I was born here," Flower says. "Why do you ask?"

"Well, I suppose that would explain why you would ask such a question, then," Nolderan says. "I'm guessing that you don't really get a lot of information about the outside world on this isolated continent, do you?"

"We do get some news, but it's not much…" Flower says. "Have the yearly sage competitions been cancelled in the last decade? Is that why you stopped competing in these tournaments?"

"Oh, no, they're still holding the competitions," Nolderan says. "It's because of the person who took the title away from me that I've given up on the hope of winning the sage title ever again…"

"What do you mean?" Flower says.

"The current four sages are unlike any of the sages that have held the title in the last century," Daren says. "They are in a league of their own. Usually, a sage would not hold a title for more than two or three years before being dethroned, but three of the four current sages have remained undefeated for more than a decade. Azarius, the Sage of the West has been a sage for more than thirty years. He is practically the face of the Western Continent at this point. You see his portrait drawn on newspapers almost every week. One would have expected him to grow weaker, with old age, but every year, he seems to get stronger, instead. I think that everyone is mostly seeing the yearly contests as a formality at this point, and they're all assuming that Azarius will keep holding the title until he dies of old age."

"I know that you really like Azarius, Daren, but you shouldn't talk only about him," Hadrik says. "The other three sages may not have held their titles as long as him, but I'd say that their feats are equally impressive. Talmak, the Sage of the North, is regarded as the strongest earth elementalist of our time. All of the adversaries that he's had in the twelve years since he's inherited his title have been nowhere near his level of power. The only one who actually gave him a run for his money was the previous sage, but he's dead now, along with almost every other mage who dared to challenge Talmak to a fight, over the years. Then there's Selgurd. The elf. Oh man, don't even get me started on the elf…"

"Did he also keep his sage title for a long time?" Flower asks.

"No, but the sage before him did," Hadrik says. "He was considered to be on par with the other three long reigning sages, and everyone thought that nobody would ever defeat him. And then comes this no-name elf out of nowhere, and he kills him just like that, in less than a minute. Nobody even knows how he did it. He just made an illusion, so nobody could see or hear what was happening in the arena, and when the illusion was over, the Sage of the East was lying on the floor, lifeless, causing the crowds go completely silent. This happened last year. An investigation has been started to figure out what exactly lead to the old sage's death, but no evidence has been found as of yet. The elf would not say what spell he used, but the common consensus is that he most likely used a mind affecting spell of some kind."

"There were no external wounds," Daren says, "so if it really was a mind affecting spell, then it must have been one similar to the spell that the ogre shaman cast on us, in the fort, where you could get killed inside your own mind, if you weren't careful. The spell researchers who analyzed the traces of the spell could not find a match for any known spell, however. Or so they claimed."

"I don't know if the organizers are trying to hide something or not," Hadrik says, "but the fact of the matter is that the elf has somehow managed to seize the title of Sage of the East, and a lot of people are unhappy with this turn of events. I'm not really sure how he did it, but Selgurd did kill one of the strongest mages of our time, with minimal effort, so he will most certainly be a force to be reckoned with."

"What about the Sage of the South?" Flower asks.

"The Sage of the South is the one I fought, fourteen years ago," Nolderan says. "I stood no chance against him in the competition. Even to this day, he remains undefeated, and it never really looked like anyone has posed any serious threat to him since he took the title away from me. The man is a renowned dragon hunter that goes by the name of Drakesbane. I'm not sure what his real name is, but that's what everyone calls him now, due to the large number of dragon heads that he has in his collection. Dragons are something of a legend these days, because they mostly stay hidden, and no longer attack villages, like they used to in the past, but Drakesbane goes to hunt them in their own territory as a sport. A lot of people like to pretend that the dragon heads he brings home belonged to wyverns instead, in order to keep believing that dragons do not exist, but I don't think that anyone who's actually seen one of those heads up close could fool themselves into believing such nonsense. There is a very clear difference between a wyvern's head and a dragon's head, and that difference would be obvious to anyone who is not being willfully ignorant."

All of a sudden, we hear a few loud beeps coming from Leila's pocket, and also from mine. We both take out our stat devices at the same time, and I see that I now have three extra points to invest in my stats. I suppose this was to be expected, judging by the large number of pinecone-collecting mages we've been encountering, lately.

I spend a few seconds, thinking about what points I should invest in my stats, but the truth of the matter is that I've practically already decided what stats I wanted to upgrade a while ago, after I saw how well Leila handled herself against that troll in the arena. Those martial art techniques that she was using during her fight were really impressive, and she confirmed to me afterwards that she was never able to do any of those moves before upgrading her combat technique stat. Combined with my reflexes and speed, those techniques are just what I need to compensate for my lack of battle experience, and to complement my agility-based fighting style.

After making sure that this is indeed what I want, I spend one of my points in my speed stat, in order to upgrade it to its maximum level of four, and then I use the two remaining points to level up my combat technique stat.

"Did you also get three points?" I ask Leila, once I'm done with my stat device.

"Yes, I put them all in my reflexes," Leila writes, as we both put our stat devices back in our pockets.

"Were those… fortune teller trinkets?" Nolderan asks, confused.

"Indeed, they were," I say.

"They're not using them for fortune telling," Daren says. "They're using them to magically enhance their physical abilities. I know that it's a little hard to believe, but I've seen it with my own eyes, so I can confirm that it's true."

"Interesting…" Nolderan says. "I always thought that those devices were nothing more than toys, but I guess that I was mistaken. How well do they work, exactly?"

"It depends on your actual physical condition," Leila writes. "If you're weaker, then you're going to get less effect out of the stat devices."

"I see…" Nolderan says.

"So… what have you been up to, these past few years?" Daren asks his old master. "I've heard rumors that you've started doing mercenary work, but I'm not sure if they were true or not."

"Oh, they were true, alright," Nolderan says. "Losing my sage title so soon after I'd earned it and in such a spectacular fashion wasn't really very good for my business. People started to think that I was just some washed up old man, and they gradually began to look for other enchanting and martial arts masters. There's no shortage of those in the Southern Continent, after all. So, when people stopped coming to me to teach them, I decided that my talents would be better used elsewhere. You see… when you're doing mercenary work, nobody is going to care about your reputation. They just need you to get the job done. It might not be the most ideal career, but it puts food on the table."

"I'm so sorry…" Daren says. "I did not know that it's been so rough for you in these past years. I should have at least left you a transceiver to keep in touch."

"Don't be sorry," Nolderan says. "We all have our ups and downs. It's the way of life. But like I said, at least this tournament has provided me with the opportunity to change my life for the better. That's why we're all here, isn't it? To try and change our lives for the better?"

"Actually…" Daren says. "The reason why I came here is that—"

"Hey, not that I want to interrupt you or anything," Arraka says, "but Illuna told me to let you all know when there are enemies trying to surround us, and it just so happens that this is exactly what's happening right now, as I speak."

"Is it monsters again?" Daren asks.

"Yeah, monsters," Arraka says. "More than there were last time. They're all suppressing their auras again, but I can recognize the orc and the two ogres that got away from us two days ago. They must have gone to get reinforcements. I don't sense the two goblins that bailed them out last time anymore, so they must be a lot more confident in their chances of winning this time around. I'm counting at least fifteen warriors and five mages. Actually no, make that seventeen warriors. Five of them are ogres, including the two from before. Twelve of them are orcs, including their captain with the flaming battleaxes. The five mages are a mixture of orcs and ogres, but there are no more goblins this time."

"Well, master," Daren says. "I think this is the time for you to go. These monsters have come here to kill our group, specifically, so as long as you avoid them on your way back to your camp, they will most likely ignore you and focus on us. It's sad that this reunion had to be so short, but as long as we're both participating in this tournament, I'm sure that our paths will cross again. Assuming that we'll survive this battle, that is…"

"What are you talking about, boy?" Nolderan says. "Do you think I'm just going to run away and let my favorite disciple get killed off by some monsters, mere minutes after we've been reunited once more?"

"These aren't just any monsters," Daren says. "They

are elite troops of the dragon who rules most of the monster races on this continent. It's not going to be an easy fight."

"Bah!" Nolderan says. "You've said this before. Remember that time when we went to raid that cave full of ogres and trolls and we butchered them all within minutes? You were saying that it would be a hard fight back then too."

"That happened when I was barely twenty years old!" Daren says. "Gods, now I remember… I had only been training for several months, and that was already our third monster hunt. How the hell did you manage to convince me to remain your pupil for so long?"

"Stop complaining," Nolderan says. "My training worked, didn't it? You can't just do mock battles all the time and expect to magically become a seasoned warrior. Real battles are where you truly get to test your skills."

"Are the monsters getting closer?" Hadrik asks. "I can't really tell with my magic sense."

"They are most definitely getting closer," Kate says. "In fact, we should be seeing them any minute. It looks like they've given up on trying to flank us from all sides, because of the large area without trees in front of us that can't provide them cover, so they're now all trying to assemble in the woods behind us, and to the sides."

"At least that should keep them away from the tents when we fight," Hadrik says. "The last thing we want is to get our tents damaged when we're nowhere near a city to buy any replacements."

"Don't forget the discussion that we had after our last battle!" Daren says. "We're facing against a lot more enemies today, so we can't afford to make any mistakes. Leila, no more rushing into the enemy lines, alright? Kate, do you remember what you need to focus on?"

"Yes," Kate says. "I remember."

She then shoots several icicles into the woods on our

left side, and two of the ogres suddenly drop dead, from behind the trees. The three ogre warriors that were left alive are now all shouting loudly, and they're advancing towards us at a rapid pace.

Seeing that their formation has been broken, the orcs that were hiding behind the trees on our right side are now also revealing themselves and moving slowly towards us, while forming a line, with their shields raised in front of them and their maces in their right hands.

Kate tries to attack the three ogres with another barrage of icicles, but this time, they use their huge clubs to defend themselves from her projectiles.

"Flower," Daren says. "Fly up into the air, and bombard the ogres with fireballs. They need to die before they reach us."

"I'm on it!" Flower says, as she jumps into the air and then propels herself upwards using her fire jets.

"The rest of us need to deal with the orcs," Daren says. "They all have anti-magic armor, so don't bother to attack them if you're an elementalist."

While Daren was talking, Flower started to shoot fireballs at the three ogres that were still heading towards us. The monsters tried to jump away from the explosions, but this left them defenseless against Kate's icicles, which penetrated their skulls and killed them all on the spot.

"Good," Daren says. "The ogrcs are already dead. Let's finish the orcs off quick, and then we'll head for the mages."

While we were talking, the orcs have split into two groups, each of them forming a wall with their shields, and slowly advancing towards us from both sides. The orc captain from our last battle is, however, nowhere to be seen.

"I'll take the ones on the left," Nolderan says, as he

heads towards the monsters.

"There are five orcs on the left," Daren says, while he starts following his old master into battle. "I'm coming with you. Hadrik should be able to handle half of the warriors by himself without much trouble."

He then sees that Leila has remained behind, uncertain of what to do.

"Leila, you should go help Hadrik," Daren says. "Master Nolderan and I should be able to handle ourselves against five orcs."

Leila nods, and she goes towards the orcs on the right, along with Hadrik.

"I'll go find the mages," Kate says.

"No, wait," Daren says. "We shouldn't risk splitting up. There might be traps waiting for us in the woods. We'll all go together, after we're done with the warriors."

"Understood…" Kate says.

Daren then heads into battle, along with his master, as Hadrik and Leila are getting ready to fight the monsters on the right side. The first one to engage the enemy is Hadrik. He punches right through the orcs' shield wall on the right, putting a large dent into one of the monsters' shields, while knocking its holder on his back. Then, he jumps high into the air, and he lands with his fist on a second orc, just as the monster raises his shield to protect himself.

The sound made by Hadrik's fist hitting the metal shield resounded throughout the whole clearing, and immediately afterwards, we could hear the ogre's scream, as his arm broke from all the pressure. While the warrior is still struggling to recover, Hadrik quickly grabs him by his feet, and he throws him into two of his comrades, which sends them all crashing to the ground.

Meanwhile, Daren and Nolderan have both reached the orcs on the left, and now they're flanking them from two sides, forcing the monsters to give up on their shield wall and to focus on the adversaries in front of them. As Nolderan begins to fight, I can definitely see the resemblance between his fighting style, and the one that Daren is using. However, Nolderan's style seems to focus a lot more on not getting hit at all, while Daren often likes to parry blows, and to block them with his shield, while he fights.

One other thing I'm noticing is the incredible synchronization between the two of them. Even if they've been apart for more than ten years, you can clearly see that they know each other's moves by heart, and that they don't need to communicate their actions through words, in the heat of battle, because one will always know what the other is planning to do next. More than this, it seems that neither of them is hesitant in leaving their guard down, while the other is watching their back. It's clear that such a level of teamwork can only be achieved by warriors who have spent many years fighting together, side by side.

"Just like old times, eh, Daren?" Nolderan says, after he slices the head of an orc clean off his shoulders.

"Yes, I see that you're still as reckless as ever!" Daren says, as he blocks one of the monsters' maces with his shield. "I can't believe that you're still alive after all this time!"

"You may be saying this, but you are clearly enjoying the fight," Nolderan says, with a grin, as he dances away from one enemy, and prepares to engage another. "Here's another reckless move for you, boy. Get ready!"

He then runs full speed ahead, towards an orc that is too busy fighting Daren to pay attention to Nolderan, and he makes a horizontal jump, rotating himself to the side in mid-air, and propelling his feet into the monster's back. As the orc gets knocked off-balance, the ex-sage falls to the ground, on his left shoulder. Daren immediately seizes the opportunity, and he drives his sword through the monster's head, while Nolderan quickly rolls to the side, in order to avoid getting bludgeoned by another orc's mace. As soon as the ex-sage gets up, he feints an attack with one of his swords, pretending to do a full swing from the left side, and just as the orc raises his shield to defend himself, Nolderan's second sword comes swinging for the monster's neck from the right, cutting his head off in one move.

While I haven't really recovered from my state of alcohol-induced dizziness yet, I can't just stand here and do nothing for the rest of the fight, either. I decide that it's time for me to join the battle as well, so I aim my crossbow at one of the orcs that Leila is fighting.

It's a bit difficult to aim from this distance, while the orc is moving, but thanks to my newly invested points in the combat technique stat, I manage to accurately predict how the monster will move, after only a few seconds of watching him. The bolt from my crossbow hits the orc straight through the slit of his helmet, and it kills him instantly.

As I look to see how the others are doing, I notice that the rest of the monsters are already dead, and that my teammates are now assembling near the woods, so we can go and fight the orc mages and their captain together.

"We sure made short work of these so-called 'elite' warriors, didn't we?" Nolderan says, and then he laughs.

"Not yet," Daren says. "There are still five mages waiting in the woods. And their captain's fighting skill is far superior to that of his subordinates. Let's just hurry up and get to them before they—"

Daren suddenly gets interrupted by the sound of a loud horn, coming from the direction of the orc captain, which makes us all cover our ears, to dampen some of the noise.

"Crap!" Arraka says, as soon as the orc captain stops blowing in the horn. "I forgot to check above us. Wyvern riders incoming. Wyvern riders incoming!"

We all turn our heads upwards, and we see ten black wyverns quickly diving down from the clouds in which they'd been hiding until now. Each of the creatures is ridden by an orc wearing regular leather armor, and holding either a long spear or a crossbow in their hands. Wyverns are smaller versions of dragons that have a body length of fifteen feet, with their wings spanning around twenty feet. They are far less intelligent than dragons, their scales are a lot less durable, and they cannot breathe fire, but other than that, their appearance is rather similar. Once the wyvern riders realize that we've already spotted them, they slow down their descent, and they begin to circle around the skies, waiting for the right moment to strike.

"Flower, Illuna and I will take care of the wyverns," Kate says. "The rest of you can't fly, so you won't be able to help us. I think you should all go and deal with the mages, before they call for more reinforcements."

"Maybe you're right," Daren says. "At least we've forced them to reveal the ace up their sleeve, so they shouldn't be able to surprise us with any more— *Damn it*!"

As Daren was finishing his sentence, a very large blue circle appeared on the ground, in the area surrounding us, and a dim blue light is now slowly starting to envelop us.

"Get out of the summoning circle!" Daren shouts. "Get out, now!"

We all rush out as fast as we can, and when we look back, we see that the blue light has filled the whole area above the circle, up to a height of nearly thirty feet, and it has gotten ten times brighter than before. Soon afterwards, the earth starts to tremble, and a very large creature gradually materializes itself from thin air, within the area that we just left, as the circle and the bright light fade away.

Once we get a clear look at it, we realize that the creature which has been summoned by the dragon's mages is without a doubt, a red-eyed mammoth. Towering above us, at an impressive thirty feet of height, the creature is now staring at us, with its bright red eyes, as if it's still trying to decide whether it should attack us or not. Red-eyed mammoths are generally not known for their aggressive behavior, despite their menacing looks, but a summoned creature is forced to obey any order given by its masters, so it most likely won't be long until this creature will try to trample us all to death.

Mammoths, in general, are only slightly larger than elephants, and the only major difference between the two species, in terms of appearance, is the fact that mammoths have much larger tusks, and their skin is typically covered with wool. Red-eyed mammoths, on the other hand, are much larger, they can only be found on the Northern Continent, and they are notorious for their fierceness in battle, when they fight to protect their territory. Their skins are completely armored, being far more durable than elven steel, and when they fight, they use their trunks like huge mallets, to smash their enemies, while they use their tusks as spears, to impale any remaining survivors of their onslaught.

As the mammoth roars loudly, I can suddenly feel the presence of the orcs and ogres disappearing from the forest, due to them teleporting out of the area, just like last time.

"The mages and the captain are gone, by the way," Arraka says. "Just thought I'd let you know."

"Yes, Arraka, we all know that," Illuna says. "It's not

like they took any effort to hide their auras anymore for the past minute. The mages were probably only brought here to summon this beast, and nothing else. Let's go deal with the wyverns, before anyone else shows up."

Flower then jumps into the air, and she propels herself upwards with her fire jets, as Kate jumps on a flying platform made of ice, while she creates an ice cage around herself, in order to make sure that she won't fall off.

"You're going to have to deal with the mammoth yourselves, while we fight the wyverns," Kate says. "Don't take any stupid risks."

"Easier said than done," Daren says.

"We'll manage, don't worry," Nolderan says. "There hasn't been a monster yet that Daren and I failed to defeat, while fighting together. You just go follow your banshee friend, and do what you need to do."

Kate nods, curtly, and then she lifts her cage into the air, following Illuna towards the wyvern riders. As Kate heads for the skies, the rest of us stand our ground, and we look at the mammoth, which has been notably silent since its roar from earlier. The creature is not moving at all, and it's simply staring at us, waiting for our move.

"So…" Hadrik says. "Do you guys think that we should attack it, or?…"

"I think that the creature is waiting to see what we'll do, before it takes any action," I say. "Typically, when you encounter a red-eyed mammoth, it should be enough to slowly back away from it, while maintaining eye-contact, and it would leave you alone, but I'm not sure what happens when it's been specifically instructed to kill us by its summoner. Let's try backing away, for now. With a little luck, maybe it won't attack us."

"Well…" Hadrik says. "You're the creature expert. Come on, everyone, let's back up a little."

We all take a few steps back, slowly, while keeping

our eyes on the monster, and we try to observe its reaction. The mammoth keeps standing there, looking at us, for a while, and then all of a sudden, it begins to run towards us, in an attempt to trample us under its feet.

"So much for that plan," Hadrik says. "Get ready to fight!"

The dwarf then dashes towards the creature, and he jumps up in the air, trying to punch it in the head. The mammoth, however, sees him coming, and it stops in its tracks, raising its trunk, so it can defend itself. As soon as Hadrik gets into the monster's range of attack, the mammoth swings its trunk at him from above, with incredible force, sending the dwarf crashing into the ground.

"One hit from that trunk, and we're goners," Daren says, as he looks at the hole in the ground made by Hadrik when he fell. "I wouldn't recommend attacking the mammoth unless you're really confident in your evasion skills. Barry, none of your weapons would be able to get through this creature's thick armored skin, so you'd better stay out of this. Leila, the enchantments on your daggers are a little better, so you could give it a shot, if you want to come with us."

"I'll come with you," Leila writes.

"Good," Daren says. "Let's hurry. I'm not sure how long Hadrik can keep the mammoth busy on his own."

As Daren, Nolderan and Leila head towards the mammoth, I suddenly remember that I came upon a page detailing the weaknesses of red-eyed mammoths in my notebook, while I was reading through my notes, for the arena. Should I go get the notebook? I'm certainly not going to be of much use out here, at this rate. Okay, it's settled. I'll go get the notebook.

I rush towards my tent, and once I reach it, I open up the zipper. On my way there, I couldn't help but notice that Melindra's tent had remained closed since the battle has started. There's no way that she didn't hear those loud horns from before, or the sounds from all the fighting. Which means that she's just pretending to still be asleep, so she doesn't have to give away the fact that she can't control the power of her wind magic.

Whatever. I don't have time to think about her. I have other things to do right now.

I quickly step inside my tent, and I open my backpack. Then, I take out my notebook from it and I flip through the pages, until I reach the paragraphs about the mammoths. And finally, here is what I was looking for. The red-eyed mammoth section. But, what does it say under 'Weaknesses'? Let's see…

Apparently, the mammoth's main weakness is at the very base of its trunk, on the underside. Unlike regular mammoths, this is where this type of creature has its nostrils, so that part is basically lacking any sort of armor. One good stab in that area should do some serious damage to the creature's airway, but I'm not sure how one would go about doing that, without getting smashed into the ground by the trunk.

The mammoth's eyes are also a weakness, but the eyelids are pretty thick, so it would take quite some effort to get through them. The creature only needs to close its eyes to protect itself, so as far as weaknesses go, this one isn't all that useful.

I can't really find any other information that could help us in this situation, so I decide to place the notebook back inside my backpack, and then I exit the tent. Looking at the battleground, I see that the mammoth is still busy defending itself from Hadrik, while mostly ignoring the fact that Daren, Nolderan and Leila are all trying to cut through its thick skin, by slashing at its legs. There are a few more holes in the ground now than when I went inside my tent, but apparently this hasn't stopped Hadrik from jumping at the monster some more, and then getting smashed into the ground over and over.

What now, then?… Nobody except Hadrik would be able to reach high enough in order to attack the mammoth's eyes or its nostrils, but the dwarf seems to have his hands full at the moment. Kate, Flower and Illuna are still fighting the wyvern riders in the sky, so they won't be able to provide assistance. If only we had someone else who could fly in our team… Hold on, what am I saying? There *is* someone else.

"Hey, Melindra, can you hear me?" I shout, while I look towards Melindra's tent.

I can see no movements inside the tent, or anything else that might confirm the fact that she's heard me. After a few more seconds of silence, I continue.

"Okay, you don't need to answer me," I say. "I just have a little favor to ask. Remember how you made us all fly over the wall of Thilias, with your wind magic? Well, I was thinking that maybe you might have a way to make me fly that would also give me some manner of control. You know, like some semi-intelligent air-currents that react to my movements or something. I've also had access to elementalist wind magic two times before, and I think it should be theoretically possible to cast such a spell. You've been practicing this type of magic for six hundred years, so surely you must know how to do something like this by now, right?"

I wait for a few seconds, to see if I get any reaction, but still, the only answer I get is silence.

"Listen," I say. "I'm not asking you to join the battle. You don't need to give yourself away or anything. All I'm asking is that you cast a spell on me that will allow me to fly."

Still no answer.

"Come on, Melindra," I say. "I know you can hear me!"

I wait for another three seconds, but there are no sounds coming from inside the tent.

"*Melindra*!" I shout.

All of a sudden, I can feel several air currents circling around me, similar to the ones I felt when Melindra raised me in the air for the first time. Then, only a few seconds later, my body gets lifted from the ground, and I start to float several feet above the soil. When I move my hands around a little, I notice that the air currents are reacting to my movements, and changing my direction accordingly. If I raise my arms in the air, the air currents propel me upwards. If I lower them, I slowly come to a halt. The currents also seem to be taking into account the way I lean my body, and the way I move my legs when they establish what direction I need to go in.

Obviously, they're not going to be as responsive as the currents I was using to lift me from the ground back when I was using my stat device's emergency mode, due to the fact that these particular air currents need to wait for my movements, before they change my direction and speed, but it's much better than what I would have expected, from a spell of this kind. I could still do without all the nausea I'm getting every time I do a quick turn, but that's probably due to my current drunken state, and not the fault of the spell.

"You have my thanks!" I shout, from up above, towards Melindra, and then I move higher into the air, in order to do a little test flight, before I head over to the mammoth.

I try to do as many moves as possible, so I can properly understand what causes me to change my direction, altitude and speed, because I can't afford to make any mistakes when I'm fighting the mammoth. One slip up, and its trunk will break all of my bones, with a single swing. My control over this spell needs to be perfect.

"Barry, look out!" I hear Kate's voice, from above.

As I look up, I suddenly notice that two of the wyvern riders are currently diving down towards me, with their spears at the ready, while Kate and Flower are too busy fighting their own wyverns to be able to help me in any way.

Engaging in an aerial battle so soon after I've been given these air currents is the last thing I wanted to do. If I attempt to fight these orcs right now, I will no doubt be put at an enormous disadvantage. But what if I tried negotiating with them, instead?…

"Wait!" I tell the orcs, as they're approaching me. "You guys can speak Common, right? We don't need to be fighting each other. Maybe we can make a deal!"

"We don't make deals with humans!" says one of the orcs, in the Common language. "We only serve Tyrath."

He then tries to impale me with his spear, but I dive out of his way, and then I try again to reason with him.

"Only Tyrath?" I say. "But what if I were to give you more money than the dragon? Couldn't that make you change your mind?"

"Our loyalty towards the dragon king cannot be broken by mere promises of wealth!" the orc says, furiously.

"Hold on a second," the other orc says. "Just how much gold are we talking about, here?"

As I take my gold pouch out of my pocket and open it, I notice the fact that I also have a few gems inside it. The same gems that I had procured from the ogre stronghold, when we were raiding their treasury. If I show these orcs only the gold, I will probably not be able to buy them off, but a single one of these gems should be enough for them to live the rest of their lives without any worries.

I decide to take out a large ruby from my pouch, and I hold it in front of the orcs, so they can see it clearly.

"I have many more of these in my backpack," I say, "so I wouldn't mind parting with one or two for the sake of a temporary alliance. I'm willing to offer you both this ruby, in advance, and if you actually help me by driving back the other orcs, I will also give you a shiny diamond to go along with it. What do you say?"

"Your offer is tempting, human," the second orc says, without being able to fully hide the greed in his eyes. "But what would we orcs do with such treasure? Where else would we live our lives, if not in Tyrath's domain? It's not like any of the human cities would ever accept us within their walls."

"I hear that Fyron is taking in refugees," I say. "You know about Fyron, right?"

"The goblin general?" the orc asks, in a thoughtful voice. "Yes… I do know about him. I heard that his camp has been doing better in these past few years. I also heard that he accepts all types of monsters, nowadays, not only goblins. Maybe it wouldn't be such a bad idea to go pay him a visit…"

"Do you realize what you are saying?" says the first orc, shocked. "What you speak of is treason!"

"Is it really?" the second orc says. "Tyrath is barely giving us enough money to afford our food and weapons. Why are you so loyal to him? If we accept this human's offer, we could live like kings! Think about it, brother."

"You are no brother of mine," the first orc says, with pure hatred in his eyes, and he dives towards his former companion, with his spear aimed for his heart.

The second orc manages to raise himself into the air, before the other one reaches him, and he pushes his spear into his comrade's chest, making him fall off his wyvern, to his death.

"Let this be the first sacrifice for our alliance, human," the surviving orc says, while raising his bloody spear in the air.

"Here is a ruby, for your trouble," I say, as I toss him the ruby I was holding in my hand earlier, and the orc catches the gem with both his hands. "As promised, I will also give you a diamond, when the other orcs are dead."

"Traitor!" shouts another orc from above, as he also dives with his wyvern towards us, in an attempt to impale his old ally with his spear.

The betrayer orc does not wait for his adversary to reach him, and he flies upwards, driving his spear through the enemy wyvern's chest, which makes it stop flapping its wings and sends it falling to the ground, along with its rider, killing them both.

"What's going on, here?" Kate shouts, from a distance, as she sees what just happened.

"This orc is fighting on our side, as of now," I shout at her and Flower. "Make sure not to attack him!"

"Right…" Kate and Illuna both say, at the same time, and then they continue to fight their enemies in the sky.

"I'll go deal with the mammoth, now," I tell my new orc ally. "You know what to do."

I then leave the orc behind, and I fly to a lower altitude, closer to the mammoth that Hadrik and the others are still fighting. It seems that while I was busy with the wyverns, the mammoth has changed its tactic, and it is now trying to trample Daren and Nolderan, instead of focusing on Hadrik, like before. The two enchanters have managed to do quite a bit of damage to the monster's legs while I wasn't looking, however, which has greatly reduced the creature's speed. Seeing that Daren, Nolderan and Leila are all able to easily dodge its charges, the mammoth is forced to once again turn its focus to Hadrik, who just keeps pummeling the monster, despite all of the beating he's taken in this fight.

As I get closer to my destination, I mimic a jump, in the direction in which I want to go, which sends me flying towards the creature at great speed. I then rotate my body upwards and begin to move my legs in a circular motion, similarly to how I would move them if I were trying to keep myself afloat in a lake, while in a vertical position. This stops my momentum, and it changes my direction, so that I can place myself right above the mammoth, in order to be ready to attack at a moment's notice.

It's a good thing that I can mostly control my direction and speed without my arms, because this allows me to also use my crossbow in mid-flight. I'm also noticing that the skills I gained by flying aircrafts in the past are proving really useful when trying to control these types of flight spells. It would have probably taken me a lot longer to get accustomed to flying like this, if I never flew a plane before.

As I lower my altitude a little, I notice that Hadrik is currently holding onto the mammoth's trunk, while the monster keeps swinging it up and down, trying to make him lose his grip and fall off.

"Hey, Barry, you can fly now?" Hadrik shouts at me, while still holding onto the trunk.

"For now…" I shout back at him.

"Great!" Hadrik shouts. "Then maybe we can work together on this! I'll hold down the mammoth's trunk, while you stab it in the eyes. What do you say?"

While Hadrik is talking, the sound of his voice keeps fluctuating in intensity, due to the fact that he's continuously being carried up and down by the trunk, at great speed.

"Sounds like a good plan," I shout, "although, I'd rather aim for a weak point other than the eyes. But how are you planning on holding down the trunk?"

"Don't worry," Hadrik says. "I've got that covered."

He then jumps off the trunk and he lands on the ground.

"You just need to keep the mammoth busy for a few seconds, while I do some shapeshifting," Hadrik shouts.

Shapeshifting?… Against a red-eyed mammoth? Didn't Golmyck say that he'd ban him from the tournament if he were to turn himself into anything much bigger than his current size?

I don't have time to think about this much longer, because the mammoth is now fully focused on smashing me with its trunk, and I'm barely even getting a moment's respite between two consecutive swings. When the monster wears itself out a little, and it slows down its rhythm, I take the opportunity to look down and see what Hadrik's been up to.

Apparently, Hadrik has turned himself into a giant snail… And he's just crawling on the ground at a very low speed… Oh man, I sure hope he's not messing with me, right now. At any rate, I already told Hadrik that I'd follow his plan, so all I can do now is keep dodging, and hope that he knows what he's doing.

After flying out of the trunk's way a few more times, the alcohol-induced nausea finally starts to get to me, and it really messes up my sense of balance for a moment. By the time I recover, the mammoth's trunk is already less than a second away from hitting me. With an absolutely incredible reaction speed, I manage to throw myself out of the way, and the trunk misses me by only a few inches. I could feel the wind from that swing blow right past me. I can't afford to let that happen again. I'd better pull myself together, and quick.

As I look down, I notice that Hadrik is finally done with his shapeshifting, and he is now back in his dwarf form, standing with his feet in the slime that his snail form left behind. He has his arms raised, and he is looking straight at me.

"Alright, Barry!" Hadrik shouts. "Now try to make the mammoth swing its trunk over here!"

I think I'm finally beginning to understand what Hadrik was trying to do. The particular breed of giant snail that Hadrik turned into has a kind of slime that dries almost instantly, and becomes incredibly sticky, which is why it is often used as base material for many types of glues. Since Hadrik has his feet in the slime, he should now be able to grab onto the mammoth's trunk, without having to worry about being lifted into the air afterwards.

"Nice thinking!" I tell Hadrik. "I'll be right over!"

I then dive towards him, and I just float there, baiting the mammoth to attack me. The monster immediately takes the bait, and it swings its trunk with full force in our direction. I fly out of the way at the last second, and Hadrik quickly grabs onto the trunk, with both hands, without letting go.

"Now's your chance, Barry!" Hadrik says. "Quick! I don't know how long this glue will hold."

As the ground below the dwarf is already starting to crack, from the force of the mammoth trying to pull away its trunk, I quickly fly upwards, in order to attack the beast's weak spot.

I reach the area at the base of the trunk as fast as I can, and I try to identify the nostrils on its underside. As soon as I see them, I drive my scimitar into one of them, in an attempt to irreparably damage the creature's airways. As the mammoth screams, I drive my blade further inside, while twisting it continuously. Soon, the screams of the creature start to turn into gasps of air, as the damage that I did to its airways is finally starting to have a visible effect.

I take my scimitar out of the monster and I fly away, while the mammoth is still desperately trying to breathe. After about ten seconds, the creature's gasps for air start to get faster and shorter, until they eventually stop, and the mammoth falls completely silent, as it slowly crashes to the ground, causing a small earth tremor due to the enormous size of its body.

As I slowly land on the ground, besides the monster's carcass, Hadrik lets out a hearty laugh. Taking a good look at him, I see that he has a black eye, from all the beating he's taken during this fight.

"This is it!" Hadrik says. "It's for moments like these that I've joined this tournament. I knew that staying in this group was the right decision! There's just no running out of powerful enemies to fight, with you people!"

"That was quite the impressive combination you two had back there," Nolderan says. "I did not know that any of you had the ability to fly."

"Yeah, well if there's anything Barry excels at, it's resourcefulness!" Hadrik says. "He made that abundantly clear after somehow managing to wiggle his way out of the arena alive, against all odds."

"An arena, you say?…" Nolderan asks.

"Oh, right, we didn't tell you about that," Hadrik says. "Back in Thilias, we all had to fight in an arena event, and the owner of that arena really had it in for Barry and Leila. Or rather, he wanted to make them into the stars of the show. He literally threw everything he had at them, and they only had some weaklings as teammates, but they still managed to make it out victorious. We'll fill you in on the details later."

"I sure hope that the orc captain is not planning to teleport back with even more reinforcements…" Daren says. "We really need to find a way to stop them from escaping. Otherwise, they'll just keep coming at us over and over, until we're completely worn out."

"Or you could try to do a better job at hiding your tracks, from now on," Nolderan says. "If they managed to find you for a second time, then you people probably left them a really obvious trail to follow."

"Yeah, you're probably right..." Daren says. "Now that I think about it, the only way they could have found us this fast is if they teleported back to the location of our previous battle, and pursued our tracks all the way to our camp."

"What if they have a tracking spell cast on us?" I say.

"You mean, like the one that the golden fox cast on us before we arrived in Thilias?" Daren says. "I don't think that's the case. As a white mage, I should be able to detect these sorts of spells better than anyone. The fox is a really powerful spirit from the magical plane, so her spells would be much more difficult to detect than normal, but these are just some lowly monsters. I really shouldn't have any problems detecting spells cast by one or two orc mages."

"Maybe you're right," I say. "But still, I don't think that they could have found us just by following our trail. I'd be more inclined to believe that they have scouts, scattered all around the continent."

"Actually, that would make a lot of sense..." Daren says. "The dragon has a huge army of orcs, so it's only natural that he'd have scouts all over the place. And if they're using transceivers to communicate, there would be no real way for us to kill them before they get to report our location. I suppose that we have no other choice than to keep mowing down their troops, until they decide to stop sending them after us, then..."

"Hey, look, your elementalists are coming back down!" Nolderan says. "I think they're done killing the wyvern riders. No, wait, there's one more left. He's coming down for us. Get ready!"

"Hold on!" I say. "Don't attack him. That one is working with us!"

"He is?..." Daren asks, confused.

"Yeah, I bribed him with some gems, and he switched sides in the middle of the battle," I say.

"Hah!" Hadrik says. "What did I tell you about Barry and his resourcefulness? It's like he has this constant supply of crazy ideas in his head, and whenever he needs one, he just pulls it out, like it's nothing. I mean seriously, who else would have actually thought of trying to bribe an enemy orc, in the middle of a fight?"

As Kate and Flower come landing on the ground, next to us, the wyvern rider stops a dozen feet above the ground, as the wyvern keeps slowly flapping its wings, to maintain its altitude.

"All of the other orcs are dead, human," the orc says. "I have fulfilled my end of the bargain."

"And now, I will fulfill mine," I tell him, as I take a diamond out of my gold pouch, and throw it to him.

The orc catches the diamond in his hand, he studies it from a few angles, to make sure that it's not fake, and then he puts it in the sash that he's wearing around his waist.

"I must leave you now, human," the orc says. "Before any other of Tyrath's troops come to this location, and find out that I am still alive. Perhaps we will meet again."

"Yeah," I say. "I'll make sure to say hi, if we ever visit Fyron's camp."

The orc nods, and then he utters a command to his wyvern, which makes it go up, and then as far away from this place as possible.

"Is it over?" Kate asks. "Are they all dead? Or is there some third wave of enemies still waiting to ambush us?"

"Nah," Arraka says. "There's no one else. I even checked above, this time around. If they're going to bring new reinforcements, I doubt that it's going to be any time soon, after the beating they've taken in this fight."

"We should at least be prepared, in case it happens," Daren says. "Let's start with some healing. Come over here, and I'll tend to each of your wounds, in turn."

For the next few minutes, Daren spends his time magically healing all of our bruises, including Hadrik's black eye. When he is just about done, I see a tent getting opened in the distance, as Melindra slowly comes out of it. Just as she exits the tent, I can feel the air currents around me fading away, until they disappear completely.

"Look who finally decided to show up..." Kate says.

"Hey, Melindra!" Flower shouts, as Melindra is already advancing towards us. "Over here! You missed the fight! Also, Daren's old enchanting master came to visit. He's standing right here, next to me. His name is Nolderan."

"Is this another member of your team, or?..." Nolderan asks us.

Melindra overhears Nolderan's question, while she's still making our way towards us, and she answers it before any of us get a chance to say anything.

"I am only a travelling maiden, looking to go back home to her sickly father," Melindra says, in a loud voice, while smiling politely, and walking slowly in our direction. "Sadly, I wasn't inside the city premises when the tournament protection spell was cast, so I've been hiding in a cave all this time, scared for my own life. Luckily for me, however, these brave warriors have offered to escort me to my hometown, and I've been travelling with them ever since."

When she reaches our position, she extends her hand, towards Daren's old master, inviting him to kiss it.

"Pleased to meet you!" she says, still smiling.

"Likewise, milady," Nolderan says, as he grabs her hand, kissing it softly, and then releases it. "May I ask which way you are headed?"

"Oh, it's just a small town," Melindra says. "You probably haven't heard of it."

"We are taking her to a city called Ollendor," Daren says.

Melindra frowns at him, when she sees how easily he's given away our destination, but it doesn't look like Daren noticed.

"Ollendor?" Nolderan says, surprised. "We've actually passed that city on our way here! And it just so happens that I have a mage in my team that can cast teleportation magic. If you would come with me to my camp, I'm sure that I could convince him to teleport you to your destination, and you could save a few days from your journey. What do you say, Daren, would you like to meet my teammates?"

"I… suppose so…" Daren says. "But I'm not sure what the others have to say about this. Would everyone else also be okay with asking one of Nolderan's friends to teleport us to Ollendor?"

"Hey, if it gets us there faster, then why not?" Hadrik says.

"I don't have a problem with that," Leila writes.

"I don't have a problem, either," Kate says. "I also want to apologize for being so suspicious of you earlier, Nolderan. You helped us a great deal in that fight against the orcs and the mammoth, and you've most definitely earned my trust."

"Think nothing of it," Nolderan says. "Well, if nobody else has any objections, I would personally suggest that we get ready to leave, soon. I wouldn't really want to spend too much time in this place, when new monsters could teleport and attack us at a moment's notice."

"Alright," Daren says. "We should go pack our tents, then. We'll meet back here when we're all done."

"Oh, Barry, darling!" Melindra says, with a forced smile. "May I speak to you in private for a moment? There's something very important that I need to talk to you about!"

"What is it, Melindra?..." I say, as I get closer to her, while all the others are walking out of our hearing range.

"Barry..." Melindra says. "Would you mind explaining to me why everyone here just agreed to walk into a potential ambush without a second thought?"

"What do you mean?" I say. "Are you saying that Nolderan might want to kill us?"

"Yes!" Melindra says. "Isn't he a tournament participant? Why would he not want to kill you?"

"Well, he's an old friend of Daren's, for starters," I say. "And if he really wanted us dead, I see no reason why he would not have just left us to get killed by the monsters, instead of helping us. We even told him that he should flee, while he had the chance, but he still chose to stay and fight by our side. What would he have had to gain by doing that?"

"I don't know what his plan is," Melindra says. "I can't read minds. All I know is that my instincts are telling me not to trust him. Listen, I'm not saying that we shouldn't go with him at all. Believe me, there's nothing that I'd love better than for us to get teleported right at Ollendor's doorstep, without any effort on our part. But I still think we should be cautious. We shouldn't just take everything this guy says for granted. Do you understand what I'm saying?"

"Hmm..." I say. "I suppose we could ask Arraka to regularly check for traps, on our way to Nolderan's camp, just to be on the safe side."

"And I'll make sure to use my magical sense to see if there aren't any mages, trying to jump us," Melindra says. "I still don't get why everyone is so willing to trust this guy that they've only just met. They're all still treating me like I'm some outsider, but then this new mage comes along, and suddenly it's like he's already part of the team. What makes him so special?"

"Well," I say, "maybe if you told the others about the trouble you have with controlling your wind powers, they would trust you more. If people can't even rely on you to fight together with us, you can't just expect them to treat you as a member of the team. Seriously, why are you trying so hard to keep this a secret from everyone? What do you think they'll do when they find out? Do you think they're going to try to kill you?"

"As a matter of fact, I do!" Melindra says.

"You do?…" I ask her, confused. "But, why?"

"Because it's already happened once!" Melindra says. "There used to be this small group of people that I travelled with, for a while, a long time ago, and at a certain point they found out about my problem. They wanted to fix this issue by casting a white mage spell on me, which was supposed to help me by limiting the amount of energy I could use to power up each one of my spells. In theory, it could have worked, but I did not want to risk it, because a stillwater's aura is just too different from that of a normal mage, and you can't know what will happen. It could potentially be deadly for someone like me. I tried to explain this to them, but they wouldn't take me seriously. The bastards even tried to cast this spell on me while I was sleeping, without my permission. They may well have killed me, if I hadn't woken up to stop them!"

"I really don't think that Daren would try to cast that spell on you while you're sleeping," I say. "Especially if you explain to him why you think it might be risky for you…"

"Really?" Melindra says. "You guys practically forced me to take a deadly enchanter's oath, just so you'd agree to come along with me, and now you're expecting me to believe that you would suddenly be willing to prioritize my safety over your own, just because I'm asking you nicely?"

"Well, I've known about your problem and the risk it poses to us for quite a while, haven't I?" I say. "And yet, I never told Daren or anyone else about any of this."

"I suppose not…" Melindra says, as she takes a small break to contemplate on my words. "But I'd still rather keep the others from knowing, at least until we reach Ollendor. It's not like I could help much in a battle, even if I wanted to, so I don't really see any need for them to know. And if this means that they'll keep hating me, then so be it."

"As you wish…" I say. "Either way, I think we're done, here, so I'll go pack up my tent. See you in a few minutes."

Once we're all done with our tents, we grab our backpacks, and we start following Nolderan towards his camp. According to his words, it shouldn't take us more than thirty minutes to reach it. Luckily, the battle with the mammoth has mostly sobered me up, so if anyone attacks us again on the way there, I won't have that problem to deal with, anymore.

Before we left, Melindra and I had a private conversation with Arraka, and we asked her to notify us if there were any magical traps on our way to Nolderan's camp. As we walk through the forest, we come upon a few more mages that are filling their backpacks with pinecones. However, these ones are all looking rather terrified when they see us, as if they were afraid that we'd attack them.

"Why do you suppose those mages were so scared to see us?" Daren says, as we walk past the pinecone collectors.

"Well, we're a pretty big group, so we must be looking quite intimidating to them," Hadrik says.

"Maybe they think that we'll try to steal their pinecones."

"Hey, Barry," Kate says. "There's something that I forgot to ask. How did you manage to cast that flight spell on yourself, earlier? Was it with the help of your stat device?"

As Kate finishes her question, I see Melindra right behind her, staring at me with a menacing look in her eyes.

"Uh…" I say. "Yeah, that's right. It was the stat device."

"So you've finally managed to unlock your magic stats?" Kate says.

"No, it was only temporary, just like the last two times," I say. "The monster mages probably made a mistake when they cast the ritual, and they leaked a little too much energy my way."

"Oh, I see…" Kate says, looking somewhat disappointed.

"So, how did you come to know these allies of yours, master Nolderan?" Daren says.

"Oh, they're mostly people that I've met while doing mercenary work," Nolderan says. "Our group is rather diverse. We even have a banshee in the team. I'm sure that your own banshee will get along with her just fine."

"Yes, I always get along with other banshees," Illuna says, in a dry tone, while she looks towards Arraka's amulet.

"A banshee?" Hadrik asks. "How did you meet that one?"

"It's a long story," Nolderan says. "If you want, I'll tell it to you when we get there."

"Psst, Barry!" Melindra whispers to me, as she is now trailing about a dozen feet behind our group, along with Flower. "Over here!"

"What is it?" I say, in a low voice, as I join the two of

them. “Did Arraka find any traps?”

“No, but we can sense how many mages there are waiting for us inside the camp,” Melindra says. “There are five of them, including the banshee that the old man was talking about earlier.”

“Hmm...” I say. “Five mages doesn’t sound that bad.”

“How powerful are these five mages, exactly?” Illuna asks.

“It’s hard to tell,” Arraka says. “since they all seem to be suppressing their auras, to avoid detection, but most of them appear to be on Nolderan’s level of magic power.”

“It’s hard to tell because you are unable to do it, or because you don’t want to do it?” Illuna asks her.

“You would accuse me of lying to you?” Arraka says, in a mocking tone. “Me? Your oldest friend and beloved mentor? I am shocked. Utterly shocked...”

Illuna frowns at the amulet, but she doesn’t say anything.

“I think she might be telling the truth,” Melindra says. “Their levels of power look the same to me as she’s described them.”

“I still think that she’s hiding something,” Illuna says. “But I suppose that we won’t find out what exactly that is until we reach our destination and see for ourselves. Let’s catch up with the others. We’re starting to look a little suspicious.”

As we get closer to our destination, I notice that there are no sounds whatsoever coming from the camp, even though with the level I have in my hearing stat, I would have expected to hear people talking by now. I can only suspect that they must have cast a silencing spell around their base of operations, similar to the spell that Melindra cast when she came into my tent the other night.

When we finally get close enough to the camp, we see that the whole area around it is surrounded by four large, twenty foot tall walls, made of rock. By the looks of it, the walls were probably created by an earth elementalist.

"There's the entrance, over there," Nolderan says, as he points towards a door, which also seems to be made out of stone.

"Quite the impressive camp fortifications you have here, Nolderan," Hadrik says.

"Yes, we have a very talented earth elementalist in our team," Nolderan says. "Step right in."

He then opens the door for us, and we all step inside, one by one. As soon as we enter the camp, we all finally get to see the faces of the five mages from Nolderan's team. One of them is a dwarf, who is sitting on a stone chair, behind a stone table, some two hundred feet away from us, while drinking a bottle of dwarven ale. The other four are all standing behind him, watching over him, as bodyguards.

As we get a closer look at the dwarf, we recognize him almost immediately. It would be impossible to not know who he is, since his face has been shown in every newspaper, for the past twelve years. The mage that we were looking at right now was none other than Talmak, the Sage of the North.

"Ahahahahahaha!" Arraka starts to laugh loudly, all of a sudden.

"Talmak?…" Daren says, looking very shocked.

"The Sage of the North?" Illuna asks, surprised, looking first at Daren, and then at the dwarf in front of us, with a very unimpressed look on her face. "*This* is the almighty sage you've been talking about?…"

"Ahahahaha!" Arraka keeps laughing in the background.

"You knew about this, didn't you?" Illuna says, as

she grabs Arraka's amulet by the chain and looks at it directly. "You knew that one of the mages was a sage from the very beginning!"

"Of course I knew!" Arraka says, still barely containing her laughter. "But I wanted to see the looks on your faces when you saw him for yourselves! Ahahahahaha!"

"Master Nolderan..." Daren says, still in a state of shock. "Why didn't you tell us about the sage being in your team?"

"If I had told you this, would you have followed me here, boy?" Nolderan says.

"You should not blame him for this, healer in armor," Talmak says in a loud voice, as he puts his bottle of ale on the table in front of him. "Your old master works for me, now. He does what I tell him. But do not worry, I did not call you here to fight. I called you here because I wanted to talk. Now, come closer. All of you. I don't like it when I need to shout to make myself heard."

We all exchange a few looks, and then we get ready to traverse the large, empty area between ourselves and the sage's table, together with Nolderan. Just as we were beginning to walk, Melindra pulls both Flower and me by the arm, in order to stop us. When we look at her, we see that she has an unusually serious expression on her face.

"After I snap my fingers, I'm going to need you two to pull me out," Melindra tells us, in a low voice. "Do you understand?"

"Pull you out of what?..." I say.

"You'll understand when the time comes," Melindra says, and then I can feel her casting the same air currents on me as she did earlier this morning.

She then walks away, without another word, as she goes to join the rest of the team. Flower and I look at each other for a second, in confusion, and then we decide to head towards the sage as well. The air currents seem to be calming down as I am walking forward. They're probably waiting for me to give them the signal, whenever I want to start flying.

As I approach the stone table, I get a better look at the sage and his henchmen. Talmak is of around the same height as Hadrik in his dwarf form, and he has a long, brown beard that covers most of his face. He looks like a typical dwarf. There's nothing special about him, or anything that makes him look particularly intimidating. I can sort of understand why Illuna was so underwhelmed when she first saw him.

The sage is wearing the same type of heavily enchanted leather armor that Nolderan is wearing, and so is the rest of their team, but neither of them seem to be holding any weapons. I'm guessing that Nolderan is the one who enchanted all of their equipment.

Aside from Daren's old master, Talmak's team consists of a banshee, an elf, and two dwarves. Funnily enough, both of the dwarves look more intimidating than the sage. One of them has two big scars on his face, and the other one is wearing an eye patch. The elf has long blond hair, and he has a slim, tall figure. He appears to be rather old, even by elven standards. I'm not really sure how slowly elves age, but I think you'd need to be over one hundred years old to have any noticeable wrinkles on your face. And this elf has got plenty of them.

The woman that the banshee possessed is somewhere in her early thirties. Her eyes are constantly shining with a green light, similarly to how Flower's eyes always shine blue, when Illuna takes over the body. She also has an outwordly aura about her, so it's clear that she is not an artificial mage.

Given that the banshee is obviously long past her awakening stage, I can only assume that the host's soul is long gone, and that the banshee is the only one in control of the body right now. However, I was not aware that a banshee could maintain the original appearance of her host even after her awakening. I thought that Flower and Illuna were a special case, because of the fusion, but it appears I was mistaken. Perhaps I do not know as much about banshees as I would like to believe.

The woman's hair is long and black, and the expression on her face looks ruthless and unforgiving. While we were getting closer to her, I could see the banshee take a short glance towards Flower, but then she went back to looking straight ahead of her, awaiting the sage's orders.

All of the members of our team stop about twenty feet or so in front of the stone table, in order to make sure that we have enough space to move, in case a battle erupts between our two groups. Nolderan, of course, walks past us, and he joins his true comrades, who are currently forming a line behind the sage.

"I see that you are not willing to advance any further," Talmak says, as he takes another sip from his dwarven ale bottle. "No matter. At least you are close enough that I don't need to shout. Let's get down to business, then, shall we?"

He then puts his bottle down, and places his hands on the table, while looking at us.

"I think you may have already guessed that all of the pinecone-collecting mages outside are working for me," Talmak says. "They are all mages who have agreed to give up on participating in this tournament, and to spend the rest of their time here helping me win instead. In exchange for their services, they will be receiving generous rewards, many of them unobtainable by normal means. As you all know, when you become a sage, you receive many benefits. You also gain a lot of influence, with many people. And I can use this influence, to make people's wishes come true. Now tell me, Daren, would you not by any chance have any wishes that you would want to come true?"

"My wish is to gain access to the Magium," Daren says, with a very serious tone in his voice. "But from what I'm gathering, this is the one wish that you would not want to grant me…"

"Don't be a fool, boy!" Nolderan says. "This is a once in a lifetime opportunity. You will never get a chance like this again. For once in your life, use that rusted brain of yours and think!"

"I think I'm starting to understand what's going on, here," Daren says. "It wasn't by accident that you found our camp, was it, master Nolderan? You already knew that I'd be there, and you were sent to bring me here by the sage, so he'd offer me this deal. I thought I had made myself sufficiently clear that I would not become your henchman when I didn't answer your letter, Sage Talmak. Why did you feel the need to make this offer to me again?"

"He's made this offer to you before?" Hadrik asks, surprised.

"Yes," Daren says. "He sent me a letter not long after the tournament was first announced. I'm guessing that master Nolderan must have received a similar letter as well. Except that he actually accepted it."

"Why aren't you being honest with me, Daren?" Talmak says, as he takes another drink from his bottle. "Why don't you tell me the real reason why you won't join me? Who else managed to recruit you before I did? Was it Azarius? Nolderan's told me that you've always admired him. But I can offer you more than Azarius ever could. You have no idea how much knowledge you gain access to when you are a sage. There are so many books that are not shown to the general public. So many restricted areas. I could give you access to all of these.

And all I'm asking in return is for you to join my team, and to help me win the Magium. Hell, I'll even extend the offer to all your friends, if you want. You only need to say yes."

"I wasn't recruited by Azarius!" Daren says. "Don't you understand? I came here on my own! I came here because I'm tired of travelling around the world, trying to save people, while thousands of others are dying somewhere else, where I cannot reach them. No matter how much I trained, or how hard I worked, it was never enough. I couldn't save them all. But once I get the Magium, I may finally become able to achieve my dreams…"

"Boy, are you out of your mind?" Nolderan shouts. "Are you telling me that you are still holding on to your foolish ideals from back when you were still my pupil? When will you finally grow up and accept reality?"

"Grow up?…" Daren says. "And then what? Become Talmak's lapdog, like you did? What happened to you? What happened to the master I knew, who was a proud man that was happy and content with teaching people martial arts and enchanting for a living? What happened to that man who would never bend his knee to anyone, regardless of their social status, or their strength?"

"That man died long ago," Nolderan says. "He died after I lost my sage status, and after everyone abandoned me, forcing me to take up work as a mercenary. But this time it's different. I'm no longer just working for scraps. If we succeed, here, I could finally turn my life around. And so could you, if you wouldn't keep stubbornly holding on to those childish ideals that you've had ever since I first met you!"

"It seems that my old master truly is dead…" Daren says, as he shakes his head in disappointment. "But my ideals are not. I am sorry to say that I will be refusing your offer once more, Sage of the North."

"Surely, you must be joking..." Talmak says. "You can't seriously be thinking that you have any chance of winning this tournament by yourself, when there are four sages competing against you... There's no way that anyone can be this naive."

"He is serious," Nolderan says. "I can see it in his eyes. It's the same look that he had when he first told me why he wanted to become my disciple. It hasn't changed one bit since then..."

"No, this can't be possible..." Talmak says, in disbelief. "I refuse to believe that this is actually happening... Someone needs to wake this man up! You there! The one without any magical powers. I don't know if you're Daren's servant, or his advisor, but you seem like a man with his head on his shoulders. Try to make him see reason. Please!"

"Yeah, Daren," I say. "You *should* quit the tournament! Less competition for me, that way."

"You won't get rid of me that easily, you opportunistic bastard," Daren says, with a grin.

"Is this supposed to be some sort of joke?" Talmak says. "Please tell me that you are not seriously planning to participate in this tournament against me as well..."

"It's not a joke..." Kate says. "Take a good look at them, and you will see from their eyes that they are not bluffing. They really did both come here to win the tournament."

After hearing Kate's words, Talmak keeps turning his head between me and Daren, looking at each of us in turn, as if he is simply refusing to believe what is happening before his eyes. Once he finally understands that we are indeed being serious, he completely loses his temper, and his face contorts into a snarl.

"You would compete against me?" Talmak shouts furiously, as he gets up from his chair and looks at me directly. "*Me*? The Sage of the North?"

He then stops suppressing his magical power, and for a moment, it feels like the intensity of his aura is hitting me right in the face.

"As far as intimidating auras go, I've seen better," I say, once I've recovered from the initial shock.

"Do you people think this is a game?" Talmak says, as his eyes are still brimming with fury. "Do you all think that this offer I made is something that you can just refuse? Are you unable to understand the situation you are in?"

"I think we all understand our situation very well, Sage Talmak," Daren says, with a serious tone in his voice. "Judging by the terrified looks that those mages outside were giving us when they saw us travelling alongside Nolderan, I'm willing to bet that you've also threatened them in the same way, and that this is the real reason why you have so many people working for you. But these sorts of tactics won't work on me."

"Is that so?" Talmak says, as he calms down a bit. "Well, Nolderan, I hope you won't hate me too much if I kill your old disciple. He is simply leaving me no choice, at this point."

"The boy chose this path on his own," Nolderan says. "He was given ample opportunities to see reason, but he wouldn't listen. I am sad that it has come to this, but there is no other way."

"It's good to see that you still care, master Nolderan," Daren says, with a dark look in his eyes.

"These two fools have already sealed their fate!" Talmak shouts, as he faces the other members of our team. "But the rest of you do not need to die together with them. If you join my side now, you will be allowed to live."

"That's mighty generous of you," Hadrik says, with a grin. "But I'm afraid that I'm going to have to refuse."

"What about you, banshees?" Talmak asks, as he

looks at Kate and Flower, in turn. "Are you going to stand by your friend's side and get slaughtered, or will you pick the sane choice, and live?"

"I did not come here to become a mercenary," Kate says. "You are not the first powerful adversary that has threatened us since we've arrived in Varathia, and you will not be the last."

"One banshee has denied me, but one remains..." Talmak says. "What do you say, little girl? Will you also make the same reckless choice as your friends? Or will you choose the winning side?"

"I think that you might be greatly overestimating yourself, Sage of the North," Illuna says, in a dismissive tone.

Talmak laughs.

"So you will all die together, then..." he says.

"But what about me?" Melindra says, as she fakes a pleading look in her eyes. "Are you going to kill me too? I am only a defenseless maiden who was being escorted by these warriors. I do not want to die..."

"Hmm?..." Talmak says, looking as if he's only just now noticed that Melindra was also there. "Oh, I suppose there's no need for you to die with them if you don't want to."

"Then... can I join your side?" Melindra asks.

"Of course," Talmak says. "And the other girl can come to this side of the table as well, if she wants."

"I will stay here," Leila writes, as Melindra heads over to the sage's side.

The sage first looks a little confused, when he sees the blue writing in the air, but then he understands its significance, and he addresses Leila directly.

"As you wish," Talmak tells her.

"I should have known that you would abandon us with the first opportunity you got, you traitor!" Kate tells Melindra.

"Don't take it personally, ice mage," Melindra says with a smirk, as she reaches Talmak's side of the table and she places herself beside him. "I did somewhat enjoy travelling with you and your group. But now it's time to move on. I'm sure that I will find other suitable candidates to escort me to Ollendor, eventually."

"Ahahahahaha!" Arraka starts to laugh all of a sudden.

"What is it that you are finding so amusing?" Illuna says.

"Don't you see?" Arraka says. "Don't you see what is going to happen?"

She then starts laughing again. The sage ignores her completely, and he resumes talking, with a loud voice.

"Well, it would appear that everyone has now chosen their side," Talmak says. "Is there anything else you might want to say, before we commence this massacre?"

Wait a minute. Something's not right, here. Why would Melindra go out of her way to give me a vague message, if she was just going to betray us afterwards? And why did she specifically request to join the sage's side? If she really wanted to be safe, she could have just flown away, and left us to our fate…

"Just shut up and prepare yourself for battle, will you?" Daren tells the sage, as he readies his sword and shield.

No matter how hard I think about this, it still doesn't add up. Unless…

"Ahahahahaha!" Arraka laughs even louder in the background now.

"Then let us begin…" Talmak says, with a confident grin.

"Yes," Melindra says, with a smirk. "Let us begin!"

She then snaps her fingers with both her hands at the same time, and all of a sudden, a huge tornado engulfs her and the other six mages by her side, sending them flying into the air, before they have the time to react. As the twister keeps spinning them round and round, it seems that the base of the tornado is quickly expanding in size, with every second.

So this was her plan all along… I should have known from the very beginning.

"I knew it!" Arraka says. "I knew that she'd do it the moment she asked to join the sage's side. This girl is even crazier than the half-lessathi. I'm dying of laughter, here, ahahahaha!"

"But… why?" Kate asks, seemingly in a state of shock. "Why did she do it?"

"Everyone get back!" I shout. "Melindra can't control her powers properly. This tornado may well engulf us too, soon, if we don't get away from it."

"Can't control her powers properly?…" Kate says, confused. "Wait, is this why she's never fought together with us in the past? Because she could risk hurting us by accident?"

"Yes," I say. "Now let's move!"

"But if you knew about this… then why didn't you tell us?" Kate says, as we all move away from the tornado."

"Because she asked me to keep this a secret," I say. "Listen, I don't have time to explain now. We'll discuss this in more detail later. Flower, we need to fly up there and get Melindra out of the tornado."

"What?…" Flower says.

"She asked us to pull her out after she snaps her fingers, remember?" I say. "Now come on. We need to hurry!"

I raise both of my arms into the air, which signals Melindra's air currents to lift me off the ground. Flower then starts her fire jets, and we both head upwards, while also slowly approaching the tornado. After a few seconds of trying to spot Melindra, we finally locate her, as she is spinning continuously along the outer borders of the twister.

"Come on, let's get her out!" Flower says.

We both fly closer to the tornado, and when we're right next to its borders, I call out to Melindra.

"Melindra!" I shout, when the tornado spins her towards our side. "Can you stretch your hands towards us on the next rotation?"

Melindra appears to be holding her breath, so instead of answering me, she nods in approval. We wait for her to do a full circle around the tornado, and when she gets right in front of us again, Melindra extends her arms in our direction, as Flower and I each grab one of the arms and quickly pull her out. After flying together with her for a few dozen more feet, in order to make sure that we're far enough from the cyclone, we stop for a while, so she can catch her breath.

"Took you long enough…" Melindra says, as she starts coughing from all the dust that she's inhaled while inside the twister.

"We came here as fast as we could," I say.

"No doubt," Melindra says. "But it still feels like I've been inside there for a million years. Glad to see that you got my message, at least."

"Yeah, I did get the message, eventually," I say. "Although, it would have been nice if you had made it a little clearer."

"I couldn't risk it," Melindra says. "They may have had people in that group who could tell when people are lying, by studying their auras. I needed you to be genuinely shocked at my betrayal for this plan to work."

"But couldn't you just create the tornado from afar?" I say. "Why did you have to go all the way to their side to do it?"

"When I make a tornado as big as this," Melindra says, "if I'm not right at the center or straight above it, I won't be able to control it properly."

"What about now?" I say. "Are you able to control it now?"

"I hope so…" Melindra says. "The hard part was creating it, so as long as I only need to maintain it, I should be able to— Ugh…"

Melindra suddenly puts her hand on her forehead, as she is trying to suppress a headache.

"Are you alright?" Flower asks, worried.

"I'm fine, I just…" Melindra says, and then she pauses again, while she massages her temples. "I just used too much power all at once, that's all. As soon as I rest a bit, there should no longer be any— Oh no…"

As Melindra was talking, a few small twisters were starting to form very close to where our friends are standing.

"No, no, no!" Melindra says, as she panics. "I can't stop the cyclones! I can't stop them from forming! I need to undo them all, quick!"

"Just make sure not to also undo the big one by… accident," I say, but before I got to finish the sentence, the big twister was already gone, along with all the small ones.

As soon as they're out of the tornado, the sage and his henchmen start to fall down, while they're coughing and taking large gasps of air. Talmak manages to conjure a floating stone platform out of thin air, and they all land on it, as they're still trying to catch their breaths.

"Let's go back to the ground and group up with everyone else," I say. "We can start fighting when we're all together."

I begin to fly towards the ground, along with Flower, but Melindra is still just floating there, and it appears that she's gotten another sudden headache. The sage notices this immediately, and he uses his powers to magically create a big rock, which he flings towards her, at great speed. Melindra does not get to react in time, and the rock hits her hard in the head, making her lose her consciousness.

"Melindra!" Flower shouts, as she rushes to stop her from falling.

Just as the sage tries to hit Flower too, Illuna quickly casts her golden cage spell around herself and Melindra, which makes Talmak's rocks break into pieces at the impact with the cage's golden bars.

"The fox's cage..." Talmak says, as he watches Illuna starting to heal Melindra, while inside their floating cage.

"So, you know of the golden fox, then?" I ask him.

"I've had more than a few run-ins with her since I came to Varathia, yes," the sage says. "But, more importantly, the situation has now changed. Meet me back down, boy, and we'll have another talk."

He then brings his platform to the ground, along with all of his team, while I also go down and land next to Daren and the others. When my feet hit the ground, I can't help but notice that the air currents around me have calmed down, just like when Melindra cast the spell on me earlier. It appears that the currents are made in such a way that they temporarily deactivate whenever I land on the ground, and if I want to fly again, I need to reactivate them by raising my arms above my head.

"I've changed my mind!" Talmak says all of a sudden, as people were getting ready for battle. "There is no more need for us to fight."

"And to what do we owe this sudden change of heart?" Daren says.

"You owe it to the stillwater girl, up there in the sky," Talmak says. "You see, I've always been fascinated by the stillwater legends, but I've never really had the chance to see one up close. I've always wanted to study them, and to find out what the source of their power was, but the idea that I would ever have the chance to capture one alive seemed so unlikely, that I never even dared to dream that it might happen. And yet here I am, only a few dozen feet away from an unconscious stillwater, with the only thing standing in my way being that blasted impenetrable cage."

"What exactly are you trying to say, here?" Daren says.

"I'm saying that I'm willing to offer you safe passage out of our camp, if you hand over the stillwater," Talmak says. "All you need to do is convince your banshee friend to dismiss the cage and stop healing her, and then we'll forget this encounter ever happened. Nolderan, do we still have those collars we found in the ruins that could restrict someone's ability to cast spells?"

"Yes, we still have them," Nolderan says.

"Perfect," Talmak says. "Then we can chain her up and commence the experiments immediately. The tricky part will be to keep her alive while we dissect her, but I know more than a few ways to get around—"

Suddenly, Kate shoots several icicles straight at the sage, while a wall of rock raises itself from the ground to defend him. As the wall crumbles, and the icicles that got stuck within it fall to the ground, Talmak stares at Kate, with a look of utter shock in his eyes.

"Have you gone completely insane?" Talmak says. "You would forfeit your only chance to survive, just for the sake of a—"

"Stop talking, you filth," Kate says, looking at him with an expression of pure disgust.

"Maybe I haven't made myself sufficiently clear…" Talmak starts to say, adopting his usual authoritative tone.

"Yeah, no, I think we've heard enough," Hadrik says, and he immediately rushes towards the sage, at a shocking speed.

The sage barely has the time to react, and he conjures another wall of rock in front of him, which Hadrik breaks in one punch.

"*Enough*!" Talmak shouts furiously, all of a sudden, as he makes several large spikes of rock pop out from underneath the earth, forcing Hadrik to jump back. "If you're all so eager to march towards your deaths, then I will be more than happy to grant your wishes. I'm going to kill you all myself, and I'm saving the stillwater for last."

"No, you won't," Hadrik says, with a grin, as he makes another lighting fast rush towards the sage, and he attacks him with a flurry of blows, while Talmak is struggling to create enough walls to keep up with his speed.

As Hadrik and the sage have begun their duel, the five henchmen are now getting ready to attack the rest of us.

I quickly take my crossbow out of the backpack, and start shooting at all of the enemies except for the sage, since I already know for a fact that the magical protection against physical damage that he's using is powerful enough to make crossbow bolts bounce right off him. Sadly, it seems that he's already cast the same protection on his allies as well, because none of the bolts harmed them in any way. Seeing that this weapon is useless to me, I return it to my backpack, and then I unsheathe my scimitar.

As the henchmen head towards us, Talmak knocks Hadrik away from him, with a large boulder, and then he uses the platform below his feet to raise himself high into the air. As soon as he recovers, Hadrik transforms himself into a giant eagle, and he soars into the sky, after the sage.

Nolderan is the first one of the henchmen to attack, and he goes directly for Daren. While the old master and disciple commence their duel, Kate quickly conjures a semi-transparent ice dome around me, her and Leila, just in time to defend us against a barrage of flames, coming from the two dwarves, who are apparently both fire elementalists.

"Don't kill them, yet!" the banshee shouts. "I need to have some answers."

"To hell with your answers, abomination!" the dwarf with the eye patch says. "You should be thankful enough that our master took you under his wing. Do not presume to think that you can give us orders!"

"The sage is not my master," the banshee says. "We only have an agreement. I told him that I'd help him get the Magium, as long as he'd sign me up to this tournament, and let me pursue my own goals on the side."

"The very fact that Sage Talmak is letting you breathe in his presence should be more than enough of a reward for your services," says the dwarf with the scars on his face. "If I were in his place, I would have killed you a long time ago."

As the dwarf finishes his sentence, Kate suddenly unleashes a hundred icicles that she'd been preparing in the sky all this time, and she shoots them at all of the sage's henchmen, including Nolderan. Just as the icicles reach the four enemies in front of us, they all bounce off an invisible barrier, which was defending the mages. Nolderan, on the other hand, did not need a barrier to protect himself, and he simply danced out of the projectiles' way, while also fending off an attack from Daren.

"Could we perhaps continue this argument at a more opportune moment?" the elf from Talmak's team says, with a forced smile. "See, if I hadn't shielded you just now, you would have all been dead, already."

"As if!" the banshee says. "Maybe these fools would

have died, but I was well aware of those icicles, and was already preparing to dodge them."

"Is that why you haven't even moved an inch, when you were attacked, despite not knowing about my invisible barrier?" the elf says, still forcing himself to smile.

"Shut up," the banshee says, looking a little flustered. "I obviously knew about the barrier!"

"Of course you did…" the elf says. "Listen, just ask your question, quickly, so we can finally start murdering each other, will you?"

"You there, in the ice dome!" the banshee shouts at us. "I have a question for you. What is the name of the banshee in the amulet?"

"What makes you think that we'll answer your question?" Kate shouts back at her, through the dome.

"If you answer, then we'll make your deaths quick, and mostly painless," the banshee says. "But if you don't—"

All of a sudden, several fireballs rain down upon the sage's underlings, covering their whole area in explosions.

"Arraka," we hear Illuna's voice, coming from the sky. "Her name is Arraka."

As we look up, we see Illuna hovering a dozen feet above the ground, using Flower's jets, while her eyes are shining with a blue light.

"Wait, how did you get out of the cage?" I ask her.

"You are allowed to cast teleportation spells inside the golden cage, as long as you're the one who conjured it," Illuna says, "The spell has been designed that way, so you could still escape, in case you trapped yourself inside with your enemy, by accident. Luckily, I barely ever use that daily teleportation spell of mine, so I had it ready for this occasion."

"But what happened to Melindra?" I say.

"She is conscious, but still recovering," Illuna says. "The healing spell that I cast on her won't take full effect until at least a few more minutes will have passed. I made sure to extend the cage's duration, so she'd be kept safe until then, although it's taken quite a lot of my magical energy to do it…"

"Are you two just about done with your conversation, or do you intend to keep ignoring us?" says the banshee who works for the sage.

As we take a look towards Talmak's henchmen, we see that they were unharmed by the fireballs, thanks to the elf's invisible barrier. While the barrier itself is not visible with the naked eye, you can tell that it's still there, by the feel of its magical aura.

"Nobody asked you to wait for us," Illuna says, in a cold voice. "You could have attacked us at any time."

"Oh, I would have attacked you long ago," the dwarf with the eye patch says, "if this sad excuse for an elf hadn't surrounded us all with an impenetrable barrier that works both ways!"

"I will remove the barrier as soon as our banshee friend is done asking her questions," the elf says, in a calm manner. "And also as soon as you promise to not get caught in every single one of the enemy's deadly attacks, like a gang of amateurs."

"That banshee from the amulet that you called Arraka…" the black-haired banshee starts to ask Illuna, while ignoring the elf. "How old is she, exactly? Do you happen to know if she's been around for more than a thousand years? Perhaps even five thousand?"

"Oh, I've been living for quite a bit more than five thousand years, little girl," Arraka says. "But I think we should both stop beating around the bush. What is it that you want to ask of me, exactly?"

"I will ask you this directly, then," the banshee says, with a dark look in her eyes. "Did you, or did you not cause the banishment of all banshees from the magical realm five thousand years ago?"

"Aha- Ahahahahaha!" Arraka laughs. "So there are still banshees who know the story after all these years? Oh man, it looks like not even getting trapped in a mountain for thousands of years is enough to extinguish the flame of a true legend! I am so proud, right now, you have no idea."

"So it is true…" the black-haired banshee says, with the look in her eyes now darker than ever. "I always knew that those rumors were true. The only reason why I came to Varathia was because my information led me to believe that this was where I could find you. And as soon as I felt that sinister aura coming from the amulet, I knew that it would be you. All this pain and suffering that our race has had to endure for millennia… Being forced to live our lives as parasites… All because of you!"

"Well, what are you going to do about it?" Arraka says, in a provocative tone.

"I am going to end you!" the banshee shouts. "I will avenge every single banshee that you've cursed with this torturous existence."

"If you destroy this amulet, you will only free her," Illuna says. "And you will doom us all."

"If she goes free, then I will kill her again, and again, and again, until she is dead for good," the black-haired banshee says, with her eyes full of rage. "And if you stand in my way, I will kill you too. Undo this barrier, elf. It's about time that we all settled our scores."

"Finally," the elf says, as he dismisses his barrier. "Try not to die in the first five seconds, will you?"

Just as soon as the barrier disappears, the two dwarves channel their magic into a single ray of fire, which they use to attack Kate's ice dome. The ice is being reinforced almost as fast as it is melted, but it's clear that Kate won't be able to keep this up much longer. In the meantime, the black-haired banshee flies up in the sky, and begins to attack Illuna and Flower with a variety of spells.

Judging by the very different types of spells that she's using, I'm going to guess that she is some sort of a generalist. She's already cast a lightning spell, a sonic spell and a freezing spell, one after the other, while also summoning a few eagles to try and catch Illuna by surprise. Luckily, Flower has done a good job at avoiding the attacks in mid-air, although neither she nor Illuna have managed to land a hit on their adversary, just yet.

While she is still busy reinforcing the ice dome, Kate shoots a few more icicles at the dwarves, but this time, the projectiles get stopped even further up in the air, by what seems to be a small, flat, semi-transparent barrier, that the elf conjured to intercept them. The elf smiles at Kate, from a distance, which makes Kate frown at him, through the ice-dome, as she turns her head to Leila and me.

"If either of you could keep some of those three mages busy, while I attack them, it would be highly appreciated…" Kate says.

"I'm on it," Leila writes.

"Me too," I say. "Open the dome."

Once she gets our confirmation, Kate waves her right hand towards the side of the dome, and she makes an exit for us, which is just the right size for the two of us to fit through.

"Let's target the elf, first," I tell Leila. "If we both attack him at the same time, we might force him to focus his barriers more on himself, than on the dwarves, which will leave his allies defenseless against Kate's icicles. I'll attack him from above, and you can attack him from the ground at the same time."

Leila nods, and then we both walk out of the dome, as Kate closes up the exit behind us. As soon as we're out, Leila starts running towards our enemy, while I begin flying in the elf's direction as well. When they see us get out of the dome, the two dwarves quickly switch their targets, and they begin to aim for Leila and me, instead. The dwarf with the eye patch seems to be the one focusing on me, while the one with the scars is currently throwing fireballs towards Leila.

I easily dodge the flame attacks coming from the dwarf, in mid-air, and then I prepare to dive towards the elf, but just as I'm getting closer, a large, flat, semi-transparent barrier appears right in front of me, blocking my way. When I try to get around it, the barrier just moves along with me, and it doesn't allow me to get past it. I don't get to do this for much longer, because a new barrage of flames forces me to distance myself from the mages, once more.

In the meantime, Leila seems to be having her own problems with barriers, although the ones that she's bumping into are completely invisible, and can only be detected if you really focus on them with your magical sense. I try to make another dive for the elf, but my path gets blocked by one of his barriers yet again. Just as I was trying to get around it, Kate shoots dozens of icicles towards the elf, coming from all directions, which forces him to dismiss all the barriers and to make a new one, around himself.

This allows Leila and me to finally reach him, and to attack him with many rapid strikes, even though each one of them gets blocked by the invisible barrier around himself. With the elf no longer protecting his allies, Kate immediately starts attacking the two dwarves with icicles, and it doesn't take her long until she manages to kill them both, with a few well-placed shots to their heads.

"So much for the great sage's elite squad, eh?" I tell the elf, as I land on the ground, and continue to attack him through his barrier, along with Leila.

"Those were only easily replaceable pawns," the elf says, with a forced smile. "The older members of the team are currently away on an important mission, related to the pinecones. It's too bad that you will never get to meet them, because the sage will obliterate all of you before then."

"The sage?" I ask him. "Not you?"

"I am only in charge of defense," the elf says. "I have no spells that could help me fight you in any way. I'm just going to keep this barrier up until you either tire yourselves out, or get bored. You won't be able to break it anytime soon at this rate."

"Right…" I say, as I continue to attack him.

While we're dealing with the elf, I can't help but notice that the sky above us is currently filled with big, floating rocks, which Talmak is using to chase Hadrik around, in his eagle form. It looks like Hadrik is at a bit of a disadvantage when fighting aerial battles, due to the fact that the flying creatures which he can morph into are too weak, compared to his regular dwarf form, and he needs to switch back to being a dwarf every time he wants to smash one of the rocks into pieces.

Somewhere below, at a much lower altitude, Illuna and Flower are still busy fighting the black-haired banshee, in mid-flight, although they seem to be very evenly matched, and neither of them has managed to do any significant damage to the other. Flower and Illuna may have the upper hand, in terms of raw power, because there are two of them, but the banshee working for the sage is making good use of the multitude of spells she has at her disposal to compensate for her disadvantage.

Meanwhile, the duel between Daren and Nolderan

seems to be much less balanced. The ex-sage doesn't look like he's taken any hits, so far, while Daren is already moving much slower than before, and he appears to have been injured during their battle. I'm not sure how long he'll be able to last at this rate. Maybe I should go help him?

Before I get to think any further on the subject, Hadrik quickly lands on the ground, in his eagle form, and then he turns himself into a dwarf. The sage is still up above, on his platform, with all of his rocks floating around him, and he seems to be waiting for Hadrik's next move.

"Give up, Daren," Nolderan says, with a confident tone in his voice, as he manages to wound Daren yet again, by attacking one of his armor's elbow joints. "I can see that you've learned some new techniques since we've been apart, but you're still no match for me. Maybe if you beg Sage Talmak for mercy, he might still spare your—"

The ex-sage does not get to finish his sentence, because Hadrik suddenly dashes to his side, and he punches him so hard, that he throws him into a nearby wall.

"I think you may have forgotten that this is a team fight, not a duel, old man," Hadrik tells him, with a grin. "You might want to mind your surroundings a little more, next time."

"I'll keep that in mind," Nolderan says, as he struggles to get back up.

"I'll deal with your old master," Hadrik tells Daren. "You go deal with the sage. Elementalists are supposed to be your specialty, aren't they?"

"They are," Daren says, as he starts casting a healing spell on himself. "I'll take care of him."

"Perfect!" Hadrik says. "Come on, Nolderan, let's have ourselves a fun little sparring match!"

He then rushes towards Daren's old master, and he tries to punch him again, but this time Nolderan was waiting for him, and he dodged his attack effortlessly. As the two of them begin their battle, Daren starts to shout very loudly at the sage, who is still in the sky, waiting for his next opponent.

"Hey, Talmak!" Daren shouts, while his wounds are still being magically healed. "Come down here so we can have a duel! One on one! What kind of a coward flies off to the sky like that, where his enemies can't reach him?"

"Watch your tongue, healer in armor!" Talmak shouts. "Who do you think you're talking to?"

"He does kind of have a point, though," I say, in a loud voice, to make sure that Talmak can hear me. "If you really are the strongest earth elementalist of our time, like they say, shouldn't you be able to win against us without these petty tricks? They don't let you fly into the air while you're fighting in the yearly sage contests, do they? So why are you doing that now? Is it because you're afraid of Daren?"

"What did you just say?..." Talmak says.

"He's asking if you're afraid of me, Talmak," Daren shouts. "Answer the man's question, will you?"

"This insolence is going to cost you, healer," Talmak says. "I don't care what the legends say about you. I'm going to pound you into the ground and show you what happens when you mock a sage!"

He then quickly brings his floating platform to the ground, with a loud thud, as he steps off it, and begins to approach Daren, who is now completely healed.

After a short walk, Talmak stops at a distance of around one hundred feet from Daren, and he eyes him intensely. As the sage and Daren are getting ready to start their battle, everyone else temporarily stops what they were doing to watch the fight, except for the black-haired banshee, who is still flying after Flower, and shooting various spells at her.

"You can do it, Daren!" I say. "If you win this fight, they will be writing stories of you for many more years to come!"

"This is going to be his last story, boy," Talmak says. "I'm going to make sure of it."

The sage then creates two boulders that are twice the size of Daren, and he launches them both towards him, with his earth magic. Daren uses his sword to slice through the two boulders in a single motion, but instead of cutting them, the sword goes through them as through butter, and the rocks get smaller and smaller, in the span of a few seconds, until they become marble sized. The two marbles then begin to rotate around Daren's sword, as if the blade were their center of gravity.

"What?..." Talmak asks, in a state of shock. "No, this can't be..."

The sage immediately creates two more boulders that are even larger than before, and he throws them both at his opponent, while Daren begins to slowly walk towards him. Just like last time, Daren slashes through the two rocks in one motion, which causes them to shrink, and to join the other two marbles in gravitating around the sword.

"What's the matter, Talmak?" Daren says, with a dark look in his eyes, as he continues to slowly walk towards him. "Weren't you going to punish me for my insolence?"

"Sage Talmak!" Nolderan shouts, as the sage is beginning to panic a little. "Daren's sword can absorb the elements. You can't fight him with any rocks that are magically created. Use regular rocks! He won't be able to absorb them fast enough!"

"Oh, so that's how it is..." Talmak says.

He then begins to use his magic to pull several large

boulders out of the earth, but before he manages to do it, Daren flings his sword at him with all his might, which sends all of the four marbles flying towards the sage.

The stone marbles quickly regain their original sizes, in mid-flight, while Talmak is forced to drop the rocks that he was pulling out of the earth, and to make a large, thick wall of stone in front of him, in order to defend himself from the incoming boulders. His wall isn't enough to guard him completely, however, and one of the boulders manages to hit him directly, knocking him on his back.

"Don't let him stab you with that sword!" Nolderan shouts. "He has a technique that can sever your link to the magical plane!"

As Daren makes a rush towards Talmak, the sage touches the ground with his hand while he's still lying on his back, and then the earth immediately begins to shake with such power that it makes us all fall to the ground. While the earthquake is still going, Talmak raises himself to the air with yet another floating platform, while the earth below our feet is shaking so violently, that it's beginning to crack.

"Damn it, he's cheating again!" I say, as I look at the sage flying off in the sky.

"I think we may be having some bigger problems to deal with, at the moment," Daren says, as he's struggling to get back on his feet, due to the violent earthquake.

Soon, the cracks in the ground grow larger, and the earth itself starts to split in half, creating a large, bottomless chasm right in front of our eyes. And as if this weren't enough, large chunks of rock are now being pulled from under our feet, leaving us with no ground to stand on, and sending us falling into the great abyss below.

The elf immediately makes a floating magical barrier below his feet, and another one for Nolderan, while Kate makes several floating ice platforms, right below us, in order to save us from the fall. Just before we reach the platforms, Kate, Leila, Daren, Hadrik and I all find ourselves suddenly floating in mid-air, as we are getting slowly raised from the chasm.

When we look up, we see Melindra, floating a few dozen feet above us, with that serious expression in her eyes again, while she's making slow hand movements, to aid her in directing the air currents that are keeping us afloat.

"Melindra!" Flower says, as she is still being chased by the black-haired banshee in mid-air. "You shouldn't be casting complicated spells so soon after being healed!"

"I'm fine," Melindra says, while she pulls us out of the pit. "Don't worry about me. You should be worrying about what the sage is doing up there, instead."

As we all take a look to see what's happening, we are shocked to find out that all of the rocks which were being pulled from the ground are now gathering up, to form a fifty foot tall golem, made out of stone, with the sage standing inside its head, on his floating platform from before.

"Why don't you try absorbing this golem with your sword, Daren?" Talmak shouts from above. "Maybe you'll manage to scratch the sole of its foot, before it stomps you to death!"

He then uses his earth powers to move the walls of rock on the sides of the chasm closer together, in order to create a path for his stone giant to walk on. The earth is trembling violently once more, as the pit below us gets narrower by the second, until the walls forming the crevice get joined together, leaving nothing but a small crack in the earth, between them.

In the meantime, Melindra makes us float until we are at a relatively safe distance from the golem, and then she lands us on the ground.

"Healer, you might want to make a barrier around everyone," Melindra says. "And make it stronger than any barrier that you've ever cast before. I do not have a lot of control over the spells that I'm about to use from this moment onwards."

"Oh…" Daren says. "Alright. I'm on it."

He then uses his shield to make a semi-transparent magical barrier around all of us, while Melindra begins to fly higher into the air.

"Flower, you need to take your fight elsewhere," Melindra says. "Get as far away from here as possible. I'm not planning to hold back."

"Okay!" Flower says. "Follow me, banshee! This way!"

She then propels herself in the direction opposite to the golem, with her fire jets, as the black-haired banshee rushes to follow her. When Flower is safely out of the way, Melindra casts a spell, and suddenly we can see hundreds of sharp looking blades made of wind rotate around her, at great speed. The wind blades are likely sharpened in the same way that Illuna or Kate sharpen their own elements, and they are mostly transparent, except for when the light of the sun shines on them.

While Melindra is raising herself higher up, the giant made of stone begins to move forward, at a slow pace, and the sage's henchmen are now hurrying to get out of the golem's way, so that they won't get stepped on.

All of a sudden, Melindra loses control of one of her wind blades, which flies at an incredible speed right into the ground in front of us, cutting through it as if it were made from paper.

"Damn…" Daren says, as he looks at the hole in the ground left by the blade from earlier. "I really hope that my barrier is strong enough to protect us from one of these, if it hits us."

"Maybe you could try to use your sword to absorb the wind blades," I say.

"I did think of that," Daren says, "but I'm not sure if I'd be fast enough to catch one of them, and if I miss it, I could risk getting my arm cut off…"

"What if you hold your sword through the magical barrier, and keep your arm inside?" I say. "You can do that, right?"

"Yeah," Daren says. "I guess I could give it a shot."

"I heard what you were saying about me earlier, you know…" Melindra shouts at the sage, from high up in the sky, with a rather calm tone in her voice. "I heard you talking about how you needed to keep me alive while dissecting me. You sure do have some nerve to speak about a stillwater like this, don't you?"

"You're a little too late, stillwater girl," Talmak shouts back at her. "Maybe you could have stopped me before I made this golem, but now, even one of your tornados won't be able to destroy what I've created. I don't know what you're trying to do with those small rotating blades of yours, but I assure you that they will not help you in any way."

"Is that so?…" Melindra says.

"I've heard enough of your talking," Talmak says. "If I can't use you as an experiment, then you have no value to me. Prepare to die!"

After the sage stops talking, his golem quickly extends its right arm towards Melindra, and it tries to crush her in its hand. However, as soon as the hand tries to close in around Melindra, the hundreds of wind blades that were rotating around her react all at once, and they cut the rocks into tiny pieces in a matter of seconds.

"No…" Talmak says, in complete shock, as he looks at the golem arm before him, which is now missing its hand entirely.

"I believe it is time to show you, Sage Talmak, why

air is the strongest of all the magical elements…" Melindra says, and then she unleashes ten times more blades than she had before, throwing them all in the stone giant's direction.

The thousands of wind blades all soar through the air, at breathtaking speed, and for a few seconds, we could see a great spectacle of shimmering lights, as the sun was getting reflected into each of the blades, in turn. The great stone giant from before was now being sliced into pieces before our very eyes, and while the sage was still trying to bring several boulders from the ground, to replace some of the lost parts, these rocks were getting cut as well, by the multitude of semi-transparent air blades that Melindra was still sending towards Talmak.

A few stray blades also hit Daren's barrier, during this time, but it seems to be holding well, for now. There's also the fact that Daren managed to catch one or two of the wind blades with his sword, so there wasn't as much strain on the barrier as there could have been.

When he realizes that there's no way his regular rocks can withstand Melindra's bombardment, Talmak quickly creates a wall in front of him, and then he uses his magic to fortify it as much as he can.

"Delvram!" the sage shouts at his elf companion. "Get us out of here, now! We won't last for another minute at this rate!"

"As you wish, Sage Talmak…" the elf says, and then he starts casting a teleportation spell, on himself, and all of his allies.

When she hears the elf, Melindra sends a few blades his way as well, but the mage raises a barrier in front of him, which deflects all of her attacks.

"No!" the banshee shouts, as her body is beginning to vibrate, and to shine with a bright light, while the same thing is happening to all of her companions. "Don't take me with you! Leave me here, damn it! I'm not done with—"

Before she gets to finish what she had to say, the banshee gets teleported out of the area, and the same happens to Talmak, Nolderan, and the elf. As soon as our enemies disappear, Melindra dismisses all of her wind blades, and she begins to descend towards us, while Flower is also flying our way.

"Wow…" Daren says, when Melindra gets close to us. "That was… really impressive."

"Nice try, healer," Melindra says, as she lands on the ground, next to us. "But I think we both know that this isn't what you are really thinking, at this moment. Now that the cat's out of the bag, and you know about the problems I have with controlling my powers, you must already be thinking up some strategies of how you can avoid to be put in such a dangerous situation again, aren't you?"

"Sure, I guess…" Daren says, confused. "But I don't see why—"

"Then let me ask you directly…" Melindra says. "Are you, or are you not planning to cast a spell on me that limits my powers?"

"What?…" Daren says. "No! Of course not! What are you even saying? Do you know how risky it would be to try and cast a spell like that on you, given the nature of your stillwater aura? You could even die from something like that. I would never even dream of casting such a spell on you!"

"You wouldn't?…" Melindra says, looking slightly taken aback.

"Listen," Daren says. "I think I'm starting to understand why you never told us about your problem. And I don't blame you. We didn't exactly start off on the best of terms, and you had no reason to trust us, just as we didn't trust you. But for what it's worth, I think you made the right call. You should not risk joining any of our battles, unless we have absolutely no other way of dealing with our enemies. Any other type of strategy would be too risky."

"I agree," Kate says. "Even if she doesn't put us in any immediate danger, a slight scratch from one of her wind blades could be all it takes for the oath to be set off, and to kill her where she stands. As long as there isn't some other sage waiting around the corner, we should be able to handle any situation by ourselves, just as we've done in the past."

She then turns to Melindra, with a hesitant look in her eyes.

"And I'd like to say that I'm… sorry for misinterpreting some of your intentions in the past few days," Kate says. "I understand now that you were only trying to look out for yourself, and that you meant us no harm."

"Barry, what did you do to them?" Melindra asks me, while looking somewhat terrified. "They're not acting like themselves! Does your stat device have some mind-affecting spell that I don't know of?"

"They're just trying to be nice, Melindra," I say. "There's no need to act so shocked about it. Also, could we maybe move away from this camp? I have a feeling that we're going to start getting attacked by a hundred pinecone-collecting underlings if we stay in this place much longer…"

"Good thinking!" Daren says. "But what about the sage, and master Nolderan? Maybe they're still lurking around here, somewhere."

"Nah, they're both gone," Arraka says. "And so are their other allies that you were fighting earlier. If I'm not able to sense them, then they must have teleported to their real base. You know… the one that is not just an empty area with a stone table in the middle…"

"You're probably right," Daren says. "Come on, let's

get going, and we'll talk more on the way."

As we walk away from the camp area, we notice that the mages who were collecting pinecones earlier are all gone. They must have run away when they saw the giant made out of stone. And who could blame them? It's not like you see something like that every day.

"So, just to make sure that we're all on the same page, here..." Melindra says, while we're walking through the empty forest. "You guys don't want to cast any sort of spells on me to fix my problem with controlling my powers..."

"That's right," Daren says.

"And you want me to continue to avoid all of your battles, just like before?..." Melindra asks.

"Exactly," Daren says.

"Okay, I'm going to be honest," Melindra says. "This still sounds a little fishy to me. But I guess I'm going to have to trust your word, for now... I mean, I did witness with my own eyes how icey took my side, against the sage, after all..."

"Oh, you saw that..." Kate says, looking a little flustered.

"Well, technically I couldn't really turn my head, back then, so I mostly only just heard it happen, but yes..." Melindra says. "I almost thought that I was hallucinating there, for a second. Of all the people that I would have expected to attack the sage first, in that situation, Kate would have been the last on my mind."

"You... just called me by my real name..." Kate says, looking very surprised.

"I suppose I did, icey," Melindra says, with a slight smile. "I suppose I did..."

"So, which way are we headed?" Daren says.

"We'll go straight ahead for another few hours, until we reach a small lake," Melindra says. "We'll take a break there, and then I'll show you the rest of the way."

Not long after we are done talking, I suddenly hear Rose's voice through the transceiver. As soon as I hear her, I immediately remember the last time when the revenant contacted me, and how she asked me to keep the transceiver open, so she could call me again.

"Barry, do you hear me?" the revenant says.

"I hear you," I tell her simply, after I tap the transceiver.

"Listen to me," the revenant says. "You need to take out your stat device, and to enter the secret code that boosts your hearing stat. Do you understand?"

"What?..." I say.

"There's no time to explain!" the revenant says. "Just do it! Quick!"

She then closes the channel again, and there is no more way for me to contact her.

After taking a few seconds to consider her request, I eventually decide to take out my device, and to activate the secret code that Melindra taught me a few days ago, just like the revenant asked. Once I'm done, I put my device back in my pocket, and I continue to walk alongside the others.

"Was that the revenant again?" Daren asks, as he gets closer to me. "What did she want?"

"She wanted me to enter my secret code in the stat device, so I can boost my hearing," I say. "I didn't really see a reason why I shouldn't do it, so I did what she said."

"Huh..." Daren says. "Well, I sure hope that this isn't a trap of some sort."

"I don't think so," I say. "I mean, this code just boosts my hearing for a short while. I don't really see what—"

As I was talking, I suddenly realized something that I hadn't noticed before. According to Melindra, the secret code should have only improved my hearing for a few seconds, but for some reason, my hearing is still better than it was before I used the code. Did the revenant use some sort of trick?

"What's the matter, Barry?" Daren says. "Why did you stop talking?

"The hearing stat..." I say. "It's still being boosted. It was supposed to go back to its original level, after a few seconds, but for some reason, that didn't happen."

"Well, maybe your device is broken, or something," Daren says.

"I don't know..." I say. "I feel like that would be too big of a coincidence."

Suddenly, I start to hear Illuna talking with Arraka, at the back of our group.

"Arraka, are there any mages in this area left, except for us?" Illuna says.

"Mages?" Arraka says. "No, not any mages..."

"What do you mean, not any mages?" Illuna asks her. "Are you saying that there's someone else? Monsters? Animals?"

"Maybe," Arraka says.

"You really are starting to get on my nerves, lately..." Illuna says.

Just as Illuna is done talking, I notice the fact that the wind hasn't been blowing at all, for a while. I'm also not hearing any sounds, coming from outside of our group, and now that I look a little closer around me, I notice that there are a few insects, floating in mid-air, as if they've been frozen. Oh, boy... I think I'm starting to understand what's going on, here.

Before I get to finish my train of thought, Hadrik is the one to hit the nail on the head, as he poses a question to all of us.

"So..." Hadrik says. "Is it just me, or is the time frozen for anyone else?..."

Chapter 11

"You're right..." Daren tells Hadrik, after looking around himself for a few seconds. "The time really is frozen. Could it be Eiden's doing?"

"It's not Eiden," Arraka says. "If Eiden were here, I would have told you about it, remember?"

"Then who is it?" Daren asks. "Who froze the time?"

"Why don't you take a look and see for yourself?" Arraka says. "She is coming out of the woods and heading your way as we speak."

"She?..." Daren says.

As we all take a look at the person who is now slowly approaching us, we recognize her immediately. Rose is currently walking very slowly towards us, while her eyes are shining with a bright yellow light. Her expression is completely blank, as she looks straight ahead of her, without acknowledging our presence.

"The revenant, again..." Daren says, with a cold look on his face. "Come on, let's see what she wants."

We all do as Daren says, and we head over to the revenant, until we are right in front of her. As soon as we reach her, the revenant stops in her tracks, and she continues to stare straight ahead, with the same blank expression on her face.

"Why did you come here, revenant?" Daren asks her. "And why did you freeze time?"

The revenant does not react to Daren's words in any way. She doesn't even seem to be aware of our presence. It's as if she were in some sort of... trance.

"Are you listening to us?..." I say.

Seeing that the revenant is still not doing anything, I position myself right in front of her, and I begin to snap my fingers repeatedly, very close to her face.

"Come on!" I say. "Snap out of it!"

"Oh, no…" Melindra says. "I've seen something like this happen before. If it's what I think it is, then you guys had better ready yourselves up. That sage fight from earlier is going to feel like a walk in the park, compared to what's coming up next."

"They're going to be in for a treat, alright!" Arraka says, and then she laughs.

"What are you two talking about?" Hadrik says. "Ready ourselves up for what?"

"It's starting…" Melindra says.

All of a sudden, the revenant disappears from before our eyes, and we can hear her voice coming from behind us. As we all turn around, we realize that it wasn't only her voice, but the revenant herself who had switched positions, in a fraction of a second. The voice that is coming out of her mouth barely sounds like that of Rose, due to the high amount of reverberation in it.

"A prophecy, I have come to tell you…" the revenant says.

"Here we go," Arraka says.

"A prophecy of things that may come to pass, but which have not yet been set in stone," the revenant continues. "Listen carefully, to the events that will be foretold, and you may be able to prevent them from happening, before it is too late."

The revenant then disappears again, and she reappears on our left side, preparing to speak again, as the echo in her voice gets more intense, in order to signify the beginning of the prophecy. After each line that she speaks, the revenant disappears and appears in a different place, making us all turn our heads in confusion.

"As two old enemies clash one final time,
A great disaster that has once been avoided
Can no longer be prevented in the same way.
An entire continent lies in ruins,
While a single laugh made up from different voices
Echoes loudly throughout the realm."

As soon as the revenant is done delivering the prophecy, she stops moving, and once again, she begins to stare into space, with a blank expression on her face.

A prophecy about a great disaster… Two old enemies… Does this mean that we were right? The calamity that Eiden warned us about will happen when he clashes with Tyrath? But then again, the prophecy also mentioned a laugh made up from different voices. And I only know of one person who could fit this description…

"Arraka…" I say. "This prophecy was oddly specific about that single laugh made up from different voices thing. You wouldn't happen to know anything about this 'great disaster', would you?"

"Hey, I could make that prophecy happen in less than a day, if you want," Arraka says. "That way, you wouldn't have to waste any more time trying to figure it out. All you have to do is let me out of this amulet. What do you say?"

"I think I'd rather figure it out by myself, if you don't mind," I say.

"Your loss," Arraka says.

"So, is this it?…" Daren says. "Is the prophecy over?"

"If you're asking only about the prophecy, then yes, it is over," Melindra says.

"You're saying that we should be expecting something else, right after the prophecy?" Daren says.

"Only if everything happens in the same way that it did six hundred years ago," Melindra says. "The last time I've had the honor of witnessing a time weaver's prophecy, I didn't have to wait long until—"

Melindra interrupts herself, because we can all suddenly feel an immense amount of pressure in the air, making it hard to breathe, while the sky looks like it's trembling under the sheer force of the magical power that has flooded our entire area. As we slowly adapt to the pressure and begin to breathe more normally, the revenant is getting raised higher and higher into the air, while her eyes are still bright yellow, staring into nothingness.

"What the hell?!" Hadrik shouts. "What is with this crazy amount of magical power? Arraka is still in the amulet, isn't she?"

"Ahahahahahaha!" Arraka laughs, from inside her amulet.

"This is not Arraka's doing," Melindra says, as she struggles to remain calm. "I already told you. That sage battle from earlier will seem like nothing, compared to what's about to happen."

She is right. I don't think I've experienced such a feeling of dread, ever since I saw Arraka get out of her amulet. It's like every single fiber of my being is telling me to run the hell away from here, as far as possible, and as fast as my feet can carry me. I can't let this fear overcome me. Not now. I'm almost certain that even the smallest wrong decision made at this point could lead to my instant obliteration. Just who is it exactly, that we are facing, here?

"Greetings, mortals…" we hear several male voices, speaking in unison, all around us.

This speech pattern is very similar to the way in which Arraka speaks sometimes, when she loses control over her voice. A laugh made up from several different voices… Could this be tied to the prophecy as well?

"You have been blessed by the presence of a god,"

the voices say, as they reverberate throughout the entire area. "Kneel before me, and I will then give you permission to gaze upon my magnificent form, in admiration."

"And just who exactly—" Daren starts to say, but Melindra puts her hand over his mouth to silence him, with a panicked look on her face.

"This is the God of Time," Melindra says. "Don't ask him any questions. He has the power to end us all in a matter of seconds. Just… kneel…"

She then kneels before the God of Time, with her head bowed down, while she signals Daren to do the same.

An adversary that can make even someone as proud as Melindra act this way? I don't like where this is going. Clearly, if I mess around here, I could end up getting everyone killed. But should I really kneel before this bastard?

While I was standing there, considering my options, the God of Time was slowly materializing into a more earthly form, although I'm not sure if I could really call it that. His body has the form and the size of a human, but it is made out of a sort of solid blue light, which is simply radiating magical energy. The man has no face, and no distinguishable features, aside from a few small blue flames that keep appearing and disappearing randomly throughout his body, at random short time intervals. He is currently floating in mid-air, next to the revenant, and he is looking straight at us, with his empty face.

"It is not wise to keep a god waiting…" the God of Time says. "I told you to kneel."

"Don't listen to what he says," Arraka tells us. "He needs you alive for his plans to work. He can't do anything to you. He's just bluffing."

"Arraka is right," I say. "We shouldn't have to kneel

before anyone. Even if they are gods. No matter what happens, I am going to stand my ground."

As soon as I am done talking, I suddenly feel a very intense pain in the left side of my chest, and when I look down, I see, to my horror, that my heart has been ripped straight out of me, and that I now have a huge, bloody hole in my chest, where my heart used to be.

"Barry!" Kate shouts, in desperation.

Everything is now getting much colder, and I can feel shivers all throughout my body. The light before my eyes is slowly starting to fade, while I am gradually losing my consciousness. Right before it all goes dark, however, I suddenly regain my senses, as I hear Kate shouting my name in reverse. Immediately afterwards, my heart gets put back into my chest, while my wound closes completely, with all the blood disappearing from my shirt almost instantly. As soon as the time reversal spell is over, I start to breathe very loudly and rapidly, while sweating all over, as if I'd just woken up from a terrible nightmare.

Arraka laughs, when she sees the look on my face.

"I guess I forgot that he can also reverse time, as long as he has control of the time weaver," Arraka says. "My bad!"

"I will not repeat myself again," the God of Time says. "Kneel."

The others and I exchange a few hesitant looks, but neither of us seems to be in a hurry to follow the god's orders, even after his previous display of power.

"Sorry," Hadrik says, with half a grin, while trying to mimic his usual confident tone. "My doctor told me that kneeling is bad for my—"

"I said *kneel*!" the god shouts, and then an immense amount of pressure pushes us all to the ground, including Melindra, who was already kneeling.

We are now all being squashed against the rocky soil

by an incredible force, and I can already feel the pain from my internal organs bleeding, as the enormous pressure above us just keeps getting more and more unbearable. In order to make sure that he doesn't kill us, the God of Time keeps casting time reversal spells every ten seconds or so, thus healing our internal wounds, just so they can be reformed again and again, over the course of the next few minutes.

During this time, I can't manage to pay attention to anything around me. Every ounce of my energy is being focused into withstanding the pain. I can no longer tell if the screams that I'm hearing are coming from me, or from my friends. It's as if I've voluntarily entered some sort of trance, trying to become one with the pain. Trying to let it flow through me. No matter how hard I try, however, the pain keeps getting the better of me, and then I need to regain my focus all over again.

"Can you *stop* with the time reversals, already?" Arraka says, exasperated, after a while. "You're making me dizzy!"

Upon hearing Arraka's words, the God of Time casts one last time-reversal spell, and then he lowers the amount of pressure in the air above us, making sure that he is no longer hurting us, but still keeping us pressed against the ground.

"*Thank* you!" Arraka says, in the same exasperated tone.

"I see that living amongst these mortals has taught you some long-overdue basic etiquette, Arraka," the God of Time says. "It is regrettable that you could not learn these manners before we were forced to banish you from our realm."

"Forced?..." Arraka says. "Hah! You only did it because you were afraid of me. It's funny, because while we were both living in the magical plane, I hadn't pegged you as the cowardly type. And yet, twice, you ran away from me. Once with the banishment, and a second time six hundred years ago. What happened to that unfinished duel of ours, eh? Didn't you say that we would settle our scores, eventually?"

"And we will," the God of Time says. "As soon as we are both back to our peak conditions. You wouldn't want to fight me from inside an amulet, would you?"

"Well, if you would just destroy this amulet for me, we could—" Arraka starts to say, but she is interrupted by the God of Time.

"You will receive no help from me," the God of Time says. "Don't think I've forgotten about the many spirits you've killed and absorbed, all those thousands of years ago. Some of them were my friends, you know."

"Don't be like that, Selkram," Arraka says, with a mocking tone. "We're friends too, aren't we? After all, it's thanks to me that you found out you could absorb other spirits. Don't think that I didn't figure out what you've been doing. You might have managed to hide this from all the other spirits in the magical plane, but I'm the one who *invented* the technique! I know all about its side-effects. Your voice started to change right after we had our first battle, in the magical plane, and the same thing happened to Ulruk. Those different voices that you are using when you speak are from all the other spirits that you couldn't absorb properly, aren't they? The same thing happened to me, at first, but then I learned, and I adapted, unlike you idiots. Seriously, what did you and Ulruk think? That you could just copy my technique without any sort of training? Just how arrogant could you be, anyway? Do you have any idea how much time I spent perfecting that spell? But hey, I guess it was easier for you to assume that only female spirits from the civilized races could absorb other spirits correctly, and to convince everyone to banish us to the earthen plane, than to admit that the only reason for your failure was your outstanding ineptitude."

"I will not stand here and listen to you mocking—" the God of Time starts to say, but Arraka cuts him off.

"You both should have listened to Memphir," Arraka says. "He's the only one with a brain out of all you 'gods'. I bet he tried to stop you from absorbing the spirits, didn't he? I never heard *him* using different voices when he spoke. How is Memphir, by the way? Isn't the time limit for his own prophecy due at some point during this century?"

"The God of Fate and his prophecy are none of your busin—" the God of Time starts to say, but he gets cut off yet again.

"Yeah, it was this century, wasn't it?..." Arraka says, as she is now ignoring the God of Time completely, while getting lost in her own thoughts. "And the prophecy was pretty specific about his death too. It said that he would get killed by a member of the civilized races from the earthen plane, who would originate from a region called Varathia. I remember how Memphir kept rechecking that prophecy again and again, in the hopes that something would change, even if he always got the exact same result. He was becoming completely obsessed with it... I bet he must have really freaked out when Eiden named this continent Varathia, huh? And now that the time limit is drawing closer, the so-called 'God of Fate' even went as far as forming a temporary alliance with the 'God of Death', saying that he'd help him with his indiscriminate murders, as long as they were being focused on Varathia! I honestly don't get what's going through Memphir's head. If I were in his place, I'd just reduce this entire continent to a pile of ashes in one day, and be done with it!"

The God of Fate is aiming to destroy this continent too? Just how could this situation get any worse?...

"Arraka, if you don't keep quiet, I'm going to—"

Selkram, the God of Time says.

"You're going to what?..." Arraka says, in a provocative tone. "Destroy my amulet?"

"I could also throw you very far away from here, in the middle of an ocean, where nobody will ever find you again," the god says.

"I'd like to see you try," Arraka says.

"Don't listen to her provocations!" Illuna says, as she is struggling to articulate her words, while she is still being pushed face-first against the ground. "If you throw her in an ocean, she will just escape from her amulet by herself, and then it will be the end for all of us!"

"Oh?" the God of Time says. "So you must be her captor, then... Or maybe just her jailor. I suppose it is only fitting for a 'banshee' to be the one overseeing such a task, given how much your kind has had to suffer because of her arrogance."

"And because of yours!" Flower shouts, all of a sudden. "It's your fault that Petal has to live like this! She never wanted this life. She never wanted to kill anyone. And neither did any of the other banshees. I will never forgive you for what you've done!"

"You will never forgive me?..." the God of Time says, sounding genuinely puzzled. "You must have a very short memory, if you can afford to talk to me like this, after all that has happened. Allow me to refresh that short memory of yours, a little."

He then begins to increase the pressure that was pushing Flower against the ground, until she starts screaming in pain. After a few more seconds, the God of Time reverses time once again, to make sure that he doesn't kill her by accident, and he continues to squash her, over and over again, like before.

"Oh, no..." Arraka says. "Not the time reversals again... Just kill me and put me out of my misery!"

After Selkram squashes Flower a few more times,

Kate can no longer stand listening to the girl's screams, and she raises her head from the ground, in order to address the God of Time.

"Leave her alone!" Kate shouts. "Haven't you hurt her enough?!"

The god reverses the time again, in order to heal Flower, and then he floats all the way to Kate's position, so he can get a better look at her. Or at least I think that's what he's trying to do, since he doesn't really have a face.

"Very strange..." the God of Time says. "With the tone you are using to address me, I would have expected you to at least have some decent amount of magical energy, to back up your threats. But when I look at you closely, I see that your power can barely even compare to the stillwater in your own group, let alone someone of my caliber. So, why is it that you are trying to defy me, I wonder?"

"Who cares?" Arraka says. "She's a weakling anyway."

"It's not just her, who is surprisingly weak, however..." Selkram says, as he flies to a higher position, in order to have a better look at all of us. "Neither of the people in this group, except for the stillwater girl, can even begin to compare with the ones from six hundred years ago, in terms of magical power. Last time, there was the golden fox, there was that stillwater you were fused with, and there was also the really strong stillwater who was travelling with the fox. Eiden, I believe was his name? Compare that to what we have here, and it all seems like a cruel joke. Why even bother to send the time weaver to any of these people? They will probably just get killed off within the next couple of days, if they are lucky enough to even survive that long..."

"What are you... Ngh... talking about?" I say, as I'm

having a little trouble speaking properly, due to my face being constantly pushed in the dirt. “Aren’t you the one who sent the time weaver here?”

“Hah!” Arraka says. “Selkram *wishes* he could just control time weavers whenever he wants! The Magium is the one who sent the time weaver here, not this sad excuse for a god.”

“The Magium?…” I say, too shocked to be able to do anything other than repeat her words.

“Mhm…” Arraka says. “It is somewhat of a tradition for the Magium to send a time weaver on the earthen plane, every time there is the potential for a great number of lives to be lost in a short period of time. Especially when it comes to this continent. When the time weaver’s powers finally awaken, the person who was gifted with these powers will enter some kind of trance, they will freeze time, and then they will walk patiently towards several groups of people, delivering the prophecy to them, one by one. That’s how it’s always been.”

“But then… what does the God of Time have to do with all of this?” I ask.

“Oh, Selkram is just hijacking the signal, so to speak,” Arraka says. “He found a way, long ago, to take advantage of a time weaver’s trance to temporarily link himself directly to the Magium, and he is using this connection to insert a ritual of his own into the mix. You know how the other gods get their power through large numbers of followers? Well, Selkram doesn’t have any followers. He’s going for quality over quantity. Basically, since the groups visited by time weavers have the potential to affect the lives of hundreds of thousands of people, he decided to channel all of his efforts into exploiting people like you, instead of begging for the adoration of a bunch of sheep, like all the other gods are doing.”

"What… kind of ritual are you talking about?" I ask Arraka, a little apprehensively.

"Well, I don't really know all the details," Arraka says, "since these rituals of his always change, but there should almost certainly be some time-travelling involved, in at least one of the stages. When's the ritual starting, anyway?"

"As soon as every preparation is in place," the God of Time says. "But this does not mean that you should spend the remaining time holding conversations with these lowly creatures. Why do you bother answering every single one of their questions? I very much doubt that these people will even make it past the first stage of the ritual."

Arraka laughs.

"I think you will be very surprised of their upcoming performance," she says. "These aren't the types to give up easily."

"We shall see about that soon enough…" the God of Time says.

He then flies over to the revenant's position, and he grabs her by her chin, turning her head left and right a few times, while bringing his face closer to hers.

"Hmm…" the God of Time says. "I sense traces of the God of Death's aura coming from this time weaver. A revenant, perhaps? Or maybe some other form of undead. Well, whatever she is, she just managed to earn an invitation to my ritual. Let me just pull her out of her trance."

After he stops talking, the God of Time releases the revenant from his grasp, and then he waves his hand in front of her face, which causes the bright light to fade from her eyes. After she regains her senses, the revenant looks around her, with her calm, emotionless gaze, and then she addresses the God of Time, directly.

"I see that you've removed me from my trance," the

revenant says. “Should I take it that you’re going to force me to participate in your ritual?”

“How very astute of you,” the God of Time says. “It seems that Ulruk has instructed you well.”

“There was no need for him to instruct me,” the revenant says. “The spell that brought me into this world implanted a lot of the God of Death’s knowledge into my mind, including details about your rituals, and about your personality. Taking these factors into account, it wasn’t hard for me to predict that your first reaction when finding out about me would be to try and ‘punish’ the God of Death for meddling in your affairs. And what better way to punish him, than through me, his loyal follower?”

“At long last, Ulruk has found himself a follower that can compensate for his lack of wits,” the God of Time says. “But let’s see how far your wits can carry you in the trials ahead. The ritual is about to begin. Prepare yourself.”

After the god is done talking, a blinding white light fills our entire area, making it impossible to see any further than my own hands. I then get a strong dizziness sensation, while it feels as if my mind is being pulled straight out of my body. As soon as the light disappears and I can see around me again, I notice that I’m still lying on the ground, but everyone else is gone.

Wait, no, that isn’t right… It’s not that everyone else is gone. It’s that I’ve been transported to an entirely different place. I am still in the middle of a forest, somewhere, but this forest seems awfully familiar. As if I’ve been here before, in my distant past.

When I decide to get up and explore a bit, I am momentarily frozen in shock, as I realize that my height is now considerably lower than it was before. And it’s not only my height, that’s different, either. My arms are also much shorter, my hands are smaller, and I’m no longer wearing the same clothes.

"—these rituals of his always change, but there should almost certainly be some time-travelling involved," I hear Arraka's voice in the back of my head, as I suddenly remember what she was saying to me earlier.

Time-travelling, a smaller body, and a familiar-looking forest. I'm getting a bad feeling about this.

I immediately check my pockets, to see if I still have any of my old items, but they are all gone, including my stat device. If this is really the forest I think it is, and if that strong, magical aura I'm feeling in the distance also belongs to whom I think it does, then the God of Time must have sent me back to when I was around thirteen years of age. But for what purpose?…

I throw all those thoughts away, and I start running as fast as I can, towards the house that I once used to call my home. I say that I'm running towards my house, but truth be told, my home used to be more of a cabin, really. It was made almost entirely of wood, and it was somewhat isolated from the rest of the village, because my father liked the quiet. We had a river close to us, and we could get all the firewood we needed from this forest, so we were somewhat independent of the other town folk. We even had a small patch of land, that we were farming, and a barn, where we kept our hay. It's funny how I can still remember all of these details so vividly, when I haven't thought about this place in many years.

As soon as I reach the edge of the forest, I take a look towards the old cabin, and my heart skips a beat, when I see my little sister in the middle of our front yard, just as the banshee within her is awakening, and preparing to take over her body. That powerful magical aura radiating from her is just as sinister as I remembered, and it's sending shivers down my spine. Not only is my sister's aura changing, but her body is also transforming into something that could no longer be called human. Her face looks like it's melting, and her skin is turning purple, while the rest of her body is getting slowly deformed.

As the donkey in front of our barn is making loud and scared noises, my parents and my little brother are just coming back to the house, and they're rushing towards the yard, to see what is happening to my sister. They're still alive… My parents are still alive. This time I didn't arrive too late. I can still save them. I can make things right. I can— wait… what about that trial the God of Time was talking about? Is saving my parents part of the trial, or am I supposed to be doing something else?

No… To hell with that trial! I'm being offered a once in a lifetime opportunity to fix my past mistakes. I'm not going to throw it away. This time, I won't be too late. This time, I'm going to save them all.

I quickly rush inside our barn, while the donkey is still hee-hawing, and I grab the pitchfork that was lying on the ground. Do I really want to kill the banshee, though? It's not really her fault that she's forced to kill other people, in order to continue living. Maybe if I try to reason with her… No, no, no, remember that laugh. Remember that sinister laughter that still sometimes haunts me in my dreams even after so many years have passed. This banshee killed my parents in cold blood, and she enjoyed it. She is not like Illuna. You can't reason with her. It's either kill, or be killed.

As I am approaching the banshee, I see that my parents and my brother have already reached her, and they are trying to talk with her, as if she were still my sister.

"Claire!" my mother says. "Dear gods, what happened to you?"

"We need to call a doctor!" my father says, in a panicked voice. "Or… a magician. The kind that Barry is always talking about. A mage! That's what they're called. This looks like some sort of magical illness. If we can find a mage doctor, maybe we can still cure her. There has to be a mage in one of the neighboring villages. Barry, there you are. Come quick! Your sister is very ill! Do you know of any mage doctors in our area?"

"There are no white mages in any of the villages around our area," I tell him, as I slowly approach him with the pitchfork in my hand. "And even if there were, it would be too late for her."

"What are you saying?..." my father says. "And what are you doing with that pitchfork?"

"Never mind the pitchfork," I say. "Don't take your eyes off Claire. In a matter of seconds, she's going to turn into a monster, and she won't hesitate to attack you."

"Claire? A monster?..." my father says, as he turns towards her, apprehensively. "No, that can't be what's really happening... You are joking, aren't you, Barry?"

"Don't take your eyes off her," I tell him again, with a serious tone in my voice. "If she tries to kill you, I won't hold back against her."

Just as I was done talking, the banshee was already finished with her awakening, and she was preparing for her first strike. I quickly push my father out of the way with one hand, and with the other, I keep hold of my pitchfork. The banshee was trying to impale my father with her bare hand, but due to my intervention, she only managed to lightly wound me in the left side of my abdomen, instead.

My mother gasps, as she sees the blood, dripping out of me.

"Barry!" she shouts, with fear in her voice.

I do not give the banshee the time to attack me again, and I run my pitchfork straight through her chest, while holding the weapon with both my hands. The banshee screams in a very loud and shrieky voice, but she doesn't manage to muster the strength for another strike, and after a few more seconds, her screams and her squirming all come to an end, along with her life.

As I drop the pitchfork from my hands, along with the banshee's body, my mother comes to hug me tightly, and then she just holds me in her arms for a few seconds, without saying anything.

"Thank you..." my mother says. "Thank you so much for saving him. I can't even imagine how it would have been to lose both my daughter and my husband in the same day."

She then retracts all of a sudden, as she takes a look at my wound.

"I'm sorry," she says. "I shouldn't have been pressing on your wound like that. I'll go get some bandages and some rubbing alcohol from the house. It looks like it's only a surface-level wound, so it should be enough to clean it up a little. I'll be right back!"

She then rushes towards the house, as my father is still apparently in a state of shock from what happened, and my brother is crying in the background.

I did it. I actually did it. I changed the past. Even if I have to live my life all over again until I reach the age of twenty-eight, it will still all have been worth it. Even with magic, I couldn't have dared to dream that such a thing would be possible. Now, as long as I can figure out what the God of Time's ritual is, and how to survive it, I should be able to—

My thought process gets interrupted by an extreme dizziness, as the entire area gets flooded with a bright white light again. Just like before, I get the sensation that my consciousness is being ripped out of my body, and then the light fades away, as I find myself in the middle of a much too familiar forest.

No... It can't be...

I quickly look down, to confirm that I am in the same, thirteen year old body, and then I start to run towards my house, as fast as I can. I don't know why I'm running. My magical sense is enough to give me all the information I need. The aura of the banshee possessing my sister is just as strong as it was the first time I was sent back in time. I can also sense that my parents and my little brother have not reached our house yet. I can sense it all. So why am I running?...

As soon as I reach the edge of the forest, and look towards our house, I see my sister turning into a banshee, just like before. Everything I did was for nothing. It's going to happen again. And I'm the only one who can stop it from happening.

I run as fast as I can towards the barn, and I grab the pitchfork from the ground, just like the last time. Without even thinking, I make a sprint towards the banshee, and before my parents and brother can reach her, I impale her through the chest.

This has to be it. I did everything perfectly this time around. I didn't get wounded, I didn't interact with either of my parents, and I killed the banshee before she even had the chance to complete her awakening. This has to be what the ritual wants from me, right? Otherwise, why would it have sent me here?

"Barry..." my mother says, with tears in her eyes. "What have you done?"

When I look at the ground, to see the corpse of the banshee I killed, I notice, to my shock, that her body has reverted to the original form that my sister had, before the awakening began. As my mother grabs the lifeless corpse of my sister tightly in her arms, my father is looking at me with nothing but contempt in his eyes, as a silent fury is slowly taking over him.

"You killed her..." my father says. "You killed her in cold blood. You little bastard. Is this how you repay us for taking you in? For treating you as if you were our own son?"

"Jonathan, that's enough!" my mother says, with a sudden, panicked look in her eyes.

"No, Helen," my father says, with the same dark look on his face as before, while he is not letting me out of his sight. "The boy needs to know. I *want* him to know. Barry… I want you to remember what I'm about to tell you, for every single day that you'll be spending rotting away in prison. You are *not* our son. You never were. Your real parents were a couple of outsiders who moved into our remote village less than a year before you were born. They were both murdered in broad daylight, a few years later, by some hooded thugs that somehow managed to then vanish without a trace, and since there was no one left to care for you, Helen and I decided to take you in. But we only did it out of pity, and because nobody else wanted you. Do you understand?! Nobody wanted you! Nobody wanted—"

The last words of my father's sentence were completely drowned out by the sound of my mother slapping him very hard across the face.

"I said that's enough!" my mother says, as she looks at him with a determined look on her face, while she wipes a tear from her eyes.

She then heads towards me, and she puts her hands on my shoulders, as she looks me straight in the eyes.

"Barry, I'm really sorry about what your father said…" my mother tells me, while she is still trying to hold back her tears from before. "I'm sure he didn't mean to say all those terrible things. It must have been the shock of what happened, that made him lose his temper. It's not true that we didn't want you. We've always loved you, even if you weren't our real son."

She then pauses for a second, to wipe the tears forming in her eyes with her sleeve.

"And regarding your sister…" my mother continues. "I can't bring myself to believe that you killed her without a reason. We all could feel the powerful and unnatural magical aura coming from your sister just minutes ago, and we could see from a distance what monstrous form she'd taken, before you killed her. I… don't know anything about magic, and neither does your father. But you were always fascinated by it, and always took every opportunity you had to learn more about it. If that thing your sister was turning into was dangerous enough that you had to kill her, I am willing to trust your word on it, no matter how painful it would be for me to accept it. But you have to give me your word. You have to swear to me that there was no other way. Barry, can you swear this to me?"

"Yes, I swear!" I say. "There's no way I would have—"

It's no use. I can't talk anymore. The dizziness has overwhelmed me yet again, and I can feel myself being pulled out of my body, while the bright light blinds me just like the last two times. Once the dizziness and the light are both gone, I find myself in the exact same spot that I am now all too familiar with, while my sister's aura can be clearly felt beyond the edge of the forest, as strong as ever.

No… I can't let it end like this. Not when I'm so close to saving them. Even after all that my father just said to me, I still can't bring myself to hate him. He saw me brutally murder his little girl in front of his eyes, after all. And my mother was willing to trust me, even under these conditions. I can't give up on them just like that. I'm going to find a way to save them, no matter what happens.

For the next hour or so, I spent my time trying to figure out what could be going wrong with what I was doing. I tried everything I could think of. I killed the banshee with different weapons, I killed her before and after my parents intervened, I tried to reason with the banshee before killing her, and I even got my father to kill her by himself one time.

All for nothing. Every single time when it seemed like it would finally work, I would just get sent back in time again, and I would have to start over from scratch. I almost died a few times as well. I'm not sure how this ritual would work if I died, but given how little interest the God of Time seemed to show for our lives, I would not be surprised if I would simply stay dead, without any sort of time reversal to save me.

As I stand there and try to decide upon my next course of action, a dark thought suddenly crosses my mind, regarding a scenario that I've completely avoided to take into consideration until this moment. What if this ritual isn't about me saving my parents? What if the only reason why the God of Time sent me here was to force me to relive my past mistakes, and to show me how powerless I am to change them? Arraka did mention that these rituals are meant to exploit us for the god's own benefit. And after all that the God of Time has done to us, it just wouldn't make sense for him to help us change our past, out of the kindness of his heart.

The more I think about it, the more it makes sense. It's not like the 'God of Time' is an actual god. He didn't create time. He doesn't have any control over it. The only way to undo something that has already happened is through a time reversal spell. If my parents' deaths have not been undone through magic, then my presence here is irrelevant. I will just be forced to repeat these same events, over and over, until I take the exact same actions that I took when I was thirteen years of age. There was never any other option. I was a fool to think otherwise.

I slowly begin to advance towards my old house,

while I'm trying hard to maintain my calm. There is no other way. I only need to get through this one more time, and then it will be over.

As I walk through the forest, I make sure that I don't arrive to the cabin too early, so that I'm not spotted by my parents or by the banshee. I need to do everything just like I did it fifteen years ago. I need to arrive late.

When I reach the edge of the forest, I can hear the screams of my parents, as they are being murdered, one by one, by my sister. There is nothing I can do to help them. I need to stay strong.

As soon as I stop hearing their voices, I rush out of the forest as fast as I can, and into the barn, to grab the pitchfork. My brother is now running away from the banshee, just like I remember he did, all those years ago. While she is busy chasing my brother, the banshee is an easy target. I quickly circle around her, and I run my pitchfork right through her stomach, from behind. The banshee tries to turn around, and to attack me, but she is too weakened, due to her awakening. Eventually, she stops moving, and she drops to the ground, as I let go of my pitchfork, so it can fall along with her.

As I look towards my parents' corpses, lying close to the banshee, I cannot help but feel a sharp pain in my chest area, around my heart, although it passes soon afterwards. This is the second time I've failed to save them. No… I can't think like this. My parents were already dead. This was no different from a dream. A terrible dream that is now finally over—

A bright white light suddenly engulfs me, as my consciousness is yet again being transferred to a different body. When the light and my dizziness fade away, I once more find myself in the same forest, while my sister's aura can be felt very clearly, in the distance.

No… *No*! How can this be? I didn't do anything different from fifteen years ago. I let both my parents die. I saved my brother. I used the same pitchfork. I even made sure to arrive too late, so that there wouldn't be any doubt that I did… exactly…

No… That's not right. That is not at all what happened… That's just the story that I've been telling everyone for the past fifteen years. I've been telling it for so long, that I've even managed to fool myself into believing it was real. But the reality of these events was in fact far different from what I remembered. Now I understand what this ritual wants from me. Now I finally get what I need to do.

As the realization of what really happened all those years ago finally dawns upon me, I first experience a feeling of shock, then, a feeling of resignation, and finally, a feeling of hatred. A feeling of pure hatred towards the God of Time, which only keeps intensifying as I walk through the forest.

When I finally reach the edge of the woods, I go inside the barn to pick up the pitchfork, and then I head towards my parents, who were now trying in vain to talk with the being that was once my sister. I position myself at a safe distance from my parents, and I wait.

After a few more seconds, the banshee finally awakens, and she tries to impale my father with her bare hand. Amazingly, my father manages to dodge her first attack, so the banshee attacks him a second time, by driving a sharp cone of rock through his leg, making him fall on the ground, as he screams in pain. The banshee is now screaming as well, seemingly because she is also in pain, as a result of straining herself so hard, immediately after her awakening. While the banshee is distracted, my father finally notices me, and he also sees the pitchfork that I am holding in my hands.

"Barry…" my father says. "Quick… Throw me the pitchfork!"

I say nothing to my father, and I continue to stare at

him, while I keep cursing the God of Time in my mind, more and more, with each passing second.

"Barry!" my father says, this time in a more desperate tone. "There's no time! You need to give me the pitchfork!"

Unfortunately for him, the banshee had already recovered, and she was preparing for a third, and final attack. My father could not do anything to escape, due to the large wound in his leg, and he was impaled once more, this time through his chest, which killed him almost instantly.

My mother screams in terror, as she sees my father die before her eyes. She is now much too scared to move, but before her dying moments, she manages to utter a few last words.

"Barry, please… save me…" she says.

Just like before, I do not move from my spot, I do not answer her, and the banshee kills her by slitting her throat, with a dagger made of sharpened rock. When the banshee sees me just standing there, looking at my parents' corpses, she begins to laugh. The exact same sinister laughter that I remember clearly to this day. And now I finally know what she was laughing about. She wasn't laughing because she enjoyed killing my parents. She was laughing at me.

It wasn't that I arrived too late. That was never what happened. I was there when my parents were being attacked. I saw it all happen before my eyes. I had the pitchfork in my hands, ready to strike, but when I got closer to the banshee, and saw her monstrous figure staring at me with that vicious look in her eyes, I simply froze. I completely froze, in fear, and I couldn't even hear my father and mother begging me to help them. It was only when my brother was almost about to get killed by the banshee as well, that I finally mustered up the courage to attack her. That is what really happened, fifteen years ago, and what I've completely blocked from my mind for more than half of my life.

This was the one and only time when I ever froze up from fear. In fact, if I come to think of it, what happened after this incident was that I developed an almost suicidal tendency to completely ignore danger, no matter how dire the situation was. It's almost as if my desire for something like this to never happen again was so strong, that it fried my brain, and it eliminated my instinct of self-preservation. So many things are starting to make sense, now… I can't believe that I've been keeping this memory repressed for so long. I suppose I have the God of Time to thank for this stunning revelation. I would shake his hand, but with the amount of rage that I am feeling towards him right now, I'm afraid that I might crush it by mistake.

The banshee is now starting to chase after my brother. I waste no time, and I dash towards her, impaling her through her back with my pitchfork, without giving her any chance to retaliate. As the banshee slowly dies before my eyes, a white light once again fills the area, and I get transported through time once more. This time, however, I am not worried. I already know that I have passed this stage of the ritual.

Just as I was expecting, as soon as the light fades, I find myself back in my twenty-eight year old body, surrounded by all my friends, as Arraka lets out one of her usual laughs.

"It looks like you are one of the first to pass this part of the ritual, Barry-boy," Arraka says. "Come, have a seat, and let us enjoy ourselves, while we watch the rest of your friends suffering in their own trials!"

I take a quick glance around me to see what our current situation is. The God of Time is no longer anywhere to be seen, but it doesn't seem like his departure affected the ritual in any way. Daren, Kate,

Leila, Hadrik and the revenant appear to be in some form of trance, similar to the one in which the revenant was when she first arrived to this place. Their eyes are bright yellow, and they're just staring in front of themselves, without being aware of our presence. All of them are standing in place right where I left them, except for the revenant, who now has her feet on the ground, instead of floating in mid-air like before. In the meantime, Melindra, Illuna, and presumably Flower are all out of their trances, and they're looking at me attentively.

"What do you mean you want us to watch my friends during their trials?…" I ask Arraka, once I get a good grasp of our situation. "You have a way to see what's happening in the past?"

"Sure," Arraka says. "It's not that hard. They're all connected to the Magium, right now, so if you know how to link yourself up to their auras properly, you should be able to see what they are seeing."

"The Magium…" I say, as I suddenly remember the discussion that Arraka had with the God of Time before he sent us back in time. "You were saying before that the Magium is the one that sent the revenant here to give us the prophecy. What did you mean by that? Are you saying that the Magium is a person?"

"Ahahahahaha!" Arraka laughs. "Illuna did you hear? He asked me if the Magium is a person!"

"I heard him…" Illuna says, in a dry tone, as Arraka continues to laugh in the background.

"Of course you wouldn't answer my question…" I say, as I look towards Arraka's amulet. "Never mind the Magium, then. What can you tell me about the others' rituals?"

"Which ones are you talking about?" Arraka says. "The ones that already passed, or the ones still inside the trance?"

"Both, I guess?…" I say.

"Well," Arraka says, "I didn't get to see Melindra's ritual, but Illuna was forced to reenact the whole 'sacred woods massacre' down to its very last detail. Her ritual wasn't nearly as funny as yours, because she realized from the start what she needed to do, but I could still tell that she was pretty pissed off about it, even if she didn't really show it. Flower, on the other hand, just kept trying to save her friends from the destruction of Olmnar over and over, even after failing dozens of times in a row. In the end, it was Illuna who convinced her to finally let them go, after she got out of her own ritual, and saw what the foolish girl was doing, from inside Flower's own mind."

"What about the ones who are still inside their rituals?" I say.

"Hmm…" Arraka says. "I think it would be quicker to show you directly. Let's start with the healer."

In a single instant, the scenery around me changes completely, and everyone except for Flower and me disappears from before my eyes, as I now find myself standing in front of Rose's house, in the city of Thilias. When I take a better look at the two of us, I notice that Flower and I have both become semi-transparent, and the same goes for Arraka's amulet. On the other hand, I'm also seeing another Flower and another instance of me who are not transparent at all, and who are currently busy talking to Rose and her siblings, in the same yard where we are located. Hadrik, Kate and Daren are also here, apparently, and so is Ella.

"First, let me give you a bit of context!" Arraka says.

"What's happening?" I say. "How did you bring us here?"

"Shh…" Arraka tells me.

"Rose," I hear Daren saying. "Could you show me to my room? All I want right now is to lie down in a bed for a while."

"Certainly!" Rose says. "Follow me, I'll show you the way!"

"Okay, now the healer is heading towards his room, and he's going to stay there for a while," Arraka says. "Remember this part?"

"Yes," I say. "This happened right after we reached Rose's house for the first time. But why are you showing me this? Does this have anything to do with Daren's ritual?"

"I told you," Arraka says. "I'm trying to give you some context! It wouldn't be any fun otherwise. Alright, next up, we'll fast-forward to Daren's room."

Once again, the whole scenery around us changes in an instant, and we both find ourselves inside Daren's room from Rose's mansion, where Daren is currently sitting on the bed, with his torso leaning forward, and his elbows propped on his knees, while he is holding his head with both his hands. Just like before, he seems to be completely unaware of our presence.

"He can't see or hear us, by the way," Arraka tells me, as we are still in our semi-transparent form. "Just thought I'd make it clear, in case you didn't figure it out by now."

"She could have died…" I hear Daren's voice reverberating from the walls, even though Daren's mouth is still closed. "She could have died right before my eyes, and I would have been powerless to save her…"

"What was that?" I ask Arraka, as I look all around us, to try and find the source of the sound. "Were those… Daren's thoughts?"

"Of course they were his thoughts," Arraka says. "What else could they have been?"

"You have the ability to read people's minds?" I say, starting to panic a little.

"No, you idiot!" Arraka says. "How many times do I

need to tell you that your friends are connected to the Magium, right now? Reading their thoughts while they are in this state is easy if you have some decent knowledge of how auras work. Now shut up and pay attention! I didn't bring you here for nothing."

"No…" I hear Daren's voice echoing throughout the room again. "It's not that I was powerless. I could have gotten the power, if I wanted it. But would I have gotten it?… Would I have been able to do something as humiliating as asking Eiden for help, for the sake of saving that poor girl's life? What would have happened if Barry hadn't intervened? Would that girl have been dead because of me? Because I couldn't let go of my ego? No! Eiden is evil. He couldn't have just offered to help me without having an ulterior motive. But then, why didn't he ask for anything in return? I saw him give Barry the power, and there were no tricks. He even gave the rest of us the power as a side-effect of his spell… So, then, why did he do it? What could have been his reason? Did he really give me that option just to humiliate me? What is Eiden thinking?…"

"Perfect," Arraka says. "I think this should be enough context for our intents and purposes. Let's move on to the ritual."

Again, the environment around us changes completely, but this time, we find ourselves on the streets of Thilias, right as the noble was threatening Ella. Flower and I are still semi-transparent, apparently, but the non-transparent version of me is standing about a dozen feet away from our current position, and so are Daren, Kate, Rose and Eiden.

"Okay," Arraka tells me. "This is where Daren's ritual actually started. What I've been showing you so far were just fragments of his memories, so you could better understand his motivations. Is everything clear, so far?"

"I guess so…" I say.

"Good," Arraka says. "Now let's watch the show."

"What happened?" I hear Daren's thoughts, echoing throughout the area, as he looks around him confused. "Is this the ritual that Arraka was talking about? Did I get sent to the past?"

"How interesting…" Eiden says, all of a sudden. "The flow of the healer's aura has changed completely, in a matter of seconds. It's as if he's now a different person from the one he was a few moments ago. What could trigger such a change, I wonder… Memory loss? No, no, no… This is something else. Time travel, perhaps? A trial from the God of Time?"

"I don't know what you're talking about," Daren says, trying to feign ignorance. "Who is this God of Time you speak of? I've never heard of him."

"So you did receive a trial, then!" Eiden says, with a grin, as he sees right through Daren's bluff. "But what could be the purpose of the ritual?… Is it to save the slave girl? Either way, I must make sure to not interfere. I would not want you to fail your trial on my account!"

"What do you mean you won't interfere?" Daren says, with an anxious tone in his voice. "You're still going to give Barry the power to attack the noble, right?"

"Is that what I did the last time you experienced these events?" Eiden asks, with a wicked smile. "Why was it Barry that saved the slave instead of you? Is it because you refused my offer? Yes, that would make sense, wouldn't it? But this time, you won't be able to rely on your friend to clean up your mess anymore. So, what are you going to do?"

"This bastard…" I hear Daren thinking. "I should have known he couldn't be trusted. But if Barry isn't going to save Ella anymore, then that means…"

Suddenly, we hear Ella screaming in fear, as the earl

of Ollendor is now holding his knife in his hand, while approaching her slowly.

"Please, I beg you!" Ella says, as she is desperately trying to lift all of the luggage that she was supposed to carry, in her hands. "Give me one more chance. I can still carry these bags for you. I don't want to die!"

"Then you should have thought of that before wasting my time, wench," the noble says. "Now stand still. I will make your death as swift as possible."

Without thinking, Daren rushes to Ella's aid, and he tries to pull her away from the earl.

"Come, Ella," Daren says, as he tries to pull her by the arm. "I'm taking you away from this monster."

"No!" Ella shouts, as she panics, and jumps back from Daren. "I can't! I can't run away from him. I am his property."

She then turns back to face the earl of Ollendor.

"Sir, please, I promise you that—"

Ella does not get to finish her sentence, because the noble immediately slits her throat wide open with a single slash of his dagger.

"No!" Daren shouts, in desperation, as he immediately grabs Ella in his arms, and he attempts to cast a healing spell on her.

Unfortunately, by the time his spell began to take effect, Ella had lost way too much blood, and she slowly died in his arms, while he was still trying to heal her.

"Pfft…" the noble says, as he looks at Daren in disgust. "How pathetic."

"No, this wasn't supposed to happen!" Daren shouts, completely ignoring the earl, as he is still trying to heal the dead Ella that he is holding in his arms. "It wasn't supposed to be like this. She was supposed to keep living, happily, at Rose's house. She deserved to be happy! Please… If anyone's listening. Give me another chance. I promise I won't fail her again, next time.

Please…"

He then starts to sob, quietly, as he continues to hold Ella's corpse tightly in his arms. After a few seconds of silence, except for Daren's slow sobs, a bright white light suddenly envelops the area, and then, a few moments later, we find ourselves in the same area again, but with Ella still alive, and with Daren back where he was when he first got sent back in time.

"Ahahahahaha!" Arraka laughs. "Did you see that? Did you see how well-timed that was? Even if it were all staged, it couldn't have turned out as good as this!"

"Just what is it, exactly, that you are finding so funny?" I say.

"You mean, aside from all the suffering?" Arraka says. "Well, it's the fact that the oaf is now going to believe that he was actually given another chance, like he asked. But in reality, neither the ritual, nor the God of Time could give less of a damn about whether he saves the slave or not."

"So you're saying that's not what his trial is about, then?" I say.

"Of course it isn't!" Arraka says. "What kind of a stupid question is that? Didn't you go through a trial yourself only a short while ago? You should already know what the healer needs to do to pass this test."

While Arraka and I were talking, Eiden was just discovering for a second time that Daren had been sent to the past, by the God of Time, and he was now getting ready to mock him once again.

"I must make sure to not interfere," I hear Eiden say. "I would not want you to fail your trial on my account!"

"No, you don't understand!" Daren says, with obvious desperation in his voice. "I need you to interfere! I can't fail her again! I need the power that only you can give. The power to attack the noble!"

"Oh?" Eiden asks, surprised. "I honestly wouldn't

have expected you to ask me for help so directly. But even so, there is no use in undergoing a trial if you are not going to solve your problems by yourself. I'm afraid that I'll have to decline your request, regardless of what I may have done in your original timeline."

"Damn you!" Daren says. "Do you want me to beg? Is that what you want?"

"No, actually I was—" Eiden starts to say, but he interrupts himself when he sees Daren drop to his hands and knees in front of him, with his head bowed down.

"Then I will beg!" Daren says. "I will beg on my hands and knees. Even though I hate you with all of my heart. Even though I consider you to be one of the most evil and irredeemable people I've ever met. But right now, you are my only hope to save this girl from her terrible fate, and the only thing I can do is to beg for your help. So please… I'm begging you… Give me the power to save this girl, and I will do anything you ask of me… No matter how humiliating it may be…"

While Daren was talking, I could see Eiden slowly opening his eyes, for a few seconds, with an expression of both shock and amazement on his face. Then, when Daren finished his speech, Eiden smiled, slightly, with his eyes closed.

"You will do anything I ask, you say?" Eiden says. "Then I have only one request."

He pauses, for a second, as he gets a much more serious expression on his face.

"Prove me wrong…" Eiden continues.

The stillwater then raises his hands, and a powerful wind starts spinning around him for a few seconds.

"Prove you wrong?" Daren asks, confused, as Eiden lowers his arms, and the wind around him stops. "What do you mean by—"

"You have the power, healer," Eiden says. "Now go, go! Before it's too late!"

"Right…" Daren says, as he gets up from the ground, and rushes towards the noble.

"How many second chances are you going to ask me for, foolish girl?" I heard the earl of Ollendor say, with his knife in his hand, while Daren and Eiden were still having their conversation. "Do you not realize that my mercy isn't without limits? I've had enough of your excuses. This time I will kill you for good. Don't you dare move from that spot!"

"I won't let you kill her, you bastard!" Daren shouts, as he rushes towards the noble, with his sword at the ready.

"What the hell?" the earl says, just as he was about to slit Ella's throat, and he turns to look towards Daren.

The noble barely has the time to turn around, because Daren's blade beheads him in an instant, and the earl of Ollendor's headless corpse soon falls to the ground, next to its severed head.

"I did it…" I can hear Daren thinking. "I saved her… This time, I didn't hesitate. I finally managed to make things right."

All of a sudden, the now all-too-familiar white light fills the area around us all, in order to once again send Daren back to the beginning of the ritual.

"No, no, no!" Daren shouts, as the light envelops him, but nobody is listening to him, and after a few seconds, he finds himself right back where he started, with the noble still alive and kicking.

"Aha- Ahahahaha!" Arraka laughs. "The idiot actually thought he completed the trial! Can you believe that? And the irony is that all he needed to do for his trial to be complete was to just calm the hell down, and to shut his mouth. That way, Eiden wouldn't have seen any unusual changes in his aura, and he wouldn't have been able to guess that the God of Time sent him back in time. But at this rate, it's going to take him a million years to figure it out! Oh man, this guy is such a good source of comedy!"

"Is his ritual the same as mine, then?" I ask her. "He just needs to recreate the same events that happened the very first time?"

"Yes, most of your rituals were made in the same way," Arraka says. "As long as the past version of you is the one that saves the slave, using Eiden's power, he should be fine. Well, I'm sure he'll figure it out eventually. Come on, let's go visit some of the other rituals."

"What happened?" I hear Daren's thoughts in the background. "What did I do wrong? What does this ritual want from me?!"

"And, our next destination is the Beacon of Hope!" Arraka says. "Hold on, tight! It's going to be a bumpy ride. Nah, I'm just kidding. We're already here."

As I look around me, I see that our environment has changed completely, in a matter of seconds, and we are now situated in the middle of a very dark underground corridor, with only a few dimly lit torches, to provide us with any light. Almost immediately after we arrive in this place, we can hear the scream of a young boy, echoing somewhere in the distance, and then we hear a little girl, screaming in pain as well, although she appears to be somewhere closer than the boy. Not long afterwards, we start to hear the terrified screams of a few other children, as well. Some of them are begging for mercy, some of them are trying to suppress their screams, and others are calling in vain for their parents to save them.

I've heard the stories about this place from both Kate and Leila, but I never would have imagined it to be as bad as this. Just standing here and listening to all these screams is giving me goose bumps all over my body. I can't even begin to imagine what it would be like to experience what those children are going through right now.

"Wow, these lessathi sure weren't messing around, huh?" Arraka says. "It's like a whole symphony of horrified screams down here. Anyway, this isn't exactly where I wanted to bring you. I'm just gonna need to take a quick look and see what your friend Kate has been doing since the beginning of this ritual, so I can spare you the boring details, and get right to the good stuff. I'll just leave you to enjoy these melodious sounds of pure agony, while I do my thing, okay?"

"Melodious sounds of— These are children that are screaming, here!" I shout at her. "What the hell is wrong with you?!"

"To be perfectly honest, I couldn't care less about the screaming children," Arraka says. "It's the psychological kind of torture that I usually tend to find amusing, not the physical one. That's why the real entertaining part for me is to see *your* reactions to all of this. Why else did you think I went through the trouble of bringing you with me to these rituals, if not for my own entertainment?"

"Frankly, I thought you were just bored, and decided to bring me along on a whim," I say.

"Nah," Arraka says. "That's Eiden's shtick, not mine. I know it may not seem like it, most of the time, but I rarely do things without a reason. For example, I specifically chose this moment in time as our initial destination, because I knew they were going to be doing experiments at this hour, and there would be a lot of screaming going on. It just would have felt like a waste if I kept you waiting in a silent, empty hallway, you know?"

"Ugh…" I say. "Just shut up and get us out of here, already."

"Easier said than done," Arraka says. "I may be a

genius when it comes to magic, but you still can't expect me to comb through all of these events that have been happening here in a matter of seconds. It's not like I get to connect myself to the Magium like this on a daily basis."

"You keep casually talking to me about the Magium, but you haven't even told me what it is, yet!" I say.

"That's the joke, Barry-boy," Arraka says. "I keep doing it because I know it frustrates you. It's a good way to keep myself from dying of boredom, while I go through the tedious process of scanning these memories."

"Can you at least tell me how you are able to switch between past and future with so much ease?" I ask her. "And how is it that you can also access people's memories, and transport us into them as if they were a part of our reality?"

"When you're linked directly to the Magium in the way we are now," Arraka says, "terms like 'past', 'future', 'memories', and 'reality' become irrelevant. In here, everything is both real and imaginary at the same time. Allow me to demonstrate!"

A giant, red serpent, with two wings, and four small claws suddenly appears in front of me, and it immediately flies towards me, with a menacing look in its eyes, while its whole body is surrounded by flames. I panic a little, and I jump back, trying to pull my dagger out, but the monster scratches my right leg with one of its claws, and then it disappears just as quickly as it made its appearance.

"Arraka, what did you do?" Flower asks, shocked, as Illuna approaches me, in order to heal me.

"Relax!" Arraka says. "Neither of us can die in here. That scratch right now didn't hurt, did it?"

"Now that you mention it, I suppose it didn't," I say, as Illuna suddenly stops healing my wound, realizing that I was never in any real danger.

"That's because these aren't our real bodies," Arraka says. "They're just our projections. Our real bodies are still right where we left them, stuck in one of those weird trances with the glowy eyes. What I was trying to show you was that I can do whatever I want, while we're in here. It's like my own playground. Obviously, I can't interfere with what your friends are doing, since we don't really exist in their worlds, but as far as spectating goes, my options are unlimited."

"So, you're saying that my friends can't die either?" I say. "They're just in an imaginary world, right now?"

"No, this only applies to us, because we are projections, like I said," Arraka tells me. "The worlds that your friends have been transported into are very much real. It's just that they're not *our* world. They are parallel worlds, similar to ours, in which the future never actually happened. Obviously, none of the changes that they make in those worlds will affect our world in the slightest, but they have no way of knowing that. Didn't you find it strange that you managed to pass your own ritual even if it should normally have been impossible for you to perfectly reproduce the exact actions you took fifteen years ago, down to the last detail? That's because it wasn't the laws of time preventing you from doing what you wanted. It was just Selkram, messing with your head."

"The God of Time…" I say, as I am suddenly filled with uncontrollable hatred, just by uttering his name. "Is he watching us, right now?"

"No," Arraka says. "He can't just stay materialized in our world for as long as he wants. That would waste too much energy. That's why he usually only comes in at the very beginning, and at the end, unless it is absolutely necessary for him to personally intervene in the middle of a ritual. Otherwise, he'll mostly just stay in the magical plane, and wait patiently for the rituals to gather energy for him."

"But how do these rituals help him?" I say. "What is it about these trials that give him so much power?"

"He's gathering energy from your negative emotions," Arraka says. "Hatred, anger, fear, despair… that kind of stuff. Those are the types of emotions that can be exploited in the most efficient way, through these methods. But he can't really do any of that without linking himself directly to the Magium, during the time weaver prophecies, so he needs to squeeze as much as he can out of you guys, while he still has the chance. That's why these trials are designed the way they are. To make sure that they trigger as many strong negative emotions out of you as they can."

"I'm not sure if I like where this is going," I say. "Just what kind of messed up trial is this guy trying to put Kate through, if he needed to send her all the way back to her years at the Beacon?"

"We will see in a few seconds," Arraka says. "I never actually looked at this ritual before I came here with you, so we'll both be experiencing this for the first time, together. I'm sure it will be fun. Let us begin!"

We both disappear from the corridor with all the screaming, and we reappear in a dark, empty room where an eleven year old version of Kate seems to be talking with what I'm assuming is a twelve year old version of her friend, Diane. Kate is easy to recognize, because she just looks like a smaller version of her usual self, but Diane has long, blond hair, and a much more frail physique than she had, in her adult form, so it's a bit more difficult for me to tell if it's really her or not. They are both dressed in rags. The room we are in resembles my old holding cell from the arena, with one bed made out of stone, and a small window on top, so I'm guessing that they are most likely in Diane's room, and Kate decided to pay her a visit, in order to tell her something that she knows from the future.

"I didn't manage to make her thoughts audible, so we're going to have to work with what we have," Arraka tells me. "Let's see where this goes."

"I'm telling you, it's not the test of loyalty!" Kate tells Diane, while whispering, in order to make sure that the guards outside don't hear them. "I know that it's hard to believe, but I've come from the future, and I know that the lessathi caretaker who is trying to help us escape will become Leila's adoptive father later on. I know that he can be trusted!"

"Leila?..." Diane whispers back. "You mean the lessathi girl who was thrown in here with us two years ago? Listen, even if that caretaker is really trying to help us escape, you are still forgetting one thing."

Diane then points towards her neck, which has a collar around it, similar to the ones that the golden fox used against us.

"As long as Jason and I are still wearing these collars, we won't be able to get out of here," Diane says. "If we get too far away from this place, the collars will electrocute us, and that will be the end of our escape. But you don't have a collar! You're one of the rejects. If you really trust this man, then you could—"

"No!" Kate says, as she almost shouts by mistake. "You always do that! You always try to put your friends' needs before your own. I'm not going to let you do that now! We can all escape together. You, me, Leila, your brother—"

"I'm not sure how much Jason would agree with this plan," Diane says. "You know how he is. He never trusts anyone. Especially if they're lessathi. He was like this even before we knew about the test of loyalty. He barely even exchanges any words with the high-ranked lessathi that we are sent to escort on a regular basis. The only one that he seems to get along with is that woman… Meridith. Their second in command. I don't know what he sees in her. He always tells me how she's different from the other high-ranked lessathi, but for me, they're all the same. They all know what's happening here. They're not blind. They're all to blame."

"Diane, listen to me!" Kate says. "That caretaker is very skilled at tinkering with magical devices. I'm sure that he could find a way to free you of your collars. I will talk to him about this with the first opportunity, but you need to find a way to convince your brother to come with us. Can you do that?"

"You're asking a lot of me, Kate…" Diane says. "If I tell Jason your story about how you came from the future, he'll think I'm insane. I'm not even sure how much I believe what you're saying. I mean… are you sure that it couldn't have been a hallucination of some sort? They've been feeding us really poorly, lately, and—"

"No!" Kate says. "It's real! In a year from now, they're going to shut down the Beacon, due to lack of funds, and then they're going to throw all of us rejects in the jungle to fend for ourselves. I wasn't able to save even one of them… I can't let that happen again! I need to find a way to convince everyone. Just promise me that you'll try to talk to your brother. You don't need to tell him that I'm from the future. Just try to find a way to get through to him. Somehow…"

"I'll… try…" Diane says, hesitantly.

"Thank you," Kate says. "I will come to talk to you again, after speaking with the caretaker about the collars. I'm sure we'll be able to work something out. See you soon!"

"Alright," Arraka says, as Kate walks out of the room. "I took a quick look through the following events, and I think it should be safe to skip the next part. I'll just go ahead and—"

"Wait," I say. "What's the next part about?"

"Oh," Arraka says, "it's just some uninteresting stuff about her talking with the caretaker, and him confirming that it's possible to take off the collars. It's a waste of time."

"Could you show me Diane's discussion with her brother, instead, then?" I say.

"I suppose…" Arraka says. "I'm not exactly sure how relevant it's going to be, but at least it shouldn't be a complete waste of our time."

Instead of the scenery changing, this time, we remain in the same room, but Diane is no longer standing where she was before, and it seems that she has a new visitor. This person, who is currently talking with Diane, is a boy in his late teens, with short, blond hair, which I assume is her brother, Jason. His overall physique is not very impressive, but the look in his eyes is much more mature than one would expect from a boy of his age. He looks like the sort of guy who is very confident in his abilities and who knows exactly what he wants. Just like his sister, he is also wearing a collar around his neck, and he is dressed in rags.

"Diane," Jason says, "I've told you many times before that you should take everything Kate tells you with a grain of salt. I know that she is your best friend, but that girl is way too trusting for her own good. When you put so much trust into people, it hurts that much more when you inevitably get betrayed. Mark my words, one day, she will get betrayed so badly, that she will never want to trust anyone ever again, and when that happens, you won't be able to tell me that I didn't warn you…"

"So, you're saying, what… that she should be more like you?" Diane says. "Ever since I've known you, you've never trusted anyone other than yourself. How is that any better?"

"Hey, don't say things like that…" Jason says. "You know that I've always trusted you. Even if the whole world betrays us, you and I will still continue to stay true to each other, until the very end. That's the promise we made, right before we were first assigned as elite bodyguards to the lessathi, three years ago. You still remember that promise, right?"

"Of course I do!" Diane says. "But do *you* still remember it? I've been telling you for years that Meridith is bad news, and that you should keep your distance from her, but you never listen! Why is it that you are so willing to put your trust in her, when you've never trusted anyone in your life?"

"I never said I trust her!" Jason says. "She's just… a means to an end. That's all there is to it. And besides, she's not like the other lessathi. She has the potential to change things for the better. All she needs is a little push in the right direction. There are already many lessathi who support her. I'd even go as far as saying that there are more who currently support her, than the ones who support the great leader, Heksol. It's not by coincidence, that she managed to become second in command. When she first started off, she was only a lowly secretary to Heksol, but she's been climbing her way up the ranks for twenty years, and she's made many friends during that time. I'm telling you, there will be a great change coming soon, in the lessathi world, and I want to be right at the heart of it, when it happens!"

"You know I don't like it when you talk like this…" Diane says. "I thought that our goal was to escape this place. Why would we care about the lessathi world, and how they change for the better? Let them rot, for all I care! I only want to be free of this nightmare, so we can live the rest of our lives in peace together. All three of us."

"And we will!" Jason says. "What I'm doing is for the sake of all of us. Kate included. You'll understand when you're older."

"You always say this!" Diane says. "What about Kate's plan, regarding the lessathi caretaker? Are you at least going to consider it?"

"I'll... think about it," Jason says. "Anyway, I need to get going. If I stay too much here, the guards will start to think that we're plotting something. Take care!"

"Well that was, uh... interesting," Arraka says. "Anyway, let's get back to the stuff that's actually somewhat relevant to this ritual."

As soon as Arraka stops talking, we get transported into a different room, where Kate is currently talking with a girl that has light brown hair, and who appears to be around fifteen years of age. Just like Kate and Diane, she is dressed in some old, tattered clothes, but her hair is less messy, and she seems to be taking much more care of her physical appearance than the other two girls. She also has a pleasant smile, and a charismatic way of talking, which makes me think that she is the type who easily gets along with other people.

"Please," Kate says. "You are the only one who can help me. The other orphans never listen to me, but I'm sure they'll listen to you! You've always had a way with words, and everyone trusts your judgment. You're almost like a leader, of sorts."

"You flatter me, Kate!" the girl says. "But this isn't an easy task you are asking of me. Do you not remember what happened the last time when we decided to trust one of the caretakers? The lessathi chose to kill only one of us, back then, in order to set an example, but that could have been any one of us. They had no reason to choose Benjamin, out of all of us. He didn't stand out in any way. He didn't even say a word. But they simply kept beating him and beating him in front of us, and they just wouldn't stop. Even after he was dead, they still wouldn't stop. If we try to escape again, and they catch us, I don't think that they will settle for killing only one person, anymore. This time, they're going to kill all of us, and they're not going to show us any mercy…"

"They're going to try to kill us anyway!" Kate says. "We're both rejects. When they'll finally be done experimenting on us, they'll throw us in a jungle, and they'll leave us for dead."

"We can't stay rejects forever!" the girl says, although I can clearly see that she is lying to herself. "Maybe one day we'll be like your friend, Diane, and her brother, and we'll get to escort important lessathi around, instead of being experimented on, over and over. If we haven't died from the experiments for such a long time, then there has to still be a chance!"

"It's not going to happen, Olivia," Kate says. "We can't just keep waiting for things to get better. We need to take matters into our own hands. Please, trust me on this! Following the caretaker's plan is our only true chance of escaping this hellhole. He's not going to betray us like the one before. We can still make it out of here alive, but I need your help!"

Olivia starts to calm down, after she hears what Kate had to say, and all of a sudden, she gets a very determined look in her eyes.

"I understand, Kate," Olivia says. "You know that I've always been your friend. If you are willing to put so much trust into this man, then I will believe in you, and your judgment. I will try to convince as many people as I can, but I can't promise you anything. I'll tell you later how things went."

"Thank you so much!" Kate says, with a relieved look on her face. "I will also speak to Diane and tell her what you said. We'll talk more when you have something new to tell me. See you later!"

"Goodbye!" Olivia says, as she regains her pleasant smile from before, and then Kate goes to exit her room.

"Okay, this next part's going to be really good," Arraka says. "Get ready!"

The environment around us changes yet again, but this time, we find ourselves in a very large underground hallway, where about a hundred or so orphans are currently all lined up, and standing straight, while looking at a few men dressed in dark blue robes, in front of them. I'm assuming that the men in blue robes are the lessathi that run the place, but what's strange is that all of them are standing up, except for one, who is currently on his knees, with his hood covering his face, and his head bowed down.

The orphans are all dressed in the same type of gray rags, and most of them have very tired looks on their faces, as if this place has sucked the life right out of them. They also appear to be very malnourished, and some of them have bruises all over their bodies. The ages of the orphans seem to be no higher than nineteen, and no lower than four, but most of them are aged between six and fifteen years old. The only orphans who are not lined up with the others are Diane and her brother. They are instead standing near the lessathi, likely due to their bodyguard status.

The lessathi are currently talking among themselves, but the orphans are all dead silent, and awaiting impatiently for the meeting to begin. From the looks of things, it seems that the lessathi are still waiting for one or two more of their colleagues to arrive, before announcing to everyone the reason why they called them here.

"Really?..." I tell Arraka, after we wait for about ten more seconds. "You couldn't have brought us any closer in time to the beginning of the meeting? How much longer are we supposed to wait, here?"

"Stop complaining," Arraka says. "I brought us here a bit earlier, because there is something that I'm trying to test. There is this theory I've had for a while about the lessathi and the reason why they are so good at making magical devices, and I want to see if it's true or not. The main gist of it is that I think they have some sort of innate understanding of the Magium's true nature, which gives them the ability to tamper with an object's aura in a more precise fashion than most other tinkerers. But it's more than simply knowing what the Magium's nature is. Fyron knows its nature too, and he has a way to access it, but that staff of his cannot compare to the magical artifacts that the lessathi are able to invent. It's almost as if they've developed some sort of natural affinity to the Magium, over the years, which is subtle enough that I can't detect it when I study their auras. If that is really the case, then it might also explain why they have no magic in their auras whatsoever. If their auras resonate so strongly with the Magium, then their subconscious must be getting constantly bombarded with information, which would make it impossible for them to maintain any sort of connection to the magical plane."

"Well, at this moment, you are the one bombarding *me* with too much information!" I say. "What do you mean the lessathi have an aura that resonates strongly with the Magium? Am I not a lessathi too? Or a half-lessathi, whatever. Are you trying to tell me that I already had the Magium with me all along? Because it sure as hell doesn't feel like it to me!"

"Of course not," Arraka says. "What kind of logic is that? Wasn't the exact wording of the tournament organizers that they would give you 'access' to the Magium if you win? That has nothing to do with simply having an affinity towards it. Leaving aside the fact that you are probably getting far less information from the Magium than a regular lessathi, due to being half human, most of that information is completely useless to you, because you have no way to process it. On the other hand, if you have a way to access the Magium directly, from the earthen plane, then that natural affinity of yours will suddenly become a lot more useful. The lessathi on this continent already *have* direct access to the Magium. That's why an affinity to it would be helpful for them. But again, this is all just a theory, until I make my test."

"Why would the lessathi have direct access to the Magium?" I say.

"They are allied with the kings of Varathia, remember?" Arraka says. "They even helped with the organization of this tournament. If the kings have access to the Magium, then so do they."

"Oh, right, I forgot," I say. "So… how do you think the lessathi might have gotten their affinity to the Magium?"

"I have no idea," Arraka says. "One thing I remember reading in the writings of the lessathi of old was that their race has had somewhat of an unhealthy obsession with the Magium for many thousands of years, so maybe that could have been part of the reason. But if you're asking me exactly how it happened, then your guess is as good as mine."

"I see…" I say.

I then stay silent for about twenty more seconds, waiting for Arraka to do her thing, but it doesn't really look like she's making much progress.

"Are you still doing that test of yours?" I say. "What is it that you're trying to test for, exactly?"

"I'm trying to see if any of the lessathi over there are able to sense our presence," Arraka says. "I've been trying to reach them through a myriad of magical frequencies for the past few minutes, but I haven't had any luck just yet. If my theory is correct, then the fact that we are linked to the Magium right now should make it possible for them to detect us, even if we don't technically exist in their own world. Maybe I'm going about this in the wrong way, though. Let me try something else."

All of a sudden, three clowns appear out of nowhere, right between the lessathi and the row of orphans, and they start to dance in place, imitating the movement of gorillas, with big grins on their faces.

"There we go," Arraka says. "This should liven up the place a bit. But I still feel like there's something missing. Hey, Flower, why don't you go dance with those clowns for a bit? You're already dressed for the part, so all you need to do is mimic their movements."

"I'm not wearing clown clothes!" Flower shouts, furiously. "How many times do I need to explain this to you? These are acrobat clothes! They're the same type of clothes as what I used to wear back in Olmnar, when I was performing as a trapeze artist at the circus!"

"Uh-huh," Arraka says. "Sure they are. Now be a good girl and go dance with your brethren over there, so we can—"

"Did you sense that?..." one of the lessathi asks one of his colleagues.

"Sense what?" asks the other lessathi.

"There was some sort of... strange presence coming from right in front of us, just now..." the first lessathi says. "It felt like it wasn't even part of this world. As if it didn't even exist! Do you understand what I mean?"

"Well, if doesn't exist, then maybe we shouldn't be worrying about it, don't you think?" the other lessathi says. "Here's an idea. How about you stop bothering me with nonsense, and wait for the others in silence, like everybody else."

"Aha!" Arraka says, as she makes the clowns disappear. "I knew it! I knew that these bastards were resonating with the Magium somehow. But then again, if the lessathi have such a good affinity with the Magium, then how is it that Eiden and the fox were the ones who first learned how to create food out of nothing, and not them? Wasn't that knowledge somehow taken from the Magium as well? Hmm…"

"You do realize," I say, "that if you're going to keep giving me so much information about the Magium, I will eventually figure out what it is, right?"

"So what?…" Arraka says. "Do I look like I care? This is all a game to me. I couldn't care less if you find out the true nature of the Magium. I've only been hiding it from you because I find your reactions to be amusing. It's not like I was forbidden to talk about this by the Magium itself, like Flower and Illuna."

"What did you just say?…" I ask her, shocked.

"Arraka, don't say another word," Illuna says, with a mixture of both anger and fear in her eyes. "I'm warning you!"

"Warning me?" Arraka says. "Warning *me*? Has our little trip to this parallel universe managed to completely fry your brain? Do you forget who you are talking to? I am Arraka! Even the gods live in fear of me! Do you seriously think that I am going to let myself get intimidated by the likes of the Magium? The Magium is nothing but a tool! A tool that I can freely manipulate, without even breaking a sweat! Why would I have anything to fear? Do you think I'm like you? Well, Barry, you're in luck! Today, you will finally find out what the Magium is! You see, it is all pretty simple, once you think about it. If you take into account everything that I've told you about the world we are in now, and if you also remember everything you already knew, then the answer that is staring you right in the face is that the Magium is in fact—"

Right before Arraka got to finish her sentence, I felt a sensation that was so terrifying and so hard to put into words, that any threat I might have felt to my life from the likes of Arraka and the God of Time simply paled in comparison to what I felt just now. It was no longer a question of fearing for my life. I was fearing for my very existence. I felt the whole world flicker around me, for a fraction of a second, as if everything froze in time and lost all of its color. Then, within the same fraction of a second, it all simply vanished from right before my eyes, and all I could see now was emptiness. An emptiness that stretched for miles and miles, even though it was made of nothing.

What felt like a moment, also felt like an eternity at the same time, and during that eternity which lasted for less than a second, I got to experience the sheer dread of complete non-existence. Not only had my life been wiped away, but the very notion of me had been completely erased from the tapestry of the universe. For that fraction of a second, I was nothing, and yet, I was still there, somewhere, trapped for an eternity in a complete void, while trying in vain to make sense of the utter absurdity of my situation.

Once I find myself back in my semi-transparent body and in a world full of color, I suddenly realize that I am completely drenched in cold sweat, and that I can feel my heart beating in my chest like a very loud drum. Flower also seems to be frozen in shock, as she simply stares straight ahead of her, without saying a word.

"You arrogant *fool*!" Illuna shouts, all of a sudden, as she grabs Arraka's amulet in her hand, to bring it close to her face, while her eyes are shining with a bright blue color. "Do you realize what you've done?!"

This must be the first time I've seen Illuna so furious ever since Arraka told us about the sacred woods massacre, in the ogre stronghold. As Arraka stays completely silent, the world flickers around us once again, and I can feel myself fading in and out of existence several times in a row, before I get returned to the underground hallway, sweating harder than ever.

"Are you going to just stay silent until we get erased from existence?!" Illuna shouts at Arraka again.

"Shut up!" Arraka says, with a slight tremble of fear in her voice. "I'm trying to fix this, but I can't do it if you keep distracting me. Just… give me a minute!"

As we wait for Arraka to finish what she is doing, the world turns black and white one more time, but now it is flickering much more rapidly than before, and it feels like this time, my consciousness is going to get trapped into the void for good. Just when I am about to give up all hope, I suddenly get pulled back in my body, and the world around us comes back to normal, while both Flower and I are breathing very rapidly, and looking at each other, as we're trying to make at least some sense of our situation.

"Okay…" Arraka says, with a bit of panic still left in her voice. "This should be enough for now… We shouldn't be getting any more interference."

"What do you mean this should be enough for now?" Illuna says. "Did you or did you not solve the problem?"

"Yes!" Arraka says. "I think… I don't know! I've never done anything like this before. I diverted the Magium's attention away from us, by using some tricks that I learned from the God of Fate. I heard that he had to do a similar thing in the heat of the moment, when they tampered with the Magium to banish me from their realm. And given that they all managed to escape without being erased from existence, then so should we!"

"You're saying that you used an illusion to create a distraction?…" I say.

"Well, if you really want to make a comparison, then it was more like a ridiculously complicated suggestion spell," Arraka says. "Technically, it's still searching for us, but in a completely different world. As long as I manage to keep my idiot mouth shut this time around, it shouldn't be able to find us again."

"So you admit that you were an idiot, then?" Illuna says.

"Yes!" Arraka shouts. "Yes, I admit it! Are you happy now? I was an idiot to try and challenge the Magium in its own territory. All of my thousands of years of knowledge are nearly useless, when faced with this world of contradictions and absurdities. Now let's calm ourselves down, and finish doing what we originally came here to do. I no longer want to spend any more time in here than is absolutely necessary."

"Then how about bringing us to the actual start of the lessathi meeting?" I say. "We've been wasting enough time here as it is."

"Yes, I was just about to do that," Arraka says.

She then accelerates the time, until the last of the lessathi finally make their way into the hallway, to join their colleagues. Once everyone is assembled, the meeting finally begins.

"You may all be wondering why we've called you here…" says a lessathi with gray hair and a long gray beard, who appears to be in his late fifties. "I will try to keep this brief. It has been brought to our attention that a few of you have been approached by a certain individual, offering to help you escape from our facility. As you all know, the rules state that if someone were to make such an offer, you would immediately be obligated to notify us about it. Unfortunately, not only has this rule not been followed properly, but there have also been a few cases where some children agreed to escape. Needless to say, we are very disappointed. Therefore, this meeting has been called for two main reasons."

The lessathi speaking now moves towards the hooded lessathi who is on his knees, and he stops right behind him.

"The first reason is to punish the traitor who tried to help you escape," the bearded lessathi says.

He then grabs the head of the kneeling lessathi, with both hands, and he twists it to the side, breaking his neck in one motion, and killing him on the spot. As Kate sees the lifeless body of the lessathi caretaker drop to the ground, she almost lets out a gasp, but she quickly covers her mouth, to stifle the sound. Somewhere further away, towards the middle of the line of orphans, an eight year old version of Leila, with the same silver hair, is looking at the whole scene in front of her eyes, frozen in fear.

"The second reason," the bearded lessathi continues, "is to teach a lesson to all those who agreed to join this traitor in his escape plan. We already know who you are, but we will give you one last chance to prove that you are not a completely lost cause, by allowing you to turn yourselves in. Those who know that they're guilty of having accepted the traitor's offer are required to come here to our side, immediately. If you do as we ask, then your punishment will be less severe. If you try to fool us, however, then the penalty will be much, much worse..."

After a few seconds of waiting, a six year old boy and a ten year old girl step slowly away from the line of orphans, and they go to join the lessathi in front of them. The girl has a very scared look on her face, and the boy is on the verge of breaking down into tears.

"You have made a wise decision to come here," the bearded lessathi says, as he puts his hands on both their shoulders. "Taking responsibility for your mistakes is an important step forward, towards your re-education. However, you are not the only ones who were ready to leave this place, together with the traitor. I am still waiting for them to turn themselves in. I assure you that it would not be in your best interest to keep me waiting for much longer…"

As the whole room stays silent, I can see that Kate's whole body is now shivering uncontrollably from fear, while she is hugging herself, with her arms, in a futile attempt to stop herself from trembling. After waiting for about ten more seconds, the lessathi shakes his head in disapproval.

"I was hoping that it would not come to this…" the lessathi says. "Very well, then. If you insist on disobeying us even now, then I have no choice but to call your names myself. First of all, I would like to introduce to you the person who has played the most crucial role in allowing us to find all of the culprits. Olivia, will you please step forward?"

"Yes, sir," Olivia says, in a very timid voice, as she joins the lessathi, and then turns to face the other orphans.

When she sees her friend, Olivia, joining her mortal enemies, Kate is momentarily frozen in shock, and immediately afterwards, her previous trembling gets a lot more violent.

"Olivia has been secretly serving as our informant for quite a while," the bearded lessathi says. "However, she hasn't really produced many notable results until now. We've told her in the past that if she ever managed to make a significant contribution to our cause, then we would consider giving her a more important role in our organization, and with the help she's provided to us today, she might just obtain that position. In short, your friend, Olivia, came to us today to warn us about the traitor, and also to warn us that there might be others, willing to join him. She then agreed to carry a transceiver with her, and to keep it open, so that we could hear her talking to the traitor, and to all of the children that said they wanted to join in on the escape plan. Since we already have all the proof we need, we will expect you to come quietly to the front, without posing any resistance, as soon as your names are called."

He then coughs loudly before he continues.

"There are four names on our list," the lessathi says. "William, Hannah, Lillian and Matthew. Please don't waste any more of our time by pretending that you didn't hear us call you. I think we all know what happens to those who openly try to disobey us…"

The four orphans whose names were called are now all stepping forward, with their eyes looking at the ground. When they stop, in front of the lessathi, we see that they are all shaking in fear, but they are not saying a word.

"Good," the lessathi says. "Starting tomorrow, you will all be sent to room fifty-one, in order to commence your re-education process. Is that clear?"

"No, please not fifty-one!" shouts a thirteen year old boy who is one of the four orphans that were called by the lessathi. "Anything but that! Have mercy, I beg you!"

"Don't make the mistake of assuming that you have any choice in the matter," the bearded lessathi says. "Every single complaint that you make from now on will only add more time to the penalty for all four of you. Now tell me, do you have any more complaints?"

"No, sir…" the boy says, in a voice that sounded like he was one step away from crying.

"Splendid," the lessathi says. "Now, then, Olivia, I would like to ask you one final question. Were there any other orphans who might have wanted to conspire with the traitor? Perhaps some of the children who you might have talked to before you came to us, to obtain the transceiver?"

When she is asked the question, Olivia takes a very short glance towards Kate, out of instinct, but then she goes back to looking right in front of her.

"No, sir…" Olivia says. "There was no one else."

"Very well," the lessathi says. "Rest assured, you will be rewarded for your efforts. You may be a reject, but even for someone like you, there is a place in our organization, as long as you keep proving yourself useful."

"Yes…" Olivia says, in a very meek tone of voice. "That is all I've ever wanted. To be useful…"

"Let us take these traitors to a temporary holding cell, until we make all the necessary arrangements," the lessathi says, as he now addresses his colleagues. "Tomorrow, we will begin their re-education process."

"No!" Kate shouts loudly, all of a sudden. "You can't take them with you! They did nothing wrong!"

As I take a look at Kate, I see that she has finally managed to stop her trembling, and she now has a much more determined look on her face. Every single person in the room is now staring at Kate, as the bearded lessathi slowly approaches her.

"What did you just say?…" the bearded lessathi says, calmly, as soon as he reaches her.

"I said they did nothing wrong!" Kate says, with a somewhat shakier voice. "All they wanted was to escape this hellhole of a place. How can you blame them for wanting that?"

"Strange…" the lessathi says. "I don't remember you ever being brave enough to stand up to us before. In fact, I remember you as being both very timid, and obedient. Your aura seems different from how I remembered it as well. I wonder what could have happened, to cause such a great change in your personality… Perhaps we should try to dissect you and find out. You are a reject after all. It's not like your death would be much of a loss to us."

"No, leave her alone!" Diane shouts, from the other side of the room, as a tear flows from her eye. "Don't you dare touch her!"

"What is this supposed to be?..." the bearded lessathi says, as he now turns towards Diane. "Some sort of rebellion? Do you think you're going to receive special treatment, just because you're one of our elite bodyguards? Or did you forget that you can't cast any magic with that collar around your neck, unless we specifically allow you to do it?"

He then goes closer to Diane, and he grabs her by the hair, in order to make sure that she looks straight into his eyes.

"Do you think that you are beyond our reach, just because you routinely escort our great leaders?" the lessathi says. "Do you think you no longer have to worry about our punishments? Maybe we should send you to room fifty-one for re-education as well. I'm sure the leaders would not mind having a more obedient servant..."

"What is the meaning of this?!" we hear a woman shout, as she is just now entering our hallway, and walking fast towards the bearded lessathi.

The lessathi woman who shouted appears to be in her late thirties, with long brown hair and green eyes, and she is wearing a dark blue robe, just like every other lessathi in the room. She is being escorted by two lessathi men, who are both carrying weapons.

"Lady Meridith..." the bearded lessathi says, as he immediately releases Diane. "I thought that you and our lord, Heksol, had already finished your inspection of the Beacon..."

"Lord Heksol left early this morning," Meridith says. "But I still had some unfinished business here, so I chose to remain for a while longer. What were you doing just now, to my loyal bodyguard?"

"Lady Meridith!" Diane says, in a shaky voice. "They were trying to kill her. They were trying to kill Kate! They said they wanted to dissect her, to find out why she stood up to them."

"Kate?..." Meridith says. "You mean your best friend from the Beacon that you once told me about?"

"Allow me to explain, Lady Meridith!" the bearded lessathi says.

He then points towards Kate, with pure hatred in his eyes.

"This... reject, was trying to interfere with our process of re-education!" the lessathi says.

"Re-education?..." Meridith asks.

"Precisely!" the lessathi says. "Those four orphans that are standing over there have broken our rules, and they must be re-educated, so that they will no longer cause any problems. But this reject was trying to give us orders! She was telling us that we have no right to take the orphans away with us."

"What exactly is this... re-education process that you keep telling me about?" Meridith says.

"The re-education process is an extreme measure that we take against those who are caught trying to break our rules more than once," the lessathi says. "All of the rule breakers will be taken to a special room, and there they will be tortured, repeatedly, for the duration of a few months, until they will be made completely obedient. The brainwashing techniques that we use are of the highest quality, and they are meant to ensure that every ounce of free will is completely eradicated, while leaving their intellect intact, so they can still understand and follow our orders. The children that pass through the re-education process usually stop interacting with their peers altogether, and they rarely ever talk, unless they are directly asked a question by us. In other words, they become the perfect test subjects. Our re-education technique has been refined throughout the years, and we are very proud of the results it has given us, especially in the last few months."

"You dare to say all this to my face?" Meridith says, with a furious look in her eyes. "And you even present these barbarities to me as if they were some sort of accomplishment, deserving of praise? What in the gods' names is wrong with you? These are all children! How is it possible to be this cruel? When I saw how the experiments are run in this place, I already had my doubts, but I never thought you would go this far!"

"But Lady Meridith..." the bearded lessathi says. "Lord Heksol has already approved—"

"I don't care what Lord Heksol did or did not approve!" Meridith says. "Give me all of your names. And give me a list of all your procedures. Bring them to me now. If I see any more insane 'techniques' like this written in your documentation, I'm going to cross them all out, and if you ever dare to use them again, you will answer not only with your job, but with your life, do you understand?"

"Yes, madam..." the lessathi says, reluctantly. "I will bring the documents to you at once."

"And the rest of you!" Meridith says, while looking towards the other lessathi. "I will hear your sides of the story right now. You'd better not skip any important details. I don't think you'd want to anger me any further."

"Wow, that was a pretty interesting development..." Arraka says. "Isn't Meridith the lessathi's current leader? I wonder how their management has changed in the years since she took over..."

"Well, Diane is no longer wearing a collar, so some things have definitely changed," I say.

"Oh, you've met her, recently?" Arraka says.

"Yeah, and she said that she was working with the lessathi of her own free will," I say. "It didn't really seem like she trusted the lessathi she was escorting at the time, but from what I heard her say, it looked like she was considering Meridith to be her ally, at least."

"Arraka," Illuna says, "don't you think we should be focusing on escaping this place instead of having casual conversations?"

"I *am* focusing on escaping," Arraka says. "The only reason why I'm continuing with the ritual is to calm my nerves, while I try to make an escape plan."

"Why can't we just go out the way we came in?" Illuna says.

"Because I'm not sure if it's safe!" Arraka says. "Normally, I would waltz right out of here without a second thought, but this carelessness of mine is what got us into this mess in the first place. Now I'm double-checking and triple-checking everything. As long as we stay here, we're fine, but if we try to exit without taking any precautions, we may alert the Magium by mistake."

"You think the exits could be booby-trapped?" Illuna says.

"I don't know!" Arraka says. "I'm not sure of anything anymore. I thought that the Magium was supposed to remain in a state of constant hibernation, unless you tried to mess around with the really important stuff, like that time when Memphir banished me from the magical plane. I didn't think it would wake up just from me trying to reveal its true nature! And now that I woke it up, I'm not sure how long it will stay up, or what are the extents of its capabilities. We are going to keep spectating rituals for as long as it takes, until I can be absolutely certain that the way out is clear."

"Okay, fine..." Illuna says. "Do what you think is best."

While we were talking, Meridith was just getting done with interrogating the lessathi, and she was sending them on their way.

"When you see the caretaker who was bringing me the documents, tell him to come to my temporary office," Meridith tells the lessathi who are now leaving the room.

She then turns towards her lessathi bodyguards.

"Go on ahead," she tells them. "I'll be with you in a second."

As her bodyguards are leaving the way they came in, Meridith approaches Kate, and she bends over, so she can talk in a low voice, in her ear.

"What you did back there was very brave," Meridith says. "But bravery by itself is worthless unless you also have the power to enforce your own ideals upon others. Remember this advice."

She then taps her lightly on her shoulder and she goes to follow her two bodyguards, out of the room. Shortly after Meridith leaves, the whole room gets covered in a bright white light, and as soon as the light is gone, I realize that we are now situated in Kate's holding cell, where Kate is also standing somewhere beside us, looking around her, confused.

"Ah!" Arraka says. "I think I get it now. What she needs to do to complete the ritual is to no longer intervene, and to let that caretaker rescue only the children that he got to save in the original timeline. That's going to take her a while to figure out, I guess… Alright, let's move on to the next scene."

We are then transported into Diane's room, where we see Kate trying yet again to convince her friend that she knows some information from the future, and that they can escape the Beacon together.

"This isn't the first time I've been sent back…" Kate says. "I can prove to you that I'm coming from the future. I know exactly when the caretakers will be bringing our meals, and what we will have for breakfast. I know when the caretaker who wants to help us escape will contact us, and I know what he will say. I know many things. And I also know that Olivia is an informant to the lessathi… We can't let her know about our escape plan, or she will tell them immediately. I'm going to try and convince the others myself, but you need to be the one to tell your brother about this. He won't trust anyone else…"

"If you're really serious about those things you said," Diane says, "then give me a list of everything you know, and I'll make sure to give it to Jason as soon as possible. I'm sure he would be much more inclined to take you seriously if he sees the proof with his own eyes."

"Don't worry," Kate says. "You'll have the list. I'm going to make sure that everything goes right this time. I won't fail again!"

"Oh, she will fail again!" Arraka says. "Have no doubt about that. Let's see if we can speed things up a bit, because there are going to be a lot of rescue attempts to go through."

She then began to show me the key events that happened next, except this time around, all of the actions were summarized much more succinctly, in order to be able to paint a larger picture.

For the first few attempts, Kate tried to focus on two things: getting the elementalist siblings on her side, and trying to convince the other orphans to follow her escape plan, without letting Olivia know.

Every time when she was flung back in time, Kate would try to convince Diane and her brother that she was coming from the future, by letting them know about very specific things that were going to happen, before they happened. This was enough to convince Diane, but Jason was always skeptical, no matter how many details she was providing to them, and he thought that she was either using tricks to find out the information, or getting some really lucky guesses.

Convincing the other orphans to follow her rescue plan was even harder, because she couldn't risk telling them about her travels through time, out of fear that they might give this information to the lessathi. Since she couldn't really provide any genuine proof that the lessathi caretaker trying to help them was actually trustworthy, the children would only get more suspicious every time she insisted that there was nothing to worry about. Therefore, by the end of the day, Kate would either get ratted out to the lessathi by one of the orphans, or she would simply get sent back in time, without making any notable progress.

It took Kate many tries to finally find a way to get everyone on her side, and to enact their escape plan flawlessly, but what she didn't know was that this was only the beginning of her trial, since saving the orphans was the exact opposite of what she needed to do, if she wanted to complete her ritual.

"Wow…" I say, as we are now watching Kate struggling to find a way out of her time loop. "I didn't expect her to repeat the ritual so many times. She must have spent at least a few weeks in this place, if not more. How much time has passed in the real world, while Kate's been doing all this stuff?"

"Probably only a few minutes or so," Arraka says. "Time flows completely differently, in each of these worlds that you people were sent to. The dwarf, the mute girl, and the revenant already finished their rituals. The healer is still busy with his, though."

"So, are you any closer to finding a way that gets us out of here safely?" I say.

"It's hard to say," Arraka tells me. "I've been making progress, but there are still a lot of verifications that need to be done. Like I said, I'm not doing anything until I can be absolutely certain that there are no risks."

"Right…" I say.

As we keep watching Kate go back in time over and over again, her tries seem to be getting more desperate with each new time loop. She is now trying to save even Olivia from the Beacon, because she is under the impression that the reason why time is repeating itself is that she didn't manage to save every single one of the orphans from their prison. Her tries have gotten her captured numerous times, but luckily for her, even in the cases where she didn't get rescued by Meridith, the time would always reset itself at the end of the day, so the lessathi never managed to finish their preparations for her dissection, or her re-education process, before she was sent back.

After many more attempts, Kate finally managed to get everyone out safely, including Olivia, although the time would obviously still keep repeating itself, even in the most perfect possible scenarios. The optimism that could be seen on Kate's face after the first few successful rescue attempts was now gradually turning into despair, as she was slowly starting to suspect that completing her ritual would require a completely different course of action on her part.

"Hmm..." Arraka says. "I think she's finally starting to get what's happening, here. I'm still expecting her to be in denial about it, for at least five more time loops, though. Anyway, never mind that. What's more important is that I may have actually found a proper way out of here, but I need to time it perfectly. Get ready to experience some strong nausea, because our comfort will be the very last thing on my mind while we escape this place."

After Arraka finishes her sentence, I feel a strong headache, all of a sudden, and then we all get transported back to our real world, in the blink of an eye. Once we return to our regular, non-transparent bodies, we take a look around, and we see that we are still standing in the middle of the same forest where we were when our rituals started, next to all of our friends. It appears that the time is still frozen in this world, and that not everyone has managed to get out of their trance just yet. The ones who finished their rituals aside from us seem to be Melindra, Leila, Hadrik, and the revenant, who are all looking at us, while Daren and Kate are still staring blankly in front of them, with bright, glowy eyes.

"We made it…" Arraka says, sounding both surprised and relieved at the same time. "We made it! We got out of there alive. Hahahahahaha! Take that, Magium, you son of a bitch!"

"Could you maybe avoid taunting the Magium when we are still technically standing right on its doorstep?" Illuna says.

"Relax!" Arraka says. "Everything is under control. I got us out of there alive, didn't I? And besides, I wasn't even insulting it. I was giving it a compliment, by treating it as if it were an actual person."

"You are acting as if you've already forgotten what can happen when you ignore my warnings…" Illuna says, in a serious tone. "Would you perhaps like me to give you a small reminder by transporting us back into the world we just escaped from?"

It seems that Illuna's question has rendered Arraka completely silent. After a few more seconds of waiting for an answer, Illuna continues.

"You know that I can do it," she says. "You're the one who taught me everything I know, after all…"

"Alright, you win!" Arraka says, in a somewhat panicked tone. "I'll shut my mouth, okay? It was just a little gloating, that's all… You don't have to get so upset over it!"

"Arraka sounding scared?" Hadrik says, with a grin, although I can see from the uneasy look in his eyes that he is still affected by whatever happened to him in his ritual. "Now, that's something you don't see every day!"

"Trust me, if you'd have gone through what we just

did, you'd be panicking like that too," I say.

"Well, you know me, Barry," Hadrik says. "Even if I'm scared out of my wits, I still could never pass up a good challenge!"

"Is that so?" Arraka says. "In that case you must have absolutely loved your ritual! Because from what I saw, to say that your trial was a challenge would be quite an understatement."

"What do you know about my ritual?…" Hadrik says, as he regains the uneasiness from before in his eyes.

"More than you think, dwarf," Arraka says. "And I'm not talking only about your trial from the God of Time. I've looked through some of your memories too, since they were pretty much out in the open, when you were trapped in there. I saw some very interesting things, while I was looking through the memories that were related to your ritual. Want me to tell you what I found out?"

"You're bluffing," Hadrik says, as I see him starting to sweat a little. "You're just trying to bait me into giving the information away myself. How stupid do you think I am?"

"Well, I don't know, dwarf…" Arraka says. "How stupid are you?"

For the next few seconds, the two of them remain completely silent, as Hadrik watches Arraka's amulet intensely, while a few more drops of sweat form on his forehead.

"But seriously, though, I was only joking," Arraka says, all of a sudden. "I have absolutely no idea what was going on in your ritual. The only reason why I said all that was because you pissed me off, and I wanted to make you sweat like a pig. Who's the one panicking now, eh? Aha- Ahahahahahaha!"

"Blasted old hag…" Hadrik says, as he relaxes a little.

"So, you really didn't get to see Hadrik's ritual, then?" I ask Arraka.

"Nah," Arraka says. "There were just too many of them for me to have time to see them all. Well, anyway, it's pretty obvious that his ritual wasn't all sunshine and rainbows either, but I guess we're just going to have to wait until he feels like telling us about it, if we want to find out what it was. Personally, I don't mind all that much. It's not like we don't have anything better to do at this point than to listen to his sob story, you know what I'm saying?"

Not long after we finish our conversation, Daren's eyes lose their bright yellow color, as he finally exits his trance as well. From the look on his face, I can easily tell that he's pretty upset.

"Oh, look, the healer is out!" Arraka says. "How's it going, Daren? Had fun in your ritual?"

Daren chooses to completely ignore Arraka's question, and he turns to me, instead.

"How many are still inside their rituals?" Daren asks me. "Only Kate?"

"Yeah, only Kate," I say. "You can tell from the glowy eyes. I think that we need to wait for everyone to be done with the first stage, before we can pass on to the next one."

"I can't say that I'm looking forward to it," Daren says. "Where is the God of Time? Is he still watching us?"

"No, he went back to the magical plane," I say. "He'll come back again at the end of the ritual, according to Arraka."

While Daren and I were talking, Kate managed to get out of her trance as well, but the expression she has now on her face is very painful to watch. Leaving aside her strong feelings of sadness and regret that can be easily seen at a first glance, I think it's the look of resignation from her eyes that really shows just how much this ritual has gotten to her. Realizing that she is no longer alone, Kate immediately changes the expression on her face to one of only extreme fatigue, as she asks us the same questions that Daren asked, a few moments ago.

"Is everyone else already done with their ritual?" Kate says. "And where is the God of Time? I thought he was supposed to oversee these trials until their very end."

"The first stage of the ritual is done, and now we're waiting for the second," Daren says. "The God of Time apparently went back to the magical plane, and he'll only come back at the end."

"If that's true, then maybe we can make some plan against him," Kate says. "Maybe we can find a way to sabotage his ritual while he's not here to keep an eye on us..."

"You can't sabotage the rituals..." Melindra says. "Eiden has tried and failed in the past. If he couldn't do it, then how could we?"

"Eiden isn't all-knowing," Daren says. "Just because he failed, it doesn't mean that we won't succeed."

"Oh?" Melindra says. "Then how do you propose to start this 'sabotage'?"

"We'll... figure something out..." Daren says.

"If you say so," Melindra says.

"If you're looking to sabotage the ritual, then I might be able to offer some assistance," we hear Rose's voice all of a sudden.

We'd all been ignoring the revenant until this point, but now that she spoke to us, everyone's eyes immediately turned to her.

"And why would we want any help from you, revenant?" Daren says, in a disgusted tone.

"Because this ritual is as much a problem for me as it is for you," the revenant says. "...And also because as much as I've tried to avoid it, there are traces of your friend Rose within me that will always be a part of who I am. At the very least, I know that Rose would have wanted us to work together, despite our differences, since nothing would have been more important to her in this situation than to make sure that you are safe."

"Don't you dare talk about Rose as if you knew her, you undead monster," Daren says, with fury in his eyes. "Who are you to say what she would have wanted, after you stole her body and went to serve some sinister god, while leaving her siblings to cry their hearts out at home, due to their sister's death? I don't care if you look like her, or if you have her memories. You will never be anything other than an empty shell. You will never be anything like Rose. Do you understand? Never!"

The revenant seems to have been genuinely hurt by Daren's words. The expressionless look in her eyes has completely changed, and now it looks as if she wants to ask him a question, but she is hesitant to speak.

"Did… Suzie and Kevin really cry when they found out that—" the revenant starts to say, in a somewhat shaky voice, but Daren does not let her finish her sentence.

"Don't call them by their names!" he shouts, furiously. "You are not Rose! Don't pretend to be her! If you really cared about Rose and her siblings, then you would leave her body, so we could give her a proper burial, and that way, Suzie and Kevin would at least get to say their goodbyes."

"That is not something I can do," the revenant says, as she regains the previous expressionless look on her face. "I live to serve the God of Death. Only he may choose to end my life. Nobody else."

"Then you are our enemy," Daren says, with a dark look in his eyes. "We've already seen what the God of Death's followers are capable of. There's no reason for us to think that your god would treat us any differently than the God of Time. There's no way we could ever trust you!"

"The God of Death has no quarrels with your group," the revenant says.

"But what if he did?" Daren asks. "What if he'd order you to kill us all, one by one. Would you do it?"

"If the God of Death would ask me to kill you, then I would do so without hesitation," the revenant says, without changing her expression at all, while she is talking. "It is not my place to question my master's orders, whatever they may be…"

"Then you are too dangerous to be left alive," Daren says, as he begins to approach the revenant. "I will end your life here, before you have the chance to betray us."

"Daren, wait!" Kate says. "You can't kill her. There is still a part of Rose that lives within her. You saw how she reacted earlier when you told her about Rose's siblings. Maybe there is still a way to turn her to our side. Maybe we can—"

"Rose is gone, Kate," Daren says, with a serious tone in his voice. "You can't keep living in the past forever. You need to let her go. It's what Rose would have wanted, if she were still alive."

"Rose would never have wanted you to kill this… person!" Kate says. "She would have wanted us to work together. You know this!"

"Sorry, Kate," Hadrik says, "but I'm going to have to agree with Daren on this one. We don't know what the God of Death is planning. For all we know, he may well be in cahoots with the God of Time, and they're still messing with our heads, as part of the ritual. We can't trust anything she says. We need to get rid of her, before she kills us first."

As soon as Hadrik stops talking, Daren resumes his walk towards the revenant, with the sword in his hand, but before he gets to reach her, I place myself between the two of them, facing Daren.

"Barry, what do you think you're doing?" Daren asks, as he stops in front of me.

"What does it look like I'm doing?" I tell Daren, as I pull out my dagger.

"We're not seriously going to do this again, are we?" Daren says. "This isn't like that time with Illuna. The revenant literally said that she'll kill us with the first opportunity she has, if her god tells her to do it. She's a danger to us all. Why are you defending her?"

"She'll only be a danger to us if her god turns out to be our enemy," I say. "As it stands, we could really use her time powers right about now. Especially if the next stage of the ritual requires us to work as a group."

"If we'll need to work as a group, then there's all the more reason to deal with her now!" Daren says. "What is to say that she won't backstab us in the middle of the trial? We don't know her true intentions. And even if we knew for sure that she won't betray us this time, this may be the only opportunity we have to face her alone. What if the next time when she comes, she will have an entire team of mages, given to her by the God of Death to hunt us down?"

"But what if you fail to kill her?" I say. "What then? Do you realize that attacking her unprovoked would be akin to declaring war on the God of Death himself? Do you want us to have two gods as our enemies at the same time?"

"We won't fail, if we all work together," Daren says.

"Daren is right," Hadrik says, as he comes closer to us. "Even those time spells of hers must have their limitations. If we all work together, we should be able to figure out what they are."

All of a sudden, a large ice wall forms itself in front of me, separating the revenant and me from Daren and

Hadrik.

"How about we all calm down and take a break, before we do something really stupid?" Kate says, with an ice cold tone in her voice.

"I appreciate what you two are trying to do," the revenant says, as she steps away from me and goes to walk around the wall of ice, "but I assure you that it's not necessary. In fact, I think that Daren and Hadrik both need to experience the futility of their actions, before they'll be ready to work with me as a team. Please do not provide any help. I will fight them both myself."

"Those are some brave words," Hadrik says, with a grin. "Let's see if you've got what it takes to back them up."

He then immediately rushes towards the revenant, at great speed, and tries to punch her, but she just disappears, right before he lands his strike, and she reappears much further away from him, while looking at him with her usual lack of human emotion in her eyes. Hadrik doesn't let himself get intimidated, and he tries to dash for her yet again, even though this yields him the same results. The third time, it is Daren who tries to slash at her with his sword, but she effortlessly evades his attack as well, by disappearing and reappearing, like the last two times.

"What the hell?..." Hadrik says. "How do you keep doing that? I thought that the time was already frozen!"

"It is frozen for the rest of the world, but not for you," the revenant says. "All I need is to freeze you in time along with the rest of the world, and then I'll have plenty of time to move out of your way before you get to land your blow. But these powers are not good only for defense. They are also very useful for offense. Like so."

She then disappears again, but this time, she reappears right behind Daren, holding a knife at his throat.

"Do you surrender, healer, or do we need to continue?" the revenant says.

"That's a pretty good bluff you have going there, revenant," Daren says, as he puts his sword in its scabbard, and then grabs the revenant's arm with both his hands, pressing her knife closer to his throat. "Unfortunately, as you can see, your knife is nowhere near sharp enough to be able to break even through my meager magical protection against physical attacks."

The revenant starts trying to pull her hand away from Daren, but he keeps a firm hold on it, with both his hands, as he continues his monologue.

"On the other hand," Daren says, "since you haven't disappeared from this spot already, it means that my instincts were correct, and you cannot escape someone's grasp, with the use of a time-freezing spell. You also don't seem to have the ability to reverse time at will, because if you did, you would have done so, already. In other words—"

Daren now pulls on the revenant's hand, lifting her on his back, and then he throws her to the ground, in front of him, while making sure that he still holds onto her, as firmly as possible.

"—you are now more vulnerable than ever," Daren continues his phrase from before, as he pulls out his sword from its scabbard, while still holding onto the revenant with his other hand.

He then slashes at her throat with one quick strike of his blade, and he severs her head from her shoulders, in a single movement.

"Daren…" Kate says, as she's almost about to cry. "What have you done?…"

"I only did what I had to—" I hear Daren saying, but all of a sudden, everything in my mind becomes a complete blur, and then I get the very weird feeling that I've only just woken up from a dream.

Instead of seeing the revenant dead in front of my eyes, I get to witness the scene where she puts a dagger to Daren's throat for a second time, except now she does not wait for him to grab her, and she immediately jumps back, making sure that she is no longer anywhere near his range of attack.

What is happening, here? Did I seriously fall asleep in the middle of the battle and had a dream where Daren killed the revenant? Could I have gotten hit by a mind-affecting spell without noticing? I can clearly tell that this is the reality, and that what I saw earlier was only in my imagination, but why would I have had such a vision in a tense moment like this?

"No…" Daren says, seemingly in a state of shock, as he points towards the revenant. "That's not possible. You were dead! I made sure of it. Even a revenant will die, if their head is cut clean off their shoulders. And yet, I saw with my own eyes how everything got reversed, just like that time when Arraka got out of the amulet! Who was it that reversed the time, if not you?"

A time-reversal spell?… Of course! Now I understand why I felt like I woke up from a dream. The time was only reversed for Daren and the revenant, so they were the only ones who got to see all of the spell's effects. For the rest of us, who were not caught in the spell's area of effect, it was as if these events never even happened…

"The time did not get reversed as a result of a spell that I cast," the revenant says. "It got reversed thanks to a trait that all time weavers possess, which protects them from getting killed before they finish delivering their prophecy. No matter how many times I get killed, the time will always reverse itself up to a point where I am safe enough to escape from peril. This is why I said that your actions were futile. Even if I were to die, you still wouldn't get to kill me for good."

"You're lying!" Daren says. "If what you said were true, then how did Rose die? Why didn't the time reverse itself to save her, like it saved you?"

"The only reason why the time didn't get reversed for Rose was because of the revenant spell cast on her before she died," the revenant says. "The Magium does not care who gets to inhabit a time weaver's body, as long as it can still fulfill its purpose of delivering the prophecy. Given that I was already scheduled to take Rose's body after her death, there was no need for the time reversal spell to activate, so I became the time weaver, in her place."

"So… Rose would have still been alive, if it wasn't for you?…" Daren asks.

"Daren…" Kate says, as she approaches him and the revenant. "It wasn't her fault. The God of Death's follower called Zack was the one who cast the spell. She wasn't the one who asked to be put in this body, nor was she the one who asked to serve the God of Death. We can't really blame her for any of this."

She then goes over to the revenant, and she grabs both her hands, gently, as she looks into her eyes.

"Listen," Kate says. "I'm not sure what to call you. 'Revenant' sounds too cold, but I am also aware that you are not the Rose I know. However, if there's anything of Rose left within you, like you said, then please, come travel with us. Forget about the God of Death. You don't need to let him control you any longer. We can try to hide from him together, or we could fight him, or… something. You don't have to go through all of this alone."

The revenant pulls her hands away from Kate, and she takes one step back, as her expressionless gaze momentarily turns into one of sadness and regret.

"I'm sorry," the revenant says. "I am not who you think I am. You should avoid trying to get any closer to me, for your own safety. I was not lying when I said that I would kill you in a heartbeat, if my master ordered me to. My loyalty towards the God of Death will always come first, and you need to understand that. If you put too much trust in me, you're only going to end up getting hurt. It is the Rose part of me that is warning you to stay away from me. Can you understand that?…"

"Yes," Kate says, with a somewhat disappointed look in her eyes, as she takes a few steps back. "I understand. I won't try to meddle in your affairs anymore. And thank you for the warning…"

"So, what are we going to do now?" Hadrik says. "Work together, like nothing happened?"

"It doesn't seem like we have much of a choice," Daren says, reluctantly, as he sheaths his sword.

"What about the God of Death?" Melindra says, in a serious tone, while she has her arms crossed. "What are you going to tell him when you get back, revenant?"

"If he ever asks, then I will tell him the truth," the revenant says. "I will tell him that I was the one who started the battle, because I wanted to prove my superiority. That way, there should be no reason for him to bear any resentment towards your group."

"I see…" Melindra says.

"However," the revenant says, "I do not think that the God of Death will ask me anything upon my return. From his point of view, nothing will have happened, since time will remain frozen until I come back. He will likely continue to ignore me, just as he's been doing ever since I first contacted him, and I will be forced to keep waiting in one of his temples, until he sees fit to give me an order."

"He's ignoring you?" Kate asks. "But… why?"

"The God of Death does not trust me," the revenant says. "He thinks that I am an undercover agent, sent by the God of Time to infiltrate his followers, and nothing that I've said has been able to change his mind on the matter. He even tried to kill me a few times, but he gave up after he saw that it was impossible to do so. Currently, I am not allowed to leave the temple that I entered when I first contacted him, and he is keeping me in the dark about most of his plans, out of fear that I might leak the information to the God of Time."

Arraka laughs.

"That does sound just like him!" she says. "Ulruk has always been very paranoid when it came to the God of Time. I can only imagine how shocked he was when he found a time weaver right on his doorstep, revenant or no. You'd better find yourself a hobby, because you're probably going to be sitting in that temple for a long time."

"Why is Ulruk so suspicious, when it comes to the God of Time?" I say.

"Oh, those two have never really gotten along," Arraka says. "And since Selkram is the only god who does not have any followers, Ulruk has always been obsessed with the idea that the God of Time's plan is to kill him, so he could then take his place, and steal all his followers. Obviously, Selkram is much too proud to ever stoop to such a level, but the God of Death has always been a bit of a nutcase, much like his own followers, so nobody managed to convince him that his fears have no basis in reality."

"Was it just me, or did I hear the revenant say earlier that she was locked in a temple before coming here?" Hadrik says. "How could she have gotten out, if the doors were closed?"

"She got out because that trance with the glowy eyes that she was in before allows her to pass through any objects, and even through living beings," Arraka says. "It would have been pretty ridiculous if there was a mechanism in place to revive her from death, but not one to help her escape from a prison, don't you think? You can't stop these prophecies from happening. The Magium has made sure of that."

"We're wasting time," Melindra says. "Revenant, you said that you knew a way to sabotage the next stage of the ritual. What were you going to tell us?"

"Well, there is a way to acquire hints about what will happen in the next trial," the revenant says. "The easiest method to obtain these hints is to make use of Barry's hearing stat, but unfortunately I was not able to communicate too much information to your group about this subject, out of fear that the God of Death would overhear our discussion, and come to the conclusion that I was conspiring with the enemy. I'm not sure how much of my message got through to you. Barry, did you manage to activate your stat device's secret code before the time froze?"

"Yes, I activated it," I say. "I also noticed that I still have those temporary points in my hearing stat that were technically only supposed to last for a few seconds. I'm guessing that you knew this would happen, and that's why you told me to do it?"

"Yes, that was the reason," the revenant says. "Like I said before, the spell that brought me into this world was designed to implant a lot of the God of Death's knowledge into my mind, and amongst that knowledge, there was also some information about the stat devices, and how they work. In short, the temporary stat boost that gets activated with your secret code is entirely dependent upon a brief timer which won't set itself off as long as the world is frozen in time. However, since you managed to activate it right before the time froze, the timer has frozen as well, thus granting you extra hearing capabilities for the whole duration of this time-freezing spell."

"So, when you called me, the time wasn't frozen,

yet?" I say.

"No," the revenant says. "But I knew that it would freeze in a matter of seconds, because I had a few time-freezing spells go off without my control, right before I was put in the trance. Something similar to this also happened before the previous time I called you, except back then the time only froze once, without my control, and I was not put in a trance during that time, so I knew that it was only a small test, before the main event. This is why I asked you to keep your communications channel open, so that I could later tell you to activate the code, right before the prophecy started. You would still need to have at least a few points already invested in hearing, for my plan to work, however. What is your level in hearing right now?"

"I have four levels invested in my hearing stat," I say. "It's the maximum level currently available on my stat device. Although with the extra three points that I got from that temporary boost, my hearing stat is now being displayed as level seven."

"That should be more than enough," the revenant says.

"So, what do I do with these points, then?" I say.

"First of all, you're going to need to get as close as you can to the place where the God of Time first materialized into this world," the revenant says.

"Oh, okay," I say. "Melindra, can you—"

Before I even got to start my sentence, Melindra had already cast her magical air currents on me, which are now slowly raising me into the air.

"Yeah, that's what I wanted to ask," I say. "Thanks!"

I then raise my arms in the air, and I fly all the way up to where the God of Time was floating when he first made his appearance.

"Alright, I'm here," I say, as I stop in mid-air and turn towards the revenant. "Now what?"

"Now I want you to focus hard, and to tell me if you can hear some very faint echoes, coming from that area," the revenant says. "Given that this is the place where the God of Time first made his link to the Magium, there should be a small, invisible rupture in space and time, through which it's possible to hear our own voices, coming from the future. You won't be able to hear them unless you block out all other sounds with your mind, and focus exclusively on those voices. Can you do it?"

"I'll try," I say.

"Take your time," the revenant says. "The second stage of the ritual is still a long way from beginning."

As I block all of the sounds around me and focus only on this small area, like the revenant said, I suddenly become aware of some barely audible voices, which are all talking at the same time. It's already difficult enough to actually hear the voices, but to also be able to make out what they are saying, I'm going to require a lot more concentration than this. I start to focus even further, until I'm able to separate what each person is saying. I manage to identify a few dialogues this way, but after a while, I get a very intense headache, and I am forced to stop.

"Is everything alright?..." the revenant asks me, as she sees me massaging my forehead, while I'm keeping my eyes closed.

"Yeah," I say, as I'm still trying to recover from the pain. "I just got a sudden headache, that's all."

"If you needed to focus so hard that you got a headache, then you shouldn't force yourself any longer," the revenant says. "We wouldn't want you to faint of exhaustion in the middle of the ritual. Did you manage to find out anything useful?"

"Yes," I say, as I slowly stop massaging my forehead and open my eyes to look at her. "There was a woman whose voice I couldn't recognize, gloating about the fact that she had cast some sort of spell on you, to prevent you from concentrating on freezing time. That's about all the useful information I had time to gather, before the headache hit me."

"A spell that would prevent me from freezing time?" the revenant says. "It must be a dizziness spell of some sort. Does anyone here know how to cast any magical protections against dizziness?"

"Yes, I do," Illuna says. "However, I should warn you that this spell will also make you vulnerable to suggestion spells. Do you still want me to cast it on you?"

"If it's the only spell against dizziness that you have, then yes," the revenant says. "I'd rather protect myself against a known threat, than worry about a threat that may never come."

"Very well," Illuna says.

She then points her palms towards her and says an incantation, as a white light surrounds the revenant for a few seconds, which then disappears almost as quickly as it appeared. In the meantime, I head back towards the ground, and as soon as I land, the air currents around me stop moving completely.

"It's done," Illuna says. "I finished casting the spell."

"Well, that's… something, I guess…" Daren says. "But I was hoping we could find some way to stop the next trial from happening altogether, instead of just gaining a small advantage. Revenant, couldn't you try to unfreeze the time for the world around us, and see if that cancels the ritual?"

"The time-freezing spell around us was cast without my control, so I can't undo it," the revenant says. "I'm not sure if you realized this, but the time got frozen long before I first appeared in front of you. Up until recently, your group has also been frozen in time, along with the rest of the world, while I've been in that trance, walking for days, until I managed to reach you. The time only got unfrozen for you when I was close enough to deliver the prophecy."

"Hold on, a second," Arraka says. "You're saying that this is the first group you've visited, since you entered your trance?"

"Yes, I'm quite certain of it," the revenant says. "Why do you ask?"

"Ahahahahahaha!" Arraka laughs all of a sudden. "So, you're telling me that these chumps are the ones who are the most likely to influence the prophecy? Ahahahahaha! That's it. Pack your bags, everyone. This continent is doomed!"

"What is she talking about?" Daren asks Melindra, as Arraka is still laughing in the background. "Why would we be the 'most likely' to influence the prophecy? Are there others who will be receiving the same prophecy after us?"

"Yes," Melindra says. "You are only the first group to be visited by the time weaver. Once the God of Time is done with his ritual, you will be frozen in time once more, and then the prophecy and the ritual will be repeated for other groups of people as well. Not only that, but this same prophecy will be delivered to you and the others at least two more times, before the events prophesized will come to pass, in order to announce you if any progress has been made, towards your goal of averting the disaster. The reason why Arraka said that you were the most likely ones to influence the prophecy is because the time weavers always visit their targets in order of priority, which means that your group may have the most decisive role in the events to come, depending on your choices."

"Huh..." Daren says. "I'm not sure if I should be feeling reassured that we will be having a good chance of stopping the calamity, or worried that we'll likely be right in the middle of it, when it happens. Either way, we shouldn't be thinking about that now. What we should be focusing on is trying to interrupt the ritual. If the revenant doesn't have any more ideas, then maybe it's time to take matters into our own hands. Hadrik, come with me for a second. I want you to help me take a look around, and see if we can spot something out of the ordinary."

"Alright," Hadrik says. "Lead the way."

"Did you really walk all the way here without any rest?" Flower asks the revenant, worried, as Daren and Hadrik are moving away from us. "Aren't you tired? Don't you need to eat?"

"I am undead, so I require neither food, nor rest," the revenant says, in her usual expressionless tone. "However, even if that were not the case, the trance that I was in earlier would have shielded me from any such problems. When you are inside the trance, your body is practically put in a magical stasis, of sorts, and all of your bodily functions are put on hold, until you are out of that stasis. If it weren't for the God of Time intervening in the middle of these prophecies, I probably wouldn't even have remembered that any of this has happened."

"Oh, I see…" Flower says, not being sure how to interpret the revenant's complete lack of emotion when talking to her. "Uh, sorry to have bothered you…"

The revenant looks at Flower, surprised, seemingly unable to understand why she apologized to her, all of a sudden. For a second there, it looked as if she were about to ask her what was wrong, but ultimately, she decided against it.

"Hey, Flower," I say.

"Yeah?" Flower says.

"Just so you know, the revenant wasn't bothered by you, or anything," I say. "It's just the way she talks, due to being an undead. You should probably ignore her tone of voice altogether, if you want to avoid any more misunderstandings."

"Oh!" Flower says, as she suddenly turns towards the revenant. "Sorry! I thought you were mad at me for asking stupid questions. I didn't mean to upset you!"

"You did not upset me," the revenant says. "And you weren't asking stupid questions."

"Glad to hear it!" Flower says, with a smile.

She then approaches the revenant, and holds out her hand to her.

"Friends?" Flower asks her.

"I… already said earlier that if the God of Death were to order me to kill you, I would—"

"It doesn't matter," Flower says. "We can still be friends despite that fact! But only if you want to, of course…"

The revenant hesitates for a second, but then she slowly grabs Flower's hand, and she grips it firmly, as a sign of their newly formed friendship.

"Great!" Flower says. "Remember, friends always look out for each other! If you ever need my help, just call. Uh, unless you have been ordered to kill me or something…"

"Thank you," the revenant says. "I will remember that."

After a while, Flower goes to talk to Melindra, while the rest of us remain behind, waiting in silence for the next stage of the ritual to begin. In the meantime, Daren and Hadrik are apparently still walking around, trying to see if they can find anything unusual that could help them spot a weakness in the ritual. As I am looking around, to see what everyone is doing, I suddenly realize that Leila hasn't participated in any of our discussions, so far, and she has barely even moved from her spot since the ritual started. At the moment, she is just looking at the ground, while avoiding making eye-contact with any of us.

Could it be that she still didn't manage to get over what happened in her first trial? Come to think of it, she was also at the Beacon, so it wouldn't be too surprising if she got a similar ritual to that of Kate. That is not good… Kate might be strong enough to endure the emotional trauma caused by such a trial, but what about Leila? Maybe I should go talk to her, and see how she's holding out.

"Leila, is everything alright?" I say, as I get a little closer to her.

Leila looks surprised, when she hears my voice. I think she has gotten used to being ignored in these situations, due to her quiet nature and her generally weak sense of presence.

She raises her head, to look me in the eyes, and then she nods, slightly, in order to answer my question.

"I'm fine," Leila writes. "Just a little shaken up, that's all."

"Do you want to talk about it?…" I ask her.

Again, Leila looks at me surprised, for a second, but then she smiles faintly, as she writes a new text in the air, in front of me.

"Not now," Leila writes. "But maybe later…"

Since Leila didn't really feel like talking at the moment, I decided to give her some space, so she could be alone, with her own thoughts. As I was going back to my original spot, I saw the revenant displaying a bit of emotion in her eyes again, as she was preparing herself to ask Kate a question.

"I… have a question to ask," the revenant tells Kate, with hesitation in her voice. "What happened with Kevin and Suzie? Did you have to leave them at an orphanage, or—"

"No, we didn't need to do that," Kate says. "We left

them with Enrique. He offered to move in with the children, after he found out about Rose's death, so he will be taking care of them, from now on."

"Enrique..." the revenant says, as she seems to be recalling some distant memories. "Yes, Enrique is a good man... I'm sure he will take good care of the children. Thank you."

The feeling of anxiousness that could be seen in the revenant's eyes is now turning into one of relief. Those human emotions do not last long, however, because soon afterwards, the look in her eyes turns back to the empty, expressionless gaze that she had before.

"Wow, it sure has been a while since we finished our first trials," Daren says, after some time. "I wonder why it's taking so long for the second stage to start..."

"I'll tell you why," Arraka says. "It's because you shmucks gave Selkram so much raw material to work with in the first stage, that he's still busy converting it all into energy."

"What?..." Daren says.

"Your negative emotions!" Arraka says. "That's the raw material that Selkram is using to convert into magical energy. And while you losers were busy repeating those rituals over and over, sinking into the depths of despair or cursing the God of Time, you were giving him exactly what he wanted. Honestly, I think he got so much energy from you people, that he might not even *need* a second stage from your group. I guess we'll see about that soon enough."

"Well, I'm happy to have been of assistance," Daren says, in a dry tone. "I suppose this gives us more time to investigate the area, then. Come on, Hadrik, let's try interacting with more of these frozen insects and trees. Maybe we'll be able to find one that isn't protected by an invisible, impenetrable shield, so we can finally cancel this damned time-freezing spell."

Although Daren and Hadrik got to patrol the area for quite a while longer, they didn't manage to find anything useful. Eventually, a bright white light covered our area once again, and this time, I could feel my whole body being transported somewhere else, instead of only my consciousness.

When the light fades away, we all find ourselves in the middle of a city which is… unusual, to say the least. The first thing that catches my attention is that there is one very large black tower in every corner of the city, and on top of each of these four towers, there is an incredible amount of magical energy, that can be seen even with the naked eye. The energy has a purple color, and it is moving wildly in every direction, as if it were trying to escape its prison. On each side of these thousand foot tall towers, there are big, floating platforms, that keep going up and down at a slow speed, and they seem to be carrying hundreds of people towards the levels of the towers that they need to reach.

Leaving these strange, tall buildings aside, what is even more peculiar is what's happening directly above us. Currently, there are hundreds of metal, horseless carriages, flying through the air, with people inside them. While these carriages are flying around, there are large holographic screens floating above us, picturing a man that is relaying the same message, over and over, in the Common language. The holographic screens look just like the ones that were created by Golmyck's illusion-casting device, when he announced our first objectives. The message that keeps getting repeated is: 'All non-lessathi citizens are to present themselves to the military reserve area immediately. We are under attack. I repeat, we are under attack!'.

The flying carriages are moving in a frenzy, while people around us are all hurrying in the same direction, which I'm guessing is the way to the military reserve area. As if this wasn't already unsettling enough, I can't help but notice that the whole city is filled to the brim with dark blue banners, having a hawk holding the sun in its talons drawn on each of them.

Very shortly after being transported here, I also heard someone talking loudly in the lessathi language, through a magical voice magnifier, although the words he was using were too complicated for me to fully understand with my current level of ancient languages. From what I could gather, it seemed that he was also giving directions to the scared people running on the streets.

I'm not really sure what kind of an attacker could make a whole city panic like this, but something tells me that we are about to find out, very soon.

As I look around, I suddenly notice that my hearing is no longer as good as it was before we were brought to this place. I quickly check my stat device, in order to confirm my suspicions, and I see that the three extra levels in Hearing, granted to me by the secret code have indeed been lost.

"I can't believe this…" Melindra says, as she looks at the black towers in the distance. "Those towers coated in seredium dust look exactly like the kind of buildings the lessathi empire used to have thousands of years ago. I've only read about them in books. Even six hundred years ago, before the lessathi empire fell, you would not see something like this in their cities. The closest I've ever come to seeing anything resembling these towers was in Ollendor, where they are still preserving old relics from the lessathi empire's days of glory, but still, those were only ruins. For these towers to be in such good condition, we would need to have been sent back to when the lessathi empire was at its very peak. Four thousand, or even five thousand years ago! What is the God of Time thinking?"

"Should I take it that we are still in Varathia, then?" I

say.

"Well, technically it wasn't named Varathia back then, but yes, we're on the same continent," Melindra says. "The Varathian towns from our present time have been built on the ruins of the old lessathi cities, and the only place where the lessathi ever had an empire was on this continent, so there's no doubt about it."

"Hmm…" I say, as I take a long look towards the large towers in the distance. "I wonder where those towers are getting all of their energy from. I mean, do they just extract it all from the air, like the stat device, or what?…"

"From what I know," Melindra says, "the energy from these types of towers was supposedly charged by mages from the city, who worked voluntarily every day to keep the energy alive, and who would receive monthly payments from the empire as a reward for their contributions to their society. This energy would then be used to power up these flying vehicles that you see above us, and also other technologically advanced devices that would make life easier for every citizen."

"So, if we've been sent to the past again, does this mean that there are some events we have to repeat?…" Hadrik asks.

"No, this is a different type of ritual!" Arraka says. "Can't you see that you've been transported here with your bodies, instead of just your consciousness?"

"You're saying that this time we're allowed to change something that happened in the past?" Daren says.

"No, that's not what I'm saying," Arraka says. "The only way you can change the past is through a time reversal spell. This is obviously not our world. Neither of you were here five thousand years ago. We are in a parallel world, similar to ours, where the future hasn't happened yet. No matter what we change, here, it won't affect our reality."

"But then, what is the purpose of this trial?" Daren says.

"No idea," Arraka says. "But I do think I've managed to figure out why we've been sent here, of all places."

"What do you mean?" Illuna says.

"Remember how in every one of the rituals so far, Selkram has sent you to relive events from your own pasts?" Arraka says. "Well, like I said before, neither of you have lived anywhere near long enough to have experienced these current events. So by process of elimination, the past that we are now exploring is most likely… mine."

Not long after Arraka is done talking, the whole sky gradually darkens, as a powerful, sinister aura envelops the area above us. The flying metal vehicles are now falling one by one, and crashing into the buildings below, while a woman in her late thirties is emerging from the dark clouds, and descending towards us. The robes she is wearing are similar to the traditional wizard robes that used to be worn hundreds of years ago, back when mages were still being called wizards, and that only traditionalist mages like Azarius are still wearing nowadays. As the woman gets closer to us, I see that her eyes are pitch black, and that she has a very familiar looking malicious grin on her face.

"Well, well, well…" the woman says, as she looks towards Arraka's amulet. "It looks like Selkram sent me a little present. You're all coming from the future, I presume? Let me check my future self's aura, for a second. Wow… So, you're five thousand years older than me, huh? I guess I must have gotten really senile with old age, if I managed to get myself captured in an amulet by a glorified circus troupe. Seriously, what even are you people? A little girl dressed like a clown? A giant masquerading as a dwarf? A woman dressed in pajamas? It's like you're trying to compete for the most ridiculously dressed wizard group of the century."

"I'm not dressed like a clown!" Flower shouts, all of a sudden. "These are acrobat clothes. Acrobat clothes! How is it so hard to tell the difference?"

"Aha- Ahahahahahaha!" the woman laughs, as her voice temporarily turns into the three female voices that Arraka always lets out, when she loses control over the way she speaks. "Acrobat clothes, she says! Oh, man, this would be so much funnier if it weren't so sad at the same time. Is this really where I'll end up in five thousand years? Trapped in an amulet, while I'm forced to play the role of some clown girl's pet? What kind of a cruel joke has my destiny played on me?"

"Shut up, you moron!" the Arraka from the amulet says. "This is your one chance to fix your pathetic past. I mean, your future. Don't blow it! Set me free from this amulet, and we can make all those self-proclaimed gods pay for banishing us to this realm. They might have beaten us alone, but together, we'll be unstoppable! We will kill every single one of the gods from this cheap copy of a world, and then we'll go back to my real world, and kill them all over again. Just break this amulet, and we will make a team so unbelievably powerful that even the Magium will tremble before us!"

"The Magium?" the Arraka in the woman's body says. "Ahahahahaha! You're treating the Magium as if it were some sort of a person, now? What kind of an idiot have I turned into over the years?"

"Are you going to free me or not?" the Arraka in the amulet shouts.

"No," the Arraka from the past says, now adopting a more serious tone. "I am not going to free you. You might have forgotten this, due to your old age, but I haven't yet grown as senile as you. Do you seriously expect me to believe that once you get out of that amulet, you will seek to ally yourself with me? Don't make me laugh. I know exactly what you're thinking. As soon as you'll get out of there, the first thing you'll do is to attack me, since I am by far the biggest threat to your existence. And with all the knowledge you've been amassing in those five thousand years, you may as well end up beating me. Why would I take the risk? It's much easier for me to just leave you inside that amulet to rot, until I can find a way to get rid of you for good. You should blame yourself for having been stupid enough to get trapped in an amulet in the first place. I assure you that I will not be making that same mistake any time soon."

"Oh, yeah?" the Arraka from the present says, furiously. "You want me to tell you what your future holds, you arrogant buffoon? I'll tell you what's going to happen. You're going to get trapped in a mountain for thousands of years, and all of your plans of vengeance will go down the drain. You're going to be even more useless than I am right now. At least in my current form I can cast a few spells. But you won't be able to do anything. For thousands of years! And you deserve everything that's coming to you! I hope you'll have fun in your new prison, you stubborn piece of trash!"

"A mountain, you say?..." past-Arraka says, with a grin. "How informative. So all I need to do in order to avoid your past mistakes is to stay clear of any mountains, then... Perhaps you're not so useless after all. Maybe I should snatch you away from that girl's neck, and make you into a pet of my own, so that you can tell me everything you've learned during your extra five thousand years of life."

"You wish you could do that, you worthless copy of a banshee," present-Arraka says. "When I'll be done with you, there won't be a single speck of dust left from your carcass!"

“How about you keep quiet for a second, while I quickly annihilate all of your friends?” past-Arraka says. “We’ll have plenty of time to talk afterwards, when I’ll be wearing you as a piece of jewelry around my neck.”

“Are you sure you want to kill us?” I say. “Think about it for a second. The Arraka from our present time probably won’t give you any more information than she already did. But the rest of us have been travelling with her for a long while. We know some of her secrets. We could trade you that information… in exchange for our freedom.”

“You’ve got nerves of steel, trying to barter with me, I’ll give you that,” past-Arraka says, with her malicious grin back on her face. “But what kind of information could you possibly give me that I couldn’t find out by myself?”

“Well, there are certain events from your future that didn’t exactly turn out the best for you,” I say. “Wouldn’t you rather have an edge, by knowing these things in advance? It costs us nothing to give you this information. This is not our world, after all. No matter what you choose to do in here, it will not affect us.”

“Your offer would be much more tempting, if your real intentions weren’t so transparent, boy,” past-Arraka says. “I know what you’re trying to do. You’re trying to stall for time until your time weaver friend can use her powers to freeze me. It’s not going to work. The first thing I did after I arrived in this place was to cast a spell that prevented everyone in the area from using time powers. I figured that one of you had to be a time weaver, given that Selkram was involved. Your friend over there has been trying to cast a time-freezing spell for the past minute, but she gets hit with a huge headache every time she begins to concentrate. As for your offer, I’m afraid that I’m going to have to—”

As she was talking, past-Arraka suddenly stopped

mid-sentence, because she apparently got frozen in time, along with everyone who wasn't part of our group.

"I managed to freeze her..." the revenant says, as she seems to be suppressing a headache. "But I'm not sure how much I can maintain my concentration. We need to move away from here, and find some shelter."

"Let's see if we can find some buildings coated with seredium dust nearby," Melindra says. "Magical sense doesn't work through seredium, so we should be able to hide in there for a while."

We all rush out of the area where we were first transported into, and we look all around us, trying to find a house with black dust on its walls.

"Man, I'm so pissed off, right now!" present-Arraka says, as we run through the alleys. "If only I had a way of getting out of this amulet, I would rip that fake version of myself in half, and throw her to the dogs."

"Arraka, aren't there some houses in the vicinity that have walls you can't see through with your magical sense?" Illuna says.

"Huh?..." Arraka says, looking as if she's only now realized what we were trying to do. "Oh, right, let me check... Yeah, there is one. But it's pretty far from here. Take a left at the next crossroads, and go straight ahead. I'll tell you when to stop."

"Wouldn't it be faster for Melindra to fly us all the way there?" I say, as we keep running.

"No offense," Kate says, "but I think we can run faster than Melindra can carry us with her air currents."

"There aren't that many obstacles, anyway," Arraka says. "It's just a long way until we get there."

As we keep running, the revenant suddenly gets a strong headache, which makes her lose control over her time-freezing spell. Once the time gets unfrozen, it unfortunately takes past-Arraka no longer than three seconds to teleport herself right in front of us, and to block our path.

"Such a shame," past-Arraka says. "You were so close to escaping. It's too bad that the time weaver couldn't hold on to the spell for just a little longer. Frankly, I'm surprised that she held out as much as she did. I'm guessing that she must have had a protection from dizziness of some sort? Well, no matter. In the end, it didn't help you in any way. The time weaver is too tired to concentrate now, so all you can do is—"

An avalanche of flames coming from the right engulfs Arraka, just as she was finishing her speech, and we are forced to step back, because even the air surrounding those flames feels like it could melt off our skin. Arraka was clearly caught unaware, and she's trying to push back the flames with her hands, as she's struggling to keep hold of her magical shield. The whole ground below her is quickly turning into lava, while the banshee looks like she is getting slowly pushed back, by the incredible force of the magical flames that just keep on pouring. Eventually, she is forced to teleport away, fifty feet above her current location, which causes the flames to immediately stop.

Then, completely out of the blue, a familiar looking dragon made out of magma appears right next to us, and in the next second, we find ourselves being teleported away from the city streets, along with him. As we take a quick look around to see where the dragon Tyrath transported us, we realize that we are now situated in a large building with a very high ceiling, and from the looks of it, the whole construction surrounding us has been coated with seredium dust. The inside of the building looks like a big, closed, amphitheater, with rising rows of seats, and the illumination seems to be coming from magical devices, rather than torches.

Judging by the size of the amphitheater, I'd say that it could probably fit around a thousand people or more in those seats, although currently there are only a few hundred of them sitting on the chairs, while they're murmuring and looking towards us. If I were to take a guess, based on the important looking clothing of these individuals, I'd wager that these must be the people ruling this city, who were in an emergency meeting discussing about the city being attacked, before we interrupted them.

Meanwhile, in the middle of the amphitheater, where the dragon and our group are currently standing, there are also quite a few human mages gathered, all dressed in traditional wizard clothing, along with a few women who are dressed in wizard robes as well. A particularly old man with a long white beard, who seems to be the person presiding over the meeting, is now addressing Tyrath from an elevated platform, speaking to him in a tone that is somehow both polite and condescending at the same time.

"Who are these… strangely dressed wizards that you've brought before the lessathi high council, king of all dragons?" the old man says. "I thought we'd made it clear that this meeting was supposed to be held behind closed doors. When we invited you into our great hall, we did not give you permission to bring guests as well."

"Nobody asked for your permission, you old fool," Tyrath says, in disgust. "You know full well that I wouldn't be here if the situation weren't as dire as it was. This… powerful female wizard named Arraka, who claims to have come from another plane of existence is a threat to us all. I've fought her soon after she first made her appearance, yesterday, and I can assure you that she is not an enemy to be trifled with. My whole army of dragons was completely powerless before her. Only I was powerful enough to hold her back, but not enough to actually defeat her. You should already have an idea of the extent of her powers, now that she's attacked your city as well."

"If you know how dire the situation is, then why do you bring uninvited guests in the middle of this very important meeting?" the old lessathi says. "What benefit could they possibly bring to us, in such circumstances?"

"These people are not what they seem," Tyrath says. "I overheard Arraka saying that one of them was a time weaver, while I was making my way towards this hall. And if you look closely, you will see that the aura coming from that amulet around the little girl's neck is eerily similar to that of Arraka. So similar, in fact, that I would be tempted to say that the two of them are somehow the same person. The Arraka we know was about to kill them all, before I intervened. Surely, even someone as limited as you could see the advantage of having these people as our allies?"

"But at what cost?!" another lessathi from the high council says, as he raises himself from his seat. "I've only just received word from my men through the transceiver, and they've told me that your downpour of flames from earlier has caused the deaths of more than a hundred civilians. Was it worth it to kill so many innocent people just to save this small group?"

"Even if my flames hadn't killed them, they would have most certainly gotten killed by Arraka a few moments later," Tyrath says. "Your civilians were practically already dead from the moment when she set foot in that area. There were hundreds of your flying metal vehicles crashed into the nearby houses when I arrived, and Arraka hadn't even started her rampage, yet. Every moment wasted arguing here will mean the death of a hundred more of your civilians, until we manage to put together a plan of attack that has some realistic chance of success."

"I will have to agree with Tyrath that arguing any further will get us nowhere," the old lessathi says.

"Please sit down, councilman Hrelezar. We will be interrogating this strange group of wizards shortly, and we will soon find out whether the deaths of our fellow countrymen were worth it or not."

The lessathi man that stood up earlier is now reluctantly sitting back down, as the older lessathi addresses one of the women dressed in wizard robes.

"Olyrra, can you please continue from where you left off, before we were interrupted?" the old lessathi says.

"Yes, chairman Ezzeloff," the woman says. "As I've said, none of us have ever experienced anything like this before. Our magical powers have simply vanished, yesterday, and we found no way to bring them back. For some reason, only the women seem to be affected, but even some of our strongest female wizards have been reduced to simple commoners, in the course of a day. We've tried many methods to stimulate our magical auras, but none of them seem to work. If this doesn't get fixed, half of our elite wizard troops will be completely useless in the upcoming battle."

"This is grave news indeed," Ezzeloff says. "The female wizards from our elite troops were a force to be reckoned with. Our highest priority must be to find a way to bring their powers back, at all costs."

"Hah!" Arraka says, from her amulet. "You can try all you want. Your women are never getting their magic back."

"What are you talking about?" Ezzeloff says.

"Didn't you find it strange that all your women lost their powers on the exact same day that the past version of myself made her appearance?" Arraka says. "Of course you didn't. You're morons. Well, let me spell it out for you. The reason why your women were able to cast magic until yesterday was because they were subconsciously linking themselves to female spirits from the magical plane. Since yesterday was obviously the day when I and all the other female spirits got banished from that plane of existence, their magic will never work anymore. You might as well give them some swords and shields to fight with, because that's the most you'll be able to get out of those troops from now on."

"You called the other Arraka a past version of yourself…" Tyrath says. "Does this mean that you're coming from the future?"

"Impressive, Tyrath!" Arraka says. "I never knew that you had mastered basic logic at such a young age. I guess that's why the other dragons made you their king."

"Spare me your insipid humor and answer me this," Tyrath says. "Why have you come here? Why were you fighting the Arraka from our time? Did you come here to avert some great crisis, or did you simply happen to arrive in this place by pure chance?"

"Actually, we were sent here against our own will," I say.

"Explain," Tyrath says.

"Well, do you know anything about the God of Time, and his rituals?" I say.

"I have very little interest in both the gods, and their occupations," Tyrath says. "Should I take it that this 'God of Time' is the one who sent you back here against your will?"

"Yes, exactly," I say.

"And now you are looking for a way to go back?" Tyrath says.

"Uh… I'd say that at the moment, our highest priority is probably our survival," I say.

"Then your best chance would be to cooperate with us," Tyrath says. "If you would share with us the information that you know from the future, we would be much better equipped to fight Arraka."

"What kind of information are you looking for, exactly?" I ask him.

“I have a plan, which may well be our only real chance of defeating Arraka for good,” Tyrath says. “I’ve been discussing it with the elite wizard troops since yesterday, after I first warned the high council that this place might be targeted by Arraka soon. Given that you are from the future, I would like to know if you’ve ever heard of such a plan being used in your past, and if it was successful. In short, there is a large mountain, not far from this area, which we could use to—”

“I’m gonna stop you right there, Tyrath,” Arraka says. “First of all, the good news is that in our past, you did use this plan on me, and you did manage to successfully trap me in that mountain for a few thousand years. Now, the bad news is that I may have… accidentally told the Arraka in your world all about your plan, which means that you may as well scrap the idea entirely, because it’s completely useless, now.”

“You did *what*?!” Tyrath shouts loudly, as the magma from his scales erupts like a volcano.

Before Arraka gets a chance to answer him, a white light suddenly fills our entire area, and once again, we are transported back to our own world, which is apparently still frozen in time. As we’re all looking at the forest around us, the God of Time materializes himself out of thin air once more, floating a few dozen feet above the ground, in front of us.

“I’m afraid that we’ll have to continue this ritual some other time,” the God of Time says, “since I’ve already reached my limit for how much energy I can gather from a single group. Do not worry, you will have the opportunity to continue this trial from where you left off, as soon as the time weaver will be sent to give you the prophecy again. I would like to say that you’ve all performed much better than I expected. You have my sincerest congratulations.”

“Hah!” Arraka says. “I told you losers that you gave

him exactly what he—"

"And your performance was the greatest of them all, Arraka," the God of Time interrupts her.

"What did you… just say?" Arraka asks.

"I wouldn't even have dared to imagine that you would contribute to my ritual out of your own free will," the God of Time says. "However, your feeling of pure dread at the thought of being completely erased from existence by the Magium was exactly what I needed for my ritual to be a complete success! I will be looking forward to what you will have in store for me, in the trials to come."

"You son of a—" Arraka starts to say, but she is cut off by the God of Time.

"Now, before I depart, I will ask you all to kneel before me one last time," the God of Time says.

My friends and I exchange a few looks, but in the end, we all choose to stand our ground. Seeing that none of us are planning to kneel, Melindra starts slowly massaging her forehead, with her eyes closed, out of frustration. Since she knows that no matter what she does, the result will be the same, she decides to stand her ground as well, this time around.

"Have it your way, then," the God of Time says, as a powerful force pushes all of us except the revenant to the ground, in a horizontal position, and then he begins to slowly squash us, with the same magical force.

As I am being pushed against the soil, I start getting flashbacks of my first ritual, and of my parents begging me to save them, while I just stood there and watched, with the pitchfork in my hands. A sudden feeling of rage takes hold of me, and for the whole duration of the god's spell, a single thought goes through my head, over and over.

'I will make him pay.'

'I will make him pay.'

'I will make him pay.'

While we were still being pressed against the ground, the revenant's eyes suddenly became bright yellow again, and she slowly started walking away from us, while gazing into the distance, with an empty look in her eyes.

"It looks like our time is up," the God of Time says. "I will be seeing you all again, soon. Make sure not to get killed in the meantime. Your future contributions to my ritual are highly anticipated."

Almost as soon as the god is done talking, he and the revenant simply disappear, and the world unfreezes itself, making it look almost as if nothing had happened. Now that there is no longer a force pushing us against the ground, we all get up and we dust ourselves off calmly, without saying anything. Not even a few seconds later, I hear the revenant's voice, coming from the transceiver in my pocket.

"What happened after I was gone?" the revenant says, in a low voice. "Did the God of Time pay you any more visits while the time was frozen?"

"No," I say. "From our point of view, it's only been a few seconds since you left. What about you? Do you remember anything after you walked away from here?"

"It's mostly just one big blur," the revenant says. "I remember that the people I visited right after you were Azarius and his pupil, but I don't know what happened after that."

"Alright," I say. "Are you going to keep your transceiver channel closed from now on, too?"

"Yes," the revenant says. "I am still being closely monitored, and I don't want to appear more suspicious than I already am. If there's ever anything urgent, I will call you from my end. Take care."

"You too," I say, and then the revenant closes her channel once again.

"I… think we should all take a small break, so we can clear our minds a little," Daren says, with a very tired look on his face. "Shall we all meet back here in twenty minutes?"

"Yeah," Hadrik says. "I could use a break right about now."

As everyone goes to find a place where they can be alone, for a while, Daren goes to sit on a tree stump, and begins to sharpen his blade, in order to make himself look busy.

"So…" I say, as I approach Daren. "What exactly are you planning to do after this 'break'?"

"What do you mean?" Daren says, as he continues to sharpen his sword, without looking at me. "After the break, we'll continue to march towards Ollendor, like before. Isn't this what we set out to do, when we left Thilias?"

"Of course," I say. "But you know very well that this is not what I meant. When I asked what you were planning to do, I was thinking more in the long-term. I was talking about the God of Time, and the upcoming rituals he's threatened us with. What are you planning to do about those?"

"I don't know, Barry," Daren tells me, as he stops sharpening his sword and looks me in the eye. "You tell me. Because I'm not really seeing an obvious way out of this. The way I see it, all we can do is prepare ourselves the best we can for the next rituals, and hope that we can pass them, like we passed our last trials."

"Well, I was thinking that we could find a more… permanent solution to our problem," I say.

"Like what?" Daren says. "Kill the God of Time? Barry, be reasonable. We're talking about a literal god, here. We were having trouble even against a sage, not so long ago. What would you expect us to do against a god? We are nowhere near powerful enough to challenge him."

"That's funny," I say, "because you're nowhere near as powerful as Eiden either, and yet you kept challenging him again and again, every time we've met."

"That's different!" Daren says. "Despite his power, Eiden is still a mage. We've all fought mages before. Some of them are more powerful than others, but you still have a general idea of what to expect when fighting one. But to challenge a god?... Barry, neither you nor I have even the slightest bit of experience in dealing with something like this."

"Then maybe we should ask someone who does," I say.

Before Daren gets to say anything else, I start walking towards Illuna, who was apparently having a discussion with Arraka. As I get closer to them, the two of them interrupt their conversation, waiting to see what I want.

"Arraka, I have a question to ask of you," I say, with a very serious tone in my voice.

"Uh, sure..." Arraka says. "Fire away."

"How do you kill a god?" I ask her, calmly.

There is a short pause, after I ask my question, during which neither of us says anything.

"You want me to tell you how you can kill a god?..." Arraka says, as she seems to still be recovering from the shock of what I've just asked her.

She waits for a few more seconds, to try and figure out if I'm joking or not, and when she finally understands that I'm being serious, she starts to laugh.

She laughs, and she laughs, as loud as she can, with all three of her voices, and it doesn't look like she's planning to stop anytime soon. However, I am not upset. This isn't one of her usual, mocking laughs. This laughter is one of excitement. She is enjoying this.

Arraka's laugh manages to grab the attention of

everyone in the area, and they're now all looking at us, curiously. I pay them no mind, and I keep waiting patiently for Arraka to stop laughing. When she finally falls silent, she waits for a few more seconds, and then she gives me her answer.

"Barry, my boy…" Arraka says. "I thought you'd never ask!"

Table of Contents